HOLE IN THE SKY

Hole in the Sky

A NOVEL

Monique Vescia

ROUGHHOUSE BOOKS · 2021

Hole in the Sky
Copyright © 2020 by Monique Vescia

ISBN: 978-0-578-81077-5

Typography by Rag & Bone Shop
First Roughhouse Books edition, 2021

For the 81 million
and the 666

"The pure products of America go crazy…"
—from "To Elsie," William Carlos Williams

"The least among us shall be the queen of heaven."
—The New Armenian Bible

1

April 2021
Miami, Florida

L east was beginning to get very tired of lying by the pool, and of having nothing to do. Once or twice she had peeked at the Kindle of the woman reading on the chaise to her right, but she saw only unbroken blocks of text, and what's the use of a screen, thought Least, without any pictures? In the open-air cocktail bar, where an arsenal of Mixmasters churned out fishbowl drinks for all the hotel guests sprawled poolside, a TV squawked about the week's latest high-profile suicide, the activist actress found hanging in her basement exercise room.

In the months before Inauguration II, the mega-jumbo flat screens began cropping up everywhere: in nail salons and pet emporiums and in every bar and restaurant, not just the businesses owned by the President but places like Babbo and Jean-Georges where cell phones and screens had always been banned, so you actually had to talk to the person sitting across from you. Now, when the conversation turned dull—and didn't it always?—you could watch television and read the crawls and stay on top of the great things happening in the country, or hear about the shocking crimes committed by illegals, while you cracked the burnt-sugar shell on your crème brûlée.

Least hadn't been exactly surprised when she heard about the actress's death; anyone could tell she'd been losing her grip. After adopting all those mismatched kids and pumping out a few of her own, she'd let the nanny lure her husband away. She used to be super-hot, but then she'd lost all that weight and looked like a corpse, long before she became one. Visiting shithole countries and saying negative stuff about the US, acting all holier-than-thou. Least wondered what it would feel like to die that way, to wrap an Hermès scarf three times around your neck and kick away the chair. What if you changed your mind while you were twisting there?

She had come down to Miami a day early, and had time to kill before the rest of the party started showing up the next morning. Plans for Angela's fortieth would tie up most of the weekend, jammed with scheduled activities that Angie's annoying sister-in-law, Margo, had detailed in an email Least hadn't bothered to read. The birthday girl's husband had rented a block of rooms at the Bentley for his wife and seven friends—definitely not the swankiest hotel in South Beach, but not exactly a dump, either. Least had sprung for an extra day; Miami had some incredible art museums, and she'd spent the afternoon at the Bass and the World Erotic Art Museum, and was determined to fit in a trip to MOCA and the Pérez before she flew back to New York.

Least thought about the Byron Luster exhibit she'd seen at the Bass. She had loved Luster's last show, a high-concept exhibition called "Carnival of Martyrs," which had drawn huge crowds at the Whitney the previous fall. The artist, dressed as a carny and stationed next to a whirling centrifuge of spun sugar, had handed out a small cone of white cotton candy to each visitor. You ate away the sugary floss to find yourself looking at the dead face of a young black man killed by the police, printed on the sticky, twisted paper. The cotton candy was champagne-flavored, and super-yummy.

She wasn't so sure about Luster's new stuff, however. Titled "Revivals," the show featured a series of small pieces in the style of religious icons, all hung at crotch-level. Each was meticulously crafted from recycled aluminum foil embellished with products of the artist's own body—fingernail clippings, earwax, blood, and dried semen. Staring somberly out of the center of each frame, one limp hand raised in blessing, was a man whose career had been destroyed by the Me Too movement: Harvey Weinstein, Bill Cosby, Louis C.K., and former presidential hopeful Joe Biden.

Least let her gaze float across the chemical expanse of the pool toward the roof edge overlooking Ocean Drive. Strolling past the white chaise lounges grouped around the rooftop patio, here came the guy she'd noticed sizing her up in the hotel lobby when she had checked in that morning. His unbuttoned linen shirt swung open as he moved, and she could see that he was slim but cut, with what looked like a Rolie Submariner on his left wrist. Next to all the flesh browning in the Florida sun he was weirdly pale. Pink pineapple-patterned swim trunks hung off his narrow hips, and black Gucci flip-flops slapped his heels as he walked. But what really caught her eye was that Anderson Cooper seen-a-ghost white hair, clipped close on the sides and arcing over his forehead like a crashing wave. Mid-thirties, she guessed—a little younger than her, and clearly money, but money that made him edgy, money he hadn't had long enough to act relaxed about. So why did he have his eye on her?

Yes, she was a Kardashian, just not one of the famous ones. Early on she'd tried to trade on that connection, but they froze her out—Kim and the rest of that clan, who thought they were too good for her branch of the family. Least had the same glossy dark flat-ironed hair, the same olive skin and long-lashed Bambi eyes, and she regularly had her limbs waxed and her brows threaded into symmetrical swoops. God had gifted her with a better-than-average rack, and she'd been working hard on her ass at Orangetheory. She would never have the trademark Goodyear blimp backside, but she suspected that was a Kanye-directed freak show requiring regular goat-fat injections and an entire second home full of custom-built clothes, and Least didn't have the resources for that kind of extreme body sculpting.

It made her physically ill to watch how her cousin's star just kept on rising. Least knew that Kim had leaked that sex tape, though she swore she hadn't. Clever bitch. It made her notorious, and once they were all on TV and their name became synonymous with drama and money, the Klan had no time for Least, or for anyone else in Least's family, though that perv Rob got drunk and hit on her at their aunt's funeral just after the election.

The thing was, when they were kids, all the cousins had gotten along just fine. Kim and Kourtney were older than Least, but they all played together, running wild around the huge party house in Beverly Hills that made her parents' Cape Cod look like a Monopoly hotel token by comparison. To Least it felt like the houses in LA were somehow more porous than the ones in Ann Arbor, because pretty people seemed to just drift in without ever knocking. All the women wore high-cut neon swimsuits under mesh cover-ups, and everyone had a pair of designer sunglasses perched on their head and a sweating drink in their hand.

That was before Least's sisters came along, and Khloé was still a baby. Kim and Kourtney shared a room like twin princesses, with ruffled pink canopy beds and a closet full of awesome dress-up clothes. Least got to stay in there, too, in a *Little Mermaid* sleeping bag shaped like a fish's sequined tail, camping out on the deep white carpet. They took a fancy oval mirror with a meringue-y frame down off the wall and put it on the bedroom floor, and they all pranced around it, pretending they were fairies and the mirror was an enchanted pond they'd found in the woods. Kourtney even let Least try her grape sparkle lip gloss. And Least would stare at Kim and think, *She's the prettiest girl in the world.*

But the next time she saw her cousins they had turned mean and snarky and snotty, especially Kim, who called her Beast, even though her name meant "shining savior" in ancient Armenian. It didn't even rhyme if you pronounced it right! Kim should talk, after naming her own spawn Saint and North and Chicago and Psalm and Deity. Those pictures of Kim in the Oval Office next to the President had been all over the Internet, like Kim was some official head of state. Least would have given anything to be standing in her cousin's Louboutins, posing for that picture. And now he'd named Kim the ambassador to some island and she'd been jetting all over the world with her spoiled kids in private planes. The whole disgusting Instagrammed spectacle made her want to lean over and puke in her raffia beach bag.

As Least's sun-stupefied brain retraced its old grudge, like a roller-coaster cart on a rusted, looping track, she watched White Hair scanning the mounds of flesh by the pool. Kardashian or not she was still a babe, even deep into her thirties, and used to men steaming up her tail. That afternoon she'd already been hit on three times, by two separate losers in business suits and a lesbian who looked vaguely like Emma Stone with a butch haircut. But every guy she met was so predictable; she knew what line would come out of his mouth before he said a word, knew which accomplishments he would trumpet, what type of music would be on his playlist, which memes he shared, what he'd want in the sack, exactly when (or if) he would call her after a hook-up. Ho-fucking-hum. When a few dates threatened to turn into a "relationship," she was already plotting her escape.

On Least's last trip home to the Mitten, it was clear her mother had finally thrown in the towel and begun concentrating her matchmaking efforts on Richie, who lived nearby and had always been susceptible to parental pressure. Alana, off in LA with her husband, Mateo, and a baby on the way, had long ago fallen prey to such machinations. The youngest, Layla, had just announced that she was bi, temporarily throwing their mother off her game.

With these few thoughts muddying a mind otherwise emptied by the sun, Least stared down at her freshly lacquered toenails, flashing red signals back at her from the foot of the chaise, and didn't bother to stifle a yawn as she waited for the white-haired man to appear.

——

"MAGA indeed." When Least looked up, he was standing there, with two umbrella-shaded drinks in his hands, the mirrored lenses of his sunglasses doubling her as she finished retying the halter straps at the back of her neck. Her swimsuit usually attracted some comments. Fire-engine red with MA embroidered on the right breast and GA on the left, those twin triangles locked together at her cleavage with a shiny gold presidential seal. If you twisted that, the top popped off. (First-term vintage deadstock, naturally. All the new merch said KAG.) White Hair extended one glass, frosty with condensation. "Thirsty?"

She was thirsty, now that he mentioned it. That scrawny, gawking waiter in the guayabera shirt had been AWOL for a while, and her bottle of Ivanka Water held just a hot inch of backwash. She reached for the glass that White Hair hadn't offered her and took a long pull on the straw, appraising him over the purple paper umbrella before answering, "Not anymore." He settled into the chaise the woman with the Kindle had conveniently vacated and pushed up his mirrored shades, fixing her with a pair of weird light-colored eyes, like a husky's. His brows and eyelashes were light, too. She idly wondered about his underarm hair, and his pubes. Up close she could see that the repeating shapes on his swim trunks weren't pineapples—they were hand grenades. She told him, "You can drink the one with the roofie in it."

He laughed and took a good sip before getting down to business. "There are still some places in this country where if you wore something like that, they would tear you to shreds." He placed a black phone facedown on the table between them.

"Not many of those left, thank God." The red tsunami from the last election had turned the map scarlet from coast to coast, with the exception of Vermont and Northern California, the final holdouts of the sputtering resistance. Since the state's financial collapse after the pandemic, the fracking-quakes, and all those wildfires, California had lost nearly one-third its population to Seattle and Canada. The last census made sure that only solidly red states received any disaster relief or federal funding. Karma was definitely a bitch.

"I am very glad, because you look so much better all in one piece." His arctic eyes scanned her Frappuccino-colored legs and settled briefly between her breasts where the sweat had begun to pool. His voice (warm, amused) had a slight accent she couldn't quite place. Russian, probably. You heard Slavic accents everywhere these days, Russia being one of the few exceptions to the worldwide travel ban. Once the alliance had been announced, wealthy Russians had started flooding in, and like many trendy places, South Beach had become a mecca for vodka-swilling oligarchs with deep pockets and sardonic laughs and their snooty blond girlfriends.

Least felt lazy, drained by the sun and the hours spent on her feet in museums, and was enjoying the sensation of the frozen drink slipping down her throat, or she might have mustered the energy to collect her things and just walk away. His name was Luka, he said, and he was in town on business, something to do with brand strategy. He kept talking, and she listened for that moment when flattery would veer into self-promotion, as it always did. At thirty-nine, Least knew the drill. Men her age were most comfortable talking about themselves, trotting their egos like show dogs past the women they wanted to impress. But unless they could claim they headed up a billion-dollar real estate empire and had been elected Leader of the Free World—twice!—she just wasn't interested. Still, she found herself mesmerized by White Hair's hand, the one with the Rolex, which traced elegant shapes in the air as he talked. Up close, the watch didn't look like a fake, but then Least had seen some pretty convincing knock-offs—she owned a closetful of them.

She reached for her phone and began scrolling through it, affecting disinterest. Undeterred, he signaled to the waiter to bring them two more of the same umbrella drinks, and commenced his pitch. "So," he began, "you have not told me your name, but I already know who you are. And I must confess I am not a fan of your family's—I do not care for their brand—it's far too obvious, it lacks class and subtlety—but I suspect that you are not like them, that you are not a typical Kardashian woman. Am I correct?"

Least appraised him over the rim of her cocktail, gauging her response. His eyes were, indeed, very strange, each iris shot through with cracks like an ice cube. A sharply carved nose bisected his long face, with its high cheekbones, before jogging slightly left over a pair of thin, faintly smiling lips. His shirt hung open over his pale hairless chest, and she could make out some initials tattooed in an ornate black font arcing over his left nipple. He had her attention, but she didn't want him to know that, not yet at least. So she shifted her eyes toward the pool with its David Hockney-esque ripples of light, where nobody seemed to be swimming. "You could say that."

Luka kept talking, in that intriguing accent, about Kardashianness, about how language is always in flux, and how the meaning of a word or a name can morph over time. "Think of the word *awful*. The liberals like to howl about how *awful* the President's behavior is. But if you follow it back to its root, you find this word once had a very different meaning, literally 'worthy of awe.' People would speak of 'the awful majesty of God.' So *awful* once meant something very good, but now it means the opposite of that.

"Now let us consider your own name, and what it has come to mean. Thanks to your famous cousins, 'Kardashian' currently behaves as a noun; you hear that word and what do you picture? What does the average American consumer see? Bottoms and lips and money. All nouns. But with you, the name becomes something more elusive: an adjective, a collection of qualities that might include captivating, impatient, ambitious, sexual, and pure." He listed them as his strange gaze flickered over her. "It's an interesting question, yes? What does 'Kardashian' mean at this moment in time, and what might it mean in the future?"

Least strained to follow, but the alcohol from the second drink had already begun to fog her brain. What Luka said definitely qualified as flattery, but she also had the unpleasant sensation of being back in college, listening to her hot young art history professor toss around terms she didn't understand like *chiaroscuro* and *trompe l'oeil* while the other students in the seats around her bobbed their heads in fawning agreement.

Maybe he sensed this, her souring, because he abruptly changed tack, tucking his sunglasses back over his eyes and asking, "Are you here on your own?"

Attractive women have antennae for this: questions that seem to probe a potential vulnerability. But something about Luka, his professorial detachment, his vocabulary, his subtle accent—or was it the vodka?—had put her at ease. She plucked the pineapple garnish off the rim of her glass and sucked the fibrous wedge while she told him about the girls' party, milking the story of Margo's war room approach to event planning for some humor. Why was she working to amuse him? she wondered.

His black phone buzzed on the glass table. Luka slid it off and glanced at the screen, then tapped his thumbs across the keypad. "Please excuse me—I have some calls to make. Since your friends won't be arriving until tomorrow, are you free to join me for dinner tonight? I promise to make it worth your while."

Before Luka had appeared on her horizon, Least's plans for the evening had included ordering in sushi while she shopped for rare MAGA gear on eBay, maybe a post-dinner stroll down Ocean Drive, and then binge-watching *Succession* in her room. Being treated to dinner by an intriguing stranger seemed like a low-risk alternative. She was just bored enough to take him up on his offer.

2

Blister Pack Moon
Sargasso Sea

Due northeast approximately 1,625 nautical miles past Least Kardashian's alcohol-glazed eyeballs, beyond the disappearing pink sand beaches of Bermuda, a former refugee named Petra Mussan was rocking gently on the bosom of the Atlantic Ocean. She lay on her back on a mattress woven from grocery bags and torn fishing nets and discarded kiddie pools and old shower curtains, and watched the sinking sun pick out the colors in the arches of interlocking plastic soda bottles that made up the low roof of her shelter.

Back in Syria, after the aspirin ran out, Petra had learned how to quiet her headaches by resting in a darkened room and envisioning all the lost beauties of Aleppo. As the war brought the ancient city down around their ears, she rebuilt it in her mind: Afternoon sun streaming through colorful glass bubbles in the dome of the neighborhood bathhouse. The heaped blocks of hand-cut soap and disks of hammered copper at the al-Zarab souk where she went with her father to collect his custom shirts from the tailor. Arabesques of iron on balconies hung with tin pots and birdcages. But the gunfire and barrel bombs made it hard to concentrate, and every day that passed it became more difficult to picture Aleppo the way it used to be.

They had no aspirins on the Patch, either, at least not until the next trade vessel arrived in three days' time. But unlike in the city she'd fled two years earlier, here Petra had found peace. Silence, or splashing water and riffling wind, the occasional querulous voice of a neighbor, sometimes the jabbering of a flock of long-flying seabirds—swifts and albatrosses—that would come down out of the sky for a while and rest their enormous wings before resuming their journeys—these were the only sounds that reached her ears as she lay there, cradled in garbage. Unlike the birds', Petra's own travels were over, at least for now.

They had all come through horrors, the days when drowned children washed up on the tourist beaches and boatloads of the desperate had been turned away from the coasts at gunpoint. Fear walled off entire nations, churned up by the powerful for their own dark purposes, sealing off every port: Alexandria, Tunis, Malta, Sardinia, Lampedusa, Algiers—uniformed soldiers had turned them away with bullhorns and Kalashnikov rifles, until finally their leaking boats were forced past Gibraltar and out into the Atlantic.

Along the way, they'd heard rumors of an island in the middle of that ocean, afloat in a tranquil sea of golden weeds, a landmass the sea couldn't gnaw away like all the other shrinking places, growing larger all the time, shaped by the hands of the tides. It might have been a legend, a watery mirage dreamed up by despairing boat people, but what choice did they have but to make for it? The last refugee boat Petra had boarded raised its sail whenever possible to conserve on fuel, but eventually the gasoline ran out. When the rotten mast cracked in a mid-ocean squall, killing some and injuring others in the overcrowded vessel, they began to drift, tossed about on the waves, jettisoning the corpses of those who died each night. And along with all the other refuse trapped in the ocean currents, they were eventually pushed westward toward the tangled mats of yellow seaweed. When the floating plants and the garbage grew dense, their boat had to be paddled slowly forward by oars and many hands.

And when at last they clambered out of the fetid, failing vessel onto the buoyant surface in the middle of the sargassum, they found themselves standing on the shore of a new world made up entirely of plastic.

At first the people lived on fish and the wretched-tasting flesh of the occasional seabird they managed to snare. When a rare storm swept over, they collected the rain. But unlike the forbidding North Atlantic whose currents surrounded it, this place was strangely warm and the winds were weak, the weather systems stable. The vast mats of sargassum sustained the animals that soon became their food: a bounty of shrimp and crabs, but also eels and marlin and dolphinfish, their bellies packed with plastic that the people repurposed or rinsed back into the sea. The seaweed nourished them, too, providing minerals and nutrients, and they slowly regained their health and strength. As they grew stronger, hope seeped slowly back into blasted hearts.

Over time, they learned to work with the available materials, building low-slung shelters with roofs that could be battened down snugly to withstand the rain and occasional winds. So many had been artisans or scientists in their old lives, robbed of those livelihoods by conflict, and their skills proved invaluable in this new environment. They adapted roofs to collect and divert rainwater, and desalinized seawater in collection pools, creating a steady source of fresh water for a growing population.

Surveying parties on rafts built from detergent bottles went out to map the size and contours of the place, one group paddling west and another heading east. As the weeks passed it was feared they'd lost their way or their vessels had sunk. Yet they returned, jubilant, eager to spread the news. Approximate measurements had been recorded and calculations made; the great plastic patch could welcome all those who came and many more. As new waves of colonists arrived and settled in the denser surfaces of the interior, they reinforced the treacherous places where the floating debris were thin and a person might slip through and vanish into the dark water. The Patch now moved as one, an island the size of three Syrias, rising and falling with the ocean swells but never pulling apart. They named their new nation Sargassa, after the masses of tangled seaweed to the east, but most of them just called it the Patch.

Eventually, new refugees found their way to Sargassa from the ruined cities in the Bahamas and Haiti, and from the starving places in Venezuela, the Dominican Republic, Puerto Rico, Senegal, and Sierra Leone; fleeing Syrians and Turks and Greeks and Cypriots made the much longer journey through the Mediterranean passage. Those who survived the voyage arrived on the Patch parched and ravenous and ragged, boats full of exhausted women and malnourished children blinking in astonishment at this new Atlantis rising from the waves. Eventually, trade vessels from Halifax and Bermuda would bring chickens and rabbits and baby goats, and soil for cultivation. Seeds germinated in greenhouses built from plastic milk jugs rooted down and grew into plants, watered by rain channeled along the greenhouse walls. Last summer Petra's own small garden had produced striped purple-and-white eggplants that didn't need to be salted.

They cut channels into the debris to create arterials for faster access to far-flung settlements on the Patch; at night phosphorescent algae lit these watery pathways snaking through the plastic that they sped along on their rafts. They learned to navigate this new land, adapted themselves to its rhythms and mastered its resources in the service of survival, and eventually the practical made way for art: Children sang songs mimicking the bursts of sound from the blowholes of migrating whales; artisans pierced the shades on the oil and battery lamps they used with decorative patterns, and strung the prettiest finds into necklaces and armbands and earrings; and architects and builders erected a mosque with a curved mosaic roof made from plastic shards and bottle caps. Work had begun on a church and a synagogue, using trash transformed by clever hands and ingenuity into structures of uncanny beauty.

But even as life improved, problems remained to be solved. Today, Petra's headache came from Adnan, not the first he'd given her. He had insisted on keeping as a pet the small dog that came in on a trade vessel, and now that malformed creature he'd named "handsome" — Wasim —

had become a nuisance to all his neighbors, begging at the kitchen tents and harassing Burak's herd of goats until one had broken through its pen in a panic and blundered into the water, where it drowned. They'd had to butcher it that day, to save the meat from spoiling.

Now Burak was demanding restitution, but Adnan had dismissed the man's claims, insisting the pen had been poorly constructed, and hadn't Burak enjoyed his goat dinner? Petra recalled when her school group had visited the National Museum and seen the cuneiform tablets, unearthed from a Babylonian merchant's house and dating from almost two thousand years before Christ. She had heard that same peevish note of complaint, inscribed in stone, translated on the little card next to the exhibit: *I have sent as messengers gentlemen like ourselves to collect the bag with my money, but you have treated them with contempt by sending them back to me empty-handed several times, and through that enemy territory....* Grievances like these were as old as time.

She might have to recommend that Adnan be censured, the dog drowned, maybe. Those who caused strife, or harm to others, were set adrift. It had become an axiom among them, "Don't bring the war here," a way of scolding children when they squabbled, but also a stern reprimand to the men still inclined to settle their disputes with their fists. Petra wielded extraordinary power, as did the other women of Sargassa, since they could be trusted to place the interests of the community above their own. Those who had been banished since they'd consolidated had all been men, and the besotted women who couldn't bear to part with them.

By necessity, the first governors of the Patch were women—so many men had been killed in the war, and they were vastly outnumbered. And as the women took on leadership roles, and made decisions about how they all might best live and thrive in their new home, they begun to speak seriously among themselves. They recognized that in this weird new life they'd been granted an opportunity. Could human beings evolve beyond the same self-destructive patterns, their perpetual lust for war and violence, if women held the power rather than men? Who was raping, who was fighting, who was killing? Always, always it was the men. So Petra and the other women closed ranks and said to the men, "Listen up, we're doing it differently from now on—you've had your chance, and look how you fucked it up. Now it's our turn." And the men had to agree. Years of war had beaten them down, made them sick of conflict, and maybe opened their brains a little, too.

The cleverest among them soon found ways to make themselves useful to the women. Adnan had been a civil engineer in Homs and applied his knowledge to the Patch. He organized teams of children to gather enough toothbrush handles and carry-out containers to build a windmill that could pump water and grind grain; he designed the shallow pools where they taught every colonist to swim, and wove Petra a surprisingly chic poncho from six-pack rings. Adnan was adept at problem solving and cunnilingus, two reasons why Petra put up with his shit.

On Sargassa, people tended to loosely coalesce in groups with members of the same nation or religion, but the governors encouraged efforts to integrate, and the dividing lines between one community and the next stayed blurry, by design—they had all had enough of walls. They were one people now, Sargassans, and they had all come from trauma; they had suffered hunger and thirst and disease, seen family members executed, or an ancient mosque bombed into rubble, witnessed gassed children gasping for air, had their life's work destroyed. Petra had lost her mother and three of her brothers in the Russian airstrikes; countless relatives had fled the city, scattered to the winds like chaff.

It gave Petra some measure of satisfaction when she heard a fellow colonist complaining about grit in the spinach or a neighbor's noisy chickens—what they once had called first-world problems. When you no longer have to struggle to survive, she thought, you start grousing about a hangnail. But she knew she must stay wary. Some of their minds had been twisted and warped by what they'd lived through, and they would never be well or whole again. One of the men who'd been set adrift, Hakim, had plotted to drown the governor of the western trust and to install his brother in her place. If the waves didn't swallow him, he might wash ashore somewhere and recruit a force on the strength of his outrage and return to make trouble. Soon they would have to start policing their own coastline.

Adnan liked to tease her that her heart was too hard, she was too swift to judge, and the punishments she meted out were excessively harsh, but she knew a leader must be strong and unafraid to do whatever was necessary to protect her people. They had all suffered too much, come too far, and worked too hard to fail at life in this final place. With a heart callused by war, she would not allow herself to be distracted from her duty by softness or sentiment. Her name, Petra, meant stone, but she was the stone that would float.

3

April
South Beach

By the time the passion fruit sorbets arrived, Least was a little drunk and laughing. Luka had been telling her about a Russian game show where contestants were given a stolen car and thirty-five minutes to elude the police. If they succeeded, they could keep the car. The show had originally been intended as propaganda, to show off the power of the police force, but eighty-five million viewers ended up cheering for the criminals.

Luka had proved to be an entertaining dinner companion, with a knack for getting her to talk about herself. So much so that nearly two hours after they'd settled into their chairs, though he'd mentioned that his family was from Belarus ("Is that a prettier version of Russia?" she'd joked), and had moved to the States when he was sixteen, she was still fuzzy on what he actually did for a living (something to do with branding, he'd said), and why he was there in South Beach. Thanks to a sparkling Mojito, followed by a bottle and a half of an expensive Vouvray, she'd already spilled the whole pathetic story of how all the famous Kardashians totally shunned her side of the family because of some longtime beef her uncle Robert had with her dad, because her dad had once asked his brother how he could live with himself, helping to defend a murderer like that. "I mean," she said, and heard a whine edge into her voice, "Kim gets to bring all her Insta-brats to the White House egg toss, and jet around the world to all these fabulous embassy parties! But she doesn't even think about throwing her own cousin a bone and getting me on the guest list for one of these events with the President she's always posting about. FYI, I was into him WAY before she was! She's only there because Kanye went off his meds and started all that dragon-brother crap. She's just using him. She doesn't give two shits about his agenda."

Luka refilled her wineglass with a deft twist of his wrist. "He is not so exclusive. He is a man of the people, right? It is not so difficult to get access to this man. I think it could be managed, if you really wanted to meet him."

The truth of Luka's words helped pull her away from the succulent carcass of self-pity. After Kim got the ambassadorship, Least's friend Resa had said something similar, trying to make her feel better: "You don't need her to get you access to the President. Remember when that Menendez brother got himself patched through to Air Force One? How hard could it be?" And Resa had a point. A man with POTUS's sexual appetites needed to surround himself with beautiful women, since anyone could tell he wasn't getting what he needed from that ice queen he'd married. So why not her? She was as hot as Stormy and Summer and Karen and all the rest, maybe even hotter. A former boyfriend of hers had once teasingly called her the Armenian Monica Lewinsky and she had been secretly flattered after she looked up that name on Wikipedia.

Least had turned slutty sixteen during the whole Clinton scandal, and had been too intent on sneaking out of the house to get sloshed at UMich frat parties while her parents were riveted by the news. Some people treated Monica like a big joke, but that curvy intern had worked that beret and flashed her thong and got to have sex with the most powerful man in the world. Some people said she was stupid to keep the dress, but if Least was lucky enough to get some presidential jizz on her clothes (even on that fake Prada sweater that had fooled everyone at the shower for the celebrity baby), she knew she would frame it like a fucking saint's relic.

But she would go Monica one better, do a Lewinsky 2.0, with a lot more finesse. *L'affair Lewinsky* was the story of a powerful man's weakness, his betrayal of the public trust. This President needed a woman who would complement and support him, not flap her gums to some faithless confidant and blow the whole game. If Monica had simply kept her mouth shut, except when it was sexually advantageous to open it, she could have become a . . . Least searched her memory for an example of a woman who'd parlayed a booty-call into a power play and came up with Madame de Pompadour, whom she'd read about in art history when they were studying rococo portraiture. Madame de Pompadour didn't become one of the most influential woman in eighteenth-century France just because she was a witty conversationalist and a great lay. She knew better than to spill her guts to the wrong people.

Least wasn't interested in being an amuse bouche, and eventually a public laughingstock; hers was a fantasy of genuine partnership. Obviously the President was on the hunt for wife number four. Melania had always been a poor fit in the role of First Lady—her habits of slapping her husband's hand away and narrowing her already narrow eyes at him in public made that very clear. Since the second inaugural, her disrespect has become more brazen; the day the President signed the executive order reversing the ban on DDT, FLOTUS was photographed wearing a jeweled beetle pin on the lapel of a blouse embroidered with songbirds.

During a lull in the conversation, Luka had caught Least staring at the TV report reflected in the mirror at the side of the restaurant: coverage from earlier that week of the groundbreaking ceremony for POTUS's Moscow tower, courtesy of TASS. The President and Vladimir Putin beaming broadly at the camera, shoulder to shoulder, each wielding a golden shovel.

"See how she loves her leader. She can't tear her eyes away!"

He was teasing her, she knew, but she flushed and felt compelled to justify her feelings. "He's an amazing man. Just look at everything he has accomplished. Against such incredible odds, against so many enemies and haters, he has inspired millions. The whole continent of India worships him like a god!" She gestured vaguely toward the screen in her tipsy enthusiasm, sloshing a little wine over the rim of her glass. It was an argument she'd tried to make to her family over the Thanksgiving holiday, in the giddy aftermath of the election. Her liberal Democrat father had quickly retreated to his den, Layla had called her a fascist and burst into tears, and her mother had made Least promise never to bring up politics again at the dinner table.

"No, I mean that you truly love him. I can see this, when I watch you looking at him. True devotion." Those weird blue eyes looked deep into hers.

Least knew there were legions of supporters who made a big show of their loyalty to the President, people who had crowed in triumph when that doddering Mueller was jailed for crimes against the state, and the know-it-all chair of the intelligence committee had been pegged by a hit-and-run driver in front of the Old Ebbitt Grill. She'd seen pictures of the scary dudes who sported MAGA forehead tattoos, and the motor-cycle gangs that crisscrossed the country in a T formation, beating up stray Mexicans they met on the road. But somehow Luka made her own obsession sound noble—as if it came from a pure and lofty place, the very best part of her. Not like those losers who regularly showed up to flash their tits at the presidential motorcade. (POTUS loved it, of course, and had his driver honk his horn at them.)

But the sudden shift in Luka's tone made her uncomfortable. She had accepted his invitation to dinner because she had nothing better to do. They'd had some laughs, but now he had turned serious and she wasn't sure if she liked it, or the idea of a near stranger grilling her about her presidential crush. It was none of his business, after all. Besides, having the right person on the job meant you didn't have to think about that stuff anymore, right? It was time to steer the conversation away from such topics and back to her, make it clear to him that he was losing her interest.

The interior of the restaurant was an appetizing buttermilk white, with shimmery accents. Massive blue and green circular columns embedded with coins created a sophisticated fish-scale effect that winked in the flattering lighting. Scanning the room, Least caught the eye of an aggressively tanned older man sitting at an adjacent table who stared at her over the spaghetti-strapped shoulder of his dinner companion. She lifted her phone from the corner of the table and scanned the texts, noticing Luka signal for the check in her peripheral vision. More bossy communiqués from Margo—God, she'd never even met the woman and she already hated her guts! When Least glanced back up she found Luka regarding her with an amused expression.

"Ah," he said, "I can see I am beginning to bore you. That is unforgiveable of me. What can I do to make it up to you?"

Luka would be picking up a hefty dinner tab, and Least didn't want to risk looking too bitchy, so she decided to throw him a bone. "No, no, it's just that I got up so early this morning to get to the airport. . . ." She shaped her mouth into a little conciliatory smile. Least fully expected he would try to invite himself up to her room for a nightcap, and she wanted to make it crystal clear she would be heading straight to bed, alone.

"I understand," Luka said smoothly, as the leather folder containing the bill materialized on his corner of the table. Sliding an American Express Platinum card inside (yes, she noticed), he told her, "It's time for you to have your beauty rest, no? And I too have some things I must take care of this evening. But perhaps you will be free again tomorrow night? To join me for a little adventure?"

"Thank you for dinner, Luka, but I am going to very busy when my friends arrive." She tucked her cell phone into the pocketbook she'd placed on her lap and forced an apology into her tone as she groped around inside the bag for a lipstick tube.

"Yes, the birthday party. But I will be going to Mar-a-Lago to meet some of my associates, and I thought you might like to come along. Have you ever been there?"

Least froze in the act of smearing lip stain across her mouth and gaped across the table at him.

"To Mar-a-Lago?"

"The President is not scheduled to be there this weekend, though sometimes his visits don't show up on the official schedule. In any case, I thought you might enjoy having a look at the place. It's not so far from here, maybe a couple hours' drive north."

"But don't you have to be a member to get in?" Least was sobering up fast as her heart rate increased. In her mind, the Winter White House had become a nearly mythical place, a wonderland out of a fever dream. And yet the man sitting across the table from her would be traveling there tomorrow. And he had invited her to come along.

"People can schedule events there. It is only a matter of money. I am meeting some business associates who are considering Mar-a-Lago as a location for a TV pilot. So perhaps your friends can spare you tomorrow evening?" By now the waiter had returned with the bill. Luka signed it and tucked his credit card back into a sleek black billfold, which he slid inside his jacket. Then he smiled and stood, extending a hand to her. "You'll come, yes?"

4

Mike Pence was not happy. He had barely set foot off the plane, and now he was being dispatched again, this time to the Slovak Republic, to mop up after POTUS's latest foreign policy blunder. The Slovakian president's nose had gotten out of joint when the "stable genius" had tweeted that the country would be better off under Russian control, like its neighbor Ukraine. Now Pence had to smooth ruffled feathers ("It was a joke!"), and flatter the president over some foie gras. And Mother would have to come along, of course, since the president was a woman.

When he got the bad news in the briefing room, his eyes had fixed on Stephen's head bowed in obeisance in the corner, sleek and muscular as a young seal's, and he had momentarily lost himself in its noble contours. When POTUS had noticed his distraction, and barked at him to pay attention (the man had a sixth sense for when he was deprived of an iota of anyone's attention), he'd had to dial up the sycophancy to 11 to cover for his mistake. He thought he saw Stephen's lip twitch in amusement at the line about what a privilege it was to act on the President's behalf.

Had he laid it on a bit thick? He prayed he would have the chance to ask him, maybe one day soon.

POTUS pointed toward the HD screen dominating one wall of the briefing room and framed by those tacky gold curtains, showing for the umpteenth time the footage of him shooting that man on Fifth Avenue in front of a crowd of tourists. "Look at them cheer!" he bellowed. "They're loving it! Best show they've ever seen!" Ever since the shooting, the President had forced everyone in the West Wing to watch the looping TV footage several times a day, crowing about "how stupid he looks when he's falling! Look at all that disgusting blood in front of my beautiful tower!" The assorted aides in the room did their best to feign enthusiasm. Pence smiled and nodded, murmuring, "You got him straight through the heart, sir," though the wild shot had clearly only grazed the man's shoulder and the Secret Service had had to finish the job. Anyone with eyes could see that the guy had leapt the barricade and welcomed every bullet, suicide by Commander in Chief. Sometimes Pence felt he would gladly accept the same fate, if death by his own hand wouldn't slam shut his escape hatch to heaven.

None of this was panning out anything like he'd hoped. He'd been playing the long game and biding his time, wearing the mask of the believer until the American people yelled, "Uncle," and demanded that he enact the Twenty-fifth Amendment. That would clear the way for the Pence presidency, or the "Pencidency," as he liked to think of it. But honestly, who could have predicted that so many Americans, and his fellow Evangelicals, of all people, would have clasped this satanic buffoon to their breasts? During the first term he'd prayed for the Mueller probe to turn up something irrefutable. Everything the FBI needed was just laying there in plain sight, twitching like piles of fish after Moses parted the Red Sea. But it was a total wash, thanks to Barr. And then when that Ukraine business cranked up the impeachment engine in the House, he'd once again dared to imagine that salvation might be within reach. But once the articles came to the Senate for a vote, Pence's hopes along with those of half the country had deflated like a farting balloon. God help him, he'd even done his part to urge the Commander in Chief to take out that Iranian nuclear scientist, knowing the repercussions would lead to decades of Middle Eastern policy collapsing like a house of cards. Yet through every scandal, the man emerged unharmed and grinning, borne aloft on the shoulders of the mob, above the rubble of the nation.

Even more mind-boggling than legions of Republicans willing to fall on their swords for this Nero? That he, Mike Pence, would lose his heart to a man—a Jew, no less. *Before I met him I didn't think I could love anyone more than my God*, he thought. He'd harbored secret feelings all his life and they had terrified him. He had suppressed his own treasonous thoughts, passing a slate of anti-gay laws as governor to shield himself from exposure. Poor Karen was the perfect beard. By swearing an oath that he'd never break bread with another woman without his wife-chaperone by his side, he'd further solidified his reputation as a man of God, determined to resist all feminine wiles—a classic case of misdirection. She'd never worried about his late-night campaign sessions with eager young aides in Indiana, and here in DC. (But he'd only looked—never touched. He had to marvel at his own restraint.) He loved her—how could he not love someone so loyal, so stalwart? Truth be told, he thought of Mother (what an apt nickname for a wife whose gazes cloaked him in devotion, and for whom he felt no carnal urges) as a kind of disciple, not as a lover. It was a miracle he'd managed to plant three successful pregnancies in her fertile Hoosier soil, considering the mental effort it took for him to climax within a country mile of her terrifying vagina. *Just close your eyes and think of Patrick Dempsey.*

But he'd grown weary of a lifetime of dissembling, of masking his true nature. *My Lord, I've served you faithfully for sixty years. How much longer must I be denied my own few morsels of joy?* His smooth cap of white hair was still intact, thank God, and his body was surprisingly muscular under his modest blue suits. But he could sense his energies waning. That first term had taken every ounce of his patience and self-control—and for what, in the end? Surely that was why his mask had slipped, just enough for POTUS to catch him eyeing that hunky Rob Porter (long gone, like so many others) and to use it against him. The man was canny—he'd give him that—and spectacularly cruel. Making cracks like "Mike wants to hang all the gays," and winking at him broadly. He knew his God wouldn't have consigned him to the purgatory of the vice presidency— under the thumb of this lummox!—if He didn't have some larger plan in store for him. And his love for Stephen had possessed him with the force of an annunciation. Glancing across Mother's meaty shoulder at the First Inaugural Ball, he'd seen that noble skull silhouetted like a Fra Angelico angel against the wall of the Walter E. Washington Convention Center and he was utterly, utterly lost.

Stephen had his own beard, as one must, and when Pence had appointed Katie Waldman as his very own press secretary, a move calculated to bring Stephen more often into his orbit, to give the boy plenty of opportunities to casually drop by the vice presidential offices, he had hoped his beloved would recognize the depth of that sacrifice. The silver-framed wedding portrait that Katie now kept propped on her cluttered desk—Mr. and Mrs. Stephen Miller, posing before a white canopy twined with roses—confronted him on a daily basis. Yet his beloved's laudable discretion only permitted the man to signal his own interest with the most subtle of glances—so subtle, in fact, that on Pence's darkest days he found himself awash in despair and flayed by doubts about whether the attraction was truly reciprocated. Must he be forever fated to play Aschenbach to Stephen's Tadzio? It was an exquisite torture to be thrown together so often, and yet they were; his beautiful boy, his lodestar of David, was the true architect of that first term's greatest hits: the travel ban, zero tolerance, that inspired first State of the Union speech, the purges, the Voting Act of 2020 (requiring mandatory proof of citizenship and a urine test, effectively ensuring Republican victories for years to come), and the total immigration moratorium. This term, Stephen had already orchestrated the magnificent spectacle of the T-shaped gibbet intended for the public hangings of MS-13 members and Antifa thugs (once the DOJ signed off on the necessary permits), erected in Lafayette Square. Stephen wasn't afraid to make a splash, but he made certain the credit always went to the clown down the hall.

As time passed, Pence worried his desires would get the better of him, that he might have to resort to self-flagellation to keep his urges in check. For now, he practiced positive visualization. He filled his lungs with the intoxicating air of righteousness, and imagined his ascension to the highest office in the land, a nation he would remake according to the Lord's own specifications, where the faithful would be rewarded and apostates punished for their sins. Where the sacred life stirring in a woman's womb would have the full protection of the government, and where abortion would be a capital offense for both provider and recipient. Where the war being fought on all fronts against what was just and right and godly in America would have its true champion, someone pure enough to wield the holy sword to carve out a path in the shape of His will. In the cathedral of his brain, he pictured a glorious stained-glass window with heaven's pure light streaming through its lozenges. President Pence on the throne of a new America, an America washed white again, with his sloe-eyed darling by his side like the Son at God's right hand.

This term they'd been operating without an official chief of staff. (The days of General John Kelly, with his habit of exaggerated eye rolling and face planting and accidentally-on-purpose turning off the lights during speeches, now seemed like eons ago. Shortly after the election the former Marine was found in bed with a Sig Sauer in his hand and his brains congealing on the pillow.) The West Wing had taken on the air of the common room in a frat house where the senior who never manages to graduate forces everyone to binge-watch his old football training videos. *Honestly, doesn't this man have any friends?* When the footage of the Fifth Avenue shooting gave way to a lurid report on another celebrity suicide (Pence's eyes flicked toward a momentary close-up of the actress's handsome former husband, grieving handsomely), POTUS started yammering about the plans for another military parade ("I want the Space Force this time!") and Pence let himself tune in to the broadcast. That made three high-profile hangings and one intentional defenestration already this month, and April wasn't even half over yet. But truly, who could blame them?

When Stephen suddenly clamped his cell phone to his ear *(Oh, lucky phone!)* and slipped from the room, Pence had to exert every last ounce of his self-control not to let his love-struck eyes trail longingly after him.

5

Felo wonders when the white lady with the narrow eyes will come back through the metal door. He assumes day and night still happen somewhere outside the room that he never leaves, but there are no windows to tell him where or when the sun is in the sky. Sometimes the lady comes when he is sleeping and he wakes to find her smiling at him. He hates her, and when she smiles he hates her even more. Hating so much makes him tired. When the lady is away he tries to sleep and to dream of Mama and Papa, to bring them back. It worries him that their faces have started to blur, and sometimes in his dreams they squint at him with eyes like the lady's. The mattress on the big, soft bed where he curls up to sleep now smells like his snot and tears, and that smell brings him a strange comfort. One of the pillows on the bed is pink and shaped like a heart and it makes the sound of a heart, or a machine with a heart. When the lady leaves he puts it in the farthest corner of the room so he won't hear it thumping.

The room where the lady visits him is much bigger than his family's home in Guatemala, but it feels smaller. It has thick gray carpet on the floor and a shelf with some picture books. One tall book shows families of rabbits and pigs dressed in clothes and a one-eyed worm with one red shoe. A big screen on the wall plays cartoons in a language Felo doesn't understand. Striped curtains on the walls hide nothing but more walls behind them. Sometimes he wraps himself up in their folds and pretends he is a cigar, or a moth waiting to be born.

A black panel at the bottom of the door slides open. A metal tray with a plastic plate of food, a small carton of milk or juice, and a bottle of water is pushed through a slot. When Felo takes the items on the tray, the tray slides backward and the panel shuts. Once he stretched out on his belly and tried to look out of the panel before it slid shut, but all he could see was a bit of the hallway floor. The lady takes the garbage bag with the empty plates and bottles away when she visits. She often brings Felo a present, a toy for him to play with. He puts these in the farthest corner, still in their boxes, behind the striped curtain.

There is a toilet with a door, and a big square mirror with a fancy gold frame. When Felo stands on his toes to peer at himself in the mirror, he looks like a famous painting of a very sad boy. There is a white bathtub and a tall cabinet with fluffy white towels that stink of bleach. The lady likes to give him a bath and brings him toys with funny faces to play with in the tub. He tries to secretly scratch off the faces with his thumbnail. Mostly he sobs into his scarred brown knees while the lady rubs his back with a soapy sponge and makes sounds he doesn't understand.

———

Felo and Mama and Papa had walked for many days and nights in the desert. After they paddled a blow-up raft across an irrigation canal and splashed out into the muddy shallows on the other side, some men in uniforms grabbed them. The men threw them into a truck with other wet men. They brought Felo and his parents to a big building with long gray halls and many rooms with no windows. Mama screamed when the uniforms took him away. They put him in a cold metal cage with a concrete floor, a cage filled with children. Most of the children cried and hid under noisy silver sheets that the uniforms gave them. Some of the older boys in the cage would punch the younger ones if they cried too much. Mama and Papa never came to the cage. One of the older boys told Felo that all their parents were dead, that the uniforms had killed them and the children would be killed next. Felo wondered how that boy knew.

A long time passed, or maybe no time. Some uniforms came and took Felo and four of the smallest boys out of the cage. Felo knew that now he would be killed and he started to shake and could not stop. The uniforms walked them down many halls and finally out to a cement lot where a black bus was parked. Felo was surprised to see the sun still there, up in the sky. Before they put the bag over his head he saw flattened cigarette butts on the asphalt and a brown lizard racing away. The inside of the bus was freezing cold, but soon the bus stopped and they were led down the steps into another place and the bags were pulled off their heads. Two of the boys had wet themselves on the bus and could not stop crying.

The uniforms made Felo and the other boys undress and took them to a cement room with a shower. They were all shaking. The uniforms used a buzzer to shave their hair. Then they sprayed the boys with a liquid from a metal tube. It made their skin hurt and their eyes sting. The uniforms turned on the water in the shower and used a hose to spray them. The boys huddled in the center of the cement room, trying to shield their faces from the hard hot water that blasted from the hose. One of the boys puked, and Felo watched the yellow vomit flow over his toes and down the drain.

After the shower, the uniforms gave them clean clothes to wear, T-shirts and sweatpants and rubber sandals, and took them into a room with high windows and some chairs and tables. They gave them juice in little boxes and plates of food—some yellow rice and red beans covered with orange cheese, and a pile of white lettuce that looked like an *abuela*'s hair. Felo tried to eat a bit but he was too afraid of dying to swallow very much.

Time passed in the room. Felo could tell from how the shadows changed shape on the floor. He began to feel a little less frightened and wanted to put his head down on his arms and sleep. Suddenly the uniforms in the room stood up fast and the door opened. Two white men in dark suits came in first, and then a lady wearing a white blouse and soft pants and a dark jacket. Her shoes had long, thin heels and made a clicking noise like a beetle when she walked. She had narrow, darting eyes and a red mouth. She went to each of the boys and crouched down in front of him and said some words. When she spoke to Felo she touched his shaved head. He was shivering but he tried to keep very still while the lady touched him. She took off her jacket and wrapped it around his shoulders. The jacket smelled like soap and flowers. Then the lady and the men in suits left the room.

One of the uniforms took Felo's hand and led him out of the room. They walked down one hallway and another hallway and stopped at a door. The uniform took away the lady's jacket and put a hood over Felo's head. He heard a door squeal and saw sunlight through the dark cloth. He heard another door open, and felt hands pushing him into a cold seat and buckling a belt across his chest. When the seat began to move he thought he might be sick inside the hood.

Now he knew he would be killed, that the boy had been right. His mama and papa were probably already dead. Now it was his turn. He tried to be brave but he could feel his heart pounding and his teeth knocking together inside his mouth.

When the car stopped, someone unbuckled the belt and lifted Felo out. He felt arms carrying him, and heat on his skin, and men's voices coming from all sides. His whole body was shaking. Then the air turned cold again and the arms carrying him put him down on a soft chair. When someone pulled the hood away from his face, he saw he was in a long, narrow place with small round windows and big white seats in rows. The lady was there and now she was smiling at him. She rubbed his head and buckled a metal belt around his waist. She gave him a juice box covered with yellow pineapples, and a little plastic straw. His mouth was very dry from breathing through the hood, but he was afraid the juice might be poison so he didn't drink it. He didn't know how they were planning to kill him, and this might be one way to do it.

———

Now, what feels like an eternity later, Felo is still alive, and he knows a little about what happened to him. The lady took him on a plane. They flew for many hours, and he ate some peanuts and chocolate and slept a bit in the chair with the belt. When the plane landed it was dark. The lady held his hand too tightly and they walked together down the steps of the plane. A white man with smooth white hair was waiting for them in a big black car with mirrored windows.

The car drove for a while on a giant road with the lights of millions of cars flashing around them. Afterward, Felo thought that a lot of what he remembered might have been a dream because he was tired and his head kept snapping backward when he caught himself falling asleep. They drove through a city with glowing buildings on all sides, and stopped at a tall gate. A uniform spoke to the driver, and the car moved forward. They stopped next to a fenced-off cage with a smooth green floor and a long net stretching across the center. Next to the cage, Felo could see a huge white building with lights on it, bigger than a cathedral. They all climbed out of the car, and he thought they would put him in the cage, but the man lifted a hidden flap in the grass and Felo saw stairs leading into the ground. The white-haired man and the lady and Felo went down the stairs into a long, cold tunnel with small bright lights in the ceiling. The man and the lady didn't speak, but their shoes were loud on the floor of the tunnel. The man's hand stayed clamped on Felo's shoulder.

At the end of the tunnel was a metal door. The man pressed a red button and the door slid open, and they stepped into a small metal room. The man put a key into a panel in the room. The metal room shook a little and, when the door opened, Felo was surprised to see they were in a different place. They walked down a fancy hallway with the lady holding on tight to Felo's hand. They went into a gold-and-pink room with flowers in vases and a fireplace and a big wooden bed with a sheet across the top, like a bed where a king would sleep. The white-haired man winked at Felo and gave a little bow to the lady and left the room.

When the man was gone, the lady led Felo to a door in the corner of the room. She opened the door and turned on a light switch. She gently pushed him in front of her into a big closet, and pulled the door shut behind them. The closet was filled with ladies' clothes, and more shoes than Felo had ever seen in his life. The lady moved some curtains hanging at the back of the closet, and she put her hands flat against the wall and pushed. When she stepped away, Felo could see a door open into the wall. The lady took his hand and led him through the door and down a skinny passage. The passage took two turns and stopped at another metal door with two big locks. Behind the door was the room with no windows, where the food tray comes in under the door and the TV is always talking.

Felo does not know if the lady is still planning to kill him. But he is very certain that he wants to die.

6

April
Miles City, Montana

When he slid onto his usual stool at the Bison Bar that night, Paul Pendegrass was definitely in the mood for something different. The evening broadcast had gone well enough, though if he had to hear Ryan make one more joke about that stupid snowflake he might just tackle him on camera. Miles City, Montana, had earned a place in the *Guinness Book of World Records* as the site of the largest natural snowflake ever measured—15 inches in diameter—back in 1887, and KYUS meteorologist Ryan Sugarman never let anyone forget it.

Since Sinclair had acquired the station from NBC in the fall of 2019, the must-airs had become wholly predictable: Obama was the devil; this country or that one was trying to screw us; second inaugural attended by largest crowd ever assembled, etc., etc. The President used to keep things lively, but even his moves were getting a tad stale: the daily outrage, walked back a step or two, and then doubled down on. You could see it all coming like a prairie thunderstorm. And earlier today Paul had heard the same old excuse from Hallie about why she couldn't visit for the weekend ("Sorry, Daddy, but I've got a Calc test on Monday, and Mom promised to take me shopping at Rimrock…"). Yep, nothing new under the sun.

After taking a long swallow from the bottle of Tumbleweed IPA that Moss plunked down on the bar in front of him (he'd cracked the top before Paul's ass was even on the stool — how sad was that?), he used the bar mirror to scan the room behind him. Thursday nights at the Bison could get busy, but it was still early, and Paul saw just a couple red-hat regulars knocking balls around the stained felt of the pool table, and Ed Toddy nursing a beer at the far end of the bar, transfixed by the Newsmax broadcast. On the sound system, Brad Paisley and Carrie Underwood were harmonizing on "Remind Me."

Moss knew enough to leave Paul alone for that first beer; they'd have plenty of time for conversation as the evening wore on, but when he came directly from work Paul needed time to decompress. As usual, he'd shucked his suit at the television station and changed into black jeans and a faded green waffle henley. He avoided his own eyes in the mirror — after all, he knew exactly what he'd find there: an artificially polished, attractive forty-something guy with a full head of smooth dark hair with just a touch of gravitas at the temples. His father's side had some Crow blood that gave Paul his dark brown eyes and wide face ("Johnny Depp without the jewelry," he'd heard someone say about his looks in college). In that mirror he would also see what most people presumably did not: the slightly stunned look of a man smashing into a wall in slow motion.

The woman at the corner table with the frizzy gray hair and black-framed glasses had her nose buried in her laptop. She wore a microfiber vest over a plaid flannel shirt, and baggy jeans, the uniform of the post-menopausal western woman. An inch of brown liquor winked blearily at him from the glass on the table. In a town the size of Miles City, you found things out fast. Dr. Helen Easterhunt liked her scotch neat. A solitary geologist who'd come to town from Oregon the previous summer to study glacial deposits, her grant funding had been frozen when the EPA (recently renamed the Exxon Power Authority — he'd have to avoid that slip again on air) had channeled all designated federal funds into fossil fuel development on public lands. Instead of bailing she'd stuck around. She had a long-term arrangement at the Stockman's Lodge in town, and lately had been doing some work for Ferris Gladwell out at his ranch.

Nothing about her appearance or her demeanor seemed to invite company, but even post-divorce Paul had sufficient confidence in his ability to charm a woman over twenty years his senior. He had television good looks, after all, and an affable manner. And he was a journalist, still possessed of some residual natural curiosity, which is why—after downing two-thirds of his beer—he decided to approach her; he'd been wondering about her work with Ferris and thought there might be the makings of a local-interest piece there. When he walked over, beer bottle in hand, Dr. Easterhunt slammed down the lid of her laptop and blinked up at him. "Yes?" Her voice was low and pleasant enough but there was an edge of impatience that Paul couldn't miss.

"Excuse me, I don't mean to interrupt your work, but I wanted to introduce myself—"

"I have a television, Mr. Pendegrass, and I watch it occasionally—I know who you are. And I assume you know who I am. What can I do for you?"

In Miles City, Paul was a minor celebrity, and now that he was unencumbered by a spouse, plenty of women would have gladly made room for him at their table. But Dr. Easterhunt's brusque manner punctured his confidence a bit, and he had a vague sense of the power balance shifting between them. Still, he soldiered on. "I ran into Ferris Gladwell and he mentioned you'd been helping him" (a small lie, but a useful one, and how would she know?) "with an art project. I'd love to hear about it, if you can spare some time to talk to me."

He saw her hesitate, and guessed at the mental calculation going on behind those shrewd blue eyes. *If I talk to him now he will leave me alone later.* He glanced at the license plate nailed to the wall above her head, featuring Montana's new state slogan, "The Last Best Place." He still wasn't exactly sure what that meant.

"All right, Mr. Pendegrass," she finally agreed is a wearily amused tone. "Why don't you have a seat."

———

Years later, Paul would think back on this as one of the more consequential conversations of his life, even before they stepped outside the bar to smoke half a joint in the sharp April wind. Not so much because of what was said, but because of all the things that came after. Would any of it have happened if he hadn't walked into the Bison that night, fed up to here with his job, his ex-wife, his daughter's excuses, and, above all else, with himself?

He settled into the chair across from her and she told him about Ferris Gladwell's metal woman. Ferris's wife had passed away from pancreatic cancer a few years earlier. Now he was building something in her honor, from scrap metal, shaped like a giant Venus of Willendorf. (Paul didn't know what that was until he Googled it later—he had initially pictured the armless Venus de Milo, tough to square with his mental image of Libby Gladwell.) As Dr. Easterhunt described it, Ferris had sketched out his plans on the back of a strip of old wallpaper. His Venus would be approximately eight feet high by five feet wide, and about three feet deep, a massive metal version of the original 30,000-year-old statuette, which was made of oolitic limestone, Paul learned, and just over four inches tall.

"Archaeologists think it's some kind of goddess figure, an homage to the eternal feminine. Or maybe it was just something a Paleolithic dude made to jerk off to. Giant breasts and thighs and a big belly roll. And the head will be wrapped with rusty barbed wire. I guess he misses his wife." This explained the talk around town that Ferris was building some kind of X-rated art piece and had paid Dr. Easterhunt to model for him. She laughed when he told her about the rumors. He saw that her laugh was the youngest part of her, much younger than the work-roughened hand that closed around her glass, before she tossed back the remains of the liquor. Ferris had hired her to search the scrap-strewn acreage behind the Gladwell ranch house for pieces of rusted metal (everyone knew Ferris was a bit of a picker, partial to car parts) that could be used for the sculpture, tagging the larger pieces they'd need to collect with the truck, and bringing the smaller ones in from the field in a wheelbarrow.

Since his beer bottle was empty and she'd finished her scotch, Paul offered to buy them another round. When he returned from the bar with two squat glasses of Johnnie Walker Red in his hands, having ignored the questioning look Moss had fixed on him when he ordered, Dr. Easterhunt extracted a crumpled baggie from the inside pocket of her vest and waggled it at him. "Have they started drug-testing you at work yet, or would you like to smoke the rest of this with me?"

Paul was momentarily taken aback—twenty minutes before she'd been annoyed at him for interrupting her, and he hadn't pegged her for a pothead. But he'd been looking for a route out of the rut he'd fallen into, and here she was throwing him a kind of rope, at least for the next couple hours. *What the hell*, he thought. Before they left, she slid her laptop into a black zippered tote, and shoved it deep into the shadows under the table, though she must have known the other Bison Bar patrons would be more interested in the fact that they were leaving together than in anything she might have stowed under there.

Outside under the neon bison sign, her eyes squinted at him from behind the glowing orange coal of the reefer she held to her lips, regarding him with amusement as he nervously checked the street, leading them around the side of the building, out of the wind, before taking the joint from her. It was too chilly to loiter in the dark after she tossed the spent end into the weeds (a low of 29 degrees tonight, Ryan had said). Once they were tucked back into their seats (she'd reached down with her hand to feel for her bag, he noticed), comfortably buzzed and sipping their drinks, Dr. Easterhunt looked him dead in the eye and asked if he'd ever considering taking his own life.

"Only every day during my divorce," he joked. Her expression warned him that she was serious. Maybe it was just the pot, and the warm fraternal buzz of the room, but he found himself liking her face and the signs of time's passage etched across it—like bird tracks pressed into the muddy edges of a marsh. In his business, most of the women reporters were blondes with Botoxed faces—he'd had some Botox himself (so far just the forehead and around the eyes) and his teeth regularly bleached like anybody who worked in front of the camera. He found it relaxing to look at this woman's face, marked with its obvious lines and flaws, the skin slowly eroding like the geological features she studied.

While he mapped her facial topography in his mind, Dr. Easterhunt told him a story. Maybe she was a pothead, but the functional kind, because she seemed unaffected by the drug, whereas Paul kept getting distracted by things like the parentheses around her mouth and his sudden, intense craving for BBQ potato chips. The pot was strong, and he felt pretty stoned. Paul pulled his thoughts back from all the different tangents they wanted to follow and tried hard to pay attention to what she was saying about suicide. When Ferris hired her to help him with his projects, he'd mentioned in an offhand way that art had given him a reason to stick around a little longer. She liked Ferris and worried he might be more depressed than he was letting on.

"So here's why I'm telling you this, Paul" (because they had switched to first names by this point). "The first time I went to the CDC website to read up on information about suicide, I found an infographic showing that suicide rates in the US have gone up an average of 30%, and here in Montana they've skyrocketed by as much as 58%. That's incredible, right? Has your station done any local reporting on that?" Paul had to admit they had not. "When I visited the page they had lots of useful information and links to other websites. But when I went back to the site a few weeks later, a lot of that information was missing. There was a generic list of warning signs to watch for, the new hotline number, and stuff like that. But all the resources I'd seen before and the links to various studies were just gone."

"What do you mean 'gone'? It's the CDC."

"Well, the site was there, but all the detailed information I'd been looking at was missing. It was incredibly odd. Like the whole CDC site has been scrubbed of everything but the most basic suicide-related information."

Paul allowed that this was indeed strange. Especially since a lot of famous people had been killing themselves. General Kelly, back in the fall, and that actress, just two days earlier. And a couple years ago, there was the designer, Kate Spade, also with a scarf, and then Anthony Bourdain hung himself, too, which really stunned people. I mean, the man seemed like a true survivor, right? Like he'd seen everything, twice, with those soulful eyes and that big grizzled mug that looked so great on TV. And after those two it just became a regular feature of the news, like the must-airs they handed him when he walked into the station every afternoon. Each time KYUS reported on the latest celebrity suicide, they put that new hotline number at the bottom of the screen for people to call, but he'd never bothered to call it. I mean, why would he?

Being stoned made Paul hyperaware of his ability to carry on one conversation while the back of his brain conducted an entirely different discourse with itself, like reading a report on the teleprompter while the producer fed him breaking news via his earpiece. The pot also made him a little paranoid. He knew his extended talk with Helen, and the fact that they had gone outside together, had registered in the minds of the bartender and the other bar patrons, who kept glancing their way. Helen definitely didn't fit the profile of the kind of woman Paul had been keeping company with, since his divorce had made him a hot property in Miles City. If anybody asked, he'd just say he was interviewing her for a piece about rock formations, and they'd stepped outside to look at the stones mortared on the outside of the bar. He took another sip of the whiskey, which tasted like earth and fire in his mouth.

And while he entertained these thoughts yet another voice began to murmur in Paul's brain. He had a strange awareness of his own alien body, his two feet planted on the sticky floor, his back and ass making contact with the vinyl chair, the points of his elbows propped on the tabletop, and his mouth hinging open to emit the required responses to whatever Helen had been telling him. That inner voice reminded him he'd become a mouthpiece, a ventriloquist dummy with good hair. He'd grown so used to parroting Sinclair-approved talking points and reporting on innocuous local stories that he had forgotten what it felt like to catch a whiff of a real story. But he thought he might be smelling one now.

Meanwhile Helen had been explaining her theory that celebrities signal trends in the larger non-celebrity community. "They're not actually trendsetters, like people think. They are trend amplifiers. They're the most visible tip of the iceberg. The public obsesses about them because they are famous and sell magazines and boost ratings—it's a closed system, a feedback loop that excludes other relevant information. What is happening to them is presumably also happening to millions of other noncelebrities, right now. And it's happening a lot right here in Montana. But somebody doesn't want us to pay attention to that."

She lowered her voice and glanced around the room. "People in this red-hat town would string you up if you said a word against *him*." She nodded toward the portrait of the President draped with dusty bunting that hung next to the bar. "Plenty of people hated Bush Two's guts, but they didn't start offing themselves. Something is definitely going on. Put this number in your phone." She rattled off a sequence of digits, and he felt helpless to do anything but pull out his cell and comply. "Now you can reach me when you find out something. And text me so I've got your number. I'm a scientist and you're a journalist, Paul. We're the last, best hope of the world. Maybe we can figure this out together."

"Okay," Paul said. "Maybe so!" And he felt something quicken inside him, a feeling that could have been his long dormant sense of journalistic integrity beginning to emerge from its long hibernation, or just a bad case of the munchies—it was hard to know. "Do you like barbecue potato chips? I'm going to get us some potato chips."

7

April
South Beach

Telling the truth was out of the question. Least Kardashian knew she had to concoct the perfect lie to get out of the Saturday night plans for Angela's fortieth so she could visit Mar-a-Lago with Luka. The super-annoying sister-in-law, Margo, had flown in that morning from New Jersey and forced Least to do a deco tour with her, followed by lunch at Bodega. Angela and the others would start arriving in Ubers from the airport any minute now. Even though an invitation to the *freaking Winter White House* should clearly preempt every other event, Angela wouldn't see it that way; Least didn't want to deal with the onslaught of shit she was sure to get from the birthday girl and her minions if she actually told them the truth about where she was going—more likely, they would try to crash that party themselves and just end up spoiling everything.

Honestly, she could hardly believe her luck. "Wear white," Luka had said, when he told her to be ready by six. "It's an incredibly sexy color on you." As Least paced her hotel room, wolfing down a rubbery veggie wrap from the minibar and trying out different combinations of accessories with the dress she'd chosen to wear, she didn't think to wonder how he might know that. The dress had a high hem and a deep, asymmetrical draping back with a swath of long fringe that dangled down toward her ass—she'd splurged on it, wanting one fabulous thing to wear over the weekend.

As she laid out different necklaces on the bed, assessing their effect, she fanned out excuses in her mind like a poker hand, from least to most elaborate, weighing the relative merits of each. She did feel kind of shitty about blowing the girls off for the night—Angie had confided in her that she was really dreading her fortieth, and Least knew exactly what she meant—she'd been dreading hers, too. Despite all the targeted workouts and the chemicals you could inject into your face, forty really seemed like the death knell for non-celebrity fuckability. (For celebrities it was fifty-eight.) And you'd better really love scented candles because you'd be getting a shit ton of those from now on. Least didn't want to spend her forties stewing in regret that she'd missed her ONE BIG CHANCE to see the President's house (and maybe even meet HIM!) just because she didn't want to hurt somebody's feelings.

Angela and the others were busy getting tarted up for dinner followed by a night at Hunk-O-Mania, and no one noticed her leaving. At 6:03 p.m., Least slipped out the Bentley's front entrance to find Luka waiting beside a purring black Lexus. He stepped around as she approached and swung open the vehicle's passenger door, nodding approvingly at the way Least's tight dress navigated her curves. He wore a smoky-blue linen suit over an open-necked cantaloupe-orange shirt, a combo that showed a certain restraint amid all the tropical neon people flaunted in South Beach. She scooched into the car's black leather interior, tucking a pashmina and her clutch next to her hip as Luka closed the door and came back around to the driver's side. He buckled himself in and smiled at Least, then swung the car's nose away from the curb and into the street. As they accelerated past the storefronts of Ocean Drive, he touched a control on the steering wheel and reggaeton filled the car's interior. "So, you made some excuse to your friends?"

She waved her hand dismissively. She'd text Angela along the way that she had to skip dinner and would meet them at the strip club—that would buy her some time. "Let's just say this seemed like a once-in-a-lifetime opportunity. So tell me again exactly what it is you do?" Judging by the Lexus and the Rolex, it was clear Luka had some bucks, though whether or not it was family money she had yet to ascertain. He ignored her question and tapped at the navigation screen, and she wondered if he was stung by the fact that she'd had to ask again. Maybe he'd described his job in detail the night before when she'd been distracted by the screens in the restaurant? But he began filling her in on the history of Mar-a-Lago—how it had been built in the twenties by the cereal heiress Marjorie Merriweather Post, who at the end of her life had wanted to give it to the government as a Winter White House, but the government turned her down. "Can you imagine? But the President saved it from the wrecking ball, and spent millions to bring it back to its original glory. We have him to thank for that, preserving this remarkable piece of American history."

They left MacArthur Causeway and headed west before merging smoothly onto 95 North toward Fort Lauderdale. Luka put the car in chauffeur mode once they reached cruising speed on the interstate. Eventually he told her, "This is an industry event, for people in the entertainment industry—production, mostly. My business is individual brand strategizing. Sometimes we … collaborate."

He adjusted the music volume and they drove for a while longer in silence, the car's contours parting the humid air. Purple dashboard lighting gave his pale hair a black-light glow. This was Least's first trip to Florida, winter home of many a Michigan snowbird, and the trunks of tall palm trees picked out by the car's headlights made her feel like she was part of a procession on a royal road. Luka got her talking, about her fascination with the President, about the origins of her interest in him long before he'd declared his candidacy. About how her support was somehow more meaningful than that of all those rabid fans who came late to the bandwagon. It was a source of pride to Least that she had been an early adopter of the man's charisma. And though she tried to play it cool, she couldn't help asking Luka if he thought there was a chance the President might make an unscheduled visit to his club that weekend. "Could be," he told her. "They don't make those plans public in advance, obviously, for security reasons. A lot of entertainment people will be there, in any case." Googling it in her hotel room earlier, she'd found that, so far this year, POTUS had already made fifteen visits to the property, traveling down to his newly adopted home state nearly every weekend, so the odds of bumping into him were definitely in her favor.

Luka turned out to be a skilled and confident driver. When traffic on the road increased, he took command of the car again, staying ahead of the speed limit and smoothly passing the other vehicles. He was courteous, too, soliciting musical preferences from Least and adjusting the car's interior environment to her liking. The blacked-out windows of the Lexus allowed for the leisurely inspection of other drivers, many of whom were actively texting as they barreled down the highway. Least saw one man watching a movie on his dashboard, a film that featured, of all things, a spectacular car crash sequence.

They'd been en route for over an hour when the disembodied female voice of the GPS spoke up, directing them toward the next exit. All this time, Luka had volunteered very little himself, so different from the M.O.s of most of the men Least dated. He answered her questions, but briefly and without self-aggrandizing embellishments. He seemed curious about her without giving the impression he intended to exploit the information he extracted from her as part of a seduction campaign. In the conversational space freed up by his reticence they talked about the incredible art Least had seen in Miami, and she told him about the sexually explicit set of Kama Sutra kitchen magnets she'd purchased at the erotic art museum, a gift for the birthday girl whose party she'd just bailed on.

They had merged onto the Ronald Reagan Turnpike when Luka turned down the music on the radio and said her name. His voice took on a confessional tone as he told her, "I should explain something to you before we arrive. I heard the rumor there was a Kardashian staying at the hotel, and I looked for you. I had an ulterior motive. I believe I can help you . . . that we can help each other."

She laughed, trying to keep the mood light. "You did? Okay . . . I'm listening."

"It may surprise you to know that I have sources close to the President. That's one reason we're going to the club tonight. My sources tell me that he likes the Kardashian brand—he sees it as sexy and powerful. So he has your cousin Kim come to the Oval Office and talk pardons with him. But in private he says he's concerned about these Kardashian girls."

"What exactly is he concerned about?" There was plenty to choose from, what with that flap about Kim hiring an armed militia to guard the Kardashian-West stockpile of toilet paper during the recent COVID-19 outbreak, and the rumors that the couple's latest baby, Deity, had been genetically modified.

"Sometimes he questions their judgment, the choices they make in their romantic life. Why do they all go with black men? It's like they think these guys are better than white men, and that bothers him. He wonders, Why do they taint their beautiful brand with these black men? And he sees how Kanye behaves, like he thinks he's Jesus running for president. His ego is out of control. He says, 'He's a showboat, like Comey and Omarosa. I don't like it.'"

These revelations took her entirely by surprise. She'd seen the rows of red-hat-wearing African Americans front and center at every rally, and she knew any claims that the President was a racist had been cooked up and circulated by his enemies. "But he just made Kim the ambassador to Bokino, or whatever that island is called."

Luka chuckled a bit. "That island doesn't even exist! You see his genius—he was looking for a way to get rid of her. It's the equivalent of sending someone to Siberia."

His hand, which had been gesturing elegantly in the dashboard lighting, paused to rest on the steering wheel. Beyond the windshield, the headlight beams picked out the mile markers speeding past. Least tugged her dress down from where it had crept up along her thighs; the air-conditioning was blasting uncomfortably between her legs, but she didn't ask Luka to adjust it.

"And then Bruce Jenner changing to a woman. That tainted their brand, too. This trans thing—it's just disgusting, he thinks. Personally, I do not care, but it bothers him. It's just not natural, he says. But the name, Kardashian, it still has value. Which is how I could get you into the party tonight. You are something very special, very rare, like a white peacock. You are an unspoiled Kardashian."

Least had to laugh out loud at that. She'd lost her virginity at fourteen to her friend Resa's older brother, Alex. As a highly attractive denizen of New York City, she'd had plenty of opportunities to misbehave over the years. And just last night she'd been half entertaining the thought of inviting Luka upstairs to do all kinds of nasty things before he'd told her he would see her the following night and left her in the lobby of the hotel. "Hate to break it to you, but the last time I was a virgin was in middle school."

Luka turned in his seat, an expression of palpable disappointment on his face. "How very 2015 of you, my dear," he chided. "What is your man's true brilliance? What has been his greatest lesson to the world, his greatest gift? *We make our own truth.* Truly powerful people create their own reality. If you repeat something often enough it will *become* true. No collusion! Rigged witch-hunt! Coronavirus hoax! Today, of course, you are not a 'virgin.'" He raised his hands from the wheel to make air quotes around the word. "Technically speaking. When I have finished with you, you will be, for all intents and purposes. I specialize in brand turnarounds. Together, we can purify the Kardashian brand and remove that taint from the family name. It is happening already. I took the liberty of starting a new Instagram account for you and it is already trending." After tapping in his passcode, he handed her his phone, which had been nestled in a compartment under the dash. "Search for 'Virgin Kardashian' and have a look."

Least wanted to spend some more time pondering the specifics of what he'd just said, but she opened the app and typed in the search term.

What she saw when she opened the Instagram account made her grab the armrest to brace herself against the sensation of a sudden and violent swerve, though the car hadn't strayed from its lane. @virginkardashian already had twenty-three posts. Least stared in astonishment at images of herself, none of which she had posed for or known were being taken. Framed in the art deco doorway of the Marlin Hotel. Backlit by the neon LOVE ME, FUCK YOU sign at Bodega, where she'd lunched with Margo. Poolside at the Bentley, with her hair heaped on top of her head. But there were also New York shots: Least in a cream silk blouse sipping a cappuccino in SoHo; walking out of the Atlantic Avenue Barneys with her phone to her ear and a bag on her arm (containing, coincidentally, the pair of underwear she was currently wearing, the single item she could afford from that store); perched on a barstool somewhere with her legs crossed and a dirty martini balanced in her hand. Her skin prickled with the first stirrings of something like fear.

"Where the fuck did these come from? Did you take these pictures?" She turned to Luka, who seemed rather pleased with himself, a smug smile twisting his mouth. He glanced at the rearview mirror before guiding the Lexus into the far right lane. Apparently, they were taking the exit. They would be slowing down soon, which meant she could get out of the car. Her four-inch silver Jimmy Choos (originally $780; scored for $250 on farfetch.com) would be hell to run in, but she could kick them off before she opened the door. Her body experienced a rush of instinctive animal responses, and the taste of pennies flooded her mouth. A light sheen of sweat rose on her skin, and the depth of her own stupidity appalled her. She had willingly gotten into a car with a strange man, and no one knew where she was. For the last hour they could have been heading in the opposite direction from Mar-a-Lago—she'd been too busy listening to Luka's mesmerizing accent and his flattering remarks to pay much attention to their surroundings. Every episode of *Dateline* had prepared her to be so much smarter than this.

He took the exit, past a sign that read "Palm Beach Island, home of Mar-a-Lago, America's most exclusive destination," and the car flew over a causeway. Nonetheless, she clutched the phone, praying they would slow down enough for her to leap out without killing herself. Luka glanced over at her frozen face and laughed out loud. "If you dial 911 on my phone we will definitely be late for the party. Don't look so spooked! I didn't take those pictures—I just curated them, and cropped them, and you look amazing in every one. It was hard to communicate the white peacock, that rare blend of sexiness and purity, but I think I hit it just right."

"But how did you get these pictures?" she repeated, pushing her back against the passenger door to put as much distance between her and Luka as she could in the confines of the car. With her right hand she groped for the door handle. She forced her voice low to keep herself from starting to shriek. "Have you been following me? Was this all a setup?" They were moving fast down a narrowing road lined with palm trees and close-clipped tall hedges, where huge parabolic mirrors marked the ends of gated drives. She guessed the sea must be somewhere off to their right.

"All the images collected by security cameras in public places are available to anyone. The facial recognition technology has become very sophisticated, and Clearview gives you access to everything. Surely you know that anytime we are out in public, cameras are watching. Now please try to relax—I have no intention of doing anything to harm you."

Least pulled her eyes away from Luka's face, somewhat reassured by his easy manner, his persuasive and reasonable tone. She gradually allowed herself to settle back into the seat. She was still holding Luka's phone, and she gazed in wonder at the most recent post, a close-up of her cleavage in her MAGA bikini, sweat and sunscreen glistening in her décolletage. She recognized the small mole on her right breast. Already, @virginkardashian had 650K followers. Her own account, the one she had started herself years ago, had barely cracked twelve hundred. So far, the MAGA image had 97,023 likes, and the comments were mostly hearts and heart-eyed frogs and flaming emojis. As she continued to stare, marveling at what had been set in motion, she felt the car slow down and execute a series of turns before easing to a stop. She looked up from the screen to see a row of arches topped by terracotta roof tiles and a pink tile-topped cupola looming over everything, like a guard tower at a prison for Barbie dolls. An eager young man dressed in a maroon uniform with gold epaulets hustled past the windshield to stand expectantly by Luka's door.

Gently, Luka took the phone from her hand and slid it into the inside pocket of his jacket. He fluffed his white forelock, checking his reflection in the rearview mirror. Then he turned to Least with a small smile. "We have arrived, beautiful lady. Are you ready?"

———

Living in New York City, and working in SoHo, Least was no stranger to opulence, vicariously enjoyed. She had sipped champagne on the terrace of a Manhattan penthouse with views of Central Park from its indoor pool and original Basquiats on the walls. She had attended lavish weddings in the Hamptons and million-dollar bat mitzvahs. Mar-a-Lago took her breath away, but not because of the beauty of the architecture. In her heart of hearts, she had to admit the place was smaller than she had imagined, and far less tasteful. The salmon exterior with its cream plaster ornaments and funny little chimneys, the lichen-spotted roof tiles, the jumble of wings topped by that jutting, boxy tower flying the presidential flag, all looked a little hokey to her, like a dictator's compound in a third-rate Caribbean nation, or one of those castles people put in their aquariums. What squeezed the air from her body was the powerful sense of nearness, of proximity to Him. Her head swam with the knowledge that somewhere in this gaudy pseudo-palace, the most powerful man in the world regularly held court; she might be inhaling some of the very same molecules of air that had migrated in and out of his powerful lungs.

Mar-a-Lago smelled like money and burnt steak. Soon after they'd mounted the scrolled-iron staircase, framed by oversized lanterns from the Rejuvenation Hardware Spanish Inquisition collection, and crossed the club's threshold, Luka guided her through several gold-splashed interiors crammed with potted palms. She noted specimens of the Palm Beach male displaying his typical plumage: open-necked plaid shirt under a linen jacket with brightly colored pants, and leather driving moccasins with a bit front. Those in ties wore them a hand's span below the belt buckle, the fashion since the second inauguration. Every woman she saw was blond, with a grouper's mouth and a Lily Pulitzer print dress. They registered Least's glossy waves of dark hair and the tight white Spandex cupping her ass, and turned away, sneering. *I already have 650K followers,* she thought. *Which of you bitches can say that?* and she lifted her chin with a surge of pride. Luka spoke to a hostess, who led them out to a large dining patio with a fabric-draped ceiling that looked, Least couldn't help thinking, like a giant anus clenching the chain of a chandelier. Soft jazz leaked out of hidden speakers, just audible over the clinking of glasses and cutlery and effervescent conversation. Through arches along the curving wall she caught the agitation of palm fronds thrashing in the breeze and sensed an expanse of dark water beyond.

Luka steered Least to a cloth-draped table on the perimeter of the dining room where an older white man and an Asian woman were already seated. The pair stood, smiling intently, as Luka and Least approached. The man extended a hand, clasping Least's in a firm, warm grip. "Miss Kardashian, what a pleasure to meet you," he said in a hearty tone, taking her in through hazel eyes behind round tortoiseshell-framed glasses. "Abbott Wunderlund, Parallax Entertainment. And this is my associate Su-mi Moon." A second hand was extended, this one cool and smooth, like its owner. A well-groomed guy in his sixties, Abbott had a full head of wavy gray hair, scraped straight back over a massive tanned forehead. The lapel of his dark-gray jacket sported an updated version of the ubiquitous American flag pin with a gold T in the place where the stars would typically be. His associate looked considerably younger—closer to Least's own age, most likely. Petite and compact with a stylish asymmetrical haircut, Su-mi wore a black 3-D printed necklace over a hot-pink sheath dress that showed off her sculpted arms. A smoky eye and a glossy nude lip gave her face drama, but her voice, when she greeted Least, was all business.

They settled into their seats, and Luka ordered cocktails from a hovering waiter. While she smiled and nodded as everyone exchanged pleasantries, Least struggled to rein in her wandering attention. If being here in this place wasn't disorienting enough, she was also trying to process everything Luka had told her in the car, and the clutch on her lap had begin buzzing with texts—no doubt the party girls wondering where the hell she was. She set the bag at her feet where the vibrations couldn't distract her. Before long the waiter returned, placing a narrow glass in front of Least—a light-green cocktail sparkling with flakes of gold. Luka tapped the rim. "Drink this," he urged her, "you'll love it." As she sipped the concoction, which tasted of melon, ginger, and star anise, she yanked the balloon of her mind down from where it had been knocking against the draped ceiling and tried to focus on the conversation at the table.

She heard Luka explain that the executives at Parallax had been working on a project to take advantage of the new right-wing media markets, "by the base, for the base." What they had in mind was a talk show with a relaxed format like *The View* but featuring a solo female host, someone new and sexy and sassy and fresh. All the celebrity guests would be hot and rich and Republican, talking freely about politics and religion and other topics that American families tended to shy away from at the supper table. The concept was "dinner TV"—a show for people to watch while they ate, a way of bringing the whole family together around a single screen. And solo viewers would be made to feel like they were part of a raucously fun dinner party where everyone was on the same political page and felt free to speak their mind. They wanted the premiere episode of the show to be filmed on location at Mar-a-Lago.

Luka's thumb tapped her elbow, as he explained how the negative trend predictor they'd hired had really hated the whole concept, which was an extremely promising sign. "This guy is one of the top negative barometers in the business, practically a legend. Back in the eighties he said Madonna would be a flash in the pan, and last year he predicted oat milk would be a bust."

A blast of Slavic laughter erupted from one of the nearby tables, and Abbott had to raise his voice, his eyebrows arcing expressively as he explained they had been meeting with women they thought might be good candidates to host the show, all of them the young, attractive trophy wives of various cabinet members, with one or two sexy right-wing influencers thrown in. He ticked off some names on his fingers. Least hadn't heard of most of them, but she nodded anyway.

Now Su-mi leaned forward. "The President's network is happy to partner with us, as long as we can guarantee that everyone appearing on the show is highly attractive." As she described the project, she tucked her black hair behind her right ear, which Least saw was missing part of its cartilage at the top, approximately the size of a mandarin orange segment. "The network would have final veto power, of course, over who we choose. And frankly, we thought the Kardashian brand was … problematic. But Luka floated his Virgin Kardashian concept with their people and the response has been super-positive."

Only at this moment did Least understand that what they were discussing had something, or rather everything, to do with her. She turned to Luka, suddenly aware that her heart had started slamming around in her chest like a sneaker in a dryer. Luka laid a possessive hand on her arm. "We know you don't have television experience, but we think that could work in your favor. A little less polish and predictability can be enormously appealing, more *authentic*, as the President knows." He smiled and then scanned the room behind her. In response to some signal Least did not see, Luka suddenly excused himself and left the table.

Abbott continued talking about the concept, about why they were there at Mar-a-Lago, and what a fantastic setting it would be for a live taping of the show's first episode. Now he had her full attention, and she stared at the broken blood vessel at the edge of his eye, a red firework going off in a white sky. Abbott told her the President liked to mingle with members of the club and Mar-a-Lago guests when he was in town, interrupting weddings and retirement parties to make cameo appearances. Unfortunately, on this particular weekend he was scheduled to meet with the Saudi Crown Prince at his Bedminster club. But on his next trip to Mar-a-Lago, he had generously agreed to pose for some publicity photos with Parallax execs, to create some buzz in advance of the show.

Near her sandaled foot, the phone in her purse continued to vibrate. Least wanted to grind it under her heel, to make it stop. What did she care about a stupid birthday party when she was sipping drinks with powerful, connected people who might be able to make her famous, maybe more famous than that washed-up bitch-cousin who treated her like a stranger, wouldn't take her calls? While Abbott talked, Su-mi had been checking her own phone. She glanced away from the screen and held up a finger to interrupt Abbott's spiel. "Yes," he said, in response. "Okay, he's almost ready. Would you please come with us?"

As she rose, rather shakily, to her feet, Least realized how much she needed to pee. And where on earth had Luka gone? She suddenly missed his steadying presence, his soothing, subtly accented voice. They threaded their way between the tables, noisy with voices amplified by alcohol and self-importance, toward the grand salon. She leaned down to Su-mi's intact ear and murmured, "I'd like to use the ladies' room, if there's time."

"Yes, of course, I'll take you there."

In the restroom (one of thirty-three, she'd later learn), Least stepped into a veined black marble stall, and lowered herself onto the commode with a rush of relief. The sight of the white material of her mini-dress bunched above her hips reminded her to feel grateful that she was right in the middle of her cycle. On the toilet, she fished her phone out of her clutch. Barely glancing at the barrage of texts from Margo and the others (*Where R U? Angie got pulled up on stage!!!! R U on yr way?*), Least checked the Instagram account for @virginkardashian, her hands shaking as she saw that the number of followers had continued to climb, to 673K. There was even a new image, posted less than an hour before, a shot of her mounting the stairs in front of the club's entrance (she recognized the diagonal slash of white fringe at the back of her dress, and her ass looked amazing, like "a white-hot valentine," as one of the comments raved). How had Luka taken that picture without her noticing?

Perched there with her legs spread over the toilet and her new thong underwear down around her knees, stunned by all that had happened to her since Luka had found her by the hotel pool, Least felt swamped by a feeling of arousal. In these surroundings, the President's markings were literally everywhere, a musky pheromone wafting through the air-conditioning vents. The revelations at the table, and the alcohol and gold leaf and flattery circulating in her system, all overwhelmed her, made her feel incredibly turned on. The two lacquered blondes staked out in front of their reflections and whining about their housekeepers finally finished adjusting their Spanx and left. Listening to make sure she was alone in the restroom, Least used her fingers to quickly get herself off. After exiting the stall, she washed her hands at the gold-fixtured sink and freshened her makeup, staring in wonder at her face in the elaborately framed mirror. She had never looked more beautiful, never felt more incandescent than she did at that moment. She would look amazing on TV.

Su-mi had instructed her to meet them in the club boutique, but when Least walked in the shop was empty except for the same pair of blondes, slathering on a sample of the club's signature lotion, Emoluments, which stank of gardenia. Her eyes scanned racks of silk scarves featuring the President's coat of arms, golf balls and tees stamped with the Great Seal, and polos with a big golden T embroidered where the little mounted rider used to be. A deck of playing cards splayed out in a glass case caught her eye—All the President's Women had Melania and Ivanka and all the other pretty women in POTUS's orbit on the face cards, plus the jokers: Elizabeth "Pocahontas" Warren wearing an Indian headdress, and Hillary Clinton in striped jail pajamas.

The persistent buzzing in her purse reminded Least that her friends would be increasingly frantic. The most recent message warned, *Calling cops if we don't hear from U!!!!* She texted back *Sorry!!—cant make it.*

Will explain later and then shut off her phone. She considered buying the joke deck for Angela, an apology gift to lump in with the Kama Sutra magnets, but what the fuck did she have to apologize for? The TV on the wall of the shop showed crawls flowing across the bottom (*Earth Day Canceled; SCOTUS Declares POTUS Above Law*) of looped footage from the White House Egg Roll, featuring a gleeful North Kardashian-West tottering through the grass in sparkly three-inch heels.

Least had just begun to seethe at this reminder of her cousin's continuing prestige when Luka reappeared. "There she is! There's someone we want you to meet." He steered her out the door of the boutique and down a long hallway lined with honey onyx console tables, each supporting an enormous arrangement of spiky tropical blooms, their masses doubled by the mirrored walls. At the end of the hall he paused to knock briefly on the dark wood paneling of a door before pushing it open and ushering Least inside.

She found herself in an overdecorated room lined with bookshelves and lit with glowing red table lamps. One wall featured an enormous gilt-framed portrait of the President in a golf sweater, looking very handsome, though about thirty years younger and sixty pounds slimmer. Black leather armchairs with nail head trim were grouped around a conference table, in front of a cold fireplace. In them sat Abbott, Su-mi, and a short bald man in a sharkskin suit who sprang to his feet as they entered the room. As the man hurried toward her, Least saw he was barely five feet tall, with a head as smooth and waxy as an anal suppository. He reached for her hand, clasping it in his two dry paws and smiling widely. "Tony Falco! Pleasure to meet you, Miss Kardashian," he said, flashing a row of Chiclet teeth.

"Tony schedules events here at the club," Luka told her.

"Among other things." Falco drew her toward the table, patting the seat nearest his own. Least took the chair, which was cold and a little slippery, and Luka settled himself on her left.

"What do you think of the place? Fantastic, am I right?" Falco asked her, spreading out his short wingspan to embrace the heavy opulence of the room, the brass chandelier and dark floral drapes, the busts of conquistadors gazing imperiously down at them from atop the bookshelves. Least looked around with what she hoped was an appreciative expression on her face, noting a framed *Time* magazine cover with a bas-relief of POTUS's profile on the gold Nobel Peace Prize medallion. Falco didn't wait for a response, but went on: "I hear this is your first visit—you'll have to come back when the President is in residence! I know he'd love to meet you."

Falco resumed his seat, and Abbott and Su-mi sketched out their vision for the show. As far as Least could tell, beyond the "dinner TV" idea, the concept didn't stray too far from other cable news program formats, except for the stipulation that all the guests and hosts would be carefully vetted for their attractiveness, right-wing bona fides, and loyalty rating. As Abbott explained, each episode would be filmed in a different location in order to showcase one of the President's many properties, beginning with the crown jewel, Mar-a-Lago. They wanted to shoot the premiere episode on the dining patio where they'd had their drinks, giving viewers a seat at the most exclusive table in the nation. "We can have cameras follow some of the guests as they explore the club," Abbott said. "It'll be the twenty-first-century equivalent of opening King Tut's tomb, all that wealth and majesty unfolding before their eyes."

"Except this king is very much alive!" Su-mi hastened to add. In addition to entrancing its target audience, the show would create extended commercials for luxury golf clubs and hotels, with POTUS himself making appearances when his schedule permitted. This bit, Luka's part of the pitch, was the piece that excited her the most, naturally. But soon Su-mi began going over the logistical details involved with staging a show at the club, not to mention the many security issues, and everything blurred together in Least's disinterested ears. Her primary function in this meeting, she assumed, was to be on display, judging by the number of times Falco's eyes swiveled in her direction. As Su-mi assured him that all the security costs would be covered by Parallax, Least did her best to seem engaged, but her gaze began to drift. On the spines of the thick volumes lining the shelves behind Abbott and Su-mi, she could make out the same series of titles repeating in a regular pattern across the width of the bookcase; the books had a suspiciously plasticine veneer, like Falco's blinding smile.

Soon after, the meeting wrapped up. Luka took several shots of her next to the President's golf portrait while Abbott and Su-mi stood chatting with Falco, and then a shot of her posing next to the *Time* cover with Falco, who flashed a thumbs-up at the camera with one hand while the other slithered around her hips. Standing by her side, his shiny head could have fit snugly into Least's armpit. Posting the images to her new Instagram site with #maralago, #POTUSproperties, #onepercentfabulous would drive her numbers even higher, Luka promised. Least was fairly certain Kim had never been to Mar-a-Lago, and it would be deeply satisfying to lord this one over her cousin via social media. Escorting them out of the conference room, Falco proudly led them on a tour of the club, and Least forced herself to gush at one oppressively appointed interior after another as they trailed in his wake. When they said their good-byes, Falco's leathery little mitt again engulfed her hand for longer than felt entirely professional.

On the way back to South Beach in the Lexus, with Falco's business card in her clutch and Abbott Wunderland's fulsome praise still ringing like a bronze bell in her ears, Least turned her phone back on just in time to stop Angie and the others from calling the police.

8

Bubble Tea Straw Moon
Sargassa

Even without a breath of wind, the scent of slow-roasted goat and melting plastic still found its way to every corner of the Patch. Petra inhaled deeply, pulling it down into her lungs. Tonight they would celebrate the quarterly lunar feast, an assembly of the governors to share news and address concerns from all regions of Sargassa. As the sun crossed the meridian, the women would begin arriving in skiffs, to gather in the common house for the Council.

Each wore the identifying necklace of her trust, the several communities under her governance; they had created these together at the first official meeting of the Council. The necklaces were hung outside each governor's shelter as a sign that she was home and "open for business," and any Sargassan could bring their concerns and disputes to her at this time. As the governor of the southeastern trust, Petra wore a necklace she'd crafted from blue monofilament fishing line, strung with alternating pieces of popped balloons and smashed Keurig cups, with a neon-green cocktail sword pendant—such ornaments were exotic tokens to those who'd left Muslim countries, and much prized by the scavenging teams, since it was rare to find one with the hilt intact.

At today's meeting, legislative matters would be discussed and the fates of lawbreakers determined until the sun's chin dipped toward the sea. After the Council announced its decisions, and dispatched messengers trusted to carry the news to all colonists of the southern Patch, they would celebrate. The long night would be full of revelry, in every region of Sargassa, but the largest celebrations took place at the four points of the compass where each council was held. Everyone looked forward to the big gathering and the opportunity to stuff their bellies—a rare event, since most days they ate sparingly and regularly fasted to avoid exhausting precious food supplies. Once the full moon laid a path down on the water, puppet shows and dances around the fire pit would tell the new fables of their world, entertainments beloved by the youngest residents of Sargassa. Watching their animated features in the firelight, Petra often found herself mesmerized by these strange children, the *vencejos*, a generation whose feet had never touched land, like the ever-flying birds for whom they were named.

Just then, Virginia Daria, the first child to be born on the Patch, raced by, her small body moving in the singular swaying gait they all had developed from walking on a floating surface. Like a kite pulling its ragged tail, she was trailed by a gang of friends, all manic with anticipation of the night's events. The girl paused to greet Petra, her tangle of braids spiked with oily feathers and multicolored bread clips, plastic tomato nets sleeved up her skinny brown arms. She grinned, revealing one crooked adult tooth nudging out of her top gum, before jerking her sargassum-crowned head to urge her flock into flight again.

Petra envied these children whom the war had never warped and twisted, who had never been deafened by a barrel bomb or gasped for air after a gas attack, never cowered at the angry buzz of drones hunting for signs of life in the rubble. Accidents still happened, of course, mostly drownings, and some parents still beat their children when they misbehaved, despite stiff penalties and growing social disapproval. But these wild new natives of the Patch were free to flourish and grow in a way their parents, their older sisters and brothers, never could. What would they make of this strange new world? she wondered.

The length of the shadows told her it was soon time for the gathering of the Council. Petra slipped her raft into the channel and paddled toward the meetinghouse, nodding to the colonists she passed along the route. She gave herself an internal scolding when she found she had half an eye out for Adnan, whom she'd sent away from her shelter just before dawn that morning. The situation with Burak still rankled her. When Petra had failed to resolve the situation to the goat herder's satisfaction, he had promised to carry his complaints to Valeria, the governor of the neighboring trust, and Petra expected to get an earful from her at the meeting.

The largest and most substantial structure in this part of Sargassa, the meetinghouse was one of only a few shelters that could be spotted from a distance. Builders had tiled its wide, arching roof with the distinctive patterned shells of loggerhead turtles, which came to feed in the rafts of sargassum and supplied the colonists with meat and other materials. The overlapping rows of shells channeled off the rains, and let in an amber light on the sunniest days. Inside, the structure measured no higher than six feet, but the taller men were the only ones who habitually knocked their heads on the ceiling. A thick wooden pole braced the low roof, the remains of the broken mast from a sailing vessel, sheathed with colorful ribbons of patterned fabric that each governor had sacrificed from the hem of a skirt or a blouse or a headscarf. Low-slung structures weathered the winds best; the colonists built their shelters close to the surface, with flaps that could be battened down in advance of a rare storm, like a turtle retreating into its shell for safety. And at the rear of the meetinghouse they stored a massive sheet of interwoven refuse, that could be dragged over the roof of the structure to camouflage it from the air.

When she pulled her raft out of the channel and approached the meetinghouse, Petra counted six necklaces hanging from the eaves around the entrance. Besides hers—which she lifted off her neck and draped over a hook to the right of the entranceway—only one was missing: Valeria's. Petra paused to rinse her hands in a shallow pool of fresh water by the door before slipping through the curtain of plastic strips that kept the flies out.

In the dim interior, arrayed on flat cushions around the central roof support, sat six governors of the southern Patch. As she settled herself on one of the two remaining cushions, Petra raised a hand to Halima; Fatou and Meryem were too deep in discussion to acknowledge her. In the Council they spoke Sargassan, a hybrid patois of Arabic, Spanish, Turkish, and African-accented French, the languages of the largest populations that had been forced out to sea in the years between 2016 and 2020. It was a practical spoken dialect, useful for communicating emergencies, political ideas, and legal decisions, but it had its limits. It had no word for boredom, for instance, or for cellulite, or money, or suicide. Many of the colonists arrived speaking some English, but that language had become tainted, and they made a conscious decision not to resort to it in the governance of their new homeland. English was the language of lies and violence and betrayal—when people wanted to lie, to wound, to insult someone beyond repair, they did it in English. Children caught speaking it were punished.

Each governor in the circle wielded equal power, but age commanded respect, and Halima had been in her late seventies when she fled an abusive husband in Mauritania. Her lumpy face wreathed by a faded blue headscarf, Halima glanced at the empty cushion to Petra's right before raising her hand to draw everyone's attention. Private conversations guttered into silence. "Governors," Halima spoke up, "should we begin? Hopefully, Valeria will join us soon, as we have much to discuss."

As the Council began to take up the dull but necessary matters that dominated these gatherings (freshwater reserves, reports on infrastructure maintenance, allocations for the regional schools and the clinics, the crimes committed in each region, deaths since the last meeting, and which colonists needed aid and support), Petra felt a growing unease at Valeria's absence. The governor was a hardass, brusque and prone to cutting off the other members in the midst of a discussion. A famine refugee from Caracas with brittle blond hair and unnerving green eyes, Valeria had arrived on the Patch with her son, Luis, just three years before, but had quickly risen to prominence. She radiated intelligence and impatience, and the first trait fed the second; Valeria didn't suffer fools, and her sharp tongue had lashed out at all of them, on occasion. More than once, Valeria had barked at Petra for being late to a meeting. So where was she? Petra made the necessary reports as they moved around the circle, but the nagging fact of the empty cushion distracted her, and Petra realized she'd missed her chance to frame the episode of the goat's drowning to Adnan's advantage.

They had been talking for nearly an hour, and Fatou had just asked the governors to submit their lists for the trade vessels, when a minor commotion at the doorway of the meetinghouse drew everyone's attention. Valeria—because it was she, of course, as Petra felt relieved to see—was speaking sharply to a hunched bundle of rags that hung on her arm. As she and several of the younger governors clambered to their feet, Petra identified the bundle as Hiranur, the haruspex who lived on the western edge of the trust.

When she'd fled her native Syria, Petra had abandoned the belief system that she knew had failed her long before the war broke out. But some colonists still clung to the old religions, and who could blame them? At the mercy of the weather around them, largely dependent on their wits for survival, they imagined that chants and sacrifices could summon rain clouds and cure sickness, and Petra did not waste her breath attempting to dissuade them. Superstitious Sargassans brought choice pieces of eel or a new sunshade to Hiranur, who scrutinized the objects she found in the split bellies of fish and seabirds like an ancient Roman oracle reading the guts of sacrificial animals to divine the future. *Has my beloved taken another lover?* one might ask her. Or *When will it be safe to return to my homeland? Will I ever tend the graves of my parents again?*

Valeria managed to yank her arm free from Hiranur's grip, and several women who had been attracted by the raised voices outside drew the haruspex away from the meetinghouse, speaking in low, soothing tones. Sweaty with annoyance, Valeria was talking even before the Council members had a chance to pose their questions. "I have been detained," she told them indignantly as she pushed through the doorway, "by a gang of idiots! And by the queen of them all!" Hiranur and several of her most ardent supporters had stopped the governor en route, demanding that she hear Hiranur's report and deliver it to the Council. And in her vehemence, Hiranur had punched her staff through the bottom of Valeria's raft, and a skiff had to be commandeered before she could continue her journey. "And then!" screeched Valeria, "the old goat decided to tag along with me!"

Ignoring Valeria's insult, Hiranur brushed aside the plastic strips at the entrance with her staff and slowly made her way to the center of the room. As she approached, Petra marveled at the abundance of colorful fabric wound around her head—surely gifts from supplicants, since such textiles were scarce on the Patch. Her skinny body was swathed in a tattered robe stitched together from a collection of ragged T-shirts. Hiranur's dark eyes swam soulfully in a face narrow as an El Greco Christ's, and with the effort of walking she thrust her tongue through the gap where several front teeth were missing. Leaning on her staff, originally the handle of a broken oar, now whittled into various geometric shapes, she stumped closer, wheezing, until she could seize the central post with a speckled hand. "I cannot trust this woman to speak for me," she declared at last, "and yet you all must hear what I have come to say."

Halima sighed and gestured to Valeria, who stood indignantly, glaring at the intruder. "Please, Valeria," she said, "come take a seat, and let us hear what is so urgent that all Council business must be stopped on its account." Halima turned to the haruspex and told her in a stern voice, "Tell your tale, and quickly. You will be asked to leave if you can't soon convince us of the value of this interruption." She instructed Meryem to fetch some water for the wheezing woman.

Once Hiranur had slurped noisily from the shallow plastic bowl she'd been handed, she cleared her throat. "I have sifted through the bellies of a month's worth of creatures brought to me by those seeking knowledge of the future. That's three seabirds, five fish, a young shark, two turtles, and a goat that drowned in the sea," she said, ticking off the victims on her skinny fingers. "Together they tell the story: A giant storm will come, larger than any before. It will suck up the very stones from the ocean's floor. It will swallow the eighth full moon, the one that brings the bottles shaped like a woman. All in its path will be lost." When Valeria and several of the other skeptics began to sputter in derision, Halima raised her hand to silence them, and Hiranur continued. "I have never known the entrails to tell this story. And by the way," she added, cutting her eyes at Valeria, "as my clients will tell you, the guts never lie."

She tucked her staff into the crook of an elbow and clawed at her robe, searching for the pocket hidden in the folds until Halima shifted and sighed with mounting impatience. When Hiranur finally pulled her hand out and held it open, all the governors except Valeria craned forward at once. Petra saw a pale T-shaped object, about an inch long and trailing a short black string, on the woman's wrinkled palm. It looked like a tiny version of the double streetlights that had once illuminated the highways around Aleppo before they were all shot out during the war. Meryem clapped a hand over her mouth, and right then Petra knew, too, where she had seen such a thing before, pinched between two latex-gloved fingers, before she lay back on the table with her feet in the metal stirrups and her knees splayed apart. Halima noted the expression on her fellow governor's face and pressed her. "What is that?"

"It's an IUD." Meryem used the Dari term, since no equivalent yet existed in Sargassan. "You put one into a woman's womb to prevent a pregnancy," she explained. Before arriving on the Patch, Meryem had worked at an underground women's clinic in Afghanistan that had been destroyed by the Taliban. The governors murmured uneasily to one another, thinking about how such a thing might have found its way into the sea, and finally into the stomach of one of those creatures.

"*What* is not important," Hiranur insisted, scoffing at the simplicity of such an interpretation. "But *where*, and *how*, that is what tells the story. Besides," she went on, "this thing is not the message. This is the exclamation point *after* the message."

———

Later that evening, the full moon cupped in the sky's dark hand, Petra reclined with a bellyful of spit-roasted goat and chicken, grilled barnacles, and braised sea greens, faintly drunk from the fermented rice that had become a feature at these festivals, despite the disapproval of some of the hardliners. Tugged this way and that by a light breeze, flames sporadically illuminated the eager faces of her fellow Sargassans seated around the fire pit, licking the last traces of grease from their fingers. Adults and children watched with rapt attention as the parade of puppets now swayed solemnly into the flickering light, enacting the creation story of Sargassa, to the accompaniment of the poet who played the oud and sang in a high and raspy voice. The puppets, built by Sargassan artisans from the assorted flotsam under their feet, were carried or worn by the puppeteers, bringing the song alive in the choreography of their dance.

By now, they all knew the fable by heart, how the kings of earth had drunk the blood of power and lost their minds. How in their madness they unleashed their seven terrible children, Ego and Greed and Hate and Violence and Ignorance and Facebook and War, who fed like jackals on the bodies of nations, driving the people into the sea. How they foundered there, crying out, and how the goddess Sargassa, who lived deep under the waves, had heard them and turned restlessly in her thousand-year sleep and arched her broad back; how her barnacled spine had crested the surface, making a place where the people could land. And as they came to make their home on the goddess's generous body, enjoying the sea's bounty, and building a new world free from famine, and drought, and war, and all the rest, the seven terrible sons became one seething mass that continued to swallow the rest of the world.

And here the smallest children shivered with anticipation, waiting for the most frightening figure of all, Chaos, to burst from the darkness into the firelight—not a human or animal form but a misbegotten mushroom crowned with sickly yellow hair. At last it staggered into the circle, spinning and screeching "MEEEEE-MEEEE-MEEEE!!!" in an unearthly voice. Chaos, the consolidation of all horrors, charged from one side of the circle to the other, terrifying and delighting the children, who shrieked with pleasure and recoiled in fear.

After the figure of Chaos had sufficiently riled up the audience, the winner of the day's scavenging contest had the honor of lifting a flaming brand from the fire and setting the monster alight. Its hair ignited and crackled, and it ran bellowing toward the nearest channel to plunge into the water. As a burst of smoke rose from the spot where it had disappeared, people could sometimes make out the legs of the puppeteer (coated with soot to hide them in the darkness), who had hurled the flaming costume into the water and then crept away into the night. He or she (the audience never knew in advance who it was, and bets would be placed) would rinse the soot off their legs and stealthily return to blend into the raucous dance party that always followed the puppet show, with music by the best local musicians.

Petra caught Valeria's eye where she sat in the circle with Luis, her teenage son, and her lover, Raiza, by her side, and nodded briefly in acknowledgment. The Council business had run late, as a result of Hiranur's interruption, and Petra still felt a lingering unease. By now word of the haruspex's prophecy had been carried, along with the Council news and decisions, to the other trusts of the southern Patch. The most sensible Sargassans would dismiss it as hoodoo, since monster storms were as rare as ice in that part of the Atlantic. But plenty of others would not. As a governor, it would fall to Petra to marshal an official response, but what exactly should that be? In the days to follow she would make a point of traveling around and listening to the people, to take a reading of how the omen was being received. After the Council, when she and Fatou stood chatting in the food line, murmurings about the prophecy had already begun to buzz around them, like clouds of gnats in the darkening air.

9

April
Washington, DC

Mike Pence had sworn himself to secrecy. The First Lady had acted impulsively when she'd taken that child from the detention facility, and he had done nothing to stop her, to talk her out of it. He couldn't help but pity her—she had taken Barron's disappearance incredibly hard. She was mourning the loss of her only child, and she clearly wasn't thinking straight. Barron had torn a raggedy, boy-shaped hole in his mother's heart, and she needed something to stuff into it, to stanch the bleeding. Pence could empathize because, after all, didn't he too have a boy-shaped hole in his heart?

Barron's decision had taken them all by surprise, but the most shocking betrayal was not that the young man wanted to transition, but that his transformation was not from male to female (as wholly unnatural as that was) but from a somebody into a nobody. The previous month, the day after his fifteenth birthday, Barron had managed to give his security detail the slip and flee the White House. The Secret Service later determined the boy had disguised himself as a commoner and boarded the Acela to New York, eventually hiding out in the home of a wealthy

New York friend who had promised to help him. This friend knew of an Upper East Side doctor skilled in identity reassignment surgery, who could help Barron change his name, erase all familiar facial features, blur his fingerprints, and even manipulate a key gene that marked him as a child of the Donald. At fifteen, Barron was old enough to know his own mind, and he recognized a truth his older half siblings clearly did not: The family name would one day be a mark of shame, like Cain's brand, or the red letter Hester Prynne wore on her adulterous breast. Saving his own soul demanded immediate action.

God knows how he was able to form an independent thought, given the conditioning that child had been subjected to in his gilded Skinner box. News coming into the White House had to be strictly controlled; FOX or OAN played 24/7 on the giant screens lining the walls. Young Barron had been brainwashed to believe his father was a giant, a genius, all-knowing and all-powerful, capable of crushing every enemy who plotted his downfall. The boy had doubtless heard it all first from his father's own mouth, before it was trumpeted from every news outlet, playing in his baby ear like a lullaby.

And yet, incredibly, the indoctrinations had failed. Maybe his mother had whispered a different story in the child's ear, draped a sheet over the flat screen on the wall of his lonely playroom. Or perhaps the evidence of his own eyes and ears was all Barron really needed to conclude that, in truth, his father was nothing more than a mendacious blowhard, elevated by conspiracy and treason to a position of immense power, an anti-Midas, who befouled everything he touched, including the body of Barron's beloved mother.

The unhappy boy had left a note, begging her forgiveness and asking that she try to forget him. The President had tweeted a few remarks ("He was only associated with the family for a very short time, actually"), and then resumed his Twitter feud with Suri Cruise, but FLOTUS had been devastated, Pence could tell. Mother and son had been extremely close, especially once the family had moved into the de facto prison of the White House. So when he'd learned she had tossed her jacket over that little brown boy and brought him on board the plane, Pence had held his tongue. A boy for a boy. He was just one child. What did it really matter? His parents were probably already dead, or deported. So many children had already fallen through the cracks. What was one more, in the scheme of things?

Since entering into the White House through the secret passage under the tennis pavilion, and leaving the First Lady at the door of the Queen's Bedroom, Pence had not seen the child. He had heard rumors of a panic room concealed behind the wainscoting, of covered trays being brought in and out at odd hours, but frankly he preferred to remain ignorant about the exact location where the boy might be tucked away and how long she intended to keep him there. He could not afford to be more deeply involved than he already was.

The First Lady detested her husband, and feared him. Pence could only assume Individual One had something on her, some *kompromat*, like he had on all of them, which kept her by his side and enforced her silence. They all lived in fear of this man who was ready to bring the world down around their ears, so long as he could save himself.

Besides, Pence had an assignment that would surely give him an ulcer the size of a manhole cover before it was all over: He was spearheading the committee for the military parade, which POTUS was determined to make happen, to hell with the cost. Pence knew the bulk of the $102 million it would take to send representatives from the combined armed forces down Pennsylvania Avenue this coming Fourth of July had been funneled directly from the Veterans' Pension Fund. Part of Pence's job was to convince the heads of every branch that the money would be returned, with interest.

He could have borne it, if it meant he and Stephen would be thrown together, brainstorming solutions and crunching numbers together late into the night. But alas, no. Stephen had been shut up for hours with POTUS, Jared, and a near-sighted balding man he didn't recognize, and the White House grapevine was humming with rumors about an ultra-hush-hush project. Roland Pinkney, the assiduous, faintly black man he had hired in January to serve as his special assistant, kept him fully informed on most matters, but even the highly efficient Pinkney had come up empty on the subject. In this house of secrets, staffers were ever on high alert, huddling and whispering, scrambling to undo all the daily damage without appearing to contradict the President's lunatic statements, and most days Pence did his best to ignore the palace intrigue. But Stephen had worn a sly smile as he fluffed his lavender pocket square ("Springtime is my playground," he'd once been heard to say) in the mirror outside the Oval Office, awaiting his summons. *What was that minx up to?*

10

April
New York City

Amid a menagerie of frosted-glass animal sculptures, Least refreshed her Instagram feed for the thirteenth time in the past half hour. It was like a drug, watching those numbers shoot up before her eyes, and she felt certain that this drab little life she had been leading—a life of interminable hours parked at the desk near the back of the gallery, interrupted only by the occasional browser wandering around the displays; a life of returning after work to her ugly apartment in Bay Ridge with a takeout bag cutting into her wrist, of going on paralyzingly dull dates with interchangeable men—all of that was racing backward in the rearview mirror. Already she could make out the faint, tantalizing outlines of what would replace it.

Late that Saturday night, when Luka had dropped her off at the Bentley, she's had to face the wrath of Angie, Margo, and the rest of the girls. *"Where the fuck were you? We thought you'd been kidnapped! We were texting you nonstop!"* On the drive back from Mar-a-Lago she'd decided just to fess up about where she'd been all night. True friends wouldn't stay mad when they heard about her incredible adventure.

Angela would have another birthday, but Least might never get another chance to take a selfie in the Winter White House. But when she told them where she'd been, they'd still seemed angry, as if the calculation she'd made (*Hello?! Once-in-a-lifetime opportunity, anyone?*) just didn't add up for them. Honestly, she was the one who should be pissed off—something absolutely amazing had happened to her, and all they could think about was how she'd blown them off at a strip club. So fuck it.

Nevertheless, the rest of the weekend had been a little awkward, and relations were still strained when they Uber'd back to the airport early Monday to catch their respective flights. Least hugged Angela's stiff shoulders and gave the other ladies an airy wave before heading off toward her gate. It didn't take much imagination to picture what the topic of conversation would be once she was out of earshot. Now that she was back in New York, she'd texted Angie a couple times, with no response. Again, fuck it.

Things were moving quickly now, and Least had plenty of other stuff on her mind besides trying to mollify an injured friend. The shot Luka had taken of her and Falco next to the President's *Time* cover had been liked 63,980 times, and her number of followers had spiked since it had been posted. Luka and she had been Skyping daily; plans for the *Foxy Friends* pilot had solidified, and they wanted to schedule her for a screen test later that week. Somewhere inside her, a little voice kept up a steady anticipatory rhythm: *This is it. This is it. This is it.* After having to watch her cousin grab all the glory, and treat her like shit, Least might finally get her shot.

One particular thought kept rolling around in her brain, until it was polished to a lovely, smooth sheen. Luka told her the President had seen a picture of her and had called Abbott to say how hot she was, and how much he'd like to see her on the show.

When Least had let herself into her apartment Monday afternoon and dropped her luggage inside the door (she'd taken the day off from work, to give herself the long weekend), the stink of pot smoke stopped her cold. Sprawled on the couch in the living room with a swirly glass pipe in her hand, her roommate, Claudia, gave Least a lazy smile. "You're back! How was the bachelorette party?" she drawled.

"Fortieth birthday party," Least corrected her, stepping across the room to shove open one of the windows. "Jesus, Claudia, it really reeks in here." Job one in her beautiful new life would be to get her own place. She had found the two-bedroom apartment on Craigslist, and Claudia came with it. Mid-forties, mixed race, frizzy light-brown hair, with a chortling laugh. She had family in Connecticut, where her dad taught sociology at Yale, and often took the train up there on weekends—a bonus, as far as Least was concerned. During the week Claudia worked at a friend's store on Atlantic Avenue selling overpriced little handmade clothes for hipster children. She sometimes worked from home, and lately more and more of that work seemed to involve getting stoned and staring at tiny knitted garments on Etsy.

As a roommate Claudia wasn't the worst—she was relatively chill and picked up after herself, though Least ended up cleaning the bathroom more often than she should have. They'd been roommates for two years, and the only major dispute they'd had was when Least put a KEEP AMERICA GREAT sign in the living room window that faced the street. "That goes, or you go," Claudia had told her. Least could have made a big stink about free speech, blah blah, but couldn't afford to lose out on an affordable apartment. So she'd taken it down and acted huffy about it for a week, just to let Claudia know she was pissed.

Now her roommate stretched her oversized striped sweater over the faded knees of her purple sweatpants and studied Least with sleepy, bloodshot eyes. "What happened? You've got weird energy."

"Nothing—the usual stereotypical Miami stuff. Male strippers, and art deco everywhere. Massive tropical drinks. We went parasailing one day. It was fun." No point in telling her about Mar-a-Lago. Least knew she'd have to hear Claudia whine about wasted tax dollars and the one percent, and that would kill her buzz more than the party girls already had. Luckily her roommate didn't ask a lot of follow-up questions. Instead, after Least had used the bathroom, Claudia launched into a story about a friend of hers whose boyfriend had disappeared off a Metro North train when they were traveling back to Manhattan from Beacon, New York. She had been staring out at the Hudson River and wondering why her boyfriend was taking so long in the restroom when she suddenly witnessed him being hustled down the platform by a couple of ICE agents and then she never saw him again.

"Well, he probably had an outstanding warrant or something," Least said.

"He's a hydraulic engineer! He works for the city of New York! He's not a felon, Least. Every Mexican American is not a felon." Least could sense Claudia working herself up into a froth of outrage, and she'd heard it all before. Time to cut this short.

"Then it's a mistake and they'll sort it out eventually." Least grabbed her bags and headed to her room. "I need to change. I smell like the plane."

———

When Least had checked in with her parents the week after her return from Florida, she gave them the same thumbnail version of the trip she'd given Claudia. No point in stirring up her dad, an old-style Democrat who'd been in a constant state of rage since the fall of 2016; his latest rants concerned the recent name change of the party, on all federal documents, to the Party of Haters and Losers, or PHAL (the President pronounced it "fail"). Her parents had lost a chunk of their retirement savings when their Amazon stock tanked after Bezos's breakdown, and her dad still blamed it on the President. "He was hounding the man! He drove him insane!" So she kept things light, feigned some interest in hearing about Alana's Braxton-Hicks contractions and the UMich professor Layla was dating ("Just thirty and a full professor!"). As usual, her parents cut each other off and veered into private disputes on the speakerphone ("She didn't say *full*—I don't know where you're getting that") until Least's impatience reached a critical mass. Before she hung up, she couldn't help dropping some hints about "starting to look for a new job," but she was superstitious enough to feel that saying anything more might jinx her chances.

It made her sad to realize how few people she could confide in about the exciting new developments in her life, when what she really wanted to do was crow from the rooftops: *I went to Mar-a-Lago! The President thinks I'm hot! I might get to be on TV!* She wanted to stop random pedestrians on the street, grab their shoulders, and shout her good news into their startled faces. She needed someone to be happy for her, but it wouldn't be her family, her roommate, or her friends. Plenty of people back in her home state shared her views, but New York was still hostile to Red Hats and she felt like a pariah whenever the subject turned to politics. Angela and the rest of that crowd didn't get it, that was pretty clear. Least had made a couple connections at a MAGA meet-up, but she had to admit that the guys who showed up at those events could be scary—talking about shoot-to-kill border policies and giving her side-eye, probably trying to suss out which part of the world her olive skin originally came from. Resa, longtime pal that she was, put up with her fixation, but Least could sense some mental eye rolling even from her.

Thank god for Luka. With him she'd felt free to open the floodgates of her obsession. He definitely got it; he understood the attraction. She could wax rhapsodic about the President's latest tweet or his genius speech at the Boys and Girls Club Breakfast, and he never cut her off or changed the subject. She assumed Luka's home must be in LA, but he was conveniently here in New York during negotiations for the TV pilot. He had spent hours coaching her on the upcoming screen test, telling her what to wear and how they would do her makeup for the lights.

Somehow, in the span of just a few days, he had become her booster, her trusted advisor, her biggest fan, and (she had begun to feel) her friend. The sound of his sexy accent during their daily phone calls bolstered her confidence that the Ferris wheel car of her fortunes might be starting to crest. He believed in her. And, she realized with an energizing jolt, so did all her followers on @virginkardashian, a community that numbered in the hundreds of thousands. So she wasn't so alone, after all.

11

May
Miles City

W hat's with the hat?"
      Helen regarded Paul quizzically as he approached from the
side road where he had parked his truck, tucked out of sight behind
a stand of catkin-covered aspen trees. She stood in their new meeting
place, leaning against one of the supports of the massive Ten Commandments billboard that could be seen from the highway. Her frizzy
gray hair moved in the breeze that blew over the Big Sheep Mountains,
still capped with snow.

      "What's the matter? Don't you like it?" Paul raised a hand to the brim
of the black Stetson shielding his eyes from the midday sun. The hat
had been a gift from a post-divorce girlfriend, an accessory he hated and
never wore. Plenty of guys wore cowboy hats in Montana, but he thought
it made him look like a poser. "I'm in disguise. I thought if somebody
saw us from a distance, they wouldn't figure it was me because I don't
usually wear a hat."

      Their first encounter at the bar and a subsequent get-together at a
coffee shop had cranked up the rumor mill in town, so they had taken

to meeting here, arriving and leaving separately, as a precautionary measure. The secrecy wasn't really necessary—they weren't trying to hide a physical relationship (God, no!) or plot a murder, but they both found these measures kind of silly and therefore amusing, and it saved them from having to explain themselves to the nosy citizens of Miles City.

"Hats give me a headache," Helen informed him. "They inhibit my thinking."

"Maybe you should wear a fake mustache so nobody knows who you are."

"I've already got a start on growing a real one."

Paul snorted and looked out at the mountains. Now that the long Montana winter had finally begun pulling back its skirts, he was reminded of why he loved it here, of why he'd never seriously considered relocating anywhere else, even though newsroom jobs were scarce in that part of the country. Two years ago he'd been aggressively courted by a DuPont-Columbia-award-winning station in Minneapolis; they'd offered him a significant salary hike along with moving expenses, but he'd turned them down—Paige had just filed for divorce and full custody, and Paul had been desperate to stay close to Hallie. Lately, however, the feeling didn't seem to be mutual. The daughter who had once delivered her own little news reports through the frame of a cardboard box (*Just like Daddy!*) now found any number of excuses to avoid him. That realization prompted a sudden ache in his chest, and he started talking to distract himself from the hurt of being rejected by his own kid, and the shame of wanting to blame her because she'd been the reason he'd sacrificed his shot at the big leagues.

"How's the project coming along at Ferris's?"

"It's coming. We got the Venus's body built, roughly at least. I'm still looking for the right scraps for her head. It's got to look like an iron medicine ball all wrapped up with barbed wire. But something happened with Ferris's cattle—a couple of days ago a bunch of the cows died."

"How many did he lose?"

"About a quarter of the herd. They ate something they shouldn't of.

Ferris found them just sprawled out dead. He sliced open one of their bellies right there in the field and found this poisonous plant in its gut."

"Was it Death Camas?"

"That's right. Do you know about that plant?"

"Yeah—it can be really toxic in the spring. But cattle mostly avoid it."

"That's what Ferris said. He said it's strange that they ate it, because there were plenty of other plants around they like much better. And now he has to dispose of all these dead cows because it would be poisonous to eat them. It's a huge waste of meat."

"That's a shame," Paul said. Ferris was not a wealthy man, and the loss would be a hardship. "You'd think those animals would have better sense."

"You would," Helen agreed. She slid into a crouch and fished around in her pockets for a lighter and the dented Altoids tin where she stashed her weed. "But it happens a lot, doesn't it? The natural world is way out of whack. All those whales that beached themselves in New Zealand last summer. Remember that? And I saw a YouTube video of a flock of birds, starlings or something, that changed direction and flew right into a wind power turbine. Why would they do that? It all seems purposeful." She pulled a joint out of the tin and cupped her hands around the end until she got it lit. "You want some?"

He shook his head—remembered about the hat. "No thanks—it'll make me too logy for work tonight." He gestured to the billboard. "That's the Eleventh Commandment: Thou shalt not get baked before a broadcast."

Helen took a deep drag, squinting up at him through the smoke. She held it in her lungs while she asked him the question he knew was coming, given the drift of the conversation. "Did you talk to the station manager again?"

Paul didn't know whether all the pot he'd been smoking lately had made him paranoid, but it seemed like ever since he'd brought up the idea of doing a story on the high suicide rate in Montana, he'd been getting a lot of pushback at work. When he'd first approached Grant, the station manager had made a joke out of it ("Geez, Paul, what a downer! Can't you think of something more positive?"). He'd brought it up a second time, and tried to explain about the CDC website being scrubbed, but Grant had given Paul the brush-off again, in a far less jocular way—in a manner that felt to Paul almost like a warning. His timing could have been better—Miles City's biggest annual event, the Bucking Horse Sale, was just a couple weeks away, and KYUS was already gearing up for its extensive coverage of all the concerts, horse races, rodeos, and bucking stock sales at the "Cowboy Mardi Gras." But Bucking Horse or not, all he'd wanted from Grant was his blessing, and the man had withheld it.

Being dismissed like that hadn't discouraged him—to Paul's surprise, he felt even more determined to follow the information, wherever it might lead. But he might have to take the story to another media outlet, or publish it anonymously online, if he ever wanted it to see the light of day.

When he explained this to Helen, she didn't look all that surprised. Over the weeks they'd known each other, she had heard him complain about changes at the station since Sinclair took over its management— the must-airs pushing narratives about Canadian invasions and the false science of climate change models, and always a nasty new wrinkle in the radical left-wing conspiracy to undermine the President. And though the station manager encouraged newscasters to bring in their own ideas for local stories, the ones they aired were relentlessly upbeat and trivial, like last night's piece about a high school kid who had built a scale model of the Montana statehouse out of shotgun shell casings.

"Well, Paul, we'll just have to figure out another way to get this out. But we don't even know what we have yet, do we? We have a lot of dots, but we don't really know how they're all connected. Dot . . . dot . . . dot . . . dot . . . dot." She used the partially smoked joint to punctuate the air before stubbing out the coal against the support pillar and tucking the roach back into the mint tin. "You know that old expression about paranoia? Just because you're paranoid doesn't mean they aren't out to get you?"

They were both quiet for a minute, staring out at the occasional car humming along the highway. Helen had stowed the Altoids tin back in her vest and pulled out a crumpled pack of gum. She offered a piece to Paul, but he shook his head. "So," she said, chomping away, and he knew something interesting was imminent. That was the way with Helen, he'd come to learn. "Last night I was hunting around online under 'suicide conspiracy' and I found something odd."

"What a surprise," he teased. "Helen, sometimes I wonder if you're actually a real scientist. Shouldn't you be looking for facts instead of following lunatics down rabbit holes?"

"A good scientist is open to all possibilities. So I found this site called Suicide Is Painless. You know, like that *M.A.S.H.* song?" Paul looked at her blankly when she hummed a few bars, so she went on. "Never mind—you're too young, obviously. Whoever runs the site has been collecting weird suicide stories from around the world—not your run-of-the-mill suicides but the ones that seem especially strange—you know, like somebody who wins the lottery and then throws himself in front of a bus the next day. That actually happened! Some guy in Rhode Island. Anyway, I was scrolling through the comments—"

"Oh my god . . ." Paul began.

"Yes, I know, it's a sewer down there, but I bet there are plenty of interesting things in the sewer. So, I found a comment from somebody named @forensickfantutti and it linked to a scientific paper written by this medical examiner. He had done an autopsy on one of these suicide cases, and when he opened up the guy's skull he found that his brain had all these masses in it that looked like yellow cotton candy."

"Like Mad Cow disease, or that thing that sounds like sauerkraut—"

Helen rolled her eyes, which looked a little bloodshot now. "Creutzfeldt-Jakob disease. It turns parts of the brain spongy, and its incredibly rare."

"So maybe it was that—people behave strangely when they have that, right?"

"Yes, they do, but what the paper describes has a different pathology—more like clumps of yellow floss throughout the brain tissue."

Paul scratched his chin, and watched a rabbit hop across an open patch of spring grass at the base of the slope they stood on. *Windigo would have been after that like a shot,* he thought. The family dog, an ugly mongrel Paul had an inordinate affection for, had been taken to Billings by Paige where he'd run into the busy street in front of her condo and been flattened by a texting driver. Paul still missed that mutt.

"Well, that does sound weird." He tried to sound intrigued, but thinking about the dog had pissed him off. Why did she want a dog in the city? He should have put up more of a fight. She'd been angry and wanted to hurt him however she could. He suspected she'd been working on Hallie, too—getting her to believe all these shitty things about her dad, to make her think that when he'd cheated on Paige he'd been cheating on them both. Pretty soon his daughter would be off at college and even harder to pin down. He didn't have much time left to make things up to her. Paul made up his mind to take Hallie on a trip before that happened—go somewhere beautiful where they could have fun together and repair their father-daughter bond. But Helen was still talking.

"What's weird is that this wasn't the only case of cotton-candy brain this coroner has seen in a suicide victim. This was the fifth case he'd seen. Creutzfeldt-Jakob happens once in a million, per year, worldwide, with about 350 cases annually in the States. This guy in Billings had seen this yellow stuff five times in three months!"

"Wait," said Paul, finally plugging into what she'd been saying. "This guy's in Montana?"

"Yep," said Helen. "See what I mean about the sewer?"

12

Bubble Tea Straw Moon
Sargassa

Nine. That was the number of scars Petra could make out on Adnan's back, even in the feeble light of the oil lamp, as he lay on the seagrass mat, turned away from her in anger. They had argued before sex, but the release hadn't softened his mood. He'd said some harsh things, called her a damaged person, but weren't they all? Inside or out, they all wore their wounds, after the world had chewed them up and spat them out into the sea.

In the week since the prophecy, the colonists had grown increasingly divided about how to respond to the threat that Hiranur had predicted. Some chose to ignore it, loudly scoffing about the absurdity of divining the future in the guts of a fish. Others called for ritual sacrifices, anything to appease a vengeful deity. Many of the men wanted to blame the women, of course—claiming they had defied God's wishes when they assumed power and upset the traditional hierarchy. Look what comes, they muttered to one another, from ignoring the Quran, the Bible, the Torah. And finally there were the pragmatists, like Adnan, who insisted that science and engineering held the solution. And it was Petra's job as a governor to broker a peace between all these factions, to not, as the Sargassans often reminded one another, bring the war here.

Earlier in the evening Adnan had been enthusiastically describing his plan to build a huge structure to deflect any storm so it would safely bypass Sargassa. He'd already sent out teams across the Patch to begin scavenging for materials. And if Hiranur was wrong and no storm materialized with the eighth full moon, one would surely come along another day, and they would be prepared, he'd told her. But Petra felt exhausted by his energy, and she had laughed and told him plastic bags and drinking straws could never stop a hurricane—after all, they couldn't even stop one rampaging goat!

It was a sore subject, she knew. After hearing the report from the Council, he had accused her of siding with Burak, of using him for her own pleasure while doing nothing to stop him from being censured or from losing his dog—the penalty had yet to be determined. And he had entered her in anger and then turned his back on her when they were finished.

She sighed and stopped herself from reaching out a finger to trace along one of his scars. Adnan had fled Homs, carrying the evidence of its desecration on his hide: bullet wounds, and the marks from an explosion that had taken his daughter and his wife. The historic city of Emesa, the celebrated "Home of Peace," reduced to dust and rubble. No wonder he chose to look forward with such ferocity; there was nothing to look back on but unendurable pain and loss.

But Petra felt the pressure of her responsibilities, and worrying about Adnan's hurt feelings, or anyone's, for that matter, made her less effective as a governor. And besides the general disagreement about how best to respond to a hurricane, there was something else troubling her mind. Along with aspirin and birth control pills and batteries and denim fabric and other things they couldn't make themselves, the most recent trading vessel had brought bad news from Bermuda. Some of the men who had been banished from the Patch over the years since the Sargassan laws had been established, rapists and murderers and child abusers (because only the worst offenders had been set adrift on flimsy rafts), had survived their expulsion and been picked up at sea or had somehow made it to shore. And they were now actively recruiting others to their cause, though they knew the penalty for returning was castration, or worse.

Over the years, some of the governors had warned of exactly this: If they allowed these offenders to live, and only banished them, what besides an expanse of water prevented them from coming back to wreak their revenge? Many, like Halima, had argued against becoming the very thing they were fleeing, and that a matriarchal society should be based on cooperation and mercy, not aggression and retribution. But Petra worried that the inherent flaw in masculinity—the impulse to dominate—could not be entirely eradicated without violence, or so it seemed. It was a discouraging thought.

Now Adnan left her bed and began gathering his clothes, without a glance her way. Once he'd pulled on his tattered shorts and laced them at his lean waist, he stepped outside her shelter and called sharply to his dog, who had likely been nosing along the transit canal to the west of the settlement. Soon she heard all six legs, those of man and beast, moving across the damp ground before the sound blended into the perpetual white noise of riffling plastic.

Petra sighed with annoyance. She left the sleeping mat to dip a rag in a plastic tub of seawater, and rinsed well between her legs. Even before she was dressed, her mind had moved on to other matters.

13

May
New York City

Least Kardashian could hardly believe her own eyelashes. She gaped at her reflection in the full-length mirror propped against the wall, wondering how Mira, the Patron Saint of Micropiercing, had managed to work miracles with such a tiny brush. When she did her own face, Least didn't stint on the mascara, and had been known to give even Kim a run for her money in that department. But after nearly an hour in the makeup chair in preparation for her screen test, Least felt like she was staring at a beautiful stranger. *Do I even know you?* she thought.

That morning, as she'd contemplated her puffy wakeup face in the cramped bathroom she shared with Claudia, her hands began to shake at the prospect of what lay ahead. After thirty-nine years of life, Least had come to know the myriad faces that peered out at her from any number of reflective surfaces: the best ones, that made her feel confident and in control, like the face she'd seen in the Mar-a-Lago restroom, and the worst, where in certain lights the pores on her nose looked grossly large, or the nose itself looked crooked, or one eye seemed slightly higher than the other, and why had she never noticed that before?

But the face in the chipped medicine-chest mirror belonged to a terrified (it hurt to say it) middle-aged woman's, and she suddenly knew, *I can't do this.* She'd slept poorly, worrying about the test, and it showed. She filled the sink with cold water and stuck her face beneath the surface, holding it there for as long as she could bear, all the while reminding herself of what Luka had said about the President's great lesson, that reality is what you make it and nothing else. But Least felt sure no amount of self-affirmation could wipe away that flawed, panicky mug staring back at her in the mirror.

Here in the depths of her thirties, Least did her best to put on a brave face, but every day she felt more like a jellyfish pulsing in the current, drifting with the tide. How she had envied the predetermined kids in her class who just seemed to *know*, from the instant they shot out of the womb, where their life paths would lead. The ones who would say, in fake modesty, "I've always loved to write," when the teacher complimented them on their English essays, or "My dad would've disowned me if I'd opted out of law school—luckily I'm good at it!" Art history had been an arbitrary decision, sticking a pin in the UMich course catalog, but she liked the sound of it, thought it gave her a veneer of sophistication. She assumed looking at pictures would be easier than reading stacks of textbooks, and she could probably bullshit her way through the exams. When her professor handed out the ten-pound syllabus to Intro to Art History: Renaissance to the Present, Least had nearly shit herself. The path Least had chosen (though it had given her a taste for contemporary artists like Yayoi Kusama and David Kramer) had marooned her at the glass gallery. *Foxy Friends* felt like her last chance to escape the sucking drain of aimless mediocrity, and now she was about to screw it up.

Luka had talked her down from the ledge, of course. When she'd reached him that morning, insisting he had to call off the screen test because she really wasn't cut out to be on television, wasn't pretty or poised enough, and everyone would know she was a total fraud, that she would only humiliate herself and waste everyone's time, and would he *please, please, please* make apologies to Abbott and Su-mi and the rest of the Parallax people? He hadn't laughed at her or teased or tried to jolly her out of her panic, which she'd been expecting. He'd just asked her to breathe with him on the phone, to sit down and breathe, and she sat on the toilet lid holding the phone without speaking, just inhaling deeply and then slowly expelling the air in her lungs, in and out, in and out again, over and over, exactly as he instructed her to do.

———

The air-conditioned loft space in Tribeca where Luka brought her for the test had tall, streaky windows facing south toward the Freedom Tower and Battery Park. A tight space in the room's center had been walled off with some scrims of dark-gray fabric. There was a camera positioned on a tripod with a monitor set up beside it, and some folding chairs arranged behind a table near the monitor, but not much else. The makeshift makeup area had been set up in a far corner, and as Least marveled at her own transformation at the hands of the pierced and pink-haired makeup artist, she watched over her shoulder in the mirror as, one by one, Luka greeted the people who would eventually be seated in those chairs. Two of them she recognized: Abbott and Su-mi, the producers from Parallax she'd met at Mar-a-Lago. The other three were strangers.

With a flourish, Mira whipped the black protective cape off Least's shoulders, exposing the white sleeveless Ivanka Couture dress that Luka had bought for her. As Least slid off the vinyl stool, he came toward them, his triumphant swoop of white hair like the piped icing on a wedding cake, his arctic eyes appraising. He took Least's hand and said, "Ah, lovely," before leading her over to meet the others milling around the space. After Abbott and Su-mi greeted her warmly, Luka beckoned a man forward whom he introduced as Victor, the casting director for *Foxy Friends*. Victor grinned at her, flashing a gap between his two front teeth she could have fed a Ballpark Frank through. A tense-looking black woman with a short, bleached haircut and artsy red plastic frames was the director, Sabine. The cameraman, an older overweight white guy with greasy hair and a beer belly filling out a faded Megadeth T-shirt, whose name she promptly forgot, waved briefly at her and went back to adjusting the video camera on its tripod.

Luka retrieved the stool from the corner and positioned it in front of the scrim, near a tall light that cast its hot cone on the floorboards, then indicated she should have a seat. He squeezed Least's arm and whispered in her ear, "You will be wonderful." Then he stepped over to reposition the light on her before moving to stand at the cameraman's elbow. The others had taken seats along the other side of the table behind the monitor and sat looking at her expectantly.

As the light's heat coated the bare skin of her arms, a sense memory flooded her body: standing on the diving board in the backyard of Kim's parents' mansion in Beverly Hills, the second and last time Least's family had been invited to visit, the SoCal sun on her shoulders, as she gathered her nerve to try a flip into the pool. Kim, giggling behind her on the board, had pinched one end of the ties on Least's bikini between her fingers just as Least darted forward, so her swimsuit top flopped to her waist just as her body left the board, exposing her twelve-year-old breasts to the eyes of Ed McMahon, and O.J., and all the other famous people drinking around the pool. Least remembered how she had frantically retied her top under the water and would have stayed there, her face flaming red with mortification, if she hadn't had to surface to take a breath.

But as Least perched there on the stool, blinking her magnificent eyelashes in the artificial light and remembering the almost bottomless shame her twelve-year-old self had suffered, exposed like that in sight of the boldface names of Hollywood, with the sound of Kim's cruel laughter in her ears, she saw that the faces facing her now were kind, and that they wanted nothing so much as for her to succeed.

———

And before she knew it, it was over. They'd had her talk about herself for a while, asking questions to draw her out. *What would you grab first if your house was on fire? What is your happy place? What did you think about the ending of* American Horror Story: Murder Hornets? They had her look up and down, and to the left and the right, and then asked her about the President and what she thought about the job he was doing. They asked her to laugh and to say the name of a new luxury sedan called the Auto de Fe. Victor and Sabine repeatedly glanced toward the monitor and then back at her, comparing the real version of Least with the televised one. Toward the end, Mira had stepped in and played the role of a visiting celebrity guest, and they had Least ask her about her latest film project and her charity work donating automatic weapons to needy school districts. Least was relieved when they didn't ask her anything about Kim, because she couldn't pretend they had any kind of relationship, and being snarky probably wouldn't have made a very good impression.

Then Victor, the casting director, said, "Okay!" rubbing his hands together and turning to the others. "Do we have what we need?" And they all smiled encouraging smiles at Least and nodded yes and began to rise from their seats. Luka strode toward her and gave her a peck on the cheek, whispering in her ear, "You killed" (which sounded like "keeled" in that accent of his) before stepping to the door to shake hands with those departing. He stood talking quietly to Abbott and Su-mi for a bit, and then they each came over to give Least a quick hug, telling her how brilliant, how natural, she'd been, before they left. After Mira packed up her makeup kit, she blew Least a kiss from the door and flashed her a thumbs-up before ducking out. Megadeth was still disassembling his camera gear when Luka returned to collect her. "I have a good feeling," Luka proclaimed, draping the sweater she'd worn in the cab over her shoulders and handing Least her pocketbook. "Let's celebrate."

14

Paul was installed at his desk in the newsroom, trying to figure out how to put a positive spin on the pipeline spill that had inundated more than 3,500 acres in the Sweetgrass Hills, when his phone buzzed. A glance at the screen told him it was from "Four Twenty," his code name for Helen. Her voice on the phone sounded low and urgent.

"Paul, you have to get over here now. Ferris is dead." Before he could shape his confusion at this news into all the necessary questions, her call had disconnected in his ear. He grabbed his jacket off the back of the chair and left the station without speaking to anyone. Ferris's ranch was about five miles to the north of town, and Paul covered the distance as quickly as he could safely manage in the truck, trailing a billowing column of brown dust in his wake.

When he parked beside Helen's Toyota in the wide dirt yard in front of the Gladwell ranch house, nothing struck him as unusual. A quick glance around took in the usual piles of scrap and the NO TRESPASSING signs, along with various surreal shapes welded together from spare parts — Ferris's art projects, he figured. He found Helen inside one of the barns, on her knees next to a large elevated wooden platform. Beside it lay a crumpled metal form resembling a giant rusted grub with a snarl of barbed wire for a head. A man's legs clad in faded jeans and worn work boots protruded from either side of the form's base. Two ranch-roughened hands seemed to grip the oxidized metal figure in the general area of where its shoulders would be, two mismatched lovers frozen in a bizarre embrace. Paul realized, with a sudden wave of revulsion, that the clotted gray-and-yellow corona in the dust around the rusted wire head had once been Ferris's brains.

Helen was crouched beside the head, holding a baggie open in her left hand and using her right to shoo away a clutch of determined chickens, who flapped around, pecking frantically at the gristly mess on the straw-strewn floor.

"Help me keep them back!" she barked at him. As Paul leaned down to try to scatter the birds away from Ferris's mortal remains, he was aghast to see Helen scooping at the matter on the floor with a little spoon.

"Have you called 911 yet?"

"Of course! That's why I'm trying to collect a sample before they get here!"

"A sample? Jesus, Helen, stop! You're interfering with the evidence!"

She tucked the silver utensil into the plastic baggie and sealed the Ziploc top.

"What are you going to do with that?" He saw the chickens had re-doubled their efforts now that both he and Helen were distracted. "Help me grab them," he yelped at her, but she was already hustling toward the barn door. Seizing a squawking bird in both hands, Paul pitched it over the wall of an empty horse stall toward the rear of the building and raced back to collar another. By the time Helen reappeared, he had most of the birds corralled. She captured one of the last ones and tossed it into the stall with the others, then stood panting, looking at Paul with an expression of mingled horror and determination on her sweaty face. She took her phone out of her pocket and he watched with astonishment as she stepped back toward the body and snapped a few pictures of the scene.

"Holy shit, Helen. What the hell happened?"

Paul stood there with his hands shaking at his sides as she ignored him to poke at her phone, breathing fast. He heard the distinctive whoosh of an image being mailed. "OK, and delete." Only then did she start to answer his question. But before she had the chance to say more than "I found him like that," Peggy Wyatt, Miles City's sheriff, bustled into the barn, her police radio squawking on her shoulder.

Paul knew Peggy, and had interviewed her on camera many times — the last occasion back in January when teen vandals accidentally torched a historic downtown building. Peggy was a short and curvy woman, her shit-brown uniform shirt gaping over her chest. She had been on the force for five years when her father, Garland, the former sheriff, had died in the saddle, so to speak, and she had fought hard for the title. Being sheriff of Miles City was a relatively low-key job. People tended to die in the usual ways — from natural causes such as being kicked in the head by a horse or from a gunshot wound or during a gender-reveal mishap, rather than being crushed to a paste beneath a giant metal woman. The sheer weirdness of the accident might have accounted for Peggy's getting there ahead of the EMTs. The sheriff took in the scene, and squatted down beside Ferris's body to search for a pulse in the left wrist. After a minute she straightened up and shook her head. "Poor guy."

They all registered that the sound of an approaching siren had just terminated somewhere beyond the barn. Peggy walked to the door, waved at someone in the yard, and called out, "In here! But he's gone," before turning her keen little brown eyes on Helen. "Did you find him like this?"

"Yes. He was working on the Venus" — Helen gestured toward the metal sculpture — "and I guess one of the supports snapped, or bent, and it crushed him. It must've happened just before I got here. I've been helping him with that sculpture. I was bringing lunch, and then we were going to get to work...." Helen pointed toward a Dairy Queen bag lying on its side on the floor.

Right then two male EMTs carrying medical equipment rushed

through the barn door. Peggy told them, "He's right there, but there's nothing to be done." The sheriff picked up the DQ bag and peered inside, then stepped back toward the sculpture and began stalking around the scene, crouching down to look at the tangle of man and metal woman from different angles, all the while speaking into the radio on her shoulder, reporting back to the station on what she'd found. The EMTs retreated through the entrance, where they stood in the yard, smoking and talking quietly as they watched the sheriff through the open door. One man was older and bald, and one was young with freckles and red, wiry hair.

Peggy looked up at Paul. "Guess you must've heard about it on the scanner." Paul nodded—better to let her conclude he'd come out on behalf of KYUS rather than in response to Helen's call. Paul suddenly felt like he needed to sit down. He sank into a dented metal folding chair near the wall and rested his damp forehead in his hands. The sight of Ferris's brains scattered across the floor of the barn brought the black coffee and cheese omelet he'd had for breakfast back up into his throat. Helen kept talking to Peggy, giving the sheriff a timeline of when she'd last spoken to Ferris and when she'd arrived at the ranch. Paul pulled his cell phone out of his pocket to distract himself, and before long he felt Helen's hand on his shoulder. "We can go," she told him. She had the lunch bag under her arm.

As they made for the door, Peggy came over and gave Paul a stern look. "I don't want this on the news until I've had a chance to notify next of kin," she said. "Check back later today." Outside, the EMTs were leaning against the ambulance, and Paul heard the red-haired kid say something snarky under his breath about "dying of an 'art' attack."

Paul walked Helen to her car. She set the paper bag on the passenger seat, then turned to him and said under her breath, "Head back into town, and call me when you're en route." He gave her a curious look but told her OK. Helen backed the Toyota out of the driveway and headed for the main road, and soon after Paul bumped down the drive after her in his truck. When Helen answered her cell phone, she rattled off more instructions: "Meet me on Park by the water tower. I'm going to leave my car there and we're going to take your truck to Billings."

"Helen—I have to get back to work—I can't drive you to Billings. Why do you need to go there?"

"Because that's where Macadangdang is."

"The what?"

"That M.E. I told you about. His name is Macadangdang. His office is in Billings."

"So why can't you just call him?"

"For crap's sake, Paul! We need to bring him this sample before it spoils!"

Finally, things began to click into place in Paul's head. He hung up and focused on the road. When he turned onto Park Street, he saw Helen's car pull alongside the curb just past the base of the water tower with the bucking bronco that loomed over Miles City like a rattle for a giant cowboy baby. She climbed out with the white lunch sack in her hand and her backpack slung over her shoulder. When he came abreast of her, she opened his door and slid into the passenger seat. As she struggled to buckle her seat belt she barked, "Drive!"

He put the truck into gear and they rolled forward slowly while he tried to talk some sense into her.

"Listen, Helen, you shouldn't have been interfering with Ferris's body—that's just plain wrong, not to mention illegal. Plus, he didn't kill himself—this was obviously an accident, so what are you expecting this Makadoo guy to tell you? And why do I have to take you there?"

"One, we don't know it was an accident. Maybe Ferris pulled the Venus over on top of himself in a suicidal frenzy. And two, if a middle-aged geologist shows up claiming she has a dead guy's brains in a Dairy Queen cup, don't you think this doctor's going to immediately call the cops?"

He blinked at her, mulling that over.

"I need you there to validate me. He'll know you from TV. If you vouch for me, he'll at least hear me out. Now speed up! This ice is melting!" She reached into the sack and pulled out a waxed blue

Blizzard cup with a plastic lid and set it into the truck's drink holder
before cranking up the AC in the cab. Then she fished out a sandwich
wrapped in red-and-white paper from the bag and asked him, "Are
you hungry?"

"I'm not eating a dead man's lunch. What the hell is wrong with you?"

"Listen, Paul, I am incredibly upset. This whole thing is just horrible.
But I'm also very hungry because I skipped breakfast. Trauma is stressful
and it burns a lot of calories!" She peeled back the greasy wrapping
and took a bite of the flattened hamburger inside. "The other one has
cheese—are you sure you don't want it?" He shook his head vehemently
and she kept eating.

Paul was surprised to find himself, as meek as a lamb, heading toward
I-94 West. He drove through the grid of streets north of the golf course,
finally heading down Haynes toward the highway. He didn't speak again
until after they'd merged onto the interstate. Once there he accelerated,
and fiddled with the controls, quieting the roar of the AC fan. Helen
had finished both burgers and wiped her hands on some napkins, and
now she had her phone out and was peering closely at it.

"What are you looking at?" he asked.

"I'm hoping that the position of his hands will show whether he
was trying to stop that thing from falling or if he was pulling it over on
himself. Maybe this doctor can tell—or if he can't he probably knows
somebody who can." She sighed and stuck her phone between her
thighs before taking the cup from the drink holder and popping off the
plastic lid. The baggie she lifted out of the melting ice held the spoon
and a smear of yellowish goo. Paul glanced over and grimaced, then
fixed his eyes back on the road, as they sped past the twin stone arches
of the county cemetery.

Incredulity in his voice, he asked, "Is that a souvenir spoon?"

"Yeah, it was the first thing I saw that looked clean. Libby had a little
collection of spoons in a rack that Ferris built. He put it in the barn after
she died because it made him sad. Look"—she held it up to show him,
pointing to the shape on the handle—"Famous potatoes, for Idaho. I

don't think they traveled very much. She only had three: this one and Wyoming and Saskatchewan."

Paul heard a little wobble in Helen's voice and turned to her in surprise. Helen tucked the baggie back into its ice bath and secured the lid, then removed her glasses and dabbed at her eyes with a napkin. "Oh god," she said, "isn't it awful?"

"Yes, it is," he agreed. "But do you think he just couldn't get over Libby's death? That he just wanted it all to be over?"

"I really don't, Paul—I spent a fair amount of time with the guy, and he was figuring it out—how to go on. He was definitely depressed, but Ferris wouldn't have done that. He has a son in Grand Rapids, and grandkids. They were coming for a visit in August, for the Eastern Montana Fair, and he wanted to finish the Venus in time for that visit. Slow down—there's a speed trap just past the ZinkCo sign."

He eased off the gas until they had passed the billboard, massive orange letters advertising the former Secretary of the Interior's new energy company, then sped up again. "So if this guy agrees to test this sample, and it looks like those other brains he autopsied, with the patches of yellow cotton candy, then maybe it's a disease or an infection that makes people suicidal?"

"Maybe so—it would be fascinating to know, right? It would explain a lot—not just about what happened to Ferris, but about those other people, too. It's a medical mystery. Since they started drilling in the national parks, the state economy has been booming, so why are all these Montanans offing themselves? There's got to be a reason why they don't want this information getting out."

Paul was listening, but he was also working out what he would say when he called the newsroom to break the news that he wouldn't be there for the broadcast. Grant could get one of the weekend anchors to cover his spot—Carla Paxton-Farley was always looking for a chance to suck up to the station manager and claw her way up the ladder. Some emergency with Paige or Hallie might explain his impromptu trip to Billings, but he would have to keep his story straight. Losing track of who he told what to was exactly what had landed him in divorce court.

———

They stopped at Hysham so Helen could use the ladies' room and refresh the ice in the cup. In the convenience store parking lot, the sun outside the truck's air-conditioned cab slammed down like a cartoon anvil. TV screens on the gas pumps all showed the same footage of federal troops aiming water cannons at a small cluster of Native Americans protesting the eminent domain action on the northern border. Paul purchased a pale, premade ham-and-Swiss sandwich from the refrigerated case, and then reluctantly stepped back outside into the June heat and called the station. Julie at the front desk answered and he got it over quickly, claiming "a family emergency," with a promise to explain more fully when he came in on Monday. Grant wasn't going to like this, he knew.

Back on the road, Helen spent some time Googling the M.E. on her cell and found out the location and contact number of the Yellowstone County coroner's office. Now she was on the phone with the guy, or his answering service, trying to convince him to see them without giving away too much. Before long, they had passed the oil derricks on the outskirts of Billings, and smoggy views of the metropolis rose in the distance. Paul recognized the black box of the Sheraton—not far from Paige's condo—and the First Interstate Building looming over the city. To their left, the dark heaps of the Pryor Mountains prompted a lecture from Helen about all the unusual geological features of those peaks, but Paul had a hard time paying attention.

He was keeping something from her, the fact that he had seen Ferris the night before at the Montana Bar, when they had shared a beer and chatted for a bit. As one of the last people to talk to Ferris (plenty of witnesses could testify to seeing them together), he would eventually have to answer some questions, if the local authorities did their job right. The reason Paul hadn't mentioned this meeting to Helen (or to the sheriff in the barn, for that matter) was because Ferris had told him he wanted to ask Helen out. He knew she had a husband in Oregon but she had mentioned her husband had a girlfriend, so maybe that meant she was looking for someone, too?

And knowing this, a thought had wormed its way into Paul's brain—that maybe something sudden and violent had happened between them. Maybe Ferris had made an unwanted pass at Helen, and she'd pushed the sculpture over on him in anger or self-defense. And could all this business with the medical examiner really be Helen trying to hide the truth about what had gone down in that barn?

Paul's gut told him he could trust Helen, that she wasn't capable of killing a man and then scooping up his brains with a potato spoon, but then why was he keeping all this from her?

15

June
Washington, DC

*S*omeone must be poisoning his mind, pouring lies into his perfectly *proportioned ear.* All month, Mike Pence had been grinding away at the plans for the military parade, chairing committees and flying back and forth across the country to meet with the heads of veterans' groups and members of the armed forces, doing his level best to sell them all on this ridiculous vanity project. That morning he and his staff had been summoned to the Oval Office for a working lunch and a progress report. And Stephen was there, an enigmatic smile curling his lips as he slouched at POTUS's side. But for the entire hour-long meeting, as Pence dutifully flattered the President and choked down his Chik-fil-A, his beloved hadn't looked his way, not once.

Stephen had looked at the television, tuned to Newsmax and reporting on the torture-murder of a blond nursing student by MS-13 gang members. He'd looked out the window at the armed guards pacing the lawn. He stared at his own beautiful hands, and adjusted his shirt cuffs, and gazed attentively at the President whenever he began pontificating about how his parade would be better than any parade, ever, in the history of the world. But he'd never spared even a glance for him, and Pence knew this (too risky, of course, to let his eyes go where they wanted) from the way his hands and feet grew cold and the terrible food dropped like gobbets of lead into his belly.

Because surely someone had been scheming to turn Stephen against him, accusing him of disloyalty, of acting the sycophant while harboring his own secret designs on the Presidency. But who would know this besides Mother and his God?—the only two to whom he dared unburden the freight of his soul. It had to be that rough beast behind the Resolute Desk, as unpredictable and dangerous as a hippopotamus. How many times had he seen Stephen emerge from this very office with an armload of legal pads and a smirk on his face? For a moment he surrendered to a nauseating fantasy: Individual One leaning across the polished expanse of oak with a TV remote in his hand, replaying footage from that last humiliating rally in Indiana, when he'd publically mocked his VP's Hoosier accent, his faith, his blue suit, his average-looking spouse. And, in his head, he saw Stephen watching and laughing right along with him.

Squirming at the image, he shook himself back into the present, made himself focus on the words spewing out of POTUS's face. He was back on the subject of the Space Force, how he wanted it marching prominently in the parade, though no one had yet been recruited to join. Apparently all that mattered were the uniforms ("I want them like *Barbarella*, but classier"), and he, Pence, was now being tasked with finding someone to design five different prototype versions for the President to choose between. Before the end of next week. He nodded and gestured to his aide, Pinkney, to make a note of it, then POTUS was rubbing his hands together and rising to his feet and shooing his VP out the door. Pinkney stood, too, and they both prepared to exit with as much dignity as possible as the President turned to Stephen and told him, "Okay, let's get to work."

He could feel himself flush as he stepped into the outer office, and, blinded by his own humiliation, he barely had time to register the presence of another person, the same man he's seen on two other occasions, in fact, meeting in private with Stephen and the President. In the moments before the guard ushered the man into the inner sanctum, he made himself take a closer look at the guy, who acknowledged him only with a brusque nod. Late fifties, balding, glasses, average build, average everything. The guy was aggressively nondescript, someone he would never have given a second look except for one thing: As the man brushed by, Pence was swamped by a powerful olfactory memory. He knew that smell, knew it with an atavistic intimacy that made his knees momentarily weak, but he didn't succeed in attaching words to it until later in the privacy of his own office bathroom, when he sat urinating into the commode and it came to him in a rush: *King David Dog*. Specifically, the Boom Boom Dog, with fried egg and cheddar cheese, the variety favored by his Irish grandfather, Richard Michael Cawley, the best man he'd ever known.

16

June
Montana

Dr. Fortunato Macadangdang stood beside a cloth-draped body on an examination table, peering intently at a little silver potato on the handle of a spoon. The medical examiner of Yellowstone County was a short man wearing latex gloves, blue scrubs, and a blue paper shower cap, with a paper mask tugged down beneath his chin. Rimless glasses disappeared into the skin of his wide and genial face. Paul thought he resembled a near-sighted Manny Pacquiao, the Filipino boxer and senator. Despite the white AirPods jutting from his ears, the M.E. seemed to be listening while Helen introduced herself and Paul before spilling the story of Ferris's accident–slash–possible suicide. Paul had been so distracted by the shrouded form under the sheet and his concerns about Helen's motives that he wasn't closely following their exchange. The fluorescent-lit room lined with cheap beige cabinets smelled sharply of chemicals, its tiled floor sloping slightly toward a central drain. A disconcerting poster of Ariana Grande looking wistful on a stool was taped above a computer desk in one corner.

"I've read your reports about the yellow fluff in the brains of the suicide cases, and I'm hoping you can test this sample, to see if it has the same pathology," she was now saying.

Dr. Macadangdang studied Helen with the same expression of bland curiosity with which he probably regarded the deceased citizens of Billings when he met them in his lab. Then he asked Helen the obvious question: Why hadn't she just taken this to the coroner in Miles City? Surely an autopsy would be carried out there, and he could ask them to share the results with his office. The potential for contamination was high, he said, casting a disapproving glance at the Dairy Queen cup full of water.

"Because," Helen said, looking intently at the M.E., "I don't really trust them, and I'm not sure you should either. Are you aware," she went on, "that none of the research findings you published on suicide victims are currently available online?"

That came as a surprise, Paul could tell. The prodigious mole nestled in Macadangdang's left eyebrow jumped halfway up the man's forehead. He set the baggie down on a nearby counter as Helen began digging through her backpack, eventually pulling out a crumpled sheaf of printouts. One by one she flipped through them, rattling off the names of various major medical journals. "Luckily I made copies, because right now all of these are missing from the web or the links are broken."

The M.E. took the pages from Helen's hand and gave her a searching look—assessing her reliability, Paul thought—before he stepped over to the desk in the corner and began typing rapidly on the computer keyboard. As he clicked away, peering at the screen, Dr. Macadangdang muttered under his breath in a language Paul assumed was Tagalog while the strains of Ariana's "Into You" trickled out of his AirPods. With the M.E. distracted, Paul moved closer to Helen and hissed, "When did you notice those studies were missing and when were you going to tell me?" He had begun to think of them as an investigative team. If they eventually went live with this story, and if he was going to stake his reputation as a journalist on the solidity of their reporting, then Helen had to quit leaving him in the dark.

"And when were *you* going to tell me that you saw Ferris last night?" Helen shot right back. Paul stood for a moment, blinking, as he registered what she had said. Glancing at Macadangdang's busy back, Helen drew Paul toward the opposite corner of the room and continued in a low voice. "I called Ferris before I drove over there this morning, and he told me you guys had a beer together at the Montana last night. But you never mentioned that to Peggy, and you never said anything about it to me. So the whole way here I'm thinking, *What the hell is up with that?*"

Helen plucked a wadded-up napkin from her front pocket and blew her nose on it before cramming it back into her jeans. "Especially when we started talking about Ferris's state of mind. I mean, you had a beer with him! Did he seem suicidal to you?" she hissed.

Just as Paul opened his mouth to respond, Dr. Macadangdang spun around in his desk chair. "Well," he announced, "it seems you are exactly right. This is very strange. Very strange." He rose and approached them. "So, I will have a look at the sample you have brought me. I am curious to see what we have there." He waved a hand at the baggie, before nodding toward the corpse on the metal table. "As you see I have other matters on my plate today, but I will be in touch with you when I have some answers. And you say you have some photographs of the body? I would very much like to see them."

———

By the time they were outside in the scorching truck it was almost four, and Paul wanted to avoid the evening traffic that clogged the highway out of the city. But as they exited the parking lot, something caught his eye and he hit the brakes. Helen was rifling through her backpack again, head down, as Paul stared across the street at some teens in red ball caps and jerseys crossing against the light. "Where the hell did I put that?" she muttered, still pawing at the crap in her bag.

He had pulled up short because he thought he recognized one of the teens. Any other day he would have rolled down his window and called out, but there was something about the way the group was moving—like coyotes intent on a sheep—that made him hold back and just watch. Now Paul could see what the group's attention was fixed on: an older Native American man riding a bicycle, with a bulging plastic takeout bag in the front basket. And as the two lines of motion converged—the teenagers' and the path of the bicyclist—Paul watched his daughter, Hallie, thrust the business end of the baseball bat she was carrying between the spokes of the bike's front tire.

17

Cotton Swab Moon
Sargassa

In the weeks since the prophecy, the progress they had managed to achieve looked impressive, even to Petra's jaded eyes. And while she feared it would all be torn to ribbons in the first blast of wind, Petra had to admit Adnan's design for a storm shield was strangely beautiful and brave. At once a parachute and a bird's wing, a nun's wimple and a white flag of surrender, it evoked all of these things and something more, maybe: hope.

Adnan hadn't visited Petra's shelter since their argument. She didn't know if he'd found another woman, but she doubted he had the time, for he and his little dog, Wasim, seemed to be everywhere at once, mustering collecting crews, consulting the fisher people and meteorologists about wind and weather conditions, and supervising construction on the materials for the shield. His workers had already begun weaving the fabric from mountains of scavenged plastic bags.

When she toured the trust during the previous weeks she had been struck by a gathering sense of purpose in the scattered communities on the Patch. Everyone seemed occupied with a task related to the storm defenses, even those who had initially dismissed the omen out of hand. One of the most vocal naysayers was Ani, whom Petra found hard at work under a ragged sunshade with a group of older women. They were hunched over a heap of plastic tampon plungers they were stringing together into long, multicolored ropes. Ani explained these would be used to anchor rafts along the coastline; the bright plastic tubes would be easy to spot and grab if one were floundering in the waves. When Petra looked skeptical, Ani shrugged, her hands still busy at her task. "We don't really believe it will save us," she told Petra, "but we are doing it anyway. What's the harm?"

Even the most devout of the refugees, accustomed to simply opening their palms to heaven and placing their fate in the hands of a supernatural being, found something practical to do in service of Hiranur's prophecy. Some of these believers collected useful materials; others helped stockpile provisions in the event the storm smashed the desalination works and leveled their gardens and chicken coops, leaving them without sources of fresh water, vegetables, and meat. Burak, who had been ready to go to war over the loss of one goat, had been placed in charge of provisioning the southern Patch with a month's supply of clean water and imperishable foods, mostly dried and salted fish and goat jerky. Petra had heard him loudly berating a youth for leaving a harvest of drying tomatoes out in a rainstorm. Burak bustled around, bristling like a puffer fish with the importance of his duties, and she had to laugh at how skillfully Adnan had maneuvered this enemy into his own camp.

As summer advanced and the air grew warmer, and the snails and roosting petrels appeared in the weeds, everywhere she traveled, Petra found Sargassans of all ages toiling in defense of their home, some jobs assigned by Adnan and his growing team of helpers, others they had dreamed up on their own. Even the *vencejos*, whipped into action by that little whirlwind of a girl Virginia Daria, were hard at work on a project. Each day they could be spotted racing by like the swift birds they were named for, as Virginia led them on expeditions to collect stray feathers from the places where the seabirds nested. As she breathlessly explained to anyone with the patience to listen, Adnan could use the feathers to build a giant pair of wings to fly them all out of the path of the hurricane. To keep their small hands free, they thrust the feathers they gathered into their hair until each was crowned by a mottled headdress of gray, white, and black plumage. The children's industry was remarkable, Petra marveled, when she passed the Darias' shelter one afternoon and noticed dozens of plastic net potato bags plump with feathers heaped against a toilet-wand fence.

But three days earlier, Sargassa's general mood of cheerfulness had been obliterated by horror and grief. Under cover of darkness, the banished Hakim had returned with a small band of marauders and made landfall on the western coast. In a stolen skiff, the men sped along the arterial channel to the governor's shelter. They seemed driven by no other purpose than to exact revenge, to sow terror. Valeria and her partner, Raiza, had been ambushed, raped, and strangled. Their screams eventually alerted other colonists nearby, who had managed to capture and restrain Hakim and several of the men after a struggle. Two of them had been wounded in the fight and bled to death, cursing the women. The governor's bodyguard had been gravely injured as well.

Petra and the other governors had been summoned immediately. In the gruel-thin light of morning, they surveyed the aftermath of the attack, the bodies of Valeria and Raiza, splayed across their mats, abused and then slaughtered where they had been peacefully sleeping just hours before. The sight of Valeria's staring green eyes, her bloodied mouth, the brittle blond hair torn in hanks from her scalp, would forever remind Petra of the cost of mercy. Afterward, in the local meetinghouse, the governors' decision had been unanimous: a sentence of death, to be carried out once Valeria and her partner had been interred at sea amid the keening of the mourners and the choked sobs of Valeria's son, Luis. During the funeral rites, dark looks had been cast at Halima and the others who had argued for clemency and swayed the group to vote for Hakim's banishment over his death. *Never again*, those eyes warned.

What use were Hiranur's prophecies if they couldn't foresee something like this? Petra wondered. Since the night of the murders, she had been staying with Meryem in her shelter near the girls' school. The other southern governors, their hair shaved in mourning, had spent the previous two nights in tents outfitted to handle the overflow during Council meetings. Now the hour had come for the punishment to be carried out. Each governor had undergone a cleansing bath in salt water and had her eyebrows daubed with greasy charcoal in preparation for her duty. At dawn they were conveyed to an ad hoc jail—formerly a collection shed for fish bones, dried and burned for fuel—where Hakim and his two surviving cohorts were held under heavy guard. Tightly bound with plastic strips, feet together and hands behind their backs, the murderers slumped morosely on middens of fish bones. Hoarse from cursing the guards who stood over them armed with machetes, they'd been given water, poured down their profaning throats with a rusty ladle, but no food since the attack. No point feeding corpses, Petra thought.

Now the guards hauled the men to their feet and dragged them outside the shed into the soft rain that had been falling since the previous night. When they saw the women waiting for them, arrayed in a grim semicircle, the two younger men blanched and fell to their knees. Hakim bared his broken teeth at Petra in an appalling grin. She fixed her stony eyes on him until he was forced to look away. Halima, her necklace of office bristling on her chest, stepped forward and raised her right arm, fisted above her shaved head, her pale face striped with rivulets of the charcoal streaming from her brows. In a surprisingly strong voice, she listed each man's crimes and informed him of his fate. Then she jerked her arm down fast to slap her thigh, and even Petra flinched at the sound, sharp as a gunshot. At this signal, the guards forced Hakim to his knees and secured their holds on the other men, who shivered and wept and begged for mercy as they struggled against the guards' grip.

Hakim said nothing. The rain kept falling.

———

Back in her shelter later that night, Petra could still see Hakim's bloodshot eyes and gasping mouth, blurred through the plastic sheet secured over his head with the woven cords looped around his straining neck.

The women had poured their collective anger and grief into the task, working together to pull hard on the cords from all sides, and the end came for each man in his turn. The weighted corpses were then disposed of, sinking far below the buoyant surface. Nothing more than fish food now, Petra knew. Despite those reproachful looks from the other governors, she refused to believe any part of the deaths of Valeria and Raiza and the bodyguard was Halima's to own. Hakim had carried all the blame down to the ocean floor with him. What ate at Petra now was a certainty that no matter how many violent men they sent to the bottom of the sea, more—and worse—would follow.

When they'd fled their homes and found their way to this improbable sanctuary, they had promised one another not to bring the war with them, yet here it came, clamoring to be fought again.

18

June
Montana

D addy, can you drive me back to Billings this afternoon?"
Paul inspected the freshly scrubbed face of his daughter across the yellow Formica table at the Pancake Corral. Without the too-heavy layer of makeup she typically wore he saw something not obvious to her friends: the traces of Crow blood that burnished her skin.

The private high school Hallie attended in Billings, the Stormfront Academy of Virtue and Excellence, had let out for the summer the previous week. Paul and Paige sat rigidly side by side, staring straight ahead as their smiling daughter—dressed in a white satin robe with a red sash draped around her neck and a white mortarboard bedazzled with the slogan 14 Words—marched forward to claim her diploma from SAVE's pompous headmaster. (When Paul had asked Hallie later what that meant, she'd told him some bogus story about it being part of the school's credo, fourteen words that all Stormfront graduates should strive for in the future, like *honesty* and *justice*. Later, Google set him straight. The fourteen words belonged to neo-Nazi Richard Spencer: "We must secure the existence of our people and a future for white people.")

Paul, dutifully videotaping the ceremony, wondered again why Hallie couldn't have attended a local public high school for her senior year, like Custer, where she'd gone when they lived in Miles City. But during the divorce Paige had made a stink about it and now he was on the hook for SAVE's ridiculous tuition, and Hallie hadn't even started college yet. Too bad the benefits he'd gotten for the mineral leasing on his family's land, because of his Native American heritage, had been terminated when the Vanishing Act was passed in 2020.

Paul had picked up Hallie in Billings on Friday afternoon. As he idled in front of Paige's condo waiting for his daughter to emerge with her overnight bags, he'd seen his ex-wife roar off in her brand-new Jeep Grand Cherokee, her severe new light-brown bob turned resolutely away from him. Now that Hallie had graduated she had fewer excuses to avoid her father's company, and she'd grudgingly agreed to this wilderness trip with him weeks before. He'd taken off a day from work so they could go kayaking in Bighorn Canyon and stay overnight in Lovell, an excursion he'd intended as a father-daughter bonding trip, part of a last-ditch campaign to improve their relationship before college life claimed her. He had planned a day of hiking, on the Upper Layout Creek trail to the falls. But now, as they dawdled over the syrupy traces of their breakfast, she was already making noises about heading back to Billings early.

All the previous day, as they kayaked through the tremendous canyons, he had stared at her shiny brown ponytail, twitching back and forth along her back as she dipped her paddle into the opaque water, and replayed the scene that had unfolded across from the medical examiner's office. The satisfaction he'd have normally taken in the rare gift of his daughter's company was muddied by the memory of what he had witnessed. But had it really been Hallie? As he'd driven away, hands clenched on the wheel, he'd already begun to question what he'd seen. The girl wielding the bat had long, straight brown hair and the same slim calves as Hallie, but didn't a lot of teenage girls look like that? His eyesight wasn't so good anymore—lately he'd caught himself squinting to read street signs at a distance. The red ball cap had shadowed part of the girl's face, and he'd seen nothing like that cap tumble out of Hallie's bag when they'd unpacked at the motel. It was so much easier to second-guess himself, to believe he'd just imagined seeing his daughter because he was in Billings and she'd been on his mind.

And there was something else, if he was being entirely honest. When Paul became a father, one thing he hadn't anticipated was that he would sometimes feel afraid of his own kid. This fear took different forms: the fear of someone who holds power over you because you love them so very much, and you know if something ever happened to that person you would walk to the closest railroad track and rest your skull against the rail. And the very different fear that comes from knowing your own authority is largely illusory—that if he told Hallie not to do something, she might just do it anyway, and what would he do then?

But now he had a new fear to add to the mix. He had seen someone who looked an awful lot like her behave with a savagery that sickened him, when the rider had sailed over the front wheel of his bicycle, and the teens had mobbed him as he sprawled facedown on the sidewalk. They had overtaken the man, gleefully walloping him, while he curled up on the ground, trying to shield himself with his arms. The violence unfolded against a soundtrack of classic rock (the final notes of Kansas's "Carry on My Wayward Son" fading into "You Shook Me" by AC/DC) that Helen had called up on the radio dial before turning her attention to the joint she was busy rolling on her lap (in the coroner's parking lot!), muttering about how this had been one hell of a day and she needed something to steady her nerves. She had missed the whole scene—while he'd just sat there gaping through the bug-speckled windshield, watching that girl with Hallie's hair, and Hallie's smile, merrily smashing the bike and the fallen rider with the bat she'd stuck through the spokes.

Paul flushed with shame when he thought of how he'd jammed the truck into gear and barreled away. In his rearview mirror, he'd seen the kids scatter, whooping, one of them clutching the takeout bag triumphantly, leaving behind the dark lump on the sidewalk, the bent bicycle frame. Just short of the highway, Paul's arms had begun to shake so badly that he told Helen he needed to use the bathroom in case they hit traffic and pulled over into a ZinkCo station lot. In the men's room he made a quick 911 call, giving a brief description of the attack and the location where it had occurred but hanging up before the operator could ask for his name. Then he steadied himself, drawing in deep, shaky breaths over the spattered enamel sink before finally walking out into the thick late-afternoon haze.

They pulled back into traffic and were soon on the highway, Helen puffing on her expertly rolled joint, riffing away in her pot-fueled enthusiasm about their visit with Dr. Macadangdang and fiddling with the radio dial. Twice Paul waved away the roach that she extended to him ("For crissakes, Helen, I'm driving!"). Here he was, he realized, keeping another secret from her, just as he had on the way to Billings, but he needed time to think, to determine what this revelation required of him, and he didn't want Helen telling him what he had to do.

With every day that had passed since that trip to Billings, Paul felt more and more like an accomplice to the crime. He'd tried to talk to his ex about it, but she'd slipped away after the graduation ceremony before he'd had the chance, and she wouldn't return his messages (*Paige, call me, it's important*). Now, as he sat across from Hallie at the diner, jabbing a fork into the gummy remains of his blueberry pancakes, his palms turned clammy at the prospect of confronting his own child. If she noticed his nerves she gave no sign; her honey-brown eyes kept straying past his shoulder to fix on the large television screen mounted over the lunch counter. Had that always been there? They had come to the Pancake Corral before, as a family, and he'd never noticed a TV. He pictured his own head, mouthing the news script, floating authoritatively over the heads of the patrons shoveling hash browns and scrambled eggs into their faces. In the morning sunlight that pierced the plate-glass window, Hallie looked as innocent as an apricot, this girl he suspected of nearly beating a man to death on a public street.

He focused on the *nearly*—the night after the attack he'd obsessively checked the newsfeed on his phone, and finally found an item about a Billings deliveryman named Parker Gallineau who had been taken to a local hospital in serious condition. Since that initial report he'd seen the story morph and change. In its latest iteration, Gallineau—a full-blooded Blackfoot—had mutated into the aggressor, intentionally plowing his bike into a group of white kids on their way home from softball practice. So Hallie wasn't an accessory to murder, thank god, but maybe that was only a matter of luck. He was terrified by what she might have done, and how she had done it—with a savage kind of glee. He was afraid that when he opened his mouth to tell her what he suspected, nothing between them would ever be the same.

It was the recognition that their relationship had already changed, even if he never said a word to anyone, that finally made him take a deep breath and heave his thoughts into his mouth, just as his cell phone rang on the Formica table. It was Helen.

"Where are you?"

"Hold on," he told her. Relief raced like a chemical through Paul's body as he made an "I have to take this" gesture to Hallie and slid out of the vinyl booth. He passed the cashier near the front door and stepped out into the restaurant parking lot with the phone pressed to his ear. "I'm in Wyoming, with Hallie. What's up?"

"I heard from Macadangdang. He tested Ferris's sample. It's the same. The yellow floss that's in the other suicide brains. The markers were all exactly the same."

"Wow. OK," was all he could think of to say, but Helen kept talking, brimming with her news. An older couple pulled into the handicapped spot in front of the restaurant and laboriously exited their silver Buick as he tried to focus on Helen's words.

"And he showed those pictures I took to one of his forensic buddies. She said the position of the hands suggests Ferris was pulling the sculpture over on him instead of pushing it away. He killed himself, Paul. But I know he wasn't suicidal. You know it, too. There's no way he would do that to himself, absolutely no way. Something happened, something went wrong inside his brain to *make* him do that. And there's something else, Paul."

"What's that?"

"The chickens are dead."

19

June
New York City

S he was dreaming about the President. Part of a cluster of reporters
behind a cordon, she waited for him to disembark from a helicopter
on the White House lawn, but her excitement shifted to alarm when he
slowly unfolded his bulk from the belly of the machine and she saw he
was extremely tall, far taller than she'd ever noticed before. As he began
to straighten she realized that he was, in fact, even taller than the helicopter, or taller than its whirring rotor, at least. She tried to warn him,
but her strangled dream voice didn't carry over the roar of the wind, or
he heard her and chose to ignore her cries and her frantically signaling
arms. The rotor caught him cleanly in the neck, lifting his head from his
body and sending it lofting over the south lawn with the grace of a well-
served shuttlecock. She opened her mouth to scream, but the only noise
she managed to produce was a low buzzing sound . . .

Least's hand started groping for the phone on her nightstand even before
she was fully awake. Her room faced east, a fact she hadn't registered
when she'd rented the apartment, and every clear morning a slim banner

of sunlight unfurled itself across her pillow before vanishing for the remainder of the day. She didn't mind that it woke her when she had to get up and onto the subway for the long ride into Manhattan from Bay Ridge. But on a Saturday morning after a shitty week, she really needed to sleep in.

Friday had been a full-on nightmare. After lunch a homeless guy had camped out in front of the gallery with all his bags, and when she had summoned the cops to move him along, he spat energetically on the plate-glass window and she'd had to clean it up—using half a bottle of Windex and a wad of paper towels the size of a dwarf planet. On the R train home during rush hour, a woman seated across from her had suddenly folded in half like a stapler and ejected the contents of her stomach onto the subway floor. Right afterward, the train ground to a halt in the tunnel and sat there for a solid fifteen minutes, and a plaintive voice asked in the silence, "How can one vomit hold up a whole train?"

When she'd finally made it home, with takeout from Golden Krust, she was thinking that if her life didn't change, and fast, she was ready to do a jackknife off the nearby Verrazano Bridge. Claudia wanted her to come see some guy she knew playing in a band called Nipple Confusion later that night, but Least had passed. *As if!* Instead, she installed her ass on the couch and binge-watched *Extreme Makeovers* while shoveling down her chicken curry, trying hard to forget the fact that she'd heard nothing from Parallax.

Since that morning in the loft something else was regularly shocking Least into consciousness, often before the sun flared through her bedroom window. The number of followers on @virginkardashian had ballooned, in response to the video of her screen test, which had already attracted over a million views. One million! Luka had posted the footage of her talking about the President, fifty-seven seconds during which she had detailed the tremendous things he'd done even though people said such terrible stuff about him, and how much she admired him, and her face had flushed the prettiest pink with pleasure and pride. Most of the comments talked about how hot she was but also about how refreshing it was to hear someone say these things, someone who wasn't the President himself or a White House spokesperson or a media pundit or the vice president or the Saudi Arabian envoy or any of the others who regularly went on TV to trumpet the President's praises and enumerate the President's accomplishments. Most incredible of all, the video had been liked and reposted on Twitter by POTUS himself.

Ever since she'd met Luka by the pool in South Beach, everyday life felt surreal to Least, as if she were going through the motions of her regular life with a VR headset strapped to her face. From the visit to Mar-a-Lago and the viral response to @virginkardashian, to the meetings about the TV show and the growing possibility that *Foxy Friends* really might happen after all . . . How could any of this be real? And yet she was staring at the evidence in her hand, on that little screen—all those likes, all those views. He had made it all happen for her, this mysterious man with the white-blond shock of hair and the ice-blue eyes and the sexy accent, who had interrupted her disappointing little life to offer her an exit strategy. Sometimes she felt so very grateful to him, especially after she'd had a few drinks, she would have gladly brought him up to her bedroom and thanked him with an orifice other than her mouth. It had been ages since she'd had sex with anyone but herself, and Least had always had a hyperactive libido. But Luka inevitably put her off, delivering her just to the stoop of her apartment building with a chaste peck on the cheek. She figured he was gay, although she didn't get that vibe from him. Once, when over dinner at Il Divo she set out to seduce him before dessert, Luka held up a finger and admonished her in a whisper, "Hashtag *virgin* Kardashian, Least—let's keep that illusion alive."

He had counseled her to be discrete about her sex life, and that was tough, because the growing buzz around her social media presence drew propositions from the men who now recognized her in bars and nightclubs, and some of them were seriously tempting. Yet Luka always managed to show up and insert himself at the critical moment, smiling and taking her arm proprietarily and steering her away from whoever had her in his sights.

Since Luka had materialized in her life, and started helping Least with her brand, her relationships with her other so-called friends were changing, too. After Angela's party, that particular group of women had frozen her out, until rumors reached them that she had become kind of a rising star on Instagram. Then Angela had called, acting all innocent, all "Hey, girlfriend, haven't seen you for a while, want to get together for a drink?" But Least had put her off, claimed she was incredibly busy, and told her she'd get back to her when her schedule freed up later in the month. Fat chance. She's seen Angie's true face by now.

She still spent time with Resa, of course, her BFF since second grade. She could still count on Resa to not act weird and treat her different now that she was becoming a person that other people recognized on the street and made a fuss over and wanted to take selfies with. Resa, who had asked her point blank, "What the hell is happening, Leasie?" Resa was curious, and genuinely excited for her, but also suspicious, and she asked Least all kinds of questions about Luka that Least couldn't answer. *Who really is this guy? Why does he want to help you? What's the quid pro quo?* The same kinds of questions Claudia had asked, Least realized, now that she thought about it. Questions that made her squirm a little, and try to act more certain than she really was about this whole evolving situation. But the fact that she hadn't slept with Luka and that he seemed to have zero interest in getting into her pants had calmed both Resa's and Claudia's fears, even though Least found it incredibly frustrating.

It wasn't like she'd never Googled Luka's name, to make sure he was actually legit. And she'd found him, and the LA consultancy firm where he worked, called Brand-Aid. His hair was more conservatively styled in his professional headshot than in real life, and his bio didn't include any personal information, though she hadn't really expected it would. She started to read the firm's mission statement ("Great branding knows no borders…") but lost interest after the first few lines.

After the screen test, Luka had seemed so confident, assuring her that she'd aced it and it was only a matter of time before the producers got back to her. She had already warned Claudia she'd probably be moving out as soon as she started making more money. But more than two weeks had passed since that afternoon in the loft without a word from Parallax, and Least was beginning to wonder if Luka's overconfidence had jinxed her chances of being chosen. She knew that having her hopes rocket up into the stratosphere only to plummet to earth again would literally gut her.

Shortly after her move to New York, she'd learned that her BA from the University of Michigan, where she had majored in art history, was worth exactly nothing in the insular and snooty New York art world. To her surprise, her very recognizable last name only seemed to inspire disdain (even at Gagosian!—so much for Armenian American solidarity), and she soon found herself answering "No relation" when the inevitable question came up in a job interview. Her first job was an unpaid, full-time internship, which gobbled up most of the money she'd managed to save by living at home while she got her undergraduate degree. Then she'd jumped from one menial gallery job to the next, finding nothing in the least bit glamorous or fulfilling about answering phones, hand-addressing envelopes, shrink-wrapping canvases, taking the owner's expensive clothing to the dry cleaner, and soothing the perpetually ruffled feathers of needy and narcissistic artists. Even at the openings, where she had once pictured herself charming the pants off some gray-haired lion of the art world, she was stuck at the back table pouring cheap Syrah into plastic cups and replenishing the cheese platter. Her puny attention span didn't help, either. Long before she might have made a case for advancement at one gallery, she had grown bored with the work on the walls and started looking for a new position, somewhere—anywhere—else.

After a decade of scraping by, Least had finally secured her current job as manager of the art glass gallery on Broome Street, but she detested the stuff on display, all the stupid frosted dolphins and dragons and howling wolves and hunting eagles, and could barely suppress her contempt while showing the occasional customer around.

Now she swung her legs out from under the duvet and sat up, gaping at the text from Luka. *Didnt I say so? Youre* . . . She had to unlock the phone to read the whole message, and her hand was shaking so much she had trouble keying in her passcode, but at last she managed it: *in! Filming for FF comm starts immed. Call me.*

Least stood up, still staring at the screen in her hand. *She had it. They wanted her. She was going to be on television.* The room began to spin around her and she had to sit back down again, yelping, "Omigod, omigod, omigod, OMIGOD!!!" until she was literally shrieking, and a bleary-eyed Claudia came busting through the door to see if her room-mate was being murdered.

20

Cotton Swab Moon
Sargassa

In the weeks after his mother's death, Petra watched Valeria's teenage son slowly lose his mind. Luis had moved in with Raiza's daughter, but Yael was grappling with her own grief and her chronic eczema and had precious little energy to spare for the kid. Blond, autistic, and alarmingly skinny, Luis began piercing his eyebrows with fish bones and drumming with his hands on his concave belly until it was purple with bruises. He had an old iPhone with a shattered screen, and though the lack of a power source on the Patch rendered such devices more than useless, Luis would swipe at the screen and make texting motions with his thumbs and mutter to himself. The other teens who might have helped distract him from his mother's loss seemed to shun him, Petra was sorry to see. Luis made people uncomfortable, had done so even before he became the boy whose lesbian mother was raped and murdered. He made Petra uncomfortable, too.

Since the executions, her sleep had been troubled. Hakim deserved it, they all did, Petra told herself, but helping to end three lives with her own hands imposed a psychic burden not easily brushed aside. How to live without either committing violence or becoming a victim to it was a perennial question—a question for the philosophers, perhaps, yet it was something she thought about every day on Sargassa. One of her responsibilities as a governor, she believed, was to find an answer to that question, or to at least come to terms with the reasons why it would never be answered.

And lately she had seen Adnan in the company of another woman, his hand on the curve of her hip, and Petra had felt the unexpected spur of jealousy, quickly replaced by anger at herself for succumbing to such a stupid emotion. Sometimes when she couldn't sleep she lay on her back and imagined her body, by centimeters, turning to stone: her fingers growing stiff, the mineral weight creeping up her legs and invading her pelvis, her arms becoming impossible to lift and her tongue growing heavy inside her mouth. And once she was entirely cold and solid and invulnerable, sleep would sometimes come.

Meanwhile, work continued on the storm preparation projects. Though Hiranur insisted the signs were unequivocal, and not a soul would survive the coming hurricane, she seemed cheerful enough and sometimes even joined in with the work parties, stripping the leaves off lengths of sargassum and braiding the strands while she hummed old melodies under her breath and gossiped with the others.

One morning, soon after Petra had hung her necklace of office at the entrance to her shelter to signal she was at home and might be approached, a movement by the gap in the door caught her eye. Virginia Daria stood there, rocking back and forth on her two small bare feet. The little girl's dark hair had been yanked roughly back into a ponytail—probably her mother's attempt to tame some of her daughter's excess energy—and the shift dress that swallowed her skinny body showed a palimpsest of salt stains along its hem. "Good morning, Virginia. Do you want to come in?" Petra asked, but Virginia stayed there at the entrance, twitchy with suppressed excitement, blurting out her news. "Governor Mussan," she lisped, and Petra could see she'd lost another tooth, "Luis had a message."

"Valeria's son? That Luis?"

"Yes, Luis had a message," the girl repeated.

"A message? From whom?"

"On his phone, a message on his phone."

It's a game, Petra thought, and she felt a burst of gratitude that these younger children hadn't been put off by Luis's strangeness, that they would befriend him even if the older kids did not.

She smiled at Virginia and kneeled down to bring herself level with the small visitor. "What was the message?" she asked.

"Luis got a message from Valeria," the girl said solemnly.

Petra forced herself not to react, to keep the sorrow out of her face as she absorbed this statement. *People grieve in different ways*, she reminded herself. *What harm to play these games, to imagine that his mother would call him from beyond the grave, to send her love? Maybe this will be how he heals*, she thought. In as neutral a tone as she could muster she asked the child, "What did Valeria say?"

Virginia's dark eyes were wide in her sun-browned face. "She told Luis he can save us."

From the yard a voice called out, "Don't forget to tell her about the—" before Virginia spun around and shouted sharply, "I *know!* I will!" at whoever had spoken out of turn. Petra looked past Virginia's shoulder, and saw some of the other *vencejos* clustered near the tomato plants by the edge of the yard.

Virginia continued in a breathless voice, hurrying to get it all out before anyone could interrupt her again. "She told him the wings won't help, with the whirlywind"—Petra smiled at Virginia's childish corruption of the word, but the girl pouted a bit, since the wings had been her idea, after all—"that she needs a sack of flies. That's the only way. That's what Valeria said."

Petra thought of the sacks of feathers the children had collected, in piles by the Darias' fence.

Then the same high voice piped up again from the yard, but Virginia twisted around and shouted the other child down. *"I'm telling it!"* she yelled back in exasperation.

Petra looked the girl in the eye and laid a hand on her bare arm. "Thank you for telling me this, Virginia. That's a very important message. Will you ask Luis to let you know if his mom sends him any more messages? Or, if he wants, he can come and tell me himself." She might as well enlist these *vencejos* to keep an eye on the troubled teen — it made sense he would feel more at ease talking to the younger children than to Yael, or the other kids his own age, who probably made fun of his odd mannerisms, the little shits.

The child nodded solemnly, then announced, "OK, I'm going now! Bye-bye!" and ran back to her friends. As the small crew hurried away, she could her Virginia reporting to them, "She said to tell her if …"

It turned out to be a busy morning. Shortly after Virginia's visit, Petra spoke with an older sourpuss whose nose was out of joint because the trust's best rat catcher, tasked with killing rodents that made their way to Sargassa on the trade vessels, hadn't been properly disposing of the vermin's bodies but instead had used them to practice his taxidermy skills. He'd been creating little vignettes with the creatures' corpses, some of which were in very questionable taste, and charging admission to see them. The neighbors were, frankly, fed up. After that, three young mothers sought her out, one of them nursing her youngest while they spoke in the shade of Petra's porch. The women had grown concerned that all the open talk about the monster storm was frightening the children. Their kids kept asking questions, and some had recurring dreams of being sucked up in the funneling winds and carried out to sea. Could the Council remind people that little ears were always listening, for everyone to be more guarded with their words? She would, Petra promised. There was a general meeting scheduled for the beginning of the new month, and she would be sure to bring their concerns to the group.

By the time the women left, the sun had crawled past the top of the sky, and Petra's stomach was complaining. She lifted her necklace off the roof pole and stowed it back inside, and then made her way to the kitchen tent, running her fingers through the short brush of hair that had grown back since she'd shaved her head for the executions. Fish soup was on the menu again—when wasn't it on the menu?—and as she sat cross-legged, sipping the warm broth, she nodded briefly to the other Sargassans. Governors were left alone at mealtimes, unless one invited you to join her. It was only then, in the relative quiet she'd earned after a long morning of meetings, that she reflected back on what Virginia had told her.

And almost as though simply thinking of Luis had the power to summon him, there he was, slipping in through the door flaps, with his downcast eyes and his self-pierced eyebrows, thin as a crane. He accepted a bowl of soup from the servers and found himself a place on the mats far removed from everyone else in the tent. As he ate, Petra watched Luis pull out his broken iPhone and jab at it with his thumbs. Two teenage boys squatting near Petra nudged each other and pointed toward Luis, snickering, but they shut up quick when she caught their eye and shook her head. She thought of the packs of young men in their conspicuously American shirts (*Hollister, Abercrombie, Adidas*) shouting happily into their cell phones as they ranged through the souk, arms slung around each other's necks; in another place, Luis might have had friends like these, instead of being shunned and teased.

Poor kid, she thought. Losing a parent so suddenly and so violently should have earned Luis a little consideration from his peers, but it seemed like teenagers just didn't see it that way. Plenty of these kids had lost parents to violence, and it had hardened them. When they sensed weakness or weirdness, they came in for the kill.

For her part, Petra was deeply ambivalent about children. She'd had a miscarriage once and felt nothing but relief. How cruel and irresponsible it seemed to bring a child into such a rotten world. Before the war she'd had an IUD inserted, and while there were doctors on the Patch who might be able to remove it, what was the point? At thirty-two, she knew her child-bearing years would soon be over, yet she could watch an infant root hungrily at its mother's breast—as she had earlier that day—and feel no desire to cradle a child of her own in her arms. She suspected she might never be ready to sacrifice her body, and her life, to another human being.

And that was when the coin dropped.

Sack of flies. *Sacrifice.*

21

The man bends over him, pries open his crusted eyes, moves dry hands across his shivering belly, and presses a cold disk to his chest. He gazes up at two little mirrors hovering there, the same strange and sorrowful face reflected in each. Two matching boys framed in silver, like the fading photographs on the tombstones in the cemetery behind his *abuela*'s house. A moving mouth smells of cooked meat that reminds him of the steam from the food cart selling *chuchitos* on the corner of his *tia*'s street, when his entire family walked from the church to her apartment for the midday meal after Mass. Sometimes his father held Felo's small hand in his large, rough hand for a moment before he let it go to point at the things they passed, full of opinions as always, about the corruption of the government, the hypocrisy of the priesthood, that funny cloud shaped like a mushroom above the mountain.

All the time he can feel himself emptying, growing dry and light as a cornhusk. Every memory that visits him carries a piece of him away when it goes: his mother's name, his own name, the taste of *algodones*. He can't remember how he came to this place, or how to move the things flopping at the ends of his wrists. The billowing walls keep lofting him up somewhere close to the ceiling before he drifts down again to rest lightly against the sweaty bedding. Even the shallowest breath sends him floating up again, like a ghost on a trampoline.

Next to the man's face another face appears, this one a woman's, beautiful and sad, speaking soft words and stroking his cheek. *Nuestra Señora de los Ojos Estrechos*, Our Lady of the Slit Eyes, he thinks, the one the women carried tenderly on heavy platforms through the teeming streets. He sees her sorrowful face, her blue mantle, her corona of golden stars. He has murmured prayers to her under his breath until his mouth is too dry to form words, when only his stammering heart can cry out, but she heard him even in his silence. La Virgen has come to bring him home.

22

June
Washington, DC

The vice president's official residence did not readily accommodate religious devotion, but they had made do. Mother had instructed the decorator to convert an underutilized side room with a skinny window into a lovely private chapel, outfitted with some simple oak pews and a narrow white marble altar. They would repair here every evening, before bed, to kneel on padded prie-dieux cross-stitched with scenes from the Crucifixion, heads bent in prayer, mouthing the beautiful, familiar words.

Mike Pence had looked forward to this moment all day. He was deeply troubled, and it always gave him solace to commune with his Lord, Jesus Christ; it helped to flush the miseries from his brain before he laid it to rest. He knew the Scriptures warned of constant evil attacks that came during the nighttime hours, and he knew prayer could shield him from the incursions of his enemies. Especially from the one man who seemed determined to turn Pence's every waking moment into a living hell.

After demanding that 110% more gold be added to the epaulets, POTUS had finally signed off on one of the concepts for the Space Force uniforms, scribbling in black Sharpie over the designer's sketch with a signature that seemed to grow larger and more jagged all the time. Fifteen skilled Honduran seamstresses were already sequestered in the basement of the Department of Labor building, sewing themselves blind to produce the sixty uniforms (thirty medium and thirty large) that had to be ready by the date of the parade. With the threat of deportation hanging over their heads, they would meet that deadline, or else.

The time he'd had to devote to the uniforms had been but a minor annoyance, however; his real problem was the lack of bodies to wear them. Since the Winnipeg skirmish, tens of thousands of troops had been deployed to the northern border to stand guard until that wall could be completed. With thousands of soldiers still camped along the southern barrier and the Navy and Coast Guard engaged in the Puerto Rico siege and guarding hundreds of newly erected coastal oil platforms, manpower and money were in seriously short supply. He was the consummate yes man, so how could he tell this President that, no, the massive military parade he wanted so badly would not happen, would never happen, no matter how many times he screamed and swore at them and pounded the table with his stubby fists?

Pence had hoped to swell the parade ranks with veterans, and issue each one a small stipend for his or her time. Lord knows they needed it, with the inflated cost of pharmaceuticals. But a week before, Pinkney had brought him a disturbing report, in the form of a secret memo from the Secretary of Veterans Affairs. Since the election there had been a sharp spike in both veteran and active-duty suicides. Exact numbers were not available, but the Secretary estimated it was somewhere in the neighborhood of 376 per month. He had had to look at the memo several times, to make sure he was seeing that number correctly. The data for May had been helpfully broken down into categories: 167 gunshot wounds (97 of these were murder-suicides involving spouses/ girlfriends and children), 102 opioid overdoses, 98 hangings, 6 subway jumps, 2 intentional drownings, and an exsanguination.

He had crisscrossed the country and called in every favor (the Carrier plant bosses wouldn't even take his calls, the ingrates!), but he found himself blocked at every turn, and time was definitely not on his side.

He closed his eyes and clenched his hands under his chin, murmuring the words from 1 Samuel 20:10, one of his favorite psalms, especially the bit about "exalting the horn of his anointed." Mother, kneeling by his side, muttered her persistent mantra: *Please, Lord, make my husband President.* Since his conversion, he had always trusted Jesus to hear his words, to come to the aid of His faithful servant. All would be well if he just reaffirmed his trust in the Lord.

Later, when they were tucked between the freshly bleached sheets of the marital bed, his heart sank when he felt his wife's chilly hand slide around his waist to tug at the strings of his pajama bottoms. She often wanted him to perform his husbandly duties after a fervent prayer session. Tonight she seemed especially insistent. He had to summon up all his choicest fantasies of Stephen to achieve climax, but at the moment of release he had a sudden thought that made all the straining and grunting worthwhile: *Just fake it.* He'd been faking it successfully for years, with his childhood friends and family, with Karen, with the press, and most of all with himself. As vice president he had had a front row seat for some of the greatest lessons in fakery in modern memory, and he'd learned at the feet of a master.

This ridiculous parade didn't actually have to be real; it only had to appear so. He thought of old-timey western towns and the false façades of buildings, propped up with slats in the back, and snake-oil salesmen peddling doctored poison in little brown bottles as a miracle cure. Faking it was the longest con of the American character, born of the need to make something from nothing, to create a nation out of a motley collection of criminals and fanatics and ne'er-do-wells, based on a survival instinct since elevated to an art form. It was the key to everything, transforming all the impossibilities that had weighed so heavily on him into opalescent soap bubbles, drifting away to vanish in wet little bursts. *Fake it till you make it.* As he lay there, the plan coalesced in his mind in all its glorious simplicity. He sighed deeply while Mother snuggled close under the double-wedding-ring quilt, believing she heard the sigh of a deeply satisfied man. *Thank you, my own dear Lord,* he thought, *for once again showing me the true way.*

23

June
Miles City

Helen had heard it from Tyler, the man she'd hired to keep an eye on the ranch and the remnants of Ferris's stock until his son could come from Grand Rapids to liquidate his late parents' estate. Tyler had ventured into the barn to have a peek at the scene of the accident when he caught a whiff of the stink coming from one of the horses' vacant stalls. "I peeped over the gate," he told Helen, "and there was nothing but a bunch of dead chickens in that stall. Not a mark on 'em. Just lying there, rotting away. Maybe some kids played a prank and throw'd 'em in there dead?"

When Helen told him they had put the birds in there to keep them away from Ferris's body after the accident, Tyler just scratched up under his battered feed cap and rubbed his bristly chin and laughed a little.

"Now I know Ferris must've raised the world's stupidest chickens. Why didn't they just fly out? A chicken can fly to the top of a horse stall. I've seen 'em do it plenty of times, to get after the grain. I have to shoo 'em out of my stalls all the time."

Helen had relayed all this to Paul as they sat on a picnic table at a rest stop on I-94 just west of Miles City, the morning after he came back from

Bighorn Canyon. They'd settled on a new place to meet because the Ten Commandments billboard seemed to be attracting graffiti artists as the weather turned warmer. Since they'd last rendezvoused there, someone had added an Eleventh Commandment to the bottom of the huge sign in bright blue spray paint: *Thou shalt not fuck butt*, followed by a plump W to illustrate the point. Vandals had also peppered out the "not" on *Thou shalt not kill* with multiple rounds of buckshot. As Helen told him what she'd found out from Tyler, she stood up and started pacing in the dust and her gestures grew more animated. "Those chickens could have escaped that stall. So why didn't they? Tyler said it didn't look like they'd pecked each other to death—'not a mark,' he said. So what else are we supposed to conclude, Paul? Every one of those birds chose to stay in there and starve to death."

Paul laughed. "You think those birds got so upset when they saw Ferris under that statue that they staged a hunger strike?"

She gave him a withering look. "You're missing the point! Those chickens were pecking at Ferris's . . . brains"—Helen winced in disgust—"just before we threw them in that stall. We know his brain was diseased! Dr. Macadangdang said so. There's no other explanation for why they would behave like that. We know Ferris killed himself, and those chickens did, too!" She dropped the spent roach they'd been smoking and ground it beneath her heel.

They couldn't prove it, of course. Much to Helen's chagrin, Tyler had bagged the rotten birds and taken them with a load of garbage to the dump days earlier, so any potential forensic evidence was likely long gone. But Helen remained adamant that the same pathology was behind all of those deaths, and that a necropsy would have shown the yellow spongiform growth Mac had identified in Ferris's sample was present in those bird brains, too.

"This is a terrifying possibility, Paul—like the coronavirus. As soon as you have a disease that can jump from an animal to a human, or vice versa, you have the potential for another pandemic."

Paul began to giggle.

"What is wrong with you?" she said, glaring at him.

"That name still kills me: Macadangdangdangadangalang... It sounds like a trolley. And did you notice that poster in his office? Do you think that guy goes home and jerks off to Ariana Grande videos?"

"You really shouldn't get stoned with me if it's going to keep turning you into an idiot," Helen admonished him, and headed over to check if the restrooms were open. While the pot helped Helen think outside the box and make unusual and intuitive connections, it just made Paul giggly and sleepy and hungry. And increasingly paranoid. After he'd made that trip to Billings with Helen, Cary Hydermaus, one of the fill-in anchors at the station, had left a voice message for him that he'd been fretting about ever since. *Hey, just a heads up, but next time you dump your shift on us at the last minute, better come up with a plausible excuse. Grant already thinks you're phoning it in.*

The warning was odd, coming from a guy who no doubt had his eye on Paul's job. And once last week when Paul was reading an EPA report about the environmental benefits of fracking, he'd seen Grant watching him from the back of the studio with a sour expression. If his job was really in jeopardy, he should be redoubling his efforts to prove his own worth, yet he'd taken off the previous Friday to go kayaking with Hallie, and here he was getting baked before lunch on a Monday, a workday.

If Paige ever spoke to him again, she'd probably say he was in the middle of a midlife crisis, and maybe she'd be right. But shouldn't he be blowing Hallie's meager college fund on a Maserati, or debating which selfie he should post on Elite Montana Singles, instead of sneaking off to smoke pot at rest stops with a postmenopausal geologist? This crazy story they were chasing had its hooks in him, for sure, but it was more than that. Paul had to admit he enjoyed hanging out with Helen. He liked her because she was smart and no nonsense and didn't try to flirt with him like most of the women he met. Paul mostly felt like himself in Helen's company, and not like some counterfeit version of himself he was trying to sell to an audience. Maybe he could relax with her because she reminded him a little of his mom—if his mom had been cool and smoked reefer and knew what an alluvial cone was and hadn't died of breast cancer when he was twenty-seven.

Paul yanked the black cowboy hat off his head and gave his skull a good scratch, then stood up and stretched. He was just turning toward the beige cement block of restrooms to see if Helen was heading back when he noticed a gray sedan with Utah plates pull into the space next to Helen's Toyota. He waited for the driver to exit the car but the man just sat there, his head turned toward the picnic area. Paul saw mirrored sunglasses, a lantern jaw, and a crew cut, silhouetted against the morning sunlight. As the man continued to stare in his direction, Paul grabbed his hat and settled it back on his head, tugging it low over his eyes. Then he took out his phone and sent Helen a text, *Stay there*, hoping she'd notice it in time.

But here she came, swinging out of the women's room and shaking her wet hands over the pavement. Paul watched the man turn her way, and then he saw Helen's hand move to the back pocket of her jeans to extract her phone. She stopped to read the text. With apparent nonchalance she glanced toward the parking lot and the gray sedan, though not toward Paul. Then Paul watched with alarm as Helen marched right up to the driver's window and rapped briskly on the glass.

Long seconds passed before the driver rolled his window partway down. Helen leaned over and started speaking to Crew Cut through the opening, and Paul felt his sweat glands open all at once. The conversation went on for a while, with Helen gesturing back toward Miles City several times. Then she stood up, went around to her car and climbed in, and headed toward the interstate on-ramp. All without a glance at him.

As he stood there, still eyeing the sedan from under his hat brim and trying to figure out his next move, his phone buzzed with a text from Four Twenty: *Stay there*. At first he mistook it for his own message bouncing back to him, but then he saw it was indeed from Helen. As he squinted down at the screen, the gray car suddenly roared to life and backed out of its parking space. Crew Cut left the lot and headed east on 94, in the same direction Helen had gone. *What the hell is going on?* Paul wondered.

Minutes passed. A crow landed and began investigating some food wrappers scattered around the trash receptacle. Paul left his hat on the picnic table and walked over to the water fountain mounted low on the wall of the restroom block, its aluminum basin gritty with dust. He took a long drink and then plunged his face into the stream, rubbing it with his palm. When he could see again he saw Helen's car pulling back into the lot. He didn't feel stoned anymore.

"What was that about? I told you to stay away! What did you say to him?" He had hurried over before she had a chance to turn off the car and stuck his damp head through the open passenger window. Helen cut the engine. She scowled at his accusatory tone and took a long sip from the Berry Blast smoothie bottle in her hand before answering Paul.

"I told him there was no paper in the restrooms."

Of all the things he'd imagined she might have said to the guy, this friendly warning about a TP shortage was definitely not on the list. "But I think he was watching us, or watching me. I got a very weird vibe from that guy. Why would you approach him?"

"How else would I find out who he was? Plus there was a high probability you were just being paranoid, Paul."

"Well, what else were you two talking about? He never used the bathroom. And then he followed you out of the lot!"

"I took the first exit and looped back. He wasn't following me. He asked me for directions—"

"So why didn't he ask *me* for directions? You were in the restroom when he pulled up."

"Honestly, Paul, I do believe you're jealous. He probably saw that stupid hat and thought you were looking to hook up, maybe get into some *Midnight Cowboy* action. You know what happens at these rest stops." She smirked and took another sip of the smoothie.

Paul was growing exasperated and felt himself flush at her last remark. With his newscaster good looks, he'd been hit on by guys before. Not so much lately, though. He made an effort to modulate his tone. "So where was he trying to get to?"

Helen broke into a grin, traces of purple smoothie on her upper lip giving her a clownish look. "The Miles City morgue."

———

As he drove back toward town, Paul's mind was buzzing, and he had to make an effort to stay focused on the road. Luckily, no one else had pulled into the rest stop before he and Helen took off toward Miles City in their own cars, leaving a brief interval between them. It could have been a coincidence that Crew Cut was heading toward the morgue, but Helen didn't think so, and he trusted her instincts.

Ferris had already been laid to rest in the Custer County Cemetery—closed casket, on account of the damage to his body—but for days before that the poor guy had been under a sheet in the morgue, until the coroner could determine exact time and cause of death. Peggy Wyatt had stopped by Helen's place and asked her a bunch more questions about her where-abouts before the murder, presumably to eliminate her as a potential suspect. And he was expecting Peggy to show up on his own doorstep any day now. Despite what they'd learned from Macadangdang, no mention of suicide appeared in the official report or in the brief obit posted in the *Star*. A short piece made it onto the KYUS evening news, reporting the death as a tragic accident, and intimating that if he had stuck to ranching instead of fooling around with scrap art, Ferris Gladwell would still be alive.

What Helen had told Paul about the chickens added a compelling new angle to the elements of the story he had already fleshed out on the newsroom computer. Grant had dismissed the topic as too depressing, but Paul hoped that with these new details he could convince his boss this story had legs—and might even get some traction on the national news, especially if he could include interviews with experts like Mac-adangdang. So he was thinking about that, fitting the pieces together, and worrying that he might wind up fired from his job before he even had a chance to put this suicide story on the air.

And finally, amid Paul's other concerns, there was the dull ache in his gut that he felt every time he thought about Hallie and what had happened when he'd dropped her off in Billings the day before. Like the coward he was, he'd half listened to his daughter's chatter all the way back from Bighorn Canyon, waiting until his truck was stopped and idling in front of the condo before he turned to her and said, "I saw what happened to that deliveryman on the bike."

What she did after that chilled him more than any of the responses he'd anticipated during the drive north: feigned shock or a flat denial, maybe a desperate attempt to spin what he'd witnessed in the same way the news report had, by claiming that Gallineau had purposely plowed his bike into her and the other kids. Instead, his daughter simply looked at him, brown eyes wide, for a beat too long before she said, "I'm pretty sure he asked for it, Daddy." Then she climbed out of the truck. He watched her go around to the truck bed and lift out her bags, then carry her stuff up the front steps of the condo and disappear through the door.

Why hadn't he gone after her, demanded she come out and explain herself? He'd simply sat there, stunned, trying to process what she'd said. Eventually he put the truck into gear and drove home, berating himself the entire way for how he'd handled the whole thing. He'd lacked the nerve to accuse her directly, and her remark contained no admission of guilt. But she seemed to know exactly what he was talking about. *He asked for it.* What on earth did she mean by that? Had Gallineau done something to Hallie, or to one of her friends? Was the attack a kind of payback?

Now Paul was coming up on Miles City and had to shake himself out of his trance, almost missing his exit. As he approached the ramp he braked sharply as another driver in a rusty Dodge Ram cut in front of him, nearly kissing Paul's front bumper. He leaned on his horn, but the guy didn't turn—just stuck his hand out the window and flipped Paul the bird, then gunned the engine. His red Keep America Great baseball cap, worn backward, was the last thing Paul saw before the

Dodge took the turn past the water tower and faded into the shimmering heat of Main Street.

When he got to work that afternoon, after a long, cold, sobering shower, Paul saw the face of a woman he had once dated smiling back at him from the TV in the studio lobby. She was a local meteorologist on the FOX affiliate out of Hardin, so that wasn't an unusual place for her to turn up. What stopped Paul in his tracks was the crawl at the bottom of the screen: *Lasix Suicide: Montana Newscaster Takes Own Life After Procedure.*

24

July
New York City

The Friday before the Fourth of July, Least found herself in a production studio in Midtown fitted out with the components of the *Foxy Friends* set. She didn't mention it to Luka as he showed her around, but the setup reminded her of the interior of the Red Queen's palace in *Adventures in Wonderland*, a musical show she and Alana had devoured as a kids. Toward one side of the space, a curved couch upholstered in pomegranate-red velvet heaped with plush accent pillows had been positioned in front of a wide glass coffee table with curvy legs. American flags on brass eagle-topped poles flanked the ends of the couch, which was backed by a large green screen. As Luka explained, this would allow them to change up the background for this commercial, showcasing an assortment of the President's luxury properties.

Least shook the director's hand ("Sabine," Luka had to prompt her in a whisper). The same fat cameraman who had filmed her screen test was there, wearing the same ragged Megadeth T-shirt, and a boom operator who introduced himself as Nash. The folks from Parallax—Abbott and Su-mi—had flown out from LA to oversee the shoot, and Mira, who had worked those miracles with Least's eyelashes, was waiting for her when they arrived.

Today they would be filming a commercial promo for *Foxy Friends*, to generate interest in advance of the actual launch, scheduled for that fall. The promo would flood the right-wing media marketplace and introduce Least to the show's target television audience. In the town car coming over, Luka had gone over the "five Ps" they were aiming for: Passionate, Positive, Polished, Patriotic, and above all, Pro-POTUS. In addition, he stressed, they wanted to see Sexy but never Slutty, in line with her Virgin Kardashian brand.

The number of followers on her Instagram account showed no signs of tapering off, and whenever it plateaued, Luka always shared an image that sent the numbers spiking again. He'd added the most recent post that morning, a shot of Least in a tight white tank and jeans, cradling an AK-47 at a shooting range in lower Manhattan. Since she'd posed for that picture something else had been Photoshopped in; the person-shaped target she'd pretended to aim at now featured the face of one of the President's many enemies, though she was pretty sure that particular governor had been neutralized as a threat by the Virginia militia. She hadn't fired the weapon—hadn't wanted to hold it, even—but minutes after Luka shared that photo, it had generated 23,601 likes and hundreds of reposts, so it was clear the guy knew what he was doing.

Lately she'd become unhealthily obsessed with reading the comments beneath the posts, despite Luka's insistence that they would only freak her out, and he'd been right. Amid all the positive comments that raved about her looks and applauded her support for the President, Least found comments that were just plain mean (*LEAST HOT KARDASHIAN!* or a long string of smiling poop icons). But the ones that really shook her seemed far more sinister, such as the one that threatened her with rape (*like to shove that gun up your MAGA-loving cunt*) and much worse. Truly horrifying suggestions that made her glad she had given notice to Claudia and was packing up for a move to a far more secure doorman building, thanks to the hefty advance Parallax had given her.

The growing buzz around her Instagram account had even attracted the attention of KKW herself, who had taken time out from sharing pictures of her nine-month-old daughter, Deity, modeling a Yeezy baby thong, to troll Least on Twitter, posting "Virgin my ass—that girl has had more dick than George Takei." As Luka reminded her, Kim's post would only help drive attention in her direction, that they couldn't pay for this kind of publicity, but it had stung nonetheless. Because in truth this whole Virgin Kardashian business made Least feel like a bit of a fraud. She wasn't worried about Resa's brother calling her on that bullshit—Alex would never do that, she knew—but there were dozens upon dozens of other guys who might.

On the phone with her parents the day before, she hadn't mentioned any of this. Her mom and dad were still trying to wrap their heads around the idea of their oldest daughter hosting a television news program (*What? You quit your job at the gallery? Why on earth would you do that?*), and neither of them had an Instagram account, at least as far as she knew. They asked a lot of questions, and she had to admit that even to her own ears the whole story sounded wildly implausible. At some point during the call her father's tone shifted from incredulous to concerned, and he said, "They haven't asked you to take your clothes off, have they, honey?" She tried not to be offended.

The conversation made her feel disrespected, like her parents still saw her as a kid who was prone to making stupid choices. When she hung up, she thought of something that had happened the summer before high school. After she and Resa's brother had hooked up that one time, without a condom, Resa had forced her to make an appointment at Planned Parenthood, where Least took a pregnancy test (negative, thank god) and got fitted for a diaphragm. That night she'd gone to a party at her friend Mark Nguyen's house, and Mark had gotten sloppy drunk on Zima and hit on her. She'd yelled at him, left the party, and biked home in tears. The next day she was naked on the bathroom rug, on her back with her knees apart, trying to figure out how to insert her new diaphragm. She'd fold the little rubber disk in half like the nurse practitioner had showed her, but it kept slipping out of her fingers and sproinging around the bathroom. In the middle of these contortions, her sister Layla started pounding on the door and yelling, "Mark is here!"

Least had just managed to cram the disk up inside her, and she scrambled to her feet and threw on her fuzzy purple bathrobe. Mark was perched on the living room couch, looking contrite and sheepish and hung-over. She stood there, her robe held closed at her throat, too startled by his presence to remember her anger from the previous night. "Hi, Mark, what's up?" He'd launched into a clumsy apology, telling her he really valued her friendship and he hadn't meant to insult her by treating her like a slut. And during his little speech she'd stared at the zits around his mouth, petrified that at any moment the diaphragm would dislodge and blast out of her snatch to land like a little UFO on the carpet between them.

She'd felt like a fraud then, and she felt like one now. She wasn't a virgin and she wasn't an exciting new television personality, so why was she trying to pretend that she was? Abbott had greeted her pleasantly when Luka showed her into the studio, and was now reviewing the script and discussing camera angles with Sabine and Megadeth. There was a rack full of Ivanka dresses in Least's size, stacks of Ivanka shoe boxes, and a portable dressing screen on casters set up in a corner. She'd tried on several styles before Luka and Su-mi had settled on the sleeveless one with the deep keyhole neckline. Now Least was parked in the makeup chair under a poncho, witnessing the final stages of her own transformation in the mirror.

As Sabine had explained as she flipped through the script, they would film Least in short sound bites, from various flattering angles, making the kind of pithy remarks that would distinguish her as a host. Of course, for the real show, all those remarks would be fed directly into her earpiece by the show's producers—she didn't need to worry about generating them herself, naturally. Least was very relieved to hear that.

Once her makeup was finished, they positioned her on the couch in front of the camera. The sound guy brought the boom in on its long black pole, and Sabine had to admonish her a couple times for letting her eyes be drawn to the mic hovering like a charred bratwurst above her head. Least took deep breaths and did her best to calm her pounding heart. At a signal from Abbott, the room grew quiet, and Sabine nodded at her to begin.

It took her a while to get the rhythms right—to vary her pace while speaking, and to lower her voice when she said an important word (like *winning* or *treason*), and to raise it when she said something exciting (like *Bedminster* or *Turnberry*). A lot of the material effusively praised the President's policies and actions; some of it derided his enemies, using cute prime-time substitutes for swear words. Packed around the guest segments would be references to recent events and a sampling of the week's best memes. Least was relieved they'd decided against including a shot of her tossing a KAG cap up in the air, Mary Tyler Moore style. She would have felt stupid doing that.

She thought she was getting the hang of it, relaxing into her new role, but then she got to the line—"U.S. carriers are now phasing in faith-based first class"—and stumbled badly. They tried it again with the same result. She blushed deeply and apologized and tried it again, but there was something about that combination of sounds that kept tripping her up. After her seventh fumbled take, Sabine and Abbott were huddled behind the camera looking concerned. Su-mi suggested Least take a break, refresh her makeup, and she led her to the chair in the corner. But once there, she waved off Mira and asked Least to take a seat. She faced her toward the mirror and stood behind her, speaking to their reflections.

"When I was a teenager in Kaesong, my friends and I were very stupid. We thought it was exciting to watch American movies in secret, so we would buy a CD on the black market, and watch it together after school when my parents were at work. We loved *The Breakfast Club*. You know this film? We watched it over and over again. It was impossible for us to imagine that kind of rebellion. We started calling ourselves the Breakfast Club. One of my friends got angry at her parents and told them about the movie, that she wanted to be like the Molly character, Claire Standish. That was a mistake. Her parents told the authorities, and they came and took all our parents in for questioning. They let them go after a few days, but my father was very ill after that. They had kicked him here"—she indicated her side, below her ribs—"and damaged his insides, and he died a week after they let him go. After my father died, they came back and took me away. My mother just stood there, looking scared, but she didn't seem surprised. Maybe she had begged them to take me instead of her.

"They brought me to a camp. They woke us every day at five and made us work very hard, for long hours. I was a young girl, just fourteen, not strong, but I had to work like a man or be punished. The only food they gave us was some corn and salt. We ate mice, bugs, whatever we could find, to stay alive. One day a guard came to rape me. When I tried to push him away, he bit off the top of my ear." She held back her hair, and Least saw the puckered skin and the gap in the cartilage she'd noticed at Mar-a-Lago. "Once I saw one of my Breakfast Club friends there, and we pretended not to know each other. But that movie helped me survive. In my head I was Allison Reynolds, the Ally Sheedy character, the one who makes it snow with her hair?" Least nodded. "Being Allison helped me to be brave. I was in that camp for seven months. I thought I would die there, many people did, but they sent me home. My mother was not happy to see me, I could tell. Maybe she expected me to die in the camp and there would be no more trouble for our family."

The woman's fingers tightened on the chair back. Least stared into Su-mi's dark eyes in the mirror, but she could feel the room had grown quiet behind them, could sense Luka and the others watching and listening. Su-mi kept talking. "One day I will tell you how I escaped from North Korea, and came to the USA, the greatest country in the world. Most Americans don't understand what it means to be in this country. You can have your bikini waxed at the ballpark, and you are not afraid to watch a movie. You are not afraid the government will come to your home and take you away. And you have a brave leader who is not afraid, either. He trusts himself to meet that devil, to shake his hand, because he knows he can beat him. He knows America is special, and he will fight every enemy to keep her safe."

Su-mi's eyes were fierce and gleaming. She cupped her hands on Least's bare shoulders. "This is what we are here for, all of us. We want to show him, to show everyone, we don't take this America for granted. Don't you want to show him how proud you are to be an American, how it feels to have someone like him steering the ship?"

Su-mi picked up a compact sitting on the makeup trolley. She spun Least around to face her and dabbed at her nose with the powder puff. "He has a very difficult job. But your job is much easier," she told her. "Okay? So let's try this again."

25

Prime Bag Moon
Sargassa

Five days without a breath of wind. The region of the ocean where the Patch was had a strange nickname, the horse latitudes, an expression Petra had never heard before, until Adnan told her about it. Back when they were at ease with each other, she had loved his ability to always offer up some obscure fact—something to amaze her or make her laugh. He told her how, when the winds died, sailing vessels would be stuck for weeks in the sargassum, their supplies running short. Those carrying cargoes of horses sometimes had to jettison them in the sea. Petra thought of those desperate animals churning their slender legs in the water, eyes rolling in terror, as they grew weak and finally sank beneath the weeds, a bounty for the sharks. When she pictured it all she sometimes saw human faces, frantic above the foam, hands grasping at anything to keep them afloat.

When Petra left Aleppo, she'd left the last shreds of her faith behind, like the torn blackout curtains in the blasted-out windows of her childhood home. Her father, if he had been alive, would have risked his life to rescue his precious copy of the Quran, but Petra left it behind to burn. The sea air on the Patch would have destroyed that book, anyway, reduced it to a heap of mold. She had abandoned it all. Who could worship a god like that? A sadist, who pitted neighbor against neighbor to prove who loved him the most. Who let children be starved and raped and beaten, for his own unfathomable reasons. That god had failed her, had failed everyone she loved who had died miserably in the ruins of a once beautiful city. There were many on the Patch, both Sunni and Shia, who still turned to Mecca and knelt to perform *salat* five times a day, bowing and muttering their prayers, but Petra was not among them.

These days, if Petra believed in anything, she believed in plastic. She was grateful to all the wasteful cultures that had produced this miraculous material, used it once, and then dumped it into the trash. As she squatted near the channel after inspecting a repair on the community waste receptacle, waiting for her raftsman and bodyguard to finish his late afternoon prayer, Petra toyed with the round plastic aperture from a drink carton, slipping it on and off her finger like a ring. When these white plastic spouts had first appeared on the juice cartons her mother bought at the market, Petra had been annoyed. The cardboard corner that folded out into a spout, and then folded back to seal the carton, was such an elegant solution. Why add a threaded hole of plastic that made the juice glug and splatter when you poured it into a glass? But now these plastic spouts and all the other indestructible bits that had accumulated here in this clearest of seas, year after year, were the only thing keeping them afloat, a surface upon which they could build a new life. All of them, who had fled their cities and been flushed like garbage into the oceans of the world, could claim this place as their home. And like these little indestructible pieces of plastic, they too would persist.

While the raftsman muttered the 'Asr, rocking back and forth on his prayer mat, Petra thought about the Council meeting, held three days before, and what she had learned there. The governors had called Adnan before them to report on the progress of the storm shield. Petra had not been under the same roof with him for weeks; it gratified her to hear her voice was steady when she greeted him, that she could offer him the same disinterested expression the others did as he entered the meetinghouse. But the news he brought to the Council concerned her.

With the hurricane now just two months away, if you believed Hiranur's prophecy, it was imperative that nothing delay their progress, but work on the shield had recently been hampered by the strange behavior of Valeria's son, Luis. He had left Yael's home to roam around the Patch, sleeping wherever he found himself when night fell, whether it provided any shelter or not. The *vencejos* had begun to follow the boy as he wandered, with his broken iPhone pressed to his ear, pausing in his ramblings to text messages to his dead mother. This odd character transfixed the children, and they brought him leftovers from the kitchen tents and little gifts that he ignored: a doll's pink plastic leg, a dried sea horse, a cracked Discover card. They chattered to anyone who would listen that Luis would save them from the *whirlywind*.

It was one thing, Adnan told the governors, that the children followed Luis around the Patch and made him the object of their devotions. They could make a game of anything, the better to amuse themselves and keep out of the way of the workers. But now some of his best people would put down their tools, set aside their tasks, to watch Luis, too, until the supervisors shouted at them to get back to work. He had heard the gossip, echoing the stories the children told, that Luis could speak to Valeria, that she had issued warnings for the Sargassans. Adnan had gone around to the crews, reminded them what was at stake if the work did not continue, but the distractions persisted.

Adnan, the clever one, the man with all the ideas, the one so adept at solving problems, had not found a solution to this one—not yet, at least. After he left, stooping to untie Wasim from the post outside the meetinghouse, the problem he had brought to them swept other Council business aside.

It did not surprise Petra that a boy who claimed he could receive messages from the dead could persuade others to believe it, too. They had all lost those they loved—family and friends—in the places they'd left or during the long journey across the water. Who could blame them for setting aside their tools to hope for a miracle, to dream that the dead might speak to them through the mouth of this troubled boy? Those prone to religious fanaticism were especially susceptible. It was sheer delusion, of course. Petra had little patience for views of existence not solidly grounded in material fact. As they discussed the matter, however, the governors disagreed about how best to respond.

To Petra, the problem seemed largely practical: how to quarantine this lunacy, and prevent Luis from infecting others with his delusions. She was not unsympathetic to his plight; after all, the kid had suffered a major trauma. But now he had become a problem for the community, and she counseled quick action. The broken phone must be confiscated and the boy taken farther west, where he could no longer interfere with work on the shield. They would arrange for him to stay with a capable person versed in the phases of grief, and Luis would remain there until this madness had passed, or the hurricane hit—after which they would have graver concerns to occupy them.

Others argued that making a martyr of the kid would only increase his allure. If Christ hadn't been crucified, would anyone know his name today? Far better to just wait for this all to blow over, for Luis's followers to grow bored with his behavior and start to drift away of their own accord. The adjustment to life on the Patch, the new privations, had been hard on all of them, but especially on the teenagers. Being deprived of their cell phones and video games and TikTok and TV had left them desperate for something to fix their scattered attentions on. Anyone who could not adapt to the simpler rhythms of life on the Patch had a hard time of it. The growing cult of Luis filled a void that had opened wide in some of their lives when they came to Sargassa. They all had these empty spaces; they just found different ways to fill them.

The problem of what to do about Luis should have been easily sorted out, to Petra's mind. Instead, the subject shone a harsh light, like an egg candler's lamp, exposing flaws in an organism that had once appeared relatively uniform. Their disagreements grew so heated that the meeting ultimately broke up before a final decision could be reached.

26

July 4
Washington, DC

As the sun beat down on the bunting-draped reviewing stands in front of the U.S. Capitol Building, Mike Pence prayed he wouldn't die of heat prostration before he had a chance to see all his plans come to fruition. The first days of July had broken heat records all across the northern hemisphere, but no place sweltered more than the Swamp. Individual One, of course, was sheltered under an enormous bullet-proof sunbrella emblazoned with a large gold T positioned above the Great Seal of State. A heavily sweating aide periodically sent a cooling blast of fine mist up toward the face of the figure in the shade. The rest of them—he and Mother, Melania, Jared and Ivanka, even poor Stephen—all suffered in the sun. *I know You don't demand more of me than I can bear, my Lord,* he thought. *I know Your suffering was greater than mine, and You chose it willingly.*

In the last week of June, when things had looked their bleakest and he'd despaired of ever fulfilling his mission, the commitment of Roland Pinkney had impressed him deeply. His aide had thrown himself at the challenge with the tenacity of a dung beetle, and it crossed Pence's mind to wonder if the misfortune of being born black conferred some advantage he'd never considered before, namely the ability to confront an insurmountable obstacle and to just keep pushing. (Though Pinkney wasn't exactly "black," but more of a lightly toasted marshmallow color, with orderly white teeth and small, neat ears close to the sides of his head.) Pinkney had worked the phones, using a combination of veiled threats and masterful wheedling, and he'd managed to extract promises from the most recalcitrant of agencies and appropriations committees.

Now, in rows beside the Navy Memorial, the assembled troops awaited the first strains of martial music to blast from the sound trucks, the signal to advance down Pennsylvania Avenue toward the Capitol. Pence had his fingers crossed that the thick white pancake makeup slathered over the faux soldiers' heads and necks wouldn't slide off wholesale in the humidity, soaking the collars of their borrowed uniforms. More than a thousand male illegals and a few token females had been bused overnight from detention centers all over the country. His instructions had been precise: Every one must be a parent whose children had been taken. He felt certain the threat that any misbehavior would result in the permanent loss of a child would effectively keep the detainees in line. That, and the warning that there were snipers positioned on every rooftop along the parade route, with orders to pick off anyone who tried to make a break for it.

With the Lord's help, and Pinkney's, he had managed it—the army, the navy, the air force, the Coast Guard, and the marines were all represented today, outfitted with dummy rifles and arrayed in ordered ranks amid the grace notes of six T-14 Armata tanks on loan from the GRU dachas in upstate New York. The Space Force was his proudest accomplishment. They looked impressively futuristic in their crisp new uniforms and gleaming moon boots, golden epaulets flashing on their shoulders. He'd arranged for ten Black Hawk helicopters and a dozen combat drones to fly through the restricted airspace above the Capitol dome. Finally, at the height of the parade, the Blue Angels would execute an impressive T-shaped maneuver overhead, laying down contrails of red, white, and blue smoke. It had all cost a mint.

In the end, much of the money for this command performance had come from the Saudis, secretly of course, but it had evaporated into the parade fund like water poured on desert sand—the cost of bribes to ICE not the least of it. He had bled every veterans' foundation dry including the widows' funds, and promised every wealthy donor's son a cabinet position or ambassadorship, as well as access to his choice of membership at one of the President's golf clubs. But even with all those foreign and domestic billions at his disposal, he'd had to economize.

Just a few days before the Fourth he'd been thrown into a panic when sixty promised bodies to fill uniforms for the Legion of the Southern Cross had failed to materialize, after a hunger strike at the Santa Claus, Indiana, detention center had ended badly. As he saw when he flew to his home state to assess their viability for himself, the handful of illegals who had survived the strike were obviously too weak to walk to the toilet, let alone down Pennsylvania Avenue. Deeply concerned, and reviewing his nonexistent options, he had insisted Pinkney schedule a short side trip to Evansville after he left the facility, so he might seek solace in the food of his youth. Despite all he'd had to worry about in the days leading up to this moment, that familiar whiff of scent he'd detected on the breath of the mysterious man in the West Wing had never left his mind.

His security team had hustled out the few patrons in the King David Dog diner so he could enjoy his lunch in peace. Walking through the smeared glass doors with the cheery red crown logo, his senses were bombarded by the familiar stink of the place where his Grandpa Cawley used to bring him and his brother, Greg, on Saturdays in Columbus. As he stood there, reviewing the Signature Dogs order board above the head of the stammering counter attendant, breathing in the hot-dog-scented air, he was more certain than ever that the man he'd seen ducking into the Oval Office had Boom Boom Dog on his breath, and this conviction gave him something new to fret about. King David Dog was an Indiana-only franchise, dying a slow death. Greg had sent him a news item a few months back about the closing of the Columbus branch, and the only remaining KDD was this one, clinging to life in Evansville. Though he wasn't a man inclined to see conspirators lurking around every corner, this nexus between the mysterious character who kept turning up in the West Wing to huddle with Stephen and the President, reeking of wiener, and his own Indiana roots gave him a frisson of concern.

He placed his order and slid into a booth by the wall. Minutes later, Pinkney materialized with a foil-lined plastic basket cradling the King David Deluxe and a diet Coke fizzing merrily in a daffodil-yellow plastic cup. He bowed his head, thanking God for this glistening cylinder of ground meat heaped with mustard and relish on a poppy seed bun. As the nostalgic bouquet of juices exploded in his mouth, he sighed deeply, and his thoughts swung back to the problem at hand. The absence of the Legion would not pass unnoticed — just the other day he'd received a memo from the Secretary of Homeland Security stressing that the President was particularly excited about reviewing these troops in the parade, whose color-blocked uniforms made up a Confederate flag when they marched in formation. In reality, the LSC was just a ragtag group of Southern survivalists living off the grid in rural Tennessee, who had trained semi-automatic weapons on the petrified postal worker who tried to deliver official invitations to the event.

The final solution came in what Pence would later think of as the Revelation of the Roller Towel. After washing down the last mouthful of his hot dog, he had stepped into the restroom to rinse the mustard from his fingers. Contemplating his own face in the smeared mirror, he saw that his eyes appeared troubled and more sunken than usual, as if his Maker had clasped his face tenderly in His hands and used both thumbs to press the eyeballs deeper into the skull. The soiled bathroom towel vanished into the slit at the bottom of the device as his damp hands yanked a fresh length of starched white cloth from the top. It was mesmerizing, really, how the cloth marred with grime emerged pristine from the clanking machine. *Like a human soul*, he thought, *being cleansed of its sins.* A letter had recently found its way to his office from a five-year-old Tucson girl named Elida Morales, who wanted to know if clouds were the people she knew who'd gone to heaven and, if so, why were they all white? *That's a very good question,* he told her, dictating his response to the staff secretary. *Clouds are white because even brown people's souls can become clean in heaven.*

And then it came to him: The parade, too, would wrap around, and the "soldiers" would be ferried back to the beginning, given different props and uniforms, and sent down the parade route in formation again. POTUS, dazzled by the display, would never know the difference. The few legitimate paramilitary and ROTC groups, high school drill teams, and battle reenacters marching amid the fakes would be instructed to assemble on Washington Avenue, a block beyond the Capitol, for post-parade refreshments, while the other marchers continued down Independence to the waiting buses.

Grasping the solution, he sank to his knees on the urine-spattered floor tiles and nearly wept with relief. Then he clasped his hands and offered up his heartfelt thanks to the Savior who had yet again come to his aid, and rose up a refreshed man, the details already falling into place. He wiped his eyes, then smoothed down his immaculate white *zucchetto* of hair and checked his teeth for shreds of meat, already drafting a memo in his mind for Pinkney; his aide would have to rent additional buses with blacked-out windows, outfitted with costumers holding LSC uniforms for the illegals to change into. They would also need additional hands to refresh each soldier's makeup during the brief ride back to the beginning of the route. The short respite inside the air-conditioned buses would cut down on the inevitable fatalities sure to occur in the heat.

It would be a miracle if he could pull it all off, he knew that—the plan depended upon countless elements that could go catastrophically wrong. Now, standing at attention in the merciless light, he reminded himself that all his suffering, every station of the Cross he had completed in the name of that golden calf under the presidential umbrella, was really for Stephen. If this obscene spectacle made POTUS happy, then Stephen would be happy—and that made it all worthwhile. Every slavish expression of devotion the President mistook for his own in truth belonged to Stephen, an enormous red, white, and blue valentine from his secret admirer. Pence risked a quick glance at his beloved, standing to the President's right, the blazing light haloing his skull. Stephen looked aloof, a mild expression on his face like that of a martyred saint dispassionately regarding his tormenters. The red pocket square peeping jauntily out of his dark suit jacket made Pence weak in the knees. How he longed to pluck out that handkerchief, to tenderly dab the silky cloth across that noble brow.

He forced his gaze away and checked his Timex—the signal to begin was scheduled for 1100 hours. Behind the viewers packing the bleachers across the road, on the murky surface of the reflecting pool, another version of the lofty white dome of the Capitol floated, obscure and wavering. He let himself dissolve into the rippling image, hypnotized by the vision of an analogous underwater world, a dreamy realm like Weeki Wachi Springs, where Stephen drifted toward him like one of those famed mermaids, with a devastating smile on his lips, and Pence started when he felt his wife squeeze his arm.

When he looked over, she gave him an encouraging nod and mouthed the words *His will be done.* The helmet of her chestnut hair gleamed in the sun. The fierce pride animating her plain features reminded him that, though he might experience an occasional dark night of the soul, his wife's faith in him had never flagged. She was, as the Bible dictated, his helpmeet, as a true wife should be. And he loved her for that, considered her a genuine partner to his ambitions, though his heart belonged to another. Then, right on time, the sound trucks blasted the first annunciatory notes of the marching music and the ranks began to move.

———

Regarding the parade guests and luminaries on the reviewing stands, Pence had issued the same invitation list they'd used for the second inaugural with a few key additions. Coal and oil barons, T-Mobile execs, Boy Scouts, Kardashian Wests, Saudi princes, QAnon congresswomen, Russian oligarchs, bikini models, recently pardoned members of the President's inner circle, and others who had benefited most from this administration fleshed out the crowd and ensured there were no empty spaces on the bleachers. No Democrats in attendance, of course—as the disgraced party, PHAL had been banished from the event, though they'd released a statement to the press claiming they were electing to stay home "in protest" and that "they didn't really want to come anyway."

So far, all seemed to be going according to plan. The "soldiers" were marching cleanly, eyes fixed straight ahead, snowy white gloves clutching dummy rifles to their shoulders. The pancake makeup on the illegals looked a little chalky, and he could see a patch or two of brown skin had been missed around the ears, but it wouldn't be noticeable to the casual observer. If nothing else, he had to agree with the President on this point: There was nothing like a military parade to show off the strength of the nation. Polished brass buttons winked in time with the military band music, and the sharp line of the soldiers' polyester trousers swinging forward mostly in unison was inspiring enough to take his mind off the river of sweat running between his shoulder blades.

He could sense POTUS's pleasure even beneath the sunshade, judging by the slight bulge in his pants, barely masked by the wide red tail of his tie. Pence could see his hands beating together in satisfaction as the ranks of each division turned to him and made a deep bow in front of their Commander in Chief before continuing past. Just around the corner of Independence Avenue he knew they were being shepherded on to the buses that would take them around to the start of the parade route, to resume marching again.

An approaching rumble alerted him that the first of the Russian tanks would soon navigate the turn off Pennsylvania at the Peace Monument before rolling past the stands in front of the Capitol. He felt a presence behind him and turned to find Pinkney there, handing him a frosty bottle of Ivanka Water and beaming a congratulatory smile.

This careful, efficient young man had risen up from the position of intern and developed a reputation for discretion, trustworthiness, and loyalty—he was, in fact, the polar opposite of the tumescent man under the bulletproof umbrella.

27

July 4
New York City

Filling the lulls between the formations of marchers, the newscaster providing color commentary sounded mildly hysterical, his voice buzzy from being forced through the cheap speaker on Claudia's crappy TV. "... text your vote for America's Hottest FLOTUS. Results will be aired immediately following our parade coverage, so stay tuned . . . ."

Least had moved into her spacious new air-conditioned one-bedroom in Chelsea three days before, but now she was back in sweltering Bay Ridge, packing up the last of her things, while the parade coverage blared in the background. Looking at the junk she had jammed into the cardboard boxes littering the living room, Least wondered why she was even bothering to move this detritus of her former life. As soon as she and Resa began unpacking in the new space, every bit of it had looked pathetic and wrong—her West Elm bedding, the leather Moroccan pouf and Mongolian lamb pillow covers she'd spent so much on, plastic tubs filled with her stretched-out bras and pilly cashmere sweaters. There were a few Ivanka pieces she decided to keep, but most of that stuff hadn't worn well, she was sorry to say. In the unimpeded sunshine of her new apartment, all her possessions looked shabby and sad, and later she had ended up shoving most of them into garbage bags and dumping them in front of the building.

She would likely do the same with the stuff she was packing up now, with the exception of some items she'd stowed in a bin marked TO KEEP: A carved sandalwood box where she kept the neon plastic mermaids her parents had once brought home from a retro cocktail party. (They hooked their elbows on the edge of your glass and thrust out their chests, and Least and her sisters fought over who got to keep the green one.) A Mouseketeer hat from a trip she and Resa had taken to Disney World, personalized with her name (the moron running the embroidery machine had to ask her TWICE if he had the spelling right). For reasons she couldn't explain, these keepsakes had survived the move from Ann Arbor to a series of grim and grimy New York City apartments.

Least's most treasured souvenirs were swag from the four rallies she had attended—various MAGA and KAG hats, pins, and bandanas, a giant foam Fuck You finger, a Nancy Pelosi voodoo doll, and the real prize of the collection, a pair of red lace bikini underwear autographed by POTUS across the crotch (with authentication papers) that she'd paid WAY too much for on eBay. But the bulk of her crap wasn't worth the effort to move, and she wanted to fully embrace the idea of a brand-new start, a rebirth. On her last day at work, the owner of the gallery had given her a going-away gift of a frosted glass unicorn rearing in front of a raging wildfire, which she intentionally left on the subway when she exited the car at her station. She had seen what that unicorn cost when she'd inventoried their stock at the beginning of the year, and it wasn't cheap, but the last thing she needed was another reminder of that boring job and her boring former life.

Claudia had been happy to keep the wineglasses and the coffeemaker along with a framed poster for the 2018 Armenia! show at the Met that Least had contributed to the household. She stepped out after Least arrived to get cold drinks and gyros for an early lunch—a nice enough gesture, Least supposed, but she could care less about hanging around this dump and reminiscing about their years as roommates. Resa was out on Fire Island for the weekend, where Least would be, too, except she had to get the last of her stuff out and clean up the room before the new tenant moved in on Monday. Luka had promised to take her out to Red Hook, where some rich associate of his was throwing a party on a roof deck with a view of the fireworks.

She was definitely in the mood to get drunk. It made her vaguely angry and a little sorry for herself that she had lived in New York for more than a decade, yet she was spending the Fourth of July with a bunch of people she didn't know. And Luka, of course. Some people had invited her out, to picnics and other roof parties, peripheral acquaintances who never gave her the time of day before she had a gazillion followers on Instagram and started getting recognized in restaurants. But the growing buzz around @virginkardashian had already propelled her into a different social stratum where the few real friends she had, like Resa, didn't really belong. Luka had said something about lions needing to lie down with lions. She was in the lion camp now, and it was time to start hanging out with her own kind.

The apartment door swung open and Claudia reappeared, her hair a dandelion in the July humidity, clutching a takeout bag in one hand and some deli flowers in the other. Panting from the climb, her freckled nose beaded with sweat, she was smiling all the same. "Ooookay, I've got sustenance and beauty, and what else does anyone really need?" She thrust the cellophane-sheathed bouquet into Least's hand before sailing into the kitchen with the food, calling over her shoulder, "Those are to prettify your new digs!"

Least grimaced at the limp little spray of red, white, and dyed-blue blooms and called, "Thanks!" with as much enthusiasm as she could muster, before tossing the bouquet onto a side table. The food smelled good, though, and she went in the kitchen to help herself to a gyro and some tabouli salad and baba ghanoush that Claudia had spread out on the counter. Once they had their plates, they brought them out with cold drinks to the coffee table, in front of the TV, where rows of stone-faced soldiers were marching. A camera cut to the reviewing stands where Least saw the President under a giant umbrella held aloft by an aide, applauding enthusiastically, his grin blazing white in the sunshine. He had wanted this so badly, she knew, and she shared in his pleasure at this celebration of American military might.

Luckily, Claudia's mouth was soon too crammed with gyro for her to make any cracks about the fact that Melania had been left to bake in the sun, and where the hell was Barron? She wasn't paying attention anyway, but had a bunch of questions for Least about the terms of her contract with Parallax and did she have to sign a massive non-disclosure agreement like all those people who'd worked on *The Apprentice* and in the White House? Least felt herself growing a little flushed as she tried to bullshit with confidence—she didn't have answers to Claudia's questions and that made her feel a bit stupid. Frankly, she'd only given the contract a cursory glance before signing and initialing it, in all the places Luka indicated with his finger.

On the screen, the coverage now cut to a prerecorded interview with members of a school group from Montana, scheduled to march in the parade. The pretty girl talking to the reporter had her shiny brown hair in a high pony stuck through the back of a ball cap and a tight white T-shirt featuring a pair of crossed bats and the words *Vigilante Volunteers*. Her little red shorts revealed the tanned curves of her trim ass cheeks, Least noticed, as the girl executed some acrobatic martial-arts-type moves with her teammates, and Claudia crowed through a mouthful of baba ghanoush, "Holy shit-snacks, if they cut those shorts any higher they'll need to change their name to the Vigilante Vaginas! Or the Volunteer Vaginas! or, no, the *Vagilantes!*"

Least laughed and took another bite. The gyro was excellent but sloppy to eat, and she had just stepped into the kitchen to grab more paper towels when Claudia shrieked, "Oh my god! Least! It's you!!" She rushed back into the living room in time to see herself magnified on the screen, looking well groomed and glossy, mouthing the phrases they'd filmed in the loft studio, now against a backdrop featuring the logo for *Foxy Friends* and a montage of patriotic and militaristic images. At first, Least had trouble reconciling the scenes she saw on TV with what they had shot in the production studio. The addition of music and spliced-in footage and a variety of camera angles (sometimes head-on, sometimes in profile, and sometimes from overhead, according to the new style protocols) gave an edgy excitement to the piece, and even the phrase "faith-based first class," which Least had had so much trouble delivering, sounded effortless now, based on whatever post-production magic they had managed to work.

As Abbott had explained, the concept for the show was a high-brow-lowbrow combo; in order to appeal to the widest possible dinner-time audience, they would cover everything from the latest political news to TikTok videos of parakeets reenacting iconic scenes from *This Is Us*, but what the promo hammered home was a combo of all caps outrage interlarded with the frothiest celebrity gossip: footage of the woman who torched herself on the steps of the Supreme Court juxtaposed with a bit about Spree Culkin sharing sweet pix of her daughter baking gourmet doggie treats for the animal shelter. The line they'd had Least say about the abortion ban, which had seemed innocuous enough at the time, was now backed by an ominous shot of the new White House gallows, implying the punishment for terminating a pregnancy was death by hanging. *Is this supposed to be funny?* she wondered.

What rattled her most, however, happened a few seconds near the end of the commercial. Least was looking directly into the camera, speaking words she was certain she had never uttered, a statement about what happens to journalists who spread lies about a ruler or a regime, and a promise to her audience that everything she reported on *Foxy Friends* would be 1000% true.

The commercial ended, and the parade coverage resumed. Despite the thrill of watching herself prominently featured in a national ad campaign, Least could smell Claudia's disapproval tainting the air. But her ex-roommate's only response was a question: "Wow, Least. Did you really agree to all that?" Claudia had turned to her with a smear of gyro sauce at the edge of her mouth and a look of bafflement in her green eyes. Least set down the remains of her sandwich in its paper sleeve and said, in a defensive tone, "I'm pretty sure it's all meant to be ironic and edgy, you know? Like early Colbert or Trevor Noah, except with a *female* host—who is an actual American! Isn't that what you're always complaining about? How 'all the talk space has been colonized by men'?" She made air quotes around the phrase she had heard Claudia utter just the other day. It annoyed her that someone who spent her days curled on the couch Googling pictures of hemp onesies saying "Locally Brewed" and "Shit Just Got Real," was judging *her* for trying to improve her life. Claudia might be content to waste her forties smoking reefer in a shitty apartment in Bay Ridge, but Least was getting the hell out and trying to make something of herself.

Luka had told her Parallax planned to air the commercial promo for the show during the parade and repeatedly the week after, for maximum exposure, and that the number of followers on @virginkardashian would hockey stick as a result. She stood up to resume her packing, while Claudia carried the lunch dishes into the kitchen, shaking her head but keeping her mouth shut. Clearly, she didn't want to sour their last moments together by debating what did and did not qualify as irony.

On the TV, the anchorman could hardly contain his ardor as a tank rumbled slowly toward the Capitol building, American flags drooping from its gun turret, spraying gravel into the packed viewing stands lining the route. But the battalion of soldiers marching about ten yards in front of the tank looked odd to Least—kind of pasty—and a camera swooping in for a close-up caught some of them glancing nervously at the nearby buildings. Least turned up the volume on the TV, to mask the clatter in the sink as Claudia noisily washed up the lunch plates. The commentator was still going ape shit about the tank, what kind it was and how heavy it was and how much firepower it packed. As they neared the stands in front of the dome, the group of soldiers marching ahead of the tank halted and starting shifting their rifles from one shoulder to the other and doing those weird coordinated goose steps that soldiers do. Their white gloves looked overly large, like Mickey Mouse hands, held to their right temples in a stiff salute.

Now the blaring patriotic sound track was overpowered by a distant roar that had been growing louder all the while, and one camera cut away to reveal a T formation of fighter jets spewing red, white, and blue smoke as they entered the protected airspace over the Capitol. A split screen showed the parade—the Mickey Mouse soldiers all swiveling back toward the route and marching forward—and the Blue Angels, screaming by overhead, as POTUS and the dignitaries all twisted their heads backward to track their passage.

Least watched one of the soldiers at the rear of the group stop, turn on his booted heel, and start back the other way. The move was executed with such precision that it must have been planned, though the parade commentator seemed at a loss for words, sputtering into silence. The soldier took several strides, his rifle on his shoulder, before he stopped, dropped the gun, and sank to his knees, clasping his gloved hands in front of him. His eyes were squeezed tightly shut in his greasy pale face and his mouth was moving.

The tank behind the platoon rolled inexorably forward, though Least assumed it would stop many yards short of the kneeling soldier, even as it continued to close the gap between them. The marching platoon, minus one member, moved on past the reviewing stand, heading for Independence Avenue. Behind them, the soldier lay facedown on the road and stretched his arms out flat on either side. The patriotic music was still playing gaily as the tank rolled forward and the man disappeared under its treads.

Least stared at the television, trying to process what she had seen. The American flags on the moving tank hung limp as the vehicle ground slowly forward. In the tank's wake straggled six rows of uniformed men, identified by the screen crawl as the Legion of the Southern Cross, several of whom swerved out of the way to avoid something in their path. On their heels came the high school group from Montana, the Vigilante Volunteers, executing back flips and turning cartwheels over the long bright smear now painted down the center of the road. They waved cheerfully and bared their perfect American teeth as they passed the reviewing stand where POTUS and the other heads of state were assembled. Least expected something to happen, for the parade to come to a screeching halt and for pandemonium to break loose as everyone began to realize one of the marching soldiers was now just a skid mark on the asphalt. But when the parade continued on without a hitch, Least began to think she had misunderstood, that her eyes had simply played a trick on her, that it was just a mirage she'd seen in the heat shimmering in distorting waves off the blacktop.

Everything must be okay, she told herself, *because the President is still smiling.*

28

July
Miles City

Before the divorce, Paul had loved spending the Fourth of July week-end with Paige's family at her parents' house. His father-in-law's birthday fell in early July, so Paige's mom always made a big sheet cake decorated like the American flag, with stripes made from strawberries arranged across the thick white buttercream in trim rows and blueberries forming a field of stars in the upper left corner.

The neighborhood kids were all invited, and they raced around the big yard, taking one gulp from a can of root beer and then abandoning it in the grass before clambering into the aboveground pool to clobber each other with noodles. The neighborhood adults, clutching Bobcat beer koozies, would greet Paul with slaps on the back or flirty smiles, depending on their gender. These reminders that she was married to a local celebrity always made Paige hot later on, and he liked that, too. When the sun went down and the cicadas unplugged their chainsaws, Hallie would tear through the yard with a sparkler in her fist, shrieking with delight when the guys at the Masonic Lodge across town started exploding M-80s in the parking lot and the dogs all ran to hide under the beds.

Paul wasn't an overly patriotic guy; being part Native American made it hard to embrace all that hoopla without irony, but having lost his own parents early he enjoyed the family stuff, liked seeing his daughter—who had no siblings to boss around—organizing the other kids into teams for the three-legged race and horseshoe pitching contest. But this holiday weekend, Hallie was away in Washington for the military parade, and Paige was probably parked in front of her new 80-inch flat screen with a bunch of her bitchy friends, waiting to see Hallie's school group on TV. Paul was stuck at the station, trying to brown-nose his way back into Grant's good graces by agreeing to anchor the parade coverage and other local Independence Day events on a weekend when most of the other newscasters had asked for time off. He had been there since seven that morning, had his makeup done as he looked over the notes for the broadcast, and now, with his earpiece in, was settling in behind the news desk to kick off the coverage, scheduled to start at nine MDT.

The satellite feed from DC would be live. Everyone on the KYUS weekend shift had stopped by his desk to say something about his daughter and wasn't he proud? But Paul felt real trepidation about seeing Hallie in action with the other Vigilante Volunteers, now that he knew exactly how those kids liked to spend their time. Paul hadn't spoken to Hallie since he'd confronted her in the truck—she'd responded airily to his texts, claiming she was too busy preparing for the trip, which was likely true, but still. He knew the group had been profiled, along with another local organization participating in the parade, and portions of the DC footage would be replayed on the six and ten o'clock news.

Paul took a final few sips of water from the bottle stowed under the desk, then looked directly into camera one, clearing his throat. "Okay, handsome, you're on," purred Jill, one of the weekend producers, in his ear. Switching on his best professional smile, Paul welcomed local viewers to the broadcast and introduced the parade segment before they cut over to the One America News Network's live coverage in DC.

As he disengaged his earpiece, Paul turned to the monitor and saw the camera come in tight on the President, who was visibly pleased, his face glowing even more orange than usual under the dome of a huge sunshade. The First Lady, the vice president and his wife, and the other VIPs in the reviewing stands looked exposed and sweaty, clearly suffering in the punishing heat. Through the open door of the production control room he could hear Jill posing the event's most compelling questions to the rest of the staff, including, "Would it kill him to share a little shade with his wife?" and "Are those Marines wearing makeup?"

After a trip to the john and a quick review of the schedule, Paul was behind the desk again and mic'ed up in time for the station ID before they cut back to the ongoing parade coverage. Hallie's fifteen seconds of fame would be coming up soon, along with the aerial maneuvers of the military jets, always a crowd-pleaser, though Paul didn't get the appeal. He'd covered a vintage airshow up near Lewistown back in 2016, and the wings of two Lockweed P-38 Lightnings had collided, causing a fiery crash that killed both pilots and a teenager watching the show from an adjacent field, and started a major brushfire that took hours to extinguish.

Seeing daredevils execute death-defying tricks above a crowd of people that included his daughter would only make him anxious, so Paul distracted himself by drafting a breakup text to a woman named April he'd met at the Montana after Ferris had left, the night before the poor guy had killed himself. Not for the first time, he wondered if Ferris might still be alive if Paul had listened to him more closely rather than bird-dogging all the attractive single women at the bar. He'd hooked up with April a few times since then, but Paul had been put off by all the yowling she did in the sack, like a wildcat with its foot stuck in a trap. It felt phony, since he knew he had his shortcomings as a lover, or so Paige had informed him. Paul figured it was probably time to end things before April came to the same conclusion.

He was making small talk with one of the cameramen, a lanky guy named Trey moonlighting from the KXGN station in Glendive, when, right after the ten-second warning before he went live again, Paul heard Jill in his ear, asking, "What the hell is that guy doing?" before her voice and the parade music were both drowned out by a deafening noise, like a whole planet was being ripped in half. Framed on the screen, the President and everyone on the reviewing stands craned their necks skyward and began applauding as the Blue Angels executed a precise maneuver over the Capitol dome, trailing thick streams of patriotic smoke.

When he snuck a peak at his phone during the commercial break, Paul saw he had a bunch of texts from Helen. *Did you see that???!* and *Are you covering this?* Some type of commotion was definitely going on in the control room, with the engineers all pointing at something on one of the monitors. But before he had a chance to find out what had happened they had rejoined the parade coverage. Paul knew, based on the day's program provided to the station, that Hallie's team would follow a paramilitary group called the Legion of the Southern Cross early in the program's second half. And here she came, right on schedule. Behind a phalanx of pale-faced soldiers whose variously colored uniforms formed the stars and bars of the Confederate flag, Paul saw Halogen Pendegrass turning cartwheels in a tight pair of red hot pants, and smiling from ear to ear.

29

Either he was suffering from heatstroke or experiencing a vision; he wasn't sure which. His ears still ringing from the Blue Angels' flyover, Mike Pence stared at the bright red cross in the middle of the road as legions of painted soldiers marched over it to halt in front of the reviewing stands, salute the President, and continue marching past. He knew it hadn't been there on the blacktop before they had assembled on the stands—he had given no such instruction to the parade staff. He'd only seen the cross after the jets had torn past, leaving their colored contrails to slowly break apart in the sky above the Capitol dome.

The sun was at the meridian, the mercury had hit 103, and his brains were surely boiling in his skull, though Pinkney, that lifesaver, continued to ply both him and Mother with icy bottles of water. Throughout the parade he'd managed to keep his expression appropriately solemn, even when he wanted to cringe at the sight of a stumbling soldier, a glitch in the formation, a uniform too large for its wearer. Now, in the latter half of the day's program, the flaws in his plan became more apparent: brass buttons were misaligned, pants didn't always match uniform jackets, and some of the white pancake makeup looked like it had been slapped on with a spackling knife. He could only hope the sweat-drenched viewers in the stands were so near collapse that such details would be lost on them. Indeed, the crowd appeared rather patchy, now that medics had carried away the first wave of attendees who had succumbed to the infernal heat. Surely more casualties would follow.

No one else seemed to notice the red cross in the road, with the possible exception of a smiling girl in shockingly brief red shorts who had turned a cartwheel, then made a face and wiped her hands, leaving brownish smears on the hem of her white T-shirt. Through it all, POTUS slapped his hands together in satisfaction, convinced it was all his doing, this show of military force and adulation that glorified his position as Commander in Chief. Stephen slouched by the President's side, an enigmatic expression on his heartbreaking face, giving nothing whatsoever away.

The First Lady wore a vague smile but had such a vacant look in her eyes that Pence had to wonder if she was overmedicated. He had hoped the little brown boy she had hidden away behind the wall would provide some distraction from her grief at Barron's desertion, but maybe she'd already had the child shipped back to Mexico or Colombia or whatever hellish spot his family had crawled out of in the first place. Since the night he had helped spirit the boy into the White House through the tunnel under the tennis courts he had washed his hands of that whole affair.

As the booted feet kept marching over the red cross in the road, he gave thanks that this whole travesty would soon be over. He had pulled it off to the best of his abilities, and tomorrow he could resume his regular duties, secure in the knowledge he had showed Stephen and all the others he could work miracles on behalf of that dotard under the umbrella. Amid the rumbling of the tanks, the flutter of the combat drones, the farting of the tubas, and the tattoo of the snare drums, it was impossible to hear himself think let alone make out his wife's words, but she squeezed his arm and nodded toward the cross still visible in the road and then he knew she'd seen it, too. He had done the Lord's work here—this vision was clear proof of that. He felt like the emperor Constantine, standing on the banks of the Tiber before the Battle of Milvian and seeing a cross of fire in the heavens, inscribed with the words *By this, thou shalt conquer.*

He wanted to close his eyes and clasp his hands in prayer, but he knew the cameras were watching. The sanctioned press only included OAN, Newsmax, and other sufficiently loyal right-wing news outlets, but his faith would become fodder for ridicule when POTUS reviewed the parade footage, as he was bound to do in the days to come. So he arranged his features into an approximation of attention and went deep into his own mind, where the words of Scripture always waited to comfort and inspire him. Colossians 1:20 would do nicely: *And through Him to reconcile to Himself all things, whether on earth or in heaven, making peace by the blood of His cross.*

But then came a voice in his ear, summoning him back to the present. He saw bonafide members of the 2nd Battalion, 2nd Marines moving past the bleachers, displaying their banner shaped like a pope's miter and featuring a sword and the nickname "Warlords." Their presence signaled the parade's finale was mere minutes away, thanks be to God. He turned and found Pinkney by his side. The sodden collar of his aide's formerly crisp white Oxford shirt made his dusky skin look darker in contrast. The unpleasant sensation of finding a black man's mouth so close to his ear—even one as light-skinned as Pinkney's—made him uncomfortable, but the noise from the military bands had climaxed as the spectacle reached its crescendo, and his aide had to practically shout to make himself heard through one cupped hand.

"I took the liberty of drafting a cover story for the press, sir, blaming PTSD and heatstroke for the soldier throwing himself under the tank," Pinkney informed him. "The mess will be swept up by the street cleaners, but the uniform seems to have wound up wrapped around the treads. The illegals have been loaded back on buses and are already en route to the camps." Pence stared as Pinkney paused and took a long swallow from an Ivanka Water bottle, curvy like its namesake's body, his sharp Adam's apple jumping up his neck. Pence tried to make sense of what his aide was saying, what it meant about the red cross he'd witnessed on the road. But Pinkney had something more to add. "Ahem—we did lose one, sir—a Guatemalan woman. Apparently she slipped past the cordon and disappeared into the crowd. We'll find her, sir," he hastened to reassure his boss. "I have agents out looking now."

30

July
Miles City

The parade footage of the tank rolling over the soldier had gone viral on the Internet, but it immediately began popping up in contexts that made it hard to divine its original significance. It was retweeted and repurposed countless times before the last regiment had trudged past the viewing stands earlier that day, after hundreds of booted feet had destroyed any remaining physical evidence of what might have once been a man.

One conspiracy site insisted it was a failed assassination attempt, and that the soldier's ill-fitting uniform had been padded with explosives that had failed to go off. Someone else claimed it was David Blaine's latest illusion, and swore they'd seen the magician alive and well, saluting from the turret of the same tank later in the parade. One theory that gained some traction argued that FLOTUS had known it was going to happen, because the First Lady was the only person in the stands who hadn't looked up to watch the Blue Angels as they blew past overhead. Instead, her gaze had remained fixed on the tank, and she hadn't so much as winced when the soldier disappeared under its treads. Whatever the hell had happened there in front of the U.S. Capitol, it had already become a meme: one version showed the tank piloted by POTUS driving over the Swedish climate activist Greta Thunberg.

Paul had finally seen the video later that day, when the engineers in the control room replayed it for him, but Grant had chosen to prominently feature the Vigilante Volunteers in the station's evening broadcasts instead of showing a sanitized version of the tank footage. "You would think you'd be happy," he told Paul in an exasperated voice. "It's your daughter and her team that we're featuring in prime time. They're local heroes! I just don't get you anymore, Paul." No one had any official confirmation from the government or could positively ID that soldier, and the station manager didn't want to air the footage until next of kin had been properly notified. As precedent Grant had cited the ban on showing images of military coffins from the wars in Afghanistan and Iran. If the video indeed showed what it appeared to show (and Grant made it clear he had his doubts), there were long-standing restrictions about airing footage of someone being smooshed to death, and he wasn't going to bring the wrath of the FCC down on their little station.

Such scruples hadn't stopped the White House–affiliated networks from going all in, however, and soon the footage was featured on every hard-right news outlet, with blurs covering the money shot. Because it had occurred in front of the viewing stands where the President stood (though he had been watching the Blue Angels at the time), one commentator claimed it was the unknown soldier's way of proving to POTUS he would make the ultimate sacrifice for his Commander in Chief, and this line had been picked up and parroted by others.

The evening of the Fourth, after the six p.m. broadcast, a weary Paul had turned the desk over to Carla Paxton-Farley, who was anchoring the ten o'clock news. On the way home he stopped by the Bison, but the place was already jammed with twentysomethings celebrating the long holiday weekend at the tops of their lungs. The big screen next to the bar was replaying the parade footage, and a raucous bunch of ranch hands had turned it into a drinking contest, doing a red-white-and-blue Jell-O shot every time the tank flattened the soldier.

Paul waved at Moss behind the bar, before heading back out to the street again, nearly colliding with two girls in tight shredded jeans on the sidewalk outside. "Hey, I know you," one of them announced in a slurry voice, bringing her mascara-fringed eyes close to Paul's face. Her breath smelled of Fireball whisky and menthol cigarettes, and her smeared pink lips lifted in a flirtatious smile. The other one was wearing an off-the-shoulder crop top that bared her sunburned shoulders, and recognition dawned slowly on her pretty, vacant face. "You're that guy on TV, the news guy my mom has a crush on," she told him. The jeweled piercing in her belly button winked at Paul. He was ashamed to find himself entertaining thoughts of offering to buy them both a drink, though they were clearly already drunk and couldn't have been much older than Hallie—hell, they might even know her—when his phone rang in his pocket. When he pulled it out he was startled to see *Miles City Sheriff* on the screen. "Excuse me, girls," he told them, stepping around the corner of the building to put some distance between himself and temptation and the din pouring out the door of the bar. He clamped the phone to his head. "Hello?"

The sheriff's no-nonsense twang filled his ear, against a background clamor of unintelligible voices. "Hey, Paul, Peggy Wyatt here. Listen, I've got someone down here in the holding area who says you can pick her up."

"Hi, Peggy. Who's that?" But he knew, he just knew.

"Lady named Helen Easterhunt, same gal who found Ferris's body. One of my deputies pulled her over for a burnt-out brake light and got a face full of pot smoke when she rolled down her window."

"O-kay," Paul said tentatively. *Jesus, Helen.*

"This is one of our busiest times of the year—I've already got a bunch of noisy drunks in here and a road-rager, and I'm gonna have to bring in some of the assholes we catch setting off M-80s. I don't have room to lock up a gray-haired hippie with a roach in her ashtray, so I'm letting her off with a warning. Do you think you can come and get her?"

———

Even after three hours in a holding cell, Helen didn't show anything approaching remorse as she climbed into Paul's truck outside the Custer County Detention Center. The sun had set by now, and explosions small and large peppered the night as Paul headed toward Riverside Park, where Helen had left her car when she'd been picked up. "Orange isn't really your color, Helen," Paul teased her, but he was annoyed at the risk she'd taken. When they eventually went public with their story, this was just the kind of dirt that would be dug up to undermine their credibility. He didn't like her compromising their investigation like this, just because she had a raging pot habit.

"I'm lucky they didn't pick me up an hour earlier," she told him, unzipping her backpack and checking inside to make sure all her possessions were there, "or they would have found an ounce of Portland's finest edibles in here."

"Wait, what? Why on earth would you be driving around with so much weed in your bag?"

"To sell it, of course. I did a pretty brisk business earlier today, and sold the last of it about an hour before that nosey parker deputy pulled me over." When Helen saw the astonishment on Paul's face she rolled her eyes and sank back into the seat. "For crap's sake, Paul, what do you think I've been living on? My grants were pulled, and I'm not getting paid by Ferris anymore, obviously, so how do you think I've been surviving here? Pole dancing is not exactly in my wheelhouse. I've been sending out resumes for BLM jobs, and I've been on some interviews, but they get one look at this face and start questioning whether I'm up to the job. It hasn't been easy! Ageism is definitely a thing, even in the geology field when you're working with the oldest shit on earth. So Gary sent me some edibles and I've been selling them, *discreetly*"—she gave him a stern look—"to some people I know around town—not kids, Paul, I would never sell pot to kids! But if I can't make some money I'll have to go back to Oregon, right when we are on the verge of blowing this whole story wide open! We are almost there, Paul, I can smell it, and I need to be here to do this—you know that."

Paul did know that, so he stayed quiet—thinking, and getting used to the news that Helen had been running her own little dispensary under his nose right here in Miles City. Off in the darkness beyond the park he saw a bottle rocket arc into the air and explode in a shower of green sparks. As he pulled up behind her car, he turned to her. "Okay, you're right, Helen. I should have thought of that. But this way is much too risky. They'll be watching you now, and if they pick you up again they're going to charge you." They sat there in silence as another two rockets sailed up over the playing field and bloomed briefly in the dark, accompanied by distant whoops and the sound of glass shattering against cement. Paul looked at Helen's eyes in the shadows of the truck's cab, and she did seem slightly worried, he realized. "Maybe I can help you find you a job."

He'd left the engine on, and the AC stirred Helen's frizzy hair on her creased forehead as she nodded, thinking too. The pale glow piercing the windshield from a streetlamp down the block and the intermittent bursts of noise and light erupting across the park had the effect of isolating them from the mayhem going on outside. For that reason, Paul felt moved to confess something to her. As with all scary truths, saying this out loud would make it real, but keeping it a secret had only helped it to fester like an ulcer in his gut. He thought of Helen as a friend; she was a smart, levelheaded woman, even when she was stoned out of her nut, and she might be able to help him see what had happened in a different way.

Without preamble, he spoke to the windshield. "Helen, my daughter is mixed up with a group of white supremacists." He went on to tell her about the beating he'd witnessed in Billings after they left the coroner's office, and his shame at fleeing the scene and saying nothing to Helen, and about how Hallie had responded when he had confronted her, how she'd made no attempt to deny it and claimed the man had deserved it. "She's my daughter, and I love her. I think she knows I won't go to the police. I tried to bring this up with Paige but we're barely speaking, and she won't trust anything I tell her, especially something like this. So, short of turning Hallie in, what the hell can I do?"

Even he could hear the desperation mounting in his voice as the story spilled out, so he forced himself to stop. A truck racing down Park Street sped past, music thumping, rattling Paul's window, affording them a glimpse of a truckbed full of hooting teenagers waving cans of Bud Light as they careened around the corner. When Helen turned back to him he could see the wheels spinning in her mind. "She's in DC right now, for that parade." It wasn't a question. She had seen the news broadcast; she'd texted him about it. And she'd likely heard all kinds of speculation about it via the lockup gossip mill while she was waiting for him to come pick her up. "She's one of those Vigilante Volunteers, marching in the parade. They were behind the tank that crushed that soldier." When he looked at her, appalled at hearing it put that way, as if causality existed between the two things, she tried to soothe him. "I don't think she had a thing to do with that, Paul—it was a suicide, *another* suicide. But"—and here Paul braced himself because this was the last bit that he had held back, as too awful to even contemplate—"after the tank steamrolled over him, that man's body must have been smeared all along the road, and those kids just marched right through it, smiling away. That tank and the group right behind it must have blocked their view of whatever happened, because the girls just kept turning cartwheels down the street."

Paul felt sick as he pictured Hallie's hands planted in human gore, the same hands he'd seen stick a bat through Parker Gallineau's spokes. He remembered a smaller version of those hands pushing up the corners of his mouth to make him smile when she'd told him about a bully at her school who had cornered her on the playground. *Don't worry, Daddy, he can't hurt you.*

"Now," Helen went on, with gathering conviction, "let's approach this scientifically. I think we should go to Billings to pay a visit to Mr. Gallineau. He doesn't need to know that one of the kids who beat him up is your daughter. You'll be there in your 'journalistic capacity.' We'll find out how he's doing and maybe he can shed a little light on this whole affair."

"Okay," Paul agreed, because it seemed like a sensible place to start. Maybe he'd been too quick to jump to conclusions, after all. Maybe Hallie's claim that Parker was to blame for what had happened pointed to a larger explanation, some episode that had preceded the attack and helped to explain its ferocity. His daughter certainly deserved the benefit of the doubt, didn't she? He felt relieved that he'd finally told Helen, because now he wasn't alone with his concerns, trapped in his own echo chamber, and they had a sensible plan of action. They settled on a date to make the trip, and Helen gathered her things. But before she climbed out of the truck, she had one more thing to say: "While I was waiting for you I heard the warden talking on the phone, and he said that one of the inmates in there hung himself last week." He just stared at her, taking that in. "We need to get our hands on that autopsy report," she said, and the smile that broke across her face made her look almost girlish as she swung open the door.

As Helen's Toyota headed up Park Street, and then stopped at the corner before turning left, Paul couldn't help but notice that both her brake lights seemed to be working just fine.

31

Prime Bag Moon
Sargassa

Since the attack on Valeria and Raiza, the Council had decided an armed guard must be posted outside each governor's shelter around the clock, and Petra had grudgingly agreed—though Angelique, the Azorean woman squatting in the yard with a machete in her belt, energetically fanning herself with a plover's wing, was far too loquacious for Petra's taste. She discovered this soon after Angelique was posted, and after some initial attempts at friendliness Petra now only responded to the woman's spigot of chatter in monosyllables, to get the point across that she had more important things to do. *Not smart, Petra,* she thought, *pissing off your bodyguard.* When the sun began to sink, Angelique's shift would be over and she would hand the machete over to Senesie, a former soldier from Sierra Leone, who knew how to keep his mouth shut.

Petra didn't have the time or the patience to listen to Angelique's litany of grievances about her ex-husband and how he'd stolen all her family money after her parents died in a tourist bus crash on Madeira. Every colonist on the Patch had a sad story to tell, but rehashing all the miserable details did nothing to move them all forward, to address the pressing issues they faced in the here and now. The pace of progress on the storm shield had continued to slow because of developing schisms dividing the Patch community, fueled by passionate disagreements about Luis. Was he a traumatized boy, or an unlikely savior, anointed by the blood of his murdered mother? Was the hurricane a climactic aberration, or God's punishment for the sacrilege of handing power over to the women, or payback for the killing of Hakim and his gang of assassins? Were the stinking entrails that Hiranur probed with her staff a magical window into the future or just a pile of fish guts? So many of the colonists, unlike Petra, had an endless appetite for these arguments, which just fatigued and irritated her. Though Petra distrusted the veracity of all omens, including those derived by haruspication, she recognized the social value in having a project, a shared goal toward which they could all strive. And the business with Luis had only served to undermine their work and impede their progress as a community.

Meanwhile, her headaches kept getting worse. Petra still had a stash of aspirin, but if she was distracted (say, by a colonist complaining that a neighbor had shirked his child care duties) and didn't take the pills at the first signs of trouble, she would wind up here, flat on her back, with a wet rag over her eyes, trying to keep her breathing steady and deep while she waited for the detonations in her skull to subside. When the migraine came, it forced down her shield, exposing her to an onslaught of images: her mother's body leaking life onto her treasured Tabriz carpet; the grocer's boy swinging a bag in his hand, caught mid-stride and spun around by a bullet, his mouth a surprised O as he went down in the dust of the road. But memories of Syria before the war could wound her, too: the oily black olives in the green glass dish on the breakfast table; the scent of gardenia and lemon blossom in the gardens; ghosts of shisha pipe smoke wafting out from sidewalk cafés . . . The remembered sights, and sounds, and tastes she had been desperate to resurrect, to help shore up her mind amid the rubble of her city, now impaled her, when her guard was down, like a spear through the heart.

Here on the Patch at the height of summer, the winds would often slacken and leave them all panting in the shade, rationing the reserves in their fresh-water cisterns. Without the breezes constantly riffling the plastic, one could hear a wife playfully scolding her husband, the dull clunk of a bell on a goat's neck, children screeching like seabirds. All these sounds and others found their way under the flaps of Petra's shelter as she lay on her mat, trying to empty her mind and focus only on the sensation of air moving slowly in and out of her lungs.

But now she heard something else, something that stood out among the now-familiar sounds of a summer evening on Sargassa. It was music — the kind of boastful song she'd once heard at the start of the American military broadcasts. On the Patch people would sometimes play snatches of recorded music at parties and celebrations, careful not to drain the precious batteries in their beat-up CD players, but the sounds she heard now were nothing like that — not like the Syrian music that poured out of the cafés and clubs before the war, a joyful stew of Arab music and reggae, or the honey flow of South Sudanese Afro-pop, or the Venezuelan *joropo* she had danced to at Valeria and Raiza's wedding. No, this was the song of the red hat and the saggy golf swing backside, the music of the self-crowned king who stands with folded arms in front of the open refrigerator and swears that it's empty. These horns trumpeted an anthem of bravado and violence, a song of lust, and fear, and bottomless greed. The music of the oil guzzlers and child cagers, the wall builders with hearts of ice and withered souls. This music was one of the reasons they were all in the middle of the ocean, trying to stay alive on a heap of garbage.

As Petra parted the door flaps, Angelique rose expectantly from her crouch, but she signaled to the guard to stay put. Following the sounds outside to the shed stacked with rafts near the channel, she found Luis leaning with his back to the sun. It was strange to see him alone like that, without the children dogging his steps, the punky teenage girls who imitated Luis's fish-bone piercings and mooned over his disinterested green eyes shot with gold, and the fanatics who insisted he would deliver them all from the fury of the coming storm. Petra peered over the boy's scrawny, sun-blistered shoulder and saw what he saw through the phone screen with its spiderweb of cracks, miraculously transmitting: the footage of Tiananmen Square and Tank Man, the protestor facing down the long row of war machines, the image that had inspired her and so many others around the world.

At first glance that's what she thought was there onscreen. But as she leaned closer Petra saw she was mistaken, that there was only one tank, flying all those fucking American flags from its turret, and that the man standing at attention, facing the tank, was a soldier. If Luis sensed her come up behind him, he did not turn around or move his eyes away from the screen as the American music gave way to a ripping sound, like a length of thick cloth being torn down the middle. The people Petra could now see lined up in a row behind the tank turned their heads in unison to stare at the sun. She watched as the soldier set aside his rifle and lay facedown in the road, arms stretched out to his sides like a saint on a cross. She watched as the tank eased forward on its treads to pass over the soldier, a piece of litter in its path. The tearing noise gradually faded away, and the American music returned.

Petra was having trouble processing what she'd seen, especially with the migraine still drilling into her temple. Cell phones didn't work on the Patch. They kept a SAT phone at each Council House, used from time to time to communicate with the trade vessels and approaching refugee boats. Was this old footage that Luis had found stored on the phone? A film of a magic trick, an illusion, like the vanishing elephant or the smiling lady being sawed in two? But the boy's precious iPhone was broken, its battery long drained. How could the small screen be anything but black? Petra had moved around to crouch beside him, by the wall of the shed, staring as his spidery fingers moved across the cracked rectangular surface and the same music, the same footage, began playing again.

"See?" Luis told her, pointing to the image on the screen. "Sacrifice."

32

July
New York City

The couch was long and curved, upholstered in a rich peacock-blue velvet with a tufted bench seat, matching bolsters, and ebonized caster legs. It had cost $12,000, plus another grand to deliver it the nine blocks from Union Square to Chelsea. This was the most Least had ever shelled out for a single piece of furniture, and now it sat in her largely empty living room like a manmade island floating in the South China Sea.

On Saturday, after a spendy lunch at Union Square Café, she and Resa had gone shopping at ABC Carpet & Home. In her former life Least would have never dreamed of buying anything in that many-leveled museum of décor porn full of the most exquisitely beautiful furnishings. The only way to avoid becoming sick with envy was to treat a trip to ABC like a visit to the Guggenheim. You don't feel bad because you can't take home a Brancusi, right? But making the shift from browser to buyer proved surprising difficult, despite Resa's encouragement; after hours of exploring the multileveled space, Least had only been able to make a single purchase—one she had already come to regret. Though the couch had looked fabulous in the showroom, it seemed marooned in her spacious new living room. Worse, after sitting on it for hour after hour while she watched the entire lineup of programming waiting for her commercial to air, which it did every nineteen minutes or so, she found that life on Peacock Island wasn't all that comfortable after all.

Besides the couch, and her queen bed, the only other item of furniture in her new apartment was a 90-inch black flat-screen TV, currently propped against one of the freshly painted walls. Since the *Foxy Friends* commercial had first started airing during the July Fourth parade, Least had seen her number of followers shoot up to two million. With each viewing, she seemed to add another 25,000, and it was a dependable thrill to track these spikes on her phone. Nowhere near KKW territory, but definitely gaining on her famous cousin. At this rate, she might give Kimbo a serious challenge by the time the show began airing in early September.

Now that she'd made the move out of Bay Ridge and up to Chelsea, rather than the sense of freedom she'd anticipated, Least felt a little lonely. She and Claudia might have occupied different ends of the political spectrum, but Least had to admit that her roommate of two years had been laid-back and respectful of her privacy; crossing paths with Claudia in the little kitchen and living room and the brief chats they'd had were not entirely unwelcome after a day spent killing time in the rarely interrupted silence of the glass gallery. Least wandered through the empty rooms of her new apartment, trying to muster the energy to unpack her few remaining possessions. Ordering Alexa to turn the lights on and off and start the microwave, and keeping the companionable outrage blaring onscreen 24/7, made Least feel less isolated.

The strange thing was that as her number of Instagram and Twitter followers continued to grow, Least watched her circle of actual friends and acquaintances shrink. She still spent time with Resa, though definitely not as much time as before. So-called friends like Angie and the other women she'd gone down to Miami with had shown their true colors

months ago, and she'd stopped returning their calls, smelling the false-
ness in their efforts to reconnect now that she had become a celebrity.

Zooming with her parents felt forced; they'd seen the commercial by
now and hated it, and said as much to Least. They seemed so clueless
and frankly suspicious about the changes in her life, and the question
they kept asking her proved hard to answer, at least to their satisfaction:
Why? Least's dad had lectured her about the evils of propaganda and
had even suggested that her exposure to FOX News would diminish her
IQ. Sometimes when they called her she didn't pick up, rather than
subject herself to yet another reminder of their disapproval. In any case,
her mom and dad had blasted off to Planet Grandparent after her sister
Alana's baby had come by C-section at the end of June, a little girl she
and Mateo had named Tasha after their favorite female character on
Star Trek: The Next Generation.

Richie called her one day, and while she'd been happy to hear her
brother's voice, Least soon realized their parents must have put him up
to it. The conversation turned testy when she heard him taking the same
line as her dad, wondering what really qualified her to host a television
show, and why on earth would she want to? The real question should
be, *Why didn't her own family want her to be famous?*

Luka remained the one constant in her new life, which made sense,
since they had work to do together. When she had first seen her commercial during the parade, once the initial excitement had evaporated, Least
was left with a residue of irritation. And she hated to admit it might have
had something to do with Claudia's reaction. She had seemed genuinely
concerned that Least had signed off on the promo's content—especially
the stuff that implied the punishment for abortion should be hanging.
Of course Least didn't believe that—if she did, her sister Layla would be
on death row. In the Lyft on the way to the Fourth of July party in Red
Hook, Least had complained to Luka about the way some of her words
had been taken out of context or twisted around, how words she'd never
spoken had been stuffed in her mouth, apparently by some deep-fake
technology. But he'd managed to convince her she was overreacting, and

that the jarring juxtapositions of words and images (abortion, gallows) were meant to be funny and hip, and with each successive viewing of the promo she could see he was right.

This week he had scheduled meetings to go over lists of potential guests for the show. The prospect of actually conducting interviews with so many A-listers made her lightheaded with anxiety, but Luka reassured her that every question and response would be fed through an earpiece; her job was to stay calm, look poised, and repeat exactly what she heard. Least was pretty sure she could do that without fucking up. He promised her by the time September rolled around she would be fully prepared to host the show, that the whole thing would seem like a cake walk, whatever the hell that was, and she had no reason not to believe him.

Least was genuinely grateful to Luka. She had this beautiful new apartment—in Manhattan! Her checking account gave her a shock of pleasure every time she checked her balance, and these were just advances—there would be plenty more once *Foxy Friends* began airing, Luka assured her. He bought Least designer clothes and ferried her around town to fabulous parties and made sure she was photographed with other influencers, and posted the most flattering shots on her Instagram account. Her burgeoning social media presence had already attracted two lucrative sponsorship offers (from Lady Dillinger, and BeautyBooty, "the next generation of anal-bleaching systems") that she was considering, with Luka's input. He had "plucked her out of obscurity," as the phrase went, and she couldn't blame him if the adjustment from being a nobody to being a boldface name had its challenges, if the price of fame meant jettisoning some people she'd once considered friends along the way. Better to know who she could count on, who was really in her corner.

She'd made a few more halfhearted attempts to seduce Luka, out of boredom, mainly, but he'd proved a master at deflecting her signals. Even worse, he had appointed himself her unofficial cock blocker, preventing Least from hooking up with any of the smorgasbord of men who had gotten a whiff of her growing fame and wanted in, literally. One night when Luka stopped her from leaving Red Square—a trendy Manhattan bar serving a new mocktail called the Virgin Kardashian—on the arm of a very hot bond trader, they'd argued right there in the middle of Varick Street, and the annoyed trader had left alone in an Uber. Apparently there was a chastity clause in the contract she'd signed with Parallax (she should have read the damn thing!), and there could be consequences for failing to honor it. Luka never tired of lecturing her about negative PR undermining her brand strategy. When she reminded him how Kim's sex tape had launched her career, Luka had only looked at her sternly and mouthed the words "virgin Kardashian," emphasis on the *virgin.* Her bitch-cousin had taken to trolling her on Twitter, pushing the hashtag #notavirgin, as if going to law school made her the boss of facts versus alternative facts. So despite the money and the attention, aspects of her new situation left Least frustrated.

So there she was, rattling around this new showroom where every surface had been painted a blinding Decorator's White. The fixtures had been installed the day before she moved in, and the tall windows still had no blinds to block the light that flooded in, revealing million-dollar views of the Hudson River and the Freedom Tower off in the distance but giving her no privacy at all when darkness fell and she stood out like the filament in an incandescent bulb. She taped up some newspaper in the bedroom to block her neighbors' views of her empty bed, and masturbated in the tangled sheets out of sheer boredom and pent-up sexual energy. One of her fantasies involved her appearing on *The Apprentice*: When she was eliminated for undermining team unity because everybody wanted to fuck her instead of working together to win the contest, she would clear the boardroom and splay herself erotically on the long table and he would take her right there, driving fiercely into her, while she yanked on his tie like the rein of a rearing stallion.

She fueled this particular fantasy by binge-watching the first three seasons of the show, and it made her nostalgic for those early days when she had first left Ann Arbor for New York, and everywhere you looked you saw the future President's name in massive golden letters on mirrored skyscrapers. He was still king of Manhattan in those days, one of those larger-than-life characters who helped rescue a crumbling city and transform it into a place of gleaming towers where no one had to apologize for making a fortune, for shouldering their way into the spotlight and seizing the public's attention as their true birthright. Time and again, he would rise above the rubble of another sensational bankruptcy, Botticelli's Venus born from the foam. She had admired him even then, though she kept quiet when her friends had dismissed him, calling him a clown and a cheat; by doing so they had clearly underestimated him. *Who's stupid now?*

When she first caught wind of a presidential bid, Least had thought, *Of course.* And once the campaign was underway, she had taped up MAGA signs and pictures torn from newspapers and magazines on her bedroom wall like a high school girl sticking pictures of teen idols on the inside of her locker door. On a trip back home in the early spring of 2016, she'd snuck away from her family to attend a rally at a community college outside of Detroit. She'd heard her parents talk about how seeing Bruce Springsteen live was a transformative experience, how the Boss knew how to connect on a deeper level with the crowd. As she stood shoulder to shoulder with the red-hatted attendees who'd been corralled to the front of the auditorium to give the appearance of a more impressive turnout, she'd felt an electric current of excitement when he stepped onstage. From the moment he began to speak, he had them all, including her, in the palm of his hand. He was the real Boss, the Great Leader, and sexy as hell, despite the orange makeup and the crazy hair. And she could see herself as someone who belonged on his arm.

Now, with Luka's help, she was rising to that level, to the upper echelons of American power. She'd set foot—hell, she'd gotten off in the ladies' room—at the Winter White House, his permanent address, even though he hadn't been there at the time. She had a swelling Instagram presence, and even the President *knew her name*, and had retweeted a number of her posts. It was incredibly intoxicating, being up here in the rarified realms of wealth and influence, and it was important that she keep reminding herself of how far she had managed to climb.

In an effort to make her new place feel a little more lived-in, she unpacked her keepsake bin and spread a few of those treasures around as the familiar voices of the right-wing pundits—and intermittently her own voice on the TV—rose and fell like soothing music in the background. Ten minutes after she had propped a KEEP AMERICA GREAT sign in the window, Least heard a polite knock at the door. It was the building manager, a skinny man with large moist eyes and a mottled nose. He apologized for disturbing her but wanted to inform Least that signage of any type in unit windows was expressly prohibited by the building management.

33

July
Billings

The cluster of scorched orange geraniums in plastic planters flanking the Weeping Pines Trailer Park sign gave way to a stretch of buckled asphalt branching off into several lanes and cul-de-sacs, each home to a collection of rusting trailer homes. A weathered post sprouting wooden arrows pointed toward different sections of the park: *Marias, Bear River*, and other names Paul had learned from his Crow grandmother, though he didn't tell Helen that until later. Even in the record-shattering heat, a posse of kids had enough energy to chase a duck toward a stagnant pond near the entrance.

No one had answered when Paul knocked on the screened aluminum door of the manager's trailer, and as he and Helen stood there, looking around, the kids drifted over to regard them suspiciously. Paul asked a tall girl with dirty blond braids and the pointed, alert face of a ferret if she knew where they could find Parker Gallineau's trailer. The girl narrowed her eyes, giving Paul the once-over, as a shrill chorus erupted from the other kids in the pack: "Are you BIA?" The Bureau of Indian Affairs had been dissolved by tweet that spring (the official announcement was

Geronimo lives rich on your dime PLUS CASINO MONEY!!!! Boro of indian afairs cheats REAL AMERCANS!!! Must close now!!), but obviously that news hadn't reached the park's youngest residents, some of whom looked Native. The ferret girl's sharp gaze kept darting to the bag of Subway sandwiches in Helen's hand and the six-pack of Budweiser tucked under Paul's arm, until Helen spoke up. "No, we're just here to check in with Mr. Gallineau and see how he's doing."

Apparently satisfied that Paul and Helen weren't government agents, the children gestured toward the depths of the park, and the ferret girl told them, "On Bear River. It's the one with all the words." It wasn't difficult to see what she meant; the place could be spotted from the intersection of two roads, where a stenciled sign confirmed they'd found the right section of the park. The proliferation of messages on Parker Gallineau's trailer simultaneously camouflaged his home and announced its existence. Signage covered the trailer, most of it with a militant Native American theme. MAKE AMERICA NATIVE AGAIN, YOU ARE ON INDIAN LAND, NO MORE STOLEN SISTERS, NATIVE LIVES MATTER, and HONOR THE TREATIES were some of the phrases Paul and Helen made out as they stood on the cracked asphalt, looking down the lane.

A skinny dog chained in the yard struggled to its feet as they approached and began to growl and then to bark in a high, strangled voice. Helen, typically fearless in all intimidating situations, had hesitated, but Paul walked forward, calling, "Hush up, doggie, hush," and soon had a firm hand on the creature's head, scratching vigorously behind its ears while it whined with pleasure at his touch. His old mutt, Windigo, hadn't been as aggressive as he looked, either. Still keeping her distance from the dog, Helen joined Paul as he reached up to rap his knuckles on the frame of the door, calling out, "Mr. Gallineau? Hello, Parker?" Paul paused and then knocked and called out several more times before a muffled response came from inside and the dog charged up the aluminum steps. After what felt like a very long time, someone demanded, "Whaddya want?"

Paul winced at the sound of the man's voice. One newspaper story had listed the sorry catalog of Gallineau's injuries: three broken teeth and a split lip, left leg busted in two places, three broken ribs, a smashed left hand, and a deep cut over one eyebrow that had bled all over the sidewalk before the ambulance had arrived. Paul had also learned that Parker Gallineau wasn't a lucky man, and that the attack had lost him the first job he'd held in eight months. Through the door, Paul introduced himself and Helen, and explained he was a TV journalist, and he had heard about the attack on the news. He said he didn't buy the version of the story circulating on the local media—that the kids had just reacted in self-defense when Parker had intentionally plowed his bicycle into them—and he wanted to give him a chance to set the record straight.

Gallineau was justifiably suspicious, refusing to open the door, either for them or for his dog, so Paul decided to try another tack. It wasn't often that he played the race card, but it was worth a shot. "Mr. Gallineau, I'm very sorry about what happened to you. It's clear the media is discriminating against you because you're Native. If you were white, they would be reporting this differently. I'm part Crow myself, so I know what that's like."

There was a very long pause. Helen's eyebrows went up, and Paul could see the wheels in her head turning, knew she was on the brink of trying some tactic of her own, and he held up a finger to silence her. Eventually, from behind the door, they heard Gallineau ask, "What part?"

"One quarter. My grandma on my dad's side was full Crow."

Again, silence, except for the dog's whining. Paul could feel the man observing him through the door's small window, only partially blocked by a stained yellow curtain. Finally, Gallineau relented. "Okay," he said. "Ah'll open the door one quarter, then. An' I'll take that six-pack."

He cracked open the door to accept the Subway sack and the beer, letting the dog slip in after unhooking it from the chain. Even in a partial view, Parker Gallineau looked like a man life had stomped all over and then kicked in the teeth for good measure. His swollen face was an aurora borealis of bruises, most of them now fading to green and yellow. Uneven rows of spidery black stitches radiated from his damaged mouth and eyebrow, and his black eyes were mournful and guarded in a broad, homely face. Most of his left hand was swaddled in a grimy bandage. He eased himself back into a metal folding chair beside a small Formica table littered with food wrappers and orange pill vials, his left leg extended awkwardly to the side, wrapped like a toddler's body in a black plastic garbage bag. The dog gave Gallineau's unbandaged hand an enthusiastic licking before it attacked a water bowl at the side of the kitchenette and then flopped down under the chair with a huff. The cooled air in the trailer smelled sour, a mix of sweaty dog and unwashed, suffering man. Paul could hear the drone of a TV coming from a room down the short hall. Gallineau set the Subway sack on the table and pulled a can from the six-pack ring, managing to grasp the pull-top with one finger that protruded from the tattered bandage.

As Gallineau took a long slurp, Helen spoke up. "I'd be careful about mixing alcohol with painkillers. Anything stronger than beer could be risky. Pot is much safer—I have a couple of joints I can leave with you."

Gallineau eyed her over the top of the beer can, clearly wondering about this woman, who looked like a congressman's mother, offering him drugs. "Ah won' say no ta that," he told her.

Hovering there on the aluminum steps, in the patch of shade beneath the awning jutting out from the side of the trailer, they spoke to Parker through the wide crack in the door, doing their best to convince him of their good intentions. The entire time Paul felt sweat trickling down his spine to soak the waistband of his jeans. Eventually Gallineau complained about the AC escaping and waved them wearily inside. He told them to help themselves to water from the faucet in the small sink heaped with dirty dishes, and Paul took the opportunity to refill the dog's water bowl. Then they stood around the cramped space of the cluttered kitchen, sipping murky water from questionably sanitary mugs, while Gallineau downed three cans of Bud and told his version of the story. Some of it was hard to make out; the man's injuries distorted his speech, and his tongue was clumsy in his mouth. But they got the gist.

Gallineau had suffered from epilepsy since he was a kid, when he had jumped into a gravel pit and slammed the back of his head. His seizures, which came on as frequently as once or twice a month, made operating a motor vehicle impossible and had lost him one shitty but necessary job after another throughout this adult life. In one instance he had stepped out for a lunch break from his job inventorying stock in a pet supplies warehouse, and come to later with a cracked and bleeding skull, staring stupidly at the feet of pedestrians hurrying past. Before the cops arrived and helped him sit up, he heard someone say "a drunk Indian was passed out on the sidewalk." No one had noticed the Medic-Alert bracelet on his wrist.

In Billings, he had spent time on the streets, educating himself about the crimes perpetrated against his people, "getting pissed off and militarized," as Gallineau put it. He saw Native women he knew among the homeless population disappearing, and no one came to look for them or ask questions about where they went. He also learned his condition was seen as sacred by some in his culture, a source of visions, evidence of a connection to the gods.

Midway through his story, Gallineau had pulled a paper-wrapped hero out of the Subway bag and began taking surprisingly dainty bites with the uninjured side of his mouth. He pulled some scraps of meat from the bun and tossed them under his chair for the dog to snap up. He gestured to the animal, saying something that Paul had trouble making out, until Helen asked, "So he can sense when you're about to have a seizure?" and Gallineau nodded, patting the dog's head gently with his bandaged hand. With government disability payments and tribal benefits, he'd been able to purchase the trailer, but the Montana winters were hard on it, and he couldn't keep up with the repairs. And now he had the price of an ambulance ride, a week's worth of hospital bills, and a prescription for Vicodin that he had to find a way to pay for. And no job.

Gallineau accepted a joint from Helen after she lit it on the electric coil of the two-burner stove and took a puff (despite Paul's disapproving frown) before handing it to him. Paul's attention sharpened as Gallineau began to describe how he'd been making a food delivery on his bike, minding his own damn business, when out of nowhere a bunch of kids with baseball bats had come at him, knocked him to the ground, and started whaling on him.

Paul had to ask: "Did you recognize any of them? Had anything happened with them, on another day, maybe? Did they come into the restaurant at some point? Did you have an argument?" He could hear the desperation creep into his tone, and now it was Helen's turn to give him a cautionary look. But no, Gallineau had never seen any of them before. The attack had taken him completely by surprise, as had the viciousness of one teen in particular. "Why did that lil gal have a beef wit' me?" The brown-haired girl who had stuck the bat through his tire, who'd brought him crashing face first onto the sidewalk, had been all set to hit him again until one of the boys pulled the bat out of her hands and yelled at her to run. "Why'd she wanna do that?" he asked them, shaking his swollen head in wonder. "She's part Native too!"

34

July
Washington, DC

As the Secret Service detail transferred him from one air-conditioned interior to another, Mike Pence peered out the tinted windows of the bulletproof SUV at the baking streets of the nation's capital and mentally patted himself on the back. It was an inferno out there, the kind of heat obliterating records up and down the Eastern Seaboard, but you'd never know it from the daily papers. Now that the *New York Times* and the *Washington Post* had been brought to heel after the Murdoch/Pecker takeover, the reporting was relentlessly upbeat, 29-point banner headlines bellowing the Good News at last: *Prez Nixes NoKo Nukes; Stock Market Hits 34,000 Again; Parade Crowd Largest Ever.* Though he knew for a fact that last one couldn't be true, what did it matter? Today's news was like one of those skinny mirrors, a medium for reflecting the President back at himself in a more pleasing form, because they all had a stake in keeping POTUS happy. And he seemed happy, for the moment. Pence had the private satisfaction of knowing he was the architect of that joy.

None of the credit, however, would go to him. In the event of a fiasco, he knew every ounce of blame would have landed squarely on his shoulders; he would have been furiously tweeted at, called out and belittled in every public forum. But the event was a success, thank the Lord, and so naturally the President had taken all the credit, crowing about crowd size and the beautiful flags and rifles, the glory of the world's mightiest land and sea and air and space forces all streaming past in formation, all doing their part to Keep America Great. And next time, he vowed, there would be missiles.

Mistakes had been made, of course, that the President knew nothing about. Pinkney had informed his boss that some of the "stand-ins" had died of heatstroke while waiting for the buses. They'd been loaded aboard for disposal elsewhere. And that Guatemalan woman, Maria Itza Marroquín, who had fled the parade, ditched her uniform in the bushes, and evaded the snipers stationed on the rooftops, had so far managed to slip through their dragnet. He knew a shadowy network of subversives had formed in the days after the total immigration ban went into effect, operating a kind of Underground Railroad for illegals, El Ferrocarril. Some so-called "maquinistas" operated right here in DC, though the punishments were severe (*see*: gibbet); he wondered whether they'd helped to spirit this woman away.

But these were minor concerns. Mostly what he experienced in the weeks following the parade, as the heat locked down the nation's capital like a lid on an Instapot, was relief. He'd pulled it off, and for a time he could relax in the brief period of relative calm; the President was too busy guzzling the elixir of self-congratulation to assign his VP another impossible task intended to feed his own insatiable ego. POTUS foamed over like a champagne fountain, wallowing in the afterglow of the pageantry, slapping his veep on the back and proclaiming it "the greatest parade in the history of America!!!" As he had done with the Fifth Avenue shooting, he played looped footage from the event throughout the West Wing, summoning staff members to admire, yet again, this spectacle of American might the nation had been forced to stage in his honor. Pence worried that with repeated viewings he might notice some of the flaws, but the President was so fixed on the sight of himself in the stands that he had so far failed to notice the sloppy makeup on one soldier, the baggy uniform on another.

Something else had siphoned off some of his attention, as well: a promo for a new program being aired in the fall, featuring one of the lesser Kardashians, a cousin of the ambassador's who had begun making her own waves on social media. The network was giving her a lot of play, and every time the spot aired the President would freeze the TV and exclaim to anyone within earshot, "She's hot, right?" She was one of those types of women who seemed to be everywhere now—all balloony breasts and cartoon-wide eyes, blowing POTUS air-kisses through the screen. Mother called them "scarlet harlots."

Despite his fixation with the latest Kardashian, Individual One did finally see footage of the soldier being crushed by the tank, as did Pence. They'd both missed this during the actual parade, when they'd turned to watch the Blue Angels blast past overhead. During a staff meeting in the Oval Office, the President grabbed his remote and paused and rewound the footage, squinting at the picture. Pence watched with horror as the man arranged his body on the road like a matador offering a cape to a charging bull and the tank proceeded over him, smearing that red cross along the asphalt.

Pinkney, who'd been at his boss's side when the President paused the footage, smoothly inserted himself, offering the same cover story he'd released to the media, with a twist: "Yes, sir, it's terribly sad. Apparently the man was suffering from PTSD. He left his wife a note saying he was sacrificing himself on the altar of your presidency, to show all the haters they were wrong."

Pence glanced at his aide in alarm. Pinkney had miscalculated; surely even the President could detect the pea of sarcasm hidden under this mattress of flattery. But no, it was Pence who had misjudged. A wide smile spread across POTUS's tangerine flesh as he replayed the scene three, four more times in eager fascination, finally summoning his press secretary to issue an announcement declaring that the soldier would be awarded a posthumous Medal of Honor. By the time the secretary appeared, however, the President's attention had already shifted back to the subject of "that Kardashian woman," and whether or not she was really a virgin.

Later in the week, when Pence arrived at the Oval Office for a planning session on deregulating the prison-farm labor pipeline, he was secretly thrilled to find Stephen there, his elegant hands briefcasing a sheaf of papers that had been spread across a coffee table. As they all filed in, Pence noted a partially erased whiteboard on an easel in the corner of the room. He made out the ghost of a graph, some numbers and symbols, and a few faint words scribbled on its surface before Stephen stepped over and turned the board to the wall.

The action felt deliberate, like a rebuke, and he flushed a bit, rearranging the fringed cushions to mask his embarrassment as Pinkney joined him on the couch. Glancing up, he found himself pinned by Stephen's eyes, and had to turn away. Once they were all settled, he risked another look, but Stephen's attention was now fixed firmly on the President, who was slurping Diet Coke and boasting about Ursa Major, his new luxury golf resort and spa scheduled to open in September. The meeting devolved, inevitably, into a contest of who could heap the most praise on the man behind the desk. All the usual toadies were in attendance, including Allison January, the White House's new press secretary and heir to the January Solutions fortune, the nation's largest food service provider to correctional facilities. When those assembled weren't nodding attentively at the President, they were—with the exception of Pinkney and Stephen and himself—eyeing Allison's considerable assets, which included two commanding breasts restrained by lime-green poplin and an abundance of coppery-red hair.

As Pence sat rigid on the couch, his face a mask of reverence, he tried to ensure that whenever his eyes found Stephen's they slid past quickly to take in, by turns, the bronze bronco buster on the sideboard, the enormous flat screen over the fireplace (thankfully muted for the meeting), the tall windows draped in acres of heavy gold damask, and the ghastly portrait of Roy Cohn mounted like a religious icon on the wall. In the midst of these ocular exercises, he became aware of a faint smell present in the room, elusive but familiar. He tried to isolate it from the dank potpourri that included the Secretary of Agriculture's garlicky Caesar lunch, whatever fragrance that buxom woman had doused herself in, and the ever-present funk of obsequiousness, topped with a trace of Pinkney's inoffensive aftershave.

By his side, his aide dutifully jotted notes on a yellow pad, though nothing of any consequence had been discussed since they'd taken their seats over an hour before. POTUS prattled continually, at one point stopping the meeting to replay the parade footage of the tank and the soldier. Chortling, he told the assembled group of vaguely perplexed faces, "And maybe there's going to be a lot of these, from now on, not heroes doing it, but lots of others, haters and losers, doing it, too, who can't help themselves, maybe we'll be seeing a lot of that very soon—" when Stephen suddenly rose, apologizing, to announce that the President was late for another meeting, and began to shoo them all from the room. They filed out, speaking deferentially to the hulking figure behind the Resolute Desk and thanking him, yet again, for the incredible job he was doing every day. The last to leave, bowing deeply, Pence found himself staring down into the well of an ornate wastebasket where a crumpled ball of daffodil-yellow sandwich paper stared back at him like a wolf's eye.

The President, still voluble with whatever excitement had gripped his fevered brain, snagged his VP by the sleeve as he moved to leave, insisting, "No, no, I want him to hear this," and beckoned to someone standing just beyond the reinforced door. Pence found himself face-to-face with the man he'd come to think of as King David Dog, though there was nothing whatsoever regal about him. He had entirely forgettable features: average height and build, silver-rimmed glasses with rectangular frames, mud-brown eyes in a pasty face, receding close-cut mouse-gray hair, anyone's mouth and chin. In his short-sleeved white button-down shirt and dark tie, King David Dog was as indistinguishable as any of the men in those famous photographs of the control room during the

Apollo 11 moon mission. If he had witnessed this person commit a robbery, Pence would have been hard-pressed to give the police sketch artist enough information to produce a likeness, couldn't have picked him out of a lineup. Yet all this blandness added up to an aggregate of menace.

When POTUS had demanded he stay, after Pinkney and the others were dismissed, Pence saw disapproval shadow Stephen's face like a passing cloud, and his highly sensitive emotional seismograph picked up the message loud and clear: He wasn't welcome. Nor did he miss the charged looks Stephen exchanged with the other man as the guard closed the door on the four of them and they awaited the President's next words. "Dr. Mobius, have you met the vice president?" An arm was extended, and he felt the momentary pressure of a dry hand tightening around his own. "Mike," the President said, grinning broadly, "meet my secret weapon."

Now POTUS was off and running, babbling about PHAL and microwaves and snowflakes and derangement syndrome and the FCC ("the project has already been a tremendous success, just phenomenal, and they tell me we're very, very close to having all the kinks worked out, right, Doctor?"), and he let the soup of words ("I guess this proves there's a least one smart guy in Indiana, ha ha") wash over him, tuning it all out as he had learned to do during these tirades. He remembered ("Because they've been very unfair to me, very, very unfair") all those times when Stephen had shut himself away with this man, whose meaty scent had permeated the West Wing; what was he to make of those charged looks, Stephen's sphinx-like smile, and his lavender pocket square?

"Look at his face!" the President guffawed, breaking into Pence's thoughts. "Mike doesn't know what hit him!" On the contrary, he knew precisely what had hit him, with the force of a javelin: jealousy. As the President gabbled away, bragging about this mysterious project they'd been working on, the greatest technology the world had ever known, an absolute game changer, etc., etc., he'd seen Stephen look at this underwhelming person with an expression he'd never seen before on that sublime face: something approaching awe.

His limited vocabulary finally exhausted, Individual One lapsed into silence. Pence sensed some response was required of him, so he forced his mouth to smile and make words, to mimic the requisite enthusiasm. "Extraordinary, sir, just extraordinary." Dr. Mobius's near-sighted eyes swam past the President to rest briefly on Stephen before fixing on Pence. "Yes, well . . . ," he said, the first words he'd spoken, in a voice as dull as his features. Now Stephen leaned close to his Commander in Chief, murmuring something into his ear, and suddenly POTUS was waving Pence out of the office, saying they had official business to attend to. Just before the door swung shut behind his back, he heard that same nondescript voice utter something in a tone too low for him to make out. But he heard every single word of the President's response: "Don't worry—that faggot won't talk."

35

July
Billings

Back in his truck after their interview with Parker Gallineau, Paul felt like Hallie had thrust a bat through his tire and sent him hurtling onto the concrete. He was spent and stunned, emptied of the small hope he'd clung to that he might have misinterpreted what he had seen. His beloved daughter was, apparently, a monster. If she hadn't been restrained she might have killed Parker—that was pretty clear from what the man had told them.

In the hot confines of the cab, with the AC cranked up, he simultaneously wanted to be as far away from Helen as possible and to burrow his face into her shoulder and have her stroke his hair like his mom used to do. Instead, he buried his head in his arms, folded on the steering wheel, and surprised them both when a sob burst from his throat. Helen laid a hand on his back, told him, "I'm going to give you a minute," and climbed out of the truck. The $500 in twenty-dollar bills Paul had left on the edge of the cracked table in Gallineau's trailer had only made him feel that much worse. The secret he had kept from Parker, that his own daughter had done this terrible thing, made it difficult to meet the man's eyes when Paul shook his unbandaged hand and said goodbye, promising to see that the truth made it into the media.

When Helen returned, about half an hour later, carrying a KFC bag, Paul had more or less pulled himself together. She handed him a can of Coke and fished a small red-and-white-striped box out of the sack. Before sinking her teeth into a chicken leg, she reminded him, "We have another stop to make. Are you up to it?" Paul nodded and put the truck in gear. Dr. Macadangdang had contacted Helen a couple days earlier, telling her he'd be in the office that Saturday and asking them to come in to discuss the results of the tests he'd run on the samples from Ferris's brain. Helen attacked her lunch, leaving Paul to his thoughts, for which he was grateful. The coroner's office was a twenty-minute drive from Weeping Pines, and by the time they turned onto N. 26th Street, Paul had started to come to terms with what he'd learned about Hallie, assessing the contours of this news as if he were probing a malignant mass in his own body. They were nearing the entrance to the coroner's parking lot when Helen suddenly hunched down and barked, "Keep driving! Drive around the block!" Once they were safely past she straightened up again and told him, "That guy with the crew cut! The one from the rest stop. He was in the lot!"

"Are you sure?" he asked before turning right at the end of the block, and then right again. "Did you get a good look at him?"

"I still have excellent distance vision, Paul," she informed him, sounding a little huffy. "I definitely recognize that guy." As they neared the office again, she directed him to pull over. "Sit tight," she said. "I'm going to walk past and check him out."

"But you talked to him," Paul protested. "He'll recognize you."

She gave him a long-suffering look. "Women my age are invisible, Paul. Don't you know that? It's our superpower." Helen set off down the sidewalk, approaching the parking lot at a relaxed lope. Paul saw her stop when she came abreast of the office and pull out her phone. She held it briefly in front of her face before clamping it to her ear. Then she stood there, shifting her weight from one foot to the other, her mouth moving as if in conversation. Eventually she tucked the phone back in her pocket. Then she resumed her stroll down the sidewalk and turned left at the end of the block. Moments later he saw a gray sedan pull out of the lot and head toward the interstate.

He had time to take a few bites of a greasy biscuit before Helen suddenly reappeared in his side mirror, having completed her circuit of the block. Her face glowed with excitement when she joined him, reporting in a breathless voice, "He was yammering on the phone when I went by, so I could hear some of what he was saying." Still talking, she showed Paul a blurry image on her phone of a man in profile leaning against a gray car with Utah plates. Looking close, Paul could see he did bear a close resemblance to the driver at the rest stop, the guy who had made him feel so paranoid. Same sculpted flattop of reddish hair, same bulbous nose and lantern jaw. "He said something about 'cleared out,' and 'don't think he'll be trouble,' and then a name." She'd taken back the phone and was busy Googling something. "Get going," she told Paul. "We need to talk to Macadangdang."

Paul pulled into the coroner's parking lot, now empty of cars. Helen was muttering, scanning some text on the screen. "Okay," she told him. "I'm going in. You stay here and keep watch!" She climbed down from the truck cab before he had a chance to object. He watched her try the door to the office, which was apparently locked, and knock several times, with no response. Then she walked around the back of the building, and he scanned the parking lot behind him in the rearview mirror, annoyed with himself for letting her boss him around. When Helen didn't immediately reappear, Paul was about to go after her when she emerged on the other side of the building and yanked open the passenger door. Again, she was sweaty and breathless and, weirdly, all smiles. "Quick, let's go!" she ordered, securing her seat belt.

"Was anyone there?" he asked as he swung the truck around and pulled into the road.

"There's blinds on the windows, but there was a crack at the bottom of one I could peek through, when I climbed up on the medical waste bin. The place looks empty, Paul. I mean, the equipment's there, but the computers and file cabinets are gone. Just bare counters, and nothing on the walls. No Macadangdang and no Ariana!"

He mulled this information over for a minute, picturing the poster of Ariana Grande looking sexy and pouty that the coroner had taped to the wall over his computer terminal. "Maybe he lost his job? Let's try to think of a rational explanation. It's possible he moved his stuff out because he got a new job somewhere else. We have to be careful not to fly off the handle here, Helen. Let's take a deep breath and not get ahead of ourselves."

But Helen was reading some text on her phone again and not paying any attention. "The guy with the crew cut said something about a Dr. Mobius, and I've been Googling that name."

"Maybe that's the doctor who's replacing Macadangdang," Paul suggested.

"Could be." Helen kept scrolling through her search results. "There's a video game character by that name — most of the results are related to that. Jesus, how can anyone get so bent out of shape about a fictional character? Honestly, Paul, the things people waste their energy on! The government poisons their drinking water and they can't be bothered to sign a petition, but Sega changes the shape of Dr. Mobius's glasses and they're ready to go to war." She continued scrolling, muttering, "Come on, come on," under her breath. "Okay! Here's a Mobius . . . associated with a microwave company in South Bend, Indiana. And there's a Dr. Mobius quoted in a piece about the sonic attacks, the ones that happened in Cuba and China a couple years back." She read aloud from the article on her phone: "Dr. Orlando Mobius, an authority on microwave technology" — "so definitely the same guy," she said, shooting Paul a triumphant look — "argues that even at very high levels, microwaves would not produce the types of symptoms reported by the diplomatic staff. 'My guess is we're dealing with a type of cicada native to Cuba and China. These insects can be deafening, registering as high as 109 decibels,' Mobius said." So this might be the same person Crew

Cut mentioned. But what's the connection here? And where the hell is Macadangdang? We had an appointment today!"

———

On the highway back to Miles City, Paul kept quiet, still ruminating on what he should do about these new revelations. Hallie had returned from her trip to DC bursting with excitement about the parade and the coverage of the Vigilante Volunteers in the local news, including on Paul's station. On the phone his daughter had sounded like her old self, telling him she'd nailed every part of her routine, even when some of the soldiers were out of step in front of her, and that she'd gotten to shake Vice President Pence's hand. Paige and Hallie would be in Miles City tomorrow to visit Paige's parents, so Hallie could share pictures of her trip, and she had agreed to meet Paul at Main Street Grind for an iced coffee and a cinnamon roll. But since he'd spoken to Parker, he knew he would never be able to sit across the café table from his daughter and feign fatherly interest in her recent adventures in the nation's capital. Clearly, something else was required of him, as a parent and as a human being. But what, exactly?

As the mountains blurred past the truck windows and these thoughts troubled his mind, he'd been only half paying attention to Helen. She'd been reviewing what they'd found at the coroner's office and online, speculating about the disappearance of Dr. Macadangdang, and reminding Paul about what she'd heard at the jail about the inmate's suicide, and how it was imperative they get their hands on that autopsy report. But he noticed she avoided bringing up Hallie and what Parker had told them, maybe because she didn't want to trigger another meltdown while he was behind the wheel. Now she told him about the job interview she had lined up with the Bureau of Land Management. Paul had promised to help find her a job, and he had started asking around, but Helen had found this position on her own, and was due at the BLM field office in Billings early next week. She wanted to poke around town after her interview and see if she could track down the doctor. "How many

Filipinos can there be in Billings, Montana?" she asked. "It's probably a relatively small population, and some of them might know him. Or maybe I can find him on one of the Ariana Grande fan sites."

As he listened, it struck Paul that if Helen got this job she might need to move to Billings, or even be off in the field somewhere, doing whatever a geologist does (and he only had a general idea of what that was). In any case, she would be far less available to chase down leads and interview people, to brainstorm ideas and theories under the creative influence of cannabis as they tried to pull together all the disparate threads of this increasingly bizarre story they were trying to untangle. Their days of clandestine meetings under billboards and at rest stops would be numbered.

Helen had succeeded in convincing him that something nefarious was going on, that Ferris Gladwell hadn't really wanted to kill himself. So what had happened in his brain, to make him flip out and pull that sculpture down on top of him? Had some of the other so-called suicides in the state been triggered by the same sickness, this yellow cotton candy the coroner kept finding in people's brains? And were these deaths somehow related to all the high-profile suicides in the news, including the soldier's under that tank? Who was invested in covering up the scientific reports about these suicides, and for what purpose? He worried that more people might die before they could figure out what was going on. Paul felt a terrible sense of urgency wash over him. He and Helen had to figure this out together, and they needed to do it soon.

36

Felo is very sad to find himself alive. He believed the Virgin had come to take him away, lifting him into her arms and flying through the air like Superman. He can still remember her breath warming his cheek as she carried him high over the land like an eagle hunting, where he looked down at the brown mountains, and saw a dry river twisting like a snake on the plain. Singing in his ear the same song his mother used to sing to help him sleep when his belly cramped with hunger.

Now he lies on his back, the air scraping in and out of his lungs, and one by one his surroundings come into focus: the gray ceiling, the tall striped curtains, the TV forever flickering on the wall. Still here, in this place where no sun comes to tell him the time, and hanging over him the sad face of a woman, not the Virgin at all but a devil, he knows now, the same narrow-eyed witch who took him away from one prison and locked him in another. As he rests there, drifting in and out of sleep and sipping broth from a spoon and water from a straw, the private places of his body wiped clean by someone else's hands, he slowly grows stronger. The man comes, too, the one with cooked meat on his breath and the silver-rimmed glasses, who pries open Felo's eyes and his mouth and looks inside his head with a tiny light. The man uses a cold silver disk to find the skin drum still beating in his chest. *Yes, I am alive*, Felo wants to tell him. *I want to be dead, but I am alive.*

As his strength returns, he feels his disappointment harden into anger. He remembers his visit to the *alfarería*, how his *tia* Ilma, the potter, shaped the soft mud with her hands, and how she showed him how to build a small bowl from clay, first rolling the mud into a long snake with his hands and then coiling it up, pinching it together with his fingers. They left his bowl to dry for days on a shelf, and when he came back she showed him how the color had changed from the brown of the wet clay to a lighter dusty color. Tia Ilma placed his bowl in an oven, and later, when the fire was strong, she let him peek through a little spy hole in the side. He could see the glow of white and orange and feel the heat on his eyeball even through the safety glasses. He saw the little cones slumping and the shaped clay stacked on the shelves, not burning up like wood but changing, because when his bowl finally came out of the oven, it rang like a bell when you flicked it with your finger.

It gives him a kind of joy to think of killing the woman, of pushing her into the oven or sticking a knife between her ribs and into the tough meat of her heart. He thinks of this—of her lying there with her black blood leaking slowly out of her side, spreading across the floor to touch each wall, soaking the bottoms of the long curtains—and he smiles at her, and she smiles back. He knows it is a sin to kill, but he thinks it might not be wrong to kill a witch, to kill a devil. There is no *sacerdote* he can ask, so he tries very hard to remember his lessons from church, the stories the Padre told every Sunday from his perch high above the people.

And Felo makes up his own story, about a boy stolen from his mother and father by a witch and locked in a cage. The cage is small and very cold. And the witch steals other children and locks them up until the cage is full. Each day the children's bellies grow empty, and they are so thirsty they must drink their own tears, and so hungry they must eat their own fingernails.

The witch creeps in every night to count the children, putting one long skinny finger through the door of the cage, and singing a little song: *¡Diez huesos para la sopa, diez niños para la olla, diez niños, ñam ñam ñam!* The boy is clever, and he knows how to count. He knows when there are ten children in the cage, they will all go into the witch's pot to make her soup. So even though the boy is small, and tired, and terribly thirsty and hungry, and he misses his parents very much, he carefully counts the children in the cage.

The first night, he counts eight children before he falls asleep. The second night the boy counts all the way to nine before his eyes grow heavy. On the third night, he knows the witch will count ten children in the cage, and they will all end up in her soup pot. So the boy waits in the dark by the door of the cage, pretending to sleep, until the witch pokes her skinny counting finger through the bars. Then the boy bites down on the witch's finger with his teeth and holds on tight. The witch shrieks and thrashes, but the boy doesn't open his mouth. The witch turns into a screaming black cat with burning white eyes, then into a hissing lizard with a whipping tail, and then into a flaming branch, but the boy keeps his jaws clamped tight around the witch's bony finger. The boy holds on all through the long night. When morning comes, at last, the boy hears a terrible scream and the witch pops like a black balloon. And when the boy finally opens his mouth, there is a long silver key on his tongue.

———

Felo is well again. His meals come through the slot under the door, as they have before, and every day the lady visits him. Sometimes she brings a book and they look at the pictures together, at the worm with the one red shoe, at the mouse flying a helicopter. When she puts her hand to his cheek, he wonders if she can feel the hate burning inside him, white and glowing like the oven where his *tia* cooked his little bowl and turned it into a bell. He knows he will find a way to kill the witch, but he isn't sure how he will do it, or when.

One day when the tray comes through the narrow slot, Felo hears a faint whispering sound, like the wind turning the pages of a book. He moves close to the door and crouches down on his bare heels, tilting his head toward the floor to listen. He keeps very still and then he hears it again, over the knocking in his chest, a voice whispering to him, softly, softly, in words from his own language. A question: *Can you hear me?* *Yes,* he whispers in his smallest voice, *I hear you.* A pause, and then the whispering comes again. *Your mother is alive. We will take you to her. Be patient.*

Then he hears someone moving away, and when he pulls the tray in and lays his head on the carpet and peers through the slot, he sees the rubber heels of two black shoes hurrying around a corner.

37

August
On the tarmac

M ike Pence drowsed fitfully on the fold-down bed bolted to the
wall in the rear of the vice-presidential plane. They had been
stuck on a Cincinnati runway for eight hours and counting, while the
latest monster weather system muscled its way through the Midwest. He
wanted to sleep, to slip into the realm of dreams, lulled by the melody
of the hymn in his head *("Softly and tenderly Jesus is calling"...)*, but
the tweets never ceased, jolting his phone and him awake every time
he felt Morpheus's hand stroking his cheek.

The most recent batch were teasers for the Ursa Major golf club
in Utah, scheduled to open to much fanfare at the beginning of next
month, coinciding with the first Russo-American business summit in
Moab over the Labor Day weekend. *Whos done more for internatonal*
relations than me??!? WHY NO NOBLE PRIZE YET FOR YOUR
FAVORITE PERSIDENT!!!!, blared the latest tweet. The luxury club,
on land formerly designated as the Bears Ears National Monument, was
the President's latest fixation now that the Independence Day parade
was just a speck in his mental rearview mirror.

Before all flights destined for points west of the Mississippi were grounded by the summer megastorms, Pence had been headed to South Dakota, to a pinprick of a town called Murdo, to deliver remarks at the site of the most recent school shooting. He'd come to think of these events, which happened regularly and to which he was regularly dispatched (this being the second one this month), as celebrations, of a sort. Those nineteen souls—roughly one-third of the middle school's student body, in this case—had been sent straight to heaven on the first day of classes, liberated by a gun-toting boy in the grip of some masculine power fantasy. That fact alone was an occasion for joy, as he would tell the Murdo-ites (or was it Murdons? Pinkney would know) assembled in the auditorium awaiting his words of comfort. *("See, on the portals He's waiting and watching"…)* And with the thoughts and prayers they looked to him to dispense he would offer them a coin of far greater value—a message of salvation.

The first time he'd done this, in the aftermath of the Bowling Green parochial school bombing, he knew he had gone off message *("Why should we tarry when Jesus is pleading?"…),* but he had felt the hand of God urge him forward, like a parent nudging a timid child toward Santa's red lap. What a blessing it was, he'd told them, to think of Ashley and Peyton and Olivia being whisked directly into heaven via God's pneumatic tube, bypassing the temptations of Four Loko and fentanyl, twerking and tattoos, lesbianism and Lululemon. Rejoice, for your daughters' souls will remain unspotted for all eternity. *("Come home, come home"…)* Afterward a small group of parents belonging to the three obliterated tweens had approached his security detail to tell him what a comfort his words had been. From then on, he'd determined to make this God-given message a regular feature of these events.

Choking on the lies spewing from the fire hose in the White House, these people craved the truth like oxygen. *("Oh for the wonderful world He has promised"…)* They responded to his message because it came directly from the heart. He had little use for this world anymore, where God's creations were despised and perverted, where young white people lost their precious innocence to drugs and rap music and Axe body spray, where men impersonated women, and women were rough and foul-mouthed and walked the streets with their bottoms spilling out of their shorts and their faces glued to their phones. The stain of sin was everywhere, and he longed for deliverance from his earthly existence like a tortured political prisoner longs for the firing squad. *("Jesus is calling, Calling, O sinner, come home!")*

If his infant grandson was crushed in his cradle by a falling tree or swallowed by a mudslide, the best, most pious part of him would have rejoiced, as hard as that might be for some to believe. What a gift to that child, to be spared the miseries of a life spent in this charnel house, this vale of tears. The signs were unmistakable: the fires and floods and famines, the plagues of locusts and lice and flies, and the contagion still cleansing the earth. Karen prayed daily for her husband's apotheosis to take place in this world *(Please, God, make my husband President)*, but he knew better now; his glory would only come in the next one.

The night before, he had dreamed a vivid and troubling dream. And rather than fade away as the day made its claims on him, his dream became clearer in his imagination with every waking hour. Even now he could conjure up that vision before his mind's eye: a shimmering white city of alabaster spires, resonating with the pure notes of a heavenly choir, an eternal home to loving souls who rejoiced in God's love. But the roots of this miraculous city formed the base of another place, a black city bristling with grotesque, twisting towers and warlike, ignorant people, a metropolis rife with blood and strife and disease, two cities conjoined like the topsy-turvy doll his mother had loved as a child. A doll with a white rag face and body whose calico skirt could be flipped up to reveal a black doll's body with a kerchief and a bright red mouth, two dolls in one, stitched together at the waist.

Near the front of the plane, his wife and his staff kept busy, waiting for the weather to clear. Karen had Skyped with little Michael (her shrill queries carried all the way to the back of the aircraft: "Where's little Mikey? Where's Gammy's big boy?"), and she was now engrossed in a challenging Sudoku based on Bible verse numbers. Pen in hand, Pinkney was drafting remarks Pence would deliver at the annual MyPillow factory Godhead Breakfast in Shakopee next week. And Stephen, where was Stephen at this moment? Did his beloved reside in the peaceful white city, or in the bellicose black one? Lately he'd had cause to wonder. No question about where the President lived, that false idol who demanded his people worship him like a god. So what did it say for his own soul that he continued to serve such a master? Ambition had whispered in his ear, persuaded him that with power would come the opportunity to manifest a pre-Rapture, to realize the kingdom of God right here on earth as President Pence. But the peach, dripping with juice and ready to be plucked, had rotted on the tree. Now only death would pry that man's stubby fingers from the rod.

Pence thought, for the umpteenth time, of what he'd overheard in the Oval Office, when the President had called him a faggot, and again felt his face flush, his belly writhe in mortification. *Faggot.* That ugly word was right at home in the devil's mouth — the foulness of it came as no surprise, since he'd heard all manner of profanity and insult spew from those lips. The threat of exposure was real, but far, far worse was what he'd heard follow the insult, just before the door clicked shut behind him: the sound of Stephen laughing.

Nobody's nails himself to a cross, he thought. *Someone has to do it for you.*

He must have dozed off at last on the squeaking vinyl, but he came to himself again when he sensed a hovering presence and startled awake. Pinkney stood by the daybed with a yellow legal pad under his arm and excitement in his eyes. "Yes, Roland?" he asked, hearing the note of annoyance in his own voice. He swung his legs to the floor and sat up, as his aide crouched beside him, speaking urgently under his breath, breath that smelled not unpleasantly of ripe banana. "Sir," Pinkney was saying, "the notes on the board ... from the planning meeting ..." As his aide went on to explain in a conspiratorial whisper, he had jotted down the words and symbols he could still make out on the whiteboard before Stephen had turned it against the wall. As they waited on the runway, he'd decided to take another crack at trying to figure out what the notations meant—

But here Pence held up a hand. "Do you mean to say, Roland, that you decided to pry into a matter that is undoubtedly secret government business?" he admonished him sharply. Or at least that's how it played out in his mind. That's what he knew a better man than Mike Pence—a man like Jesus, for instance, or Richard Michael Cawley, his beloved grandfather—would have said in the same situation. Yet he allowed Pinkney to continue. After all, the President himself had been excited to tell him about this "secret weapon" they had supposedly developed, but he had been so distracted by the looks passing between Stephen and that loathsome Mobius that he hadn't been able to pay attention. It had been something technical in nature, he knew that, judging from the isolated words and phrases he could recall, but Individual One's grasp of anything scientific was nonexistent and he'd surely garbled whatever he was trying to describe. So there was no harm, Pence reasoned, in hearing what his aide had learned; it might even help him appear informed in the future if the President ever brought up the subject again. Pinkney showed him the legal pad, where he'd written the following notes:

R. Silvestri
"weaponizing" despair
TDS
Beta trials (Havana, China)
1st wave test mkts: CA, NY, MT

"I Googled that name, Silvestri, and nothing came up that made sense. But I kept thinking I'd heard it before, and then I remembered where." Pinkney glanced toward the front of the plane, checking that no one was close enough to overhear them before he continued. "My

the news was so upsetting. My wife complained about it a little when I visited her, but it didn't seem like a big deal.' Silvestri had worked for the Baltimore Department of Parks and Recreation since 1995 and was an avid tennis player."

The name Silvestri and the news story didn't ring a bell, but it reminded him of what the President had said that day in the Oval Office. Something about all the haters and the liberal nut jobs going bananas ("They call it *derangement syndrome*"), and how his reelection made them all crazy. About good TV and bad TV, and what can happen if somebody's got a screw loose.

But then a member of the security team stepped toward the rear of the plane, saying, "Excuse me, sir, but we have clearance. The pilot needs everyone buckled in," and the pilot's voice came over the intercom to announce a break in the weather. "Thank you, Roland," he told his aide as they both rose to their feet. "We'll discuss this later." As he moved up the aisle to resume his seat, Mother waved her completed Bible Sudoku at him like a checkered flag.

38

August
Montana

The first thing Helen bought when she cashed her paycheck was a pair of burner phones. "I'm not taking any chances," she told Paul, handing him a matching one in its molded plastic packaging, "and neither should you." She'd been hired by the Bureau of Land Management, stationed in Billings, but her first field assignment was in the southeast corner of the state, at a site in the Powder River Coal Basin forty-five miles south of Miles City.

Paul met her at the Dairy Queen outside of Rosebud, a sad array of trailer homes and rotting barns tucked into the low hills along the Yellowstone River. She was wearing new olive-green cargo pants and a crisp khaki shirt with epaulets, with a large triangular patch on the left arm that featured a tiny snowcapped mountain and a giant oil rig. A white plastic card was clipped to one of her front shirt pockets.

When she saw Paul glance at it, Helen lowered her voice, and he could scarcely hear her over the wheezing of the ancient air-conditioner. "Check this out," she told him, tapping the plastic with her finger. "They call this a 'vision card.' We all have to wear these. They changed the

Bureau mission — it used to be about protecting land for public use, and now there's all this garbage about 'serving shareholders' and 'multi-use commercial management.' They dock your pay if you forget to wear it."

She dunked the tip of her corndog into a blob of mustard and took a bite. As she stared at him, chewing, she shook her head. "It's incredible, Paul, what these assholes are up to. It would curl your hair," she said, fluffing her frizz, which was flattened by the hat she'd taken off when they sat down. "I almost didn't take this job," she told him, "on account of the hat. And the drug test."

Helen had explained she'd been doing soil sampling and other data gathering at a new extraction site being developed in the basin. Some of her work was out in the field, baking under a blistering early-August sun and breathing in the smoke from the wildfires drifting east from western Montana and Alberta; sometimes she worked in a mobile lab, analyzing data and running computer models and a bunch of other technical stuff, but he understood enough to be surprised and a little disappointed. He sat back, taking in the sight of Helen in her government uniform, delicately gnawing on the blob of deep-fried batter at the base of the wooden skewer. "So," he teased her, "the earth mother is now in the coal business. Who would have thunk it? Is this really what you want to be doing?"

"Of course not!" Helen jabbed at him with the empty stick. "We need someone working on the inside, to figure out exactly what's going on. I'm an *embed*," she hissed, "a spy in the house of coal. And this job is already paying dividends."

Lately, more espionage terms had been creeping into Helen's vocabulary. From her "recon," she knew this Dairy Queen had no security cameras, which was why she'd wanted to meet here. Helen looked around to make sure no one was in earshot, but the bored teenage girl working the counter had disappeared into the back room. Paul strained to hear Helen when she said, "That soldier during the parade, under the tank? Every creep on the web had a theory about that and the other high-profile suicides, and in one alt-right chat room someone said these people offing themselves are probably registered Democrats, because they're such snowflakes and devastated about the election."

When Paul looked at her skeptically, Helen told him, "I know, but Ferris was a Dem, not that he wanted any of his neighbors to know that. And that newscaster you knew, the woman, was too." Paul recalled, from their one and only date, the Shepard Fairey poster of Obama looking down on him disapprovingly as she pulled Paul into bed. "They still don't know who the soldier was, but that activist actress was a leftie, of course, that football player and the Kennedy kid—all hardcore Dems. Well, BLM maintains a huge pool of demographic files because that information influences land-use decisions in every state. God forbid they delegate any federal funds to critics of the President! So they keep current population statistics, broken down by county, socioeconomic class, age, race, marital status, etc., etc. And yes, by *political party*."

She let that sink in for a moment. The DQ girl reemerged lugging a rectangular metal pan heaped with coleslaw and began slopping it into the reservoirs behind the counter. Helen pulled a notebook from her backpack and held it up briefly for Paul to see. The scribbled page read: *MT: 2nd highest suicide rate in US. 58% increase 2016–2020, 89% PHAL.* "So," she said loudly enough for the counter attendant to hear, "I'm really loving this new job because I get to use my computer skills."

A dusty truck rattled up outside, and shortly after the glass door swung open and a man and woman in jeans and matching red KAG ball caps stepped into the Dairy Queen. The man glanced over at Paul and then continued to scrutinize him for an unpleasantly protracted moment, finally turning to scan the menu before he and the woman placed their order. People sometimes recognized Paul's face from TV, but he knew that look (a friendly "Don't I know you?" that turned to mild embarrassment when they eventually placed him) and this wasn't it. They loitered near the counter waiting for their food, not speaking to each other, and Helen made innocuous small talk—asking Paul when Hallie would be starting her term at Montana State and what was the deal with those extra-long dorm sheets? Finally, the couple left with their order. After their truck backed out of the lot and drove away, Paul asked Helen, "Am I nuts or did I sense some hostility from that guy?"

"Probably both," she said, then dropped her voice again. "I'm going to send you what I've found, plus some more stuff about that Mobius guy that I dug up. I think you'll find it illuminating. How's the piece coming?"

In the free time he'd had since Helen started her job, Paul had been hard at work on the story, trying to weave together all the threads they had so far: all the Montana suicides; the yellow cotton candy in the victims' brains; the suspicious deaths, both animal and human; the disappearing coroner and Crew Cut; the mysterious Dr. Mobius and microwaves and the sonic attacks in various embassies. Maybe none of these things fit together, maybe some or all of them did. When he couldn't sleep, he sometimes felt all the random pieces flapping over his face in the dark like a bat trapped in the room. He had come up with various ledes for the piece, including *Fifty Ways to Leave Montana. Our state economy is booming. So why do Montanans keep killing themselves?*

Following Helen's cautionary example, he kept all of his notes and drafts on a flash drive that he brought to the office when he wanted to work on the piece there, and he took all the files home with him when he left. Sometimes when he was writing at the station, Ryan Sugarman drifted by and hung over Paul's shoulder, forcing him to click the window closed and snap, "Do you mind, Ryan? This is private," and the weatherman would wink broadly and announce to the backs of the editors hunched over their terminals, "Looks like Paul's surfing Big Sky Singles again!"

Paul needed something rock-solid before he brought it to the station manager, but he also suspected that this story, however well researched, would never make it on the air. After he'd promised Parker to get his version of the assault story out there, KYUS management had nixed the piece, claiming the *Billings Gazette* had already covered it (they had, if a one-line item on page B-16 counted as "coverage"), and the new information Paul had dug up didn't really warrant their attention.

Grant even had the nerve to hint that his interest in Parker's attack was driven by pro-Native bias. He reminded Paul he had once claimed he didn't want to be pigeonholed doing only tribal news, which made Paul want to clock him.

As for the suicide story, it was "too depressing," as Grant had complained before, and it reeked of conspiracy. Crazy theories still churned up the bowels of the Internet, but they weren't typically aired on the Sinclair-sanctioned 10 o'clock news. If Grant told him no, categorically, Paul needed to figure out what his next move was going to be, which outlet to approach with the story. All the old leftist sites had been smothered to death under the new FCC regulations: Buzzfeed, Vox, ProPublica, HuffPo, forced to lay off 80% of their writers and staff, and even the college stations wouldn't touch anything controversial for fear of having their broadcast licenses revoked. He had to find a way to spread the word in a medium that wouldn't instantly delegitimize the message. Because he knew they had *something*, though he didn't yet know what that *something* was. He wasn't going to just kill it and move on.

The sudden disappearance of the medical examiner showed they were on the right track. When the counter girl stepped out with her arms full of toilet paper rolls, heading for the restroom around the back of the building, Helen leaned in to ask him, "Do you think they offed Macadangdang?" Even before the second term began, hundreds of government scientists had been forced out of their jobs during the purges. Maybe the M.E. had been reassigned to some backwater, or pressured to quit. Imagining him dead was the stuff of a bad spy novel, but Paul had gotten a very menacing vibe from Crew Cut. The fact that the guy had turned up again at the coroner's office just as Macadangdang went missing did not bode well at all.

And Paul had something else weighing on his mind since that day he and Helen had gone to Billings to talk to Parker Gallineau. After learning the truth about the attack, he'd felt called upon to take some action, to address the matter with Hallie in some meaningful way. But how? A good father was supposed to impart some moral wisdom to his child. Paul's own dad hadn't been around long enough to teach him much about his own Native ancestry or pass on many life lessons, though his paternal grandmother and his mom had done their level best to take up the slack.

Even when his marriage was falling apart Paul had tried to be a good dad to his daughter, but he had clearly failed Hallie in some essential way. The little girl who had ridden through the Crazy Mountains in his backpack, shrieking at the marmots on the trails; who'd flashed a proud thumbs-up at him in the stands after she scored a triple during a middle school softball tournament—somewhere along the way she'd gotten the idea that beating up someone was justified by that person's race, by the color of his skin. She'd targeted Parker, despite the fact that they shared a common heritage.

Paul and Helen both fell silent as more customers trickled in and placed their lunch orders, filling some of the nearby tables with bodies (some of them dressed in the same uniforms as Helen) and the low rumble of conversation. Paul had managed to wrestle the packaging off the burner phone without severing a finger and was storing Helen's new number in its memory while she doodled in her notebook. As the clock on the wall closed in on one, time for Helen to get back to work, she took a final slurp from her straw. Then she turned her notebook his way again, so he could see what she'd drawn on the page. It was a cartoon equation:

She grinned at him and mimed taking a hit off a joint.

Paul went home and showered for the second time that day. When he padded out of the bathroom with a towel around his waist, the day's mail had been shoved through the slot and was scattered across the weather mat inside his front door. Amid the junk mail and utility bills and Albertsons circulars he found a postcard. It featured a glamour shot of Manila Bay and a carefully printed message with a phone number: *Sorry we lost touch. Call me here. PS: Ariana sends her love.*

39

She is not his mother. She will never be his mother. But he knows she wants to pretend, to have him sit on her lap like a child and move the pages of the big book, pointing at the pictures and turning her face to smile at his face. Her hands with their sharp painted nails slowly move the pages, and Felo looks at all the places where the finger points. *Look there, and there. Do you see?*

He sees a mouse with goggles flying a plane, and another mouse digging a ditch. A dog in pants places stones edge to edge on a bridge. He sees the animals doing things that people in his village used to do, planting corn and baking bread, knitting a warm sweater, crowding onto a bus for a bouncing ride down the twisty mountain road into the city—all things people he knew did before the rains stopped and the ground cracked and the coffee plants didn't grow anymore. Before the men came, yelling, and dragged Felo's neighbor out of his home, punching and kicking him in the road. How the neighbors only crept out much later, when they knew the man was dead. The smiling animals in the book do the things his family once did, before his mama and papa leaned their heads together and talked late into the night. Before they packed some T-shirts for Felo into one small cloth bag and walked away from their home, following the stars to the north.

As the narrow-eyed lady turns one page and then another page of the heavy book, Felo sees pigs and rabbits and cats and bears wearing clean clothes, and dancing, and driving tractors. But he doesn't see crowds of animals fighting their way onto la Bestia, *el tren de la muerte*, or one falling off the outside and under the wheels when the train begins to move. No animals are locked into the back of a truck and left in the sun to die and rot along the road. No picture shows the smallest animals taken away from their parents and locked into cages made of chains, shitting themselves with fear in the freezing air under the ice-white lights, hungry and trying to sleep on their feet.

He does not know how long he has been in this room where the slit-eyed lady comes to read to him. As it was when he lived in the cold cage, no sunlight falls on the floor to tell him *morning* or *afternoon*, no absence of light to say *night*. Before he was sick, he saved a tiny piece of bread or meat, a wrinkled pea or a kernel of corn, to mark each time the food came through the door on its tray. At home they had eaten once a day, on most days, so he knew that each time the food came counted as one day. He hid all the little pieces behind the striped curtains, lined up next to the wall at the edge of the carpet. When he was well again and could leave his bed he had checked behind the curtain and found all the bits of food were gone.

As Felo sits on the lap that is nothing like his mother's lap, nothing at all, he sees that he has grown, that his legs now hang down farther than they once did and his bare heels brush the tops of the lady's shoes. Felo sees that the arms sticking out of his sleeves are longer than they once were, and the hands holding the sides of the book are bigger than the little hands that once clung tight to the rough and familiar hands of his parents. He guesses he might be seven or eight now, no longer six, the age he was when they left their village, and stronger than when he and Mama and Papa walked away from their little home, leaving the door open behind them.

Felo thinks of a picture he's seen in another book: a white girl with long yellow hair and a blue dress with round sleeves. The girl ate a cake and grew so tall she had to fold in half to fit inside her house, and put her foot up the chimney and stick her arm out the window. He wonders if one day he will grow too big for this room with no window, too big for the bed, and have to sleep on the floor with his head in the bathroom. It frightens him and makes him angry when he thinks of growing old in this place, and never again seeing a hummingbird or a sapodilla tree or a cloud shaped like a horse, never feeling the wind sting his eyes or the sun smile on his skin. Since the tiny voice whispered to him at the door he has heard no other messages, and he wonders now if he only dreamed that voice and the sight of the black shoes hurrying away down the hall.

As the witch talks softly to him and turns the pages of the big book, Felo thinks about all these things. The happy animals in their funny clothes look blurry to him as his eyes grow wet, and he wants to cry out, in his loudest voice, about every terrible thing happening to him that will keep happening forever. And the anger that flares inside his body is so strong, he thinks the witch must surely feel it burning along his back and his legs, making his body glow white and orange like a pot inside his *tia's* kiln.

He jumps off her lap with a shout, swinging the big book back over his shoulder with all the new strength in his arms. He hears a loud crack and sees the lady's eyes open very wide. Then a scream pours out of the red hole of her mouth, and blood drips down from her nose.

When the two locks click and the thick door opens, a man in a black suit rushes inside. Felo is still holding the book in his hands. He throws the big book at the man's head, as hard as he can. As the man turns his face away, Felo dodges the grabbing hands and slips out into the long hall, as fast as a lizard on his new legs. He digs his bare toes into the soft carpet and he flies.

40

August
New York City

As Least scrolled through the celebrity news feed on her phone, wondering if there was any truth to those Kimye divorce rumors, she realized with a start that almost an hour had passed without her once checking her Instagram account. Watching those numbers tick up had once been as energizing as a key bump, but now she'd become numb to the thrill. Two million followers, three million—what the hell did it really matter?

Those numbers definitely translated into money, but while Least enjoyed the comfort and security afforded by her new wealth, at heart she wasn't really an acquisitive person; her mostly empty apartment with its tufted teal couch testified to that. What she craved was the company of someone exciting enough to alleviate her perpetual boredom, someone dynamic and unpredictable and charismatic and a little crazy, someone with an attention span as minuscule as her own, because attracting the interest of a person like that would finally prove to her that she was worthy.

The novelty of her new life had already worn off, leaving Least with no one to blame for this state of affairs but Luka, the "Abominable Snowman," as she sometimes thought of him. With his frosty hair and his pale eyes and his asexual vibe — was he gay? Straight? Bi? Or nothing at all? Sometimes she thought of him as a eunuch guarding a harem of one, the loyal gatekeeper to her newly moated life. He still pimped her around on the party circuit, telling her what to wear and how to act and who to charm when they got there, but despite the free-flowing Armand de Brignac Ace of Spades and the Kobe beef sliders and the designer heroin, Least had come to hate these gatherings and the people she met there. A party should be at least entertaining enough to make you forget your feet were killing you in those four-inch heels. If you've seen one wraparound travertine terrace with a view of the park, or one powder room with an original de Kooning lithograph, you've seen them all.

The same celebrities and socialites who circulated in their beautiful clothes, yakking about their cleanses and their vacations on Ibiza, talked about the President like he was a villain instead of an American hero. And in their arrogance they assumed she shared their opinion that the people who had voted for him were all idiots and nutcases, morons too stupid to see that his policies had made them all poorer and sicker, taken away their food stamps and poisoned their kids, or so they claimed. They didn't even bother to lower their voices when they wished aloud that someone would assassinate him, all the while watching their stock portfolios increase in value. And when she showed up defiantly sporting an Ivanka bag or a KAG pin, they either studiously ignored her or gave her the stink-eye from across the room.

Least had lived in the liberal enclave of New York long enough to know her devotion to the President put her in the minority, but it still shocked her to hear such wealthy and privileged people railing against the very guy responsible for keeping them in their current tax bracket. They were all snobs and hypocrites; ten years earlier the President would have been at that party, the straw that stirs the drink, and the same people would have been flirting with him and buddying up and kissing his ass. All of them bored her silly.

She missed the friends she used to have, and the friends with benefits, even the ones who disagreed with her politics and who she only made the effort to hook up with a couple of times a year. At least in her previous life there had always been a revolving cast of characters in the mix, other Michigan transplants and Williamsburg hipsters and Manhattan day traders and Hoboken magazine editors, to keep things lively. Now Least felt like she was trapped in a one-act play, one of those artsy claustrophobic pieces where the actors insulted the audience, like the one a bad date had once dragged her to see at PS 122.

As Resa used to say about boyfriends, "When you're down to one, you're down to none," and it seemed to apply to girlfriends, too. She was currently down to Resa, as loyal and supportive as ever and who knew her history and her heart better than anyone. Resa was the only person she could really confide in about how nervous she was to host the show, and how much she hated all the glamorous assholes she was meeting, and how frustrated she felt now that she had her best body, ever, and no one to share it with. Resa had been suspicious of Luka from the start. Was he Least's "handler" now? And what did that actually mean? How did Least know, Resa had asked, that Luka truly had her best interests in mind? Whose interests was he really looking out for? A chastity clause—honestly? Was that even legal? Maybe Least should get a lawyer to take a closer look at that contract.

But Resa had a boyfriend now, an egghead-y graphic designer named Eldon, and though she did her best to make time for Least, Resa just wasn't as available as she'd been when she was single. One night the three of them went out to Hunan Balcony and they drank too much and the boyfriend got in an argument with Least about the President and he called her a sycophant. She didn't know exactly what that meant, but it sounded like an insane Republican and she knew it was an insult. So that was the end of hanging out with Resa and her boyfriend, and even though Resa had yelled at Eldon and defended Least, she had stopped short of dumping him, so Least wasn't seeing much of Resa, either.

She'd spent the morning slathered in 150+ SPF sunblock, posing in a white Ivankini in the Jeff Koons red balloon flower fountain next to the 9/11 memorial as Luka took pictures to post to her account. Heading home afterward, with the dirty fountain water still sticky on her skin under her cover-up, she worried someone who'd seen her at the shoot might have followed her. Least kept glancing back at the cars behind them, and the Lyft driver kept looking at her in the rearview mirror as he drove her north along the West Side Highway. When she scurried past the doorman toward the elevator bank, she felt grateful she now lived in a secure building instead of in a mouse-infested dump in Bay Ridge.

Resa and Least had a friend from Ann Arbor who had moved to New Orleans, where she'd been raped. The guy had entered her ground-floor apartment through an open window, and she'd woken to find him standing over her, warning her not to scream. Least and Resa agreed the absolute worst part of the story was that she had scrambled out of bed and made a break for the door, had even managed to get the door open an inch before the man reached past her shoulder and slammed it shut. He slapped a hand over her mouth and dragged her back to the bedroom where he held a knife to her throat and raped her for hours. The fact that she had almost escaped somehow made what happened after that even worse. Least shuddered whenever she thought about it, and she double-checked the locks on her doors and windows every night before she went to bed.

Every crazy thing Least had agreed to in the last few months of her life, all the dangerous new possibilities she had opened herself up to in her new high-profile existence, had, in her mind, one true goal: access to Him. Kim had proved what a Kardashian was capable of, how far up the rope a girl could climb on beauty alone, a reverse Rapunzel using her own hair to scale the slippery sides of the tower of power. But so far the closest Least had come to that stratosphere was the fact that the President had "liked" her *Foxy Friends* commercial and retweeted it and reposted some of her Instagram posts. And despite all of Luka's promises about "access," the closest she had come to the object of her desires was getting herself off in the bathroom at Mar-a-Lago. As they liked to say about the Mueller report and the Ukraine hoax, it was all just a big nothingburger.

By the time Luka arrived back at her apartment that evening to take her to the launch party for BeautyBooty, Least had downed a bottle and a half of Chardonnay and worked herself into a lather of frustration. In her XL red MAGA sweatshirt and black bikini underpants, with OAN blaring on the tube, she was sprawled across a pile of nearly identical white body-con dresses and strappy sandals, glaring at Luka from a makeup-free face when he let himself in (and since when did he have a key to her apartment?). Luka's pale eyebrows hovering in surprise up near his Mister Softee hairline made Least think of a pair of seagulls, floating above fresh landfill.

"What's this? Why aren't you ready to go? The car will be here in ten minutes."

"Fuck the car," she shot back, slurring a bit. "I'm not in the mood for a party. I'm staying home to watch TV in my underwear, like the rest of the country." It was an act of solidarity—most of the people she could see from her windows did the same thing every night in their own apartments. Then, as an afterthought: "How dare you just walk into my apartment? I want that key back. I don't remember giving you my key, and I want it back now." She was on her feet, a little unsteady, her voice rising along with her body. She vaguely recalled giving Luka a key so he could drop off clothes and props at her place when she wasn't at home, but it bothered her that a man with murky motives could just invade her space whenever he felt like it.

Luka's initial look of surprise shaded into his typical demeanor of studied coolness. He began lifting dresses from the couch, smoothing out the wrinkles where they'd been balled up under Least's inebriated ass and slipping them back on their hangers and onto the rolling rack at the side of the living room. "You should respect the dresses, Least. These are on loan from the designer." His placid surface, as always, was maddening. She wanted to heave a rock into that pond. The room spun a bit, and Least remembered she hadn't had any dinner with her wine. Scrounging around in the too-bright kitchen she unearthed a bag of white cheddar rice cakes and shoved one into her mouth, finding it had the exact flavor and squeakiness of Styrofoam packing peanuts. Her next words came at Luka in a spray of white-cheddar dust: "I'm sick of wearing white dresses! I want a lawyer to look at that contract. I don't think a chastity clause is even a thing!"

Luka's phone buzzed in his pocket and he stared at the caller ID for a beat before he answered it. "Yes, yes, hello! Yes, I am her manager. (Pause.) That's right." She followed him out of the kitchen, inhaling particles of rice cake dust and beginning to sputter and cough. Listening intently to the voice at the other end of the line, he stared at her with a strange exultant expression on his face, holding up an index finger to silence her, and Least pictured herself snipping off that digit at the knuckle with her mother's pruning shears. Still listening, his shoulders tensed, Luka crossed quickly to the other corner of the apartment with one hand cupped protectively around his phone.

The part of Least's brain that wasn't fuzzy with wine knew she'd never heard Luka sound so excited before. He was always such a cool customer, but as he reacted to whoever was on the other end of the line, he appeared almost giddy with gratitude. "Oh, that's absolutely wonderful! What an incredible opportunity! She will be so honored to hear this. . . ." Still coughing, she went back into the kitchen to fill a glass with tap water, but Luka caught her at the sink and spun her around and planted a kiss right smack on her rice-cake-dusted mouth.

"What the fuck!? What was that about?"

His hands were clenched uncomfortably around her forearms and his euphoric face was so close to hers she could see into the ice-cave depths of his eyes. "Least!" he breathed. "We did it!"

———

Luka's cold white fingers had wrapped around her waist and lifted her onto the granite countertop, knocking her water glass to smash in the sink as he hastily stripped off her black lace underwear. There had been an awkward hesitation when they realized neither of them had a condom, but with fingers, hands, and mouths, they succeeded in getting each other off, right there under the blazing kitchen lights against the expensive cabinetry, no doubt in full view of the neighboring apartments.

Luka's pubic hair was not, as she had always imagined, the same frosty white as the hair on his head and his eyebrows, but a rather surprising black. He also had a tattoo, the one she'd glimpsed the day they'd met by the pool in Miami, a design featuring two intertwined S's and a T. As if by mutual consent, they didn't say much while all this urgent groping was going on, so she didn't stop to ask him why now, and what it meant. They went through the motions, emitted the appropriate noises, but the whole time Least felt like a third person was present in the room — someone more intoxicating than either of them. The sex was forgettable, in part because it was so hurried, but also because Least forgot about it almost immediately, and turned her thoughts to what truly excited her, the mind-blowing news that had arrived via that phone call. Besides, the whole hook-up felt perfunctory to Least, an act to inaugurate this new phase of her fame, like smashing a bottle on a ship's prow. The broken glass, the foaming champagne, wasn't the point, but what it all signified: launching something beautiful and glossy and expensive on its maiden voyage into the world.

The call had been an invitation for Least to accompany the President on his upcoming trip to Utah for the soft opening of his Ursa Major golf club. She would be flying aboard *Air Force Fucking One* with POTUS and some of his aides and a senator or two; FLOTUS would apparently remain behind in DC, attending to some pressing Be Best business. As Luka enthused post-coitus, cleaning up the shards of glass in the sink, this was the most insane PR boost *Foxy Friends* could have ever dreamed of — Abbott Wunderland had apparently pulled a gazillion strings to wrangle her that invitation. But Least didn't give two shits about the show and its ratings. This was it, her Oval Office moment, Monica flashing her thong at the leader of the free world, a wink with the force to change the future. In a few short weeks she would be soaring above the planet with the most powerful man on earth, locked in a shining metal tube for four blissful hours—enough time for anything—for *everything*—to happen.

41

Orange Pill Bottle Moon
Sargassa

Even the most skeptical among them could see something was wrong. You didn't have to be another Nostradamus to know that a seabird flying backward is a bad omen. The clouds took on strange, ominous shapes—an octopus, a scythe, the Amazon smirk—which remained in place for hours before suddenly unraveling.

A small gray whale was spotted off the southeastern coast of the Patch, moving in an erratic path through the weedy waters, its back a moonscape of barnacles and lice and the trenches cut by ship propellers and orca teeth. Those who knew the habits of these whales were astounded that a resident of the frigid waters of the Bering Sea would show up here in the warming Atlantic. Lookouts on the coast sighted the whale offshore for five days, surfacing from time to time to lift its tapered head above the surface and spew a fetid blast from its double blowhole, rolling almost languidly in the weeds to flash its ridged belly, shockingly white, before sinking out of sight. Petra wondered what the creature, with its fist-sized eye, had seen when it looked toward Sargassa. Had it wondered at the strange forms waving and shouting in the distance, or were the humans indistinguishable from the garbage they lived on, all part of the same stuff that packed its guts, killing it slowly and painfully?

Everyone's nerves had been on edge since Luis had seen that footage on his phone. Only the children, the *vencejos*, had actually viewed the same scene Petra watched over the boy's shoulder; the screen had gone dark again soon after, and like a game of Chinese whispers the tale had changed in the telling, passed from mouth to ear. The ominous gray tank with its fluttering flags had become the hurricane, inexorable, grinding toward them, gathering strength and mass with every mile, and Luis was the soldier who spread himself like a martyr in its path in a bid to save them all.

Increasing numbers of his followers trailed him in his wanderings. Like desperate people everywhere they placed their faith in visions and miracles, much to Petra's frustration and to Adnan's as well. With just a month remaining to finish the shield, the chief engineer had lost nearly a quarter of his workforce to this madness, with more drawn off every day. Though Adnan had dispatched Burak, the goat farmer who now functioned as his lieutenant, to try to control the damage, to cajole and threaten, the converts now spent their time in prayer, invoking Luis as a new savior who would sacrifice himself to deliver them safely through the storm.

At the most recent Council meeting, Adnan had asked the governors to compel the deserters to return to their tasks. He had struggled to listen respectfully, at first, as Halima reminded them all that the bylaws of Sargassa permitted freedom of worship, and that work on the storm shield was strictly voluntary. Then each governor took her turn at the center post to air her views before the Council. Esther, the distractingly beautiful governor of the west central trust, chastised Adnan for wasting community resources on a masculine ego project while the gardens needed weeding and the produce had to be harvested. As she spoke, Petra watched his frustration mass like a thunderhead.

When Esther resumed her seat, Adnan stood abruptly and grabbed the post to steady the shaking in his arms. He addressed Halima but included them all in his anger. "Enough talk! The time for discussions is past. The clouds have spoken, the birds have spoken, the fish have all had their say. It is time to act, to commit to a plan—this plan. There is no time for anything else. Every one of us must pour our energies into building this thing that may help us survive. This has been our challenge, through all history, hasn't it? To know what is the right project at the right moment and to do whatever is necessary to make it happen. This is how we live! No Rome without the aquaducts. No cliff homes, no Anasazi. No London without the Thames Barrier! All the engines of human survival!"

He was panting now, his face wet with sweat. "We must work together to build a future where we can live. Here, in this place! What will you say," he demanded, his voice hoarse with outrage, "when Virginia Daria asks you why you insisted on following the rules of order when the hurricane broke down the door? What will you tell her? That the tomatoes needed picking? Or that you were on your scabby knees, praying for salvation? That you trusted a kid with a broken brain to save you?" Spittle flew from his mouth as he clutched the post, his chest heaving and his eyes wild.

This was a dangerous outburst. The governors only tolerated male anger to a point, and Adnan had tested their patience before. His loss of control could easily put the whole project at risk, if they determined Sargassan resources would no longer be allocated to support a zealot's folly. As he slumped, spent now, Petra stood and took his arm, steering him past the scowling governors and out into the hazy light. She waved away the armed guard who came forward as they emerged. The dog, Wasim, had been tethered to a fence at the edge of the yard, and he lunged toward them, whining.

"Listen," Petra told Adnan once they were out of earshot of the Council, "you will risk everything if you take this approach. Please, calm yourself." She looked at him, her hand on his quivering arm, waiting for the fury to drain from his face, and noticed how thin and unkempt he'd grown, how haggard, his lovely dark eyes rimmed with yellow and shot through with broken blood vessels. When she took one of Adnan's hands in her own she saw the skin of his knuckles was split, the fingernails dirty and torn. Looking at his body, a body she had once known intimately, she saw what it had already cost him to come this far and to see it all falling apart. In the sudden urgency of wanting to help him, an idea came. "Listen," she said again.

———

When Petra returned to the meetinghouse, the governors were reviewing long-established plans for hurricane response. Since Sargassa had been settled, they'd been concerned enough about disrupted weather patterns and their vulnerable location in the middle of the ocean to have put some plans in place, including instructions about where the people should assemble in advance of a storm, where provisions would be stored, and how rebuilding would commence. But so far they'd been lucky; every season the storms swept past them, sparing the Patch, fostering a belief among some that the Almighty had blessed Sargassa and would protect her while the world went to pieces around them. Halima gave her a searching look as she resumed her seat in the circle, so Petra acknowledged her with a brief nod, and made a show of turning her attention to the discussion and even asked a question or two.

The plan she had sketched out for Adnan as they paced by the channel had its seeds in something she'd witnessed two days earlier: Luis kneeling near the kitchen tent, gesticulating before an audience that listened, rapt, to his words. His fluttering hands conjured patterns in the air and tapped out a rhythm on the drum of his belly. He chanted and sang in a high, strained voice that Petra recognized as the one she sometimes heard through the walls of her shelter late at night.

Petra had been tasked with overseeing arrangements for the puppet play, always a high point of the quarterly feast, to be celebrated under the coming full moon, and plans for the event would still go forward despite worries about the hurricane. The Council had determined it was just what the Sargassans needed—a diversion to bring them together and give them all something to think about besides bad omens and the strange weather. Petra had coordinated with puppet makers, musicians, choreographers, and storytellers, and she had originally thought Luis might be convinced to help, that the work might take his mind off Valeria. But now she would use the pressure of her authority to insist he join her team, and help produce the puppet play.

Art is the safest channel for madness, Petra believed. Luis's growing influence had to be contained and neutralized before he placed himself, and Sargassa, at risk. For she could see that what Luis had come to represent would pit the believers against the skeptics, and tear their patchwork society apart after Petra and the other governors had worked so very hard to stitch it together.

Petra gave no credence to Hiranur's prophecies. Pieces of plastic lodged in the guts of sea creatures weren't coded omens from the gods—they were unequivocal signs from the planet itself, all spelling out the same message: *Look what you have done in your colossal stupidity.* Adnan's shield might help protect them from a hurricane, it might not—either way, it struck her as a practical solution, something worth trying if only because it gave them a common cause, a way to strengthen the bonds of their community. But the metastasizing cult of Luis, his growing number of followers, would divide them and ultimately destroy them all. She saw this clearly, and she was determined to stop it.

42

August
Billings

Paul stood on the rusty steps of Parker Gallineau's trailer with his hand clamped on his daughter's shoulder. Hallie's presence here, with just an aluminum inch separating her from the man whose blood she'd sprayed across a Billings sidewalk, was a testament to the efficacy of blackmail. Paul had threatened to report Hallie to the police and to testify against her in court, as an eyewitness to the attack, if she didn't agree to his terms. She was here to face up to the consequences of her actions and to help Parker during his recovery. Paul had enlisted the kids in the trailer park — the ferret-faced girl, whose name was Montana, and the others — to keep an eye on things, reporting back to him if Hallie cut out early or troubled Parker in any way. Paige believed their daughter had volunteered to do community service for two weeks that summer, before starting her freshman year at MSU, and in Paul's eyes that was exactly what Hallie would be doing.

When she caught sight of the array of militant signage sprouting from the trailer, Hallie had balked, saying Parker was an obvious lunatic. She accused her father of putting her in danger, and threatened to call her mom and expose the whole scheme. She was likely experiencing a storm of emotions: fear and humiliation and rage and shame, maybe something like what he'd felt at age nine, when his mother had marched him back to the Town Pump to return the pack of Little Debbie Cosmic Brownies he'd swiped, to 'fess up and apologize and offer to help out in the store as punishment for his petty larceny. Paul would never forget the sick churn in his belly as he faced the acne-scarred manager and admitted to his crime, but it had cured him of his sticky fingers forever.

Revealing to Parker that his own daughter had wielded the baseball bat during the assault had terrified Paul, because he knew if Parker went to the authorities, Hallie might never speak to him again. He trusted Parker not to do that, but the man was well within his rights. In truth, Paul felt deeply anxious. After a divorce that had flensed him of more than half his earnings and the hefty tab for Hallie's tuition at Stormfront, Paul's salary and savings could only be described as modest. He was in no position to cover Parker's hospital bills, if that was the price of his silence. So after weeks of heartburn, Paul was left with this, a plan that might go horribly wrong for all concerned.

His brisk rap on the aluminum frame set the dog to yapping inside, and Paul had to shout, almost, to be heard. "Mr. Gallineau? It's Paul Pendegrass. I'm here with my daughter. May we come in?" He could make out Parker's mumbled assent, so he cracked the door on its creaky spring and the mutt lunged through the gap, causing Hallie to jerk back in alarm. Once again Paul had cause to question the storied loyalty of dogs when Ringo hurled himself at her bare knees, all smiles, tail cranking with excitement at this newcomer in cut-off jeans and a gray Yellowjackets T-shirt. She knelt and scratched the dog's shaggy back, putting off meeting her victim for a few seconds longer, while Paul took a good look at Parker, trying to gauge his mood and the degree to which the man's battered body had healed since they were last face-to-face. "That's Ringo," Parker said.

"And you remember Mr. Gallineau," Paul told Hallie as she rose reluctantly. At her father's urging, she reached out to shake Parker's uninjured hand, then continued looking rather defiantly at the man sinking back into his chair, his left leg still in its bulky cast, five grimy toes protruding from the gap at the bottom. Parker's bloodshot brown eyes regarded Hallie with weary amusement. The bruising had faded and the swelling in Parker's face had ebbed, though ugly black sutures still held together his split lip and right eyebrow.

"Okay," Paul launched in, "this is how it's going to go. Halogen is here to help you, Parker. She'll show up every weekday at nine a.m. sharp and will stay here until three. She will clean, prepare meals, run errands, walk Ringo, whatever you need her to do. During that time you'll attempt to educate her about your common heritage. She clearly has a lot to learn about that. If Hallie holds up her end of the bargain, I am asking you not to take any legal action against her. If she reneges, or gives you any cause to regret your generosity, then I will go to the police with what I know. There's something you'd like to say to Mr. Gallineau, right, Hallie?"

This was perhaps the moment Paul had dreaded most; he'd asked Hallie to prepare a brief statement of apology, but he could not predict exactly what his daughter would say in this moment, and he knew the wrong words from her could derail the whole agreement. That look he'd seen in her eye made him nervous. But before she could open her mouth, Parker spoke up. "I'm sure the little gal regrets what she done, and I'm glad she's here and willing to help. I got plenty of stuff that needs doing around here, as you can see." He gestured around the cluttered space with his bandaged hand. "How about you start with them dishes?"

———

At five minutes to three that same day, Paul parked near the entrance to Weeping Pines and climbed out into the blast furnace of the afternoon with a box of Popsicles. Montana and her grubby little gang were waiting for him, and as he doled out their frozen rewards he knew every single skinny arm would be striped with fruit juice within seconds. Montana slurped the melting grape ice while she delivered her report with the precision of an army corporal detailing the movements of the enemy: ". . . She walked Ringo for ten minutes, texting on her phone. She went to the Wendy's around the block, texting, and came back with a bag, texting. She and Parker had lunch outside his trailer. He sat outside for a while and she brought a garbage bag out to the can by the road. They went back in the trailer, but Ringo had to stay outside. . . ." She went on like this for a while, until one of the littler kids piped up. "We peeked through the window. They were looking at some cards on the table." The boy drew a small rectangle in the air with a sticky red index finger.

Paul was pondering this revelation when he spotted his daughter on the road leading from Parker's place, freeing her hair from its high ponytail, running her hands through it as she approached. "Okay, kids, thanks for the information," he told them, trying to read Hallie's mood in the aftermath of her first day of penance. She knelt to retie the lace on her shoe, momentarily hiding her face in shadow. Then she was upright again, striding along, calling, "Run along, little spies!" after the retreating backs of the children before she climbed into the truck. By the time he was back in the driver's seat and buckling his shoulder strap, Hallie was deep in her phone, and he left her there, turning up the radio for the duration of the drive back to Paige's. Better to let Hallie decompress from the experience instead of grilling her about how her first day with Parker had gone. He'd learned a few things, at least, about dealing with a teenager.

When they pulled up in front of the condo, Hallie was out of her seat almost before he could get the damn car in park. He sighed and watched her race up the front stoop and punch in the key code before disappearing through the ugly paneled door. To his mind, the day had gone about as well as he had any right to expect. Hallie would be riding her bike to Parker's from now on. If she could survive nine more days just like this one she would be absolved of her crimes, and hopefully they could begin to put the whole rotten business behind them. When Paul glanced at the passenger seat his daughter had just vacated, he saw the creased cardboard face of Jacoby Ellsbury, the Native American center fielder, smiling confidently at him.

———

While Hallie was at the trailer park atoning for her sins, Paul had killed a couple of hours answering emails at a local coffee shop before driving across Billings at the appointed time, to the appointed location. The whole way there he kept checking in the rearview mirror to make sure he wasn't being followed, but a flattop silhouette driving a gray sedan with Utah plates never appeared, to his relief.

When he arrived at the piano practice space that Helen had reserved — on account of its soundproofing — Dr. Macadangdang was waiting in a light-blue guayabera shirt and gold-rimmed aviator-style lenses, picking out "Love Me Harder" on the Yamaha upright. For a man who'd gone "underground," as Helen phrased it with relish, Macadangdang appeared well rested and untroubled, looking more like a casino patron than a Montana medical examiner. In contrast, Helen's BLM uniform looked noticeably less crisp than the last time Paul had seen it, with sweat stains around its khaki collar.

When he'd reached the M.E. at the number on the postcard, using his burner phone, "Mac" had asked Paul if he could set up a meeting with Helen, in a safe place where they all could talk. Helen had thought of the practice rooms and now here they were. Mac told them how he'd received, out of the blue, an email terminating his position and invalidating all his passwords, effective immediately. Soon after, Crew Cut (aka Agent Ross Tart) had descended on the office with a team of very efficient and burly helpers. Tart had asked him to surrender his passkey and any materials related to the two corpses he'd been processing in the morgue. He'd been allowed to take his Ariana Grande poster, but everything else had been cleared out. Then the agent had escorted him into one of the back rooms and sat him down at a table covered with official-looking papers, and informed him that if he refused to sign them his medical license would be revoked. Other more sinister repercussions were implied. He'd signed and initialed everywhere the agent indicated and then Tart had shown him the door.

"So," Paul concluded, as his dream of a Pulitzer Prize sputtered out like a dud sparkler, "that means we've lost all the evidence of what you found in Ferris's brain and the other suicide victims. We're back to square one."

"Not exactly," said Macadangdang, slipping something out of one of the little front pockets of his shirt. When he held out his hand, a black flash drive was cupped in his palm. Helen barked a laugh as the coroner explained how, after hearing his research papers had been yanked off the Internet, he had created backups of all his notes and reports on the thumb drive, which he secured behind the Ariana Grande poster with a binder clip. The drive wound up tightly rolled inside the poster, hidden "like Cleopatra in the rug meant for Julius Caesar," Dr. Macadangdang told them with roguish glee.

Paul set up his laptop on the back of the piano and slid the drive into a port on the side. Since time was limited, they agreed he'd just copy the files and review them later at home, but as he slipped the cache of materials onto his desktop he could feel his heart accelerate and a cold feeling pass through his body like a ghost. What they were doing was likely illegal. What if he was arrested and found with this stuff in his possession? What was his exposure, anyway? He thought of Marie Colvin snuffed out covering the siege of Homs in Syria, of Jamal Khashoggi butchered like a hog in the Turkish embassy, Daniel Pearl's grisly end, and, just last week, the Molotov cocktail hurled through a window at the *LA Times*. This shit was no joke. Forget crab fishing—*the story* was the deadliest catch. He knew journalists risked their freedom and their lives every day to get the news out. What was he, Paul Pendegrass, really willing to risk?

Macadangdang was giggling at something Helen had said about a scene in *The Walking Dead*, when a zombie gets high after feasting on the brains of a stoner. Yes, he told her when she asked, he did a tox screen on every cadaver that came through the lab. They needed to know which drugs were in the system of a suicide victim, so they could rule out a bad drug reaction as a factor. Ferris Gladwell's brain tissue showed no evidence of cannabis use, no cannabinol or cannabidiol or THC-COOH, and neither did the blood of the majority of the suicide cases he'd recently processed through the morgue in Billings. That fact had surprised him, given the prevalence of pot use in the western states and the propensity for self-medication in those individuals suffering from clinical depression.

By now, their time in the practice room had expired, so they came up with a backup plan for making contact if phone communication became risky or impossible, though the coroner seemed more tickled by the subterfuge than worried about his own skin. "I, Fortunato Macadangdang, stare death in the face every day," he declared. "Ha ha, old coroner's joke." Taking the flash drive back from Paul, he tucked it away, then patted his little pocket with a conspiratorial smile. "My family has survived cyclones, tsunamis, earthquakes, volcanic eruptions, and Duterte—it takes more than one U.S. government guy with a flattop to spook a Filipino."

43

Orange Pill Bottle Moon
Sargassa

Petra was feeling rather pleased with herself. Her scheme to involve Luis in the preparations for the puppet show had already born fruit. In the weeks leading up to the feast, Luis and the *vencejos* who stuck to him like remoras on a shark's chin had roved over the trust in search of materials to refurbish the different puppets and props. Since the figure of Chaos was set alight and drowned at the culmination of each feast, that puppet—unlike the figures of Greed and Facebook and the others—had to be constructed anew each time. The screaming mouth, the sickly yellow explosion of hair—these features always identified Chaos for the audience, but the puppet makers took great pride in creating something different and newly terrifying each time, a monster that would give the children nightmares. As always, the Sargassan chosen to embody Chaos remained a closely guarded secret, the subject of much speculation and wagering before the performance.

These days, as her duties took her from one community to another, Petra would often see Luis on the common near the Council House, helping to assemble props and watching the rehearsals of the ritual dances and other amusements that would be part of the celebration. By now, the children — ever fickle in their attentions — had drifted off to other games. But Luis had always been obsessive and deeply focused, and gave himself wholeheartedly to whatever captured his interest. As the moon puffed up like a pita in the sky, he also seemed brighter and more present, no longer mesmerized by the shattered screen of the broken phone or conducting one-sided conversations with his deceased mother late into the night. Petra noted that the bruises on his chest had faded. He had even stopped sleeping outside under eaves and in sheds and returned to Yael's shelter, where his mother's lover's daughter was happy to tolerate his tics and habits: rocking and humming while he ate, grimacing unexpectedly, enumerating every Lego character head he'd seen lined up on a blanket at the weekly swap market. Petra had taken the precaution of checking with Benjamina, the woman stage-managing the puppet show, but nothing she heard concerned her. Luis had made no effort to inject his own agenda into the plotline, hadn't been overheard scaring the kids with tales about sacrificial virgins. So Petra allowed herself to relax and to hope the crisis had been averted.

When she spotted Adnan before the feast, part of the crew searing meat on the grill he'd built from the metal wreckage of a boat's canopy, Petra forced herself to smile and approach him, inwardly chiding herself for the effort it took. He appeared more at ease than he had in many weeks, joking with the others as they flipped the sizzling chunks of goat over the coals in the fatty, fragrant smoke. As they chatted, she noted the relief that softened Adnan's face — now that Luis was otherwise engaged and his messianic antics had ceased to distract the workers, real progress could again be made on the shield. Adnan had dedicated himself to ensuring the construction would be completed in time.

The most recent trade ship had arrived from Turks and Caicos, bringing — along with its cargo of batteries and cooking pots and knives and morphine — some unwelcome news. Numerous weather forecasters had reported that conditions in the Atlantic were ripe for a parade of unusually large tropical storms, extreme weather that might delay the next trade vessel for many weeks.

For Petra, who had disciplined herself not to waste her energies worrying about events she could not control, this potential confirmation of Hiranur's prophecy was jarring. Another member of the grill crew, a short and muscular Azorean named Rui who made no effort to hide his interest in her, broke into their conversation, flashing bright teeth in a tanned face, greasy from the fire, and teasing Petra that no hurricane would blow her away if he had his strong arms locked around her. Rui's flirting was unusually bold, since men didn't often speak this way to the governors, but what bothered Petra most was that Adnan seemed so unbothered by it. She bid them both a cool goodbye.

As the late-summer sun crossed the meridian, Sargassans began arriving on foot and by raft from all corners of the trust, adorned for the celebration: mothers with nursing infants, wearing elaborate headdresses built from broken fidget spinners; older colonists helped along by dutiful grandsons daubed with homemade face paint in wild patterns; gangly teenagers with chicken feathers and plastic barrettes in their dreadlocked hair, who clustered near the canals to flirt and try to shove one another into the water. And, always underfoot, the *vencejos*, sporting rag tails and fish-fin horns, whooping and darting away from the admonishments of the men assigned to keep an eye on them. But the celebration had a muted quality, Petra thought. After the other revelers had helped themselves, she filled her plate from the offerings spread across the makeshift tables but had to force herself to finish it all. Governors had to set an example and must never be seen wasting food.

It would have been too much to hope that Luis had found some kids his own age to hang out with at the feast, but Petra first searched for him near the other knots of teens before scanning the groups seated on woven mats or milling around. At last she spotted him, a solitary figure with his back to the crowds. He was flicking his hands by the sides of his head with its blond cockatiel crest, apparently talking to himself, maybe rehearsing his part in one of the plays that made up that evening's entertainment. In his ragged T-shirt and shorts, he looked as scrawny as ever, his sinewy legs almost stork-like, and she noticed a raw patch on his right shin where the skin had been freshly scraped away.

As she stood watching him, a projectile slammed into her legs and she turned to find Virginia Daria smiling up at her and apologizing. "Sorry, Governor! I'm chasing my brother!" The girl had her matted auburn hair gathered on top of her head and spraying out like a fountain, and her brazen little face was iridescent with fish scales smeared along her eyebrows and cheeks. Petra looked in the direction Virginia pointed and saw a skinny boy with a long seaweed tail tied to the back loop of his ragged shorts, sticking out his tongue and dancing away. "Raul says that Chaos is so scary I'll piss my pants! He'll be the one pissing himself! Ha!" She yelled this last bit toward her brother, grabbing an imaginary penis and spraying from side to side while he taunted her from a distance. Petra was glad to see the boy so full of health; when the Daria family had landed on the Patch, two-year-old Raul was severely malnourished and covered with sores. An older boy, Martí, had died before the family left Cuba. Virginia waved goodbye and ran off after her brother, and when Petra looked for Luis again, he was gone.

By now the sea had eaten the sun and the bonfires would soon be lit. The colonists had started taking their seats for the entertainments to follow. Petra saw Ani beckon to her and pat a tattered FedEx bubble bag by her side, so she came over and sank down next to her. The older woman had recently had a rotten tooth pulled, and Petra could tell her jaw was still sore; she was chewing on a fistful of parsley that turned her teeth a shocking green. As had many of the other non-Muslim adults, she had also imbibed a generous amount of *kumis*, the alcohol made from fermented milk that they brewed up north. As they listened to the music—a rhythmic blend of oud and cuatro accompanied by an *adufe* made of goatskin—and stared into the fire, they shared news of the community and discussed progress on the shield.

When Petra brought up the worrisome weather report from the trade vessel, Ani waved a hand dismissively. "That's the least of our troubles," she told Petra. Some intelligence had arrived with the vessel, she said, lowering her voice and breathing a quantity of alcohol fumes into Petra's ear. The ship's cook had a brother stationed at an air base in Florida, where they were ramping up to begin weapons testing in the Sargasso Sea, a "next-generation" nuke—something that used massive microwave blasts. The abundance of life in the sargassum made it a perfect place to gauge the effects of microwaves on everything from the smallest organisms to the big brains of the whales now migrating through the region. They also wanted to see what nuking might do to large concentrations of plastic in the area. Petra gaped at Ani in surprise, trying to wrap her mind around the news. "When?" she croaked. Ani bared her bright green teeth in a ghoulish smile and shook her head. "I don't know, but if the whirlwind hits us there'll be nothing left to nuke."

The night's entertainments finally got underway as Petra tried to process this revelation. She was dimly aware of some silliness taking place in front of her, one child dressed like a flying fish and another mimicking the lithe body of an eel, legs flashing in the firelight, and the audience's bursts of raucous laughter. But the thunder in her ears made it hard to hear anything beyond the limits of her own body. She sat very still and felt despair's rank lily sink its roots into her heart.

Through the years of war, the slaughter of family and friends, and cities turned to rubble, the desperation of the journey when one nation after another turned its back on them, driving them away from their ports with plastic bullets and sound cannons—through all these hardships Petra had cradled her own heart like a stone in her chest, a material as old as earth, strong enough to withstand life's bludgeons, whatever the gods hurled down from the sky. And then, when they made landfall on the Patch and came together to establish a home in this place, building shelters and growing food and making children and enacting laws, choosing the best parts of their old cultures to assemble a new one, a more just society, a homeland to cherish and protect and kill for, for crap's sake—she had killed for Sargassa! Through all those times she had never once allowed herself the luxury of despair, that temptation to do nothing but throw your hands up and wail.

How stupid they'd been, to believe their greatest threat was the wild planet itself. Even if the nuke story turned out to be just a rumor, Petra now saw that well enough would never be left alone. The world was too small, and the men who ruled it too greedy, to permit them even this: an Atlantis of garbage all to themselves. When the other seas had been emptied, the fishing fleets would anchor in the sargassum to take the turtles and the dolphins and the eels and eventually even the weeds themselves, and grind them all down into money. And when the colonists had been driven back into the sea, the American king would turn the Patch into a luxury golf course where the other monsters would come to play.

Suddenly feeling as if the air were too solid to breathe, Petra rose unsteadily to her feet and picked her way through the seated crowds just as the final puppet show began. She stumbled past mats and blankets spread in a semicircle facing the fire pit: children nestled in their parents' laps, lovers entwined in each other's arms, grandmothers squinting toward the spectacle unfolding behind Petra's retreating back, as the insane kings of earth and their hideous children, War and Ego and all the rest, tottered into the light. She saw Adnan's worried face as she staggered past and stood heaving at the back of the crowd, her hands braced on her knees, the gorge rising in her throat as she surveyed all those doomed souls, young and old, frozen in place and gawking, while the puppets orbited the flames in their frantic dance.

Struggling to master herself, Petra heard the show reach its crescendo as the figure of Chaos lurched into the light, and the children screamed in delight and terror. Now Adnan was by Petra's side, touching her arm and asking her if she was all right, but she hardly marked his presence. The prop builders had outdone themselves this time; the firelight revealed not one red mouth but dozens ringing the figure's hideous head, each leaking something foul. The misshapen body was covered with carbuncles, and the ghastly white eyes glowed like moonstones.

The salt wind snarled the creature's bile-yellow hair and sucked at the flames of the torch that a grinning Virginia, proud winner of that honor, held aloft. As she extended her small arm toward the monster, the figure inclined its horrible mask, in a grotesque parody of a knight's courtly bow, to touch its forehead to the torch, before its hair erupted into a fiery corona. And even from the back of the cheering crowd, Petra could make out the raw patch on the shin of the puppeteer as he ran toward the channel, the blazing head now fully aflame.

She saw the arc of orange light as Chaos dove headfirst into the black water, and watched the clouds of bubbling gray smoke as the fire sizzled and died. The spectators roared their approval and turned back to the fire pit as the musicians began to play again. But as much as Petra strained her eyes to peer through the smoke and the darkness, she never saw the boy's skinny legs, with the bright red brand on the naked shin, stealing away into the night.

44

August
Billings

Paul felt ashamed that he hadn't given Hallie a chance to explain. What kind of father assumes the worst about his child? According to the regular reports from Montana, Hallie had been showing up at the trailer park on time and not skipping out early. By all accounts, she and Parker actually seemed to be finding common ground and starting to forge some sort of friendship, if the occasional comments Hallie dropped to him could be trusted. She'd even helped Parker set up a GoFundMe page to assist with his hospital bills. For the first time in Paul's experience, his daughter appeared genuinely curious about her heritage and interested in what Parker had tried to teach her about some of the six gazillion highly imaginative ways in which the federal government continued to screw Native people.

Yet when he'd heard Parker had been taken back to the hospital, Paul had immediately launched into an attack. "What the hell happened with you and Parker, and where the hell did you go?" he'd barked at Hallie when she finally answered her phone. It was only when she described the behavior of the dog, Ringo, in the moments before Parker's collapse that Paul began to grasp what had actually happened. Parker had fallen and split open his recently healed forehead on the corner of the counter, spilling blood all over the floor of the little trailer kitchen. Hallie had dialed 911, and when the ambulance screamed into the trailer park, the dog had scrambled out the door and fled in terror, with Hallie hot on his heels.

She'd left her phone behind on the counter and had spent the afternoon roaming the neighborhood, calling Ringo's name into the wind. Hours later, Hallie was back at the trailer park in tears, without the dog. She retrieved her phone and her bike, and had been pedaling home when Paul finally reached her with his recriminations. The injustice of it, heaped on top of her heartbreak about the missing dog and her concerns about Parker, reopened the wounds in their relationship.

The next time Paul made the trip to Billings, he found Parker perched on a chair in the long shadow thrown by the largest signs on his trailer, his leg cast stuck out in front of him and a fresh set of sutures snaking across his brow. "Christ, Parker, you look like shit . . . again," he told him. Parker corroborated Hallie's version of events. He didn't recall the seizure itself, but before he'd blacked out he remembered Ringo frantically licking his face and his hands. He'd been adamant that Hallie hadn't threatened him in any way.

"She probably saved my life," he assured Paul. "If I'd been alone I might have bled right out. I'm grateful to her. Turns out we get along just fine, that little gal and I." Hallie had brought Parker home from the hospital earlier that week, in her mom's SUV. Montana and the Weeping Pines kids had papered the neighborhood with hand-drawn flyers describing Ringo, and Hallie had called around to all the animal shelters, but so far the mutt was still missing. He wasn't chipped, unfortunately.

Parker heaved himself up on his crutches, and Paul followed him as he stumped past Ringo's abandoned chain coiled in the dust of the yard and up the steps of the trailer. The park manager, Montana's mom, had wiped up the blood in Parker's absence and left a glass of chickory flowers and oxeye daisies on the counter, along with half a huckleberry pie in the fridge. Parker cranked up the old AC, and they each sat down at the little table with an oozing slice and a beer. When he'd come to in the hospital and heard how he wound up there, Parker had been worried that seeing all that blood might have traumatized Hallie. "I don't guess you know this, because she told me she didn't tell you, but she was pretty upset after she went to D.C. and saw that guy smeared along the road."

Paul froze with a purple forkful midway to his mouth. He'd seen the footage, and he knew Hallie's view of the kneeling man had been blocked by the marchers ahead of her group and by the giant tank crawling down Independence Avenue in front of them. He'd assumed she was too focused on her routine to notice what was on the pavement. Easier to think that than it was to watch the parade footage and see her execute that exuberant cartwheel and then wipe her hands on her shirt, still smiling, knowing exactly what she was wiping away. Paul put the fork down and stared at Parker as the significance of this revelation slowly dawned on him. His daughter had chosen to tell this man about her trauma, a guy she had bloodied just a few weeks before, but she hadn't told her own father. And since when had Hallie become so squeamish about bloodshed, considering what she'd done to Parker with that bat?

After he left Parker's place, Paul sat in his truck for a long time with the air running, checking the newsfeed on his phone. The fan noise and the clamor of his thoughts were so loud he startled at a sudden sharp rapping on the window, and saw Hallie peering in at him through the smudged glass. A bag labeled "MSU Bookstore" and a plastic sack of groceries dangled from her fingers, and he realized he'd shown up at Parker's empty handed. Paul rolled down the window and looked into his daughter's unsmiling face, flushed from her bike ride over there in the late summer heat.

"Hey, Dad. Are you coming or going?"

"Just about to leave. Hell of a thing, right? The poor guy can't win for losing. Get in, okay? I want to talk to you for just a minute."

Hallie hesitated, and then came around and climbed into the cab, slamming the door behind her. She stuffed her bags around her feet and looked at him warily and with impatience, the same way Helen had looked at him when he'd first approached her at the bar. Nothing to do but get right into it, he thought. But he didn't really know where to begin.

Paul noticed that Hallie's face was free of makeup. She wore silver earrings with amber stones, golden-brown like her eyes, and her long hair unbound, a woven sweet-grass bracelet knotted around her left wrist. Worn blue jean shorts and a gray tank with a faded flag patch on the front, not hiding the skinny pink bra straps on her smooth shoulders. No Vigilante Volunteers gear—she'd quit that group not long after the parade, according to Parker. The curved white scar in the tanned skin of her left knee, stitches from when she'd tumbled off the trampoline at the rec center during a friend's tenth birthday party. His daughter, yet a virtual stranger to him, his time with her nearly over.

He had been there too little when she was ready to receive whatever wisdom he had to impart, and the divorce had set her against him. A sponge, she would soak up whatever influences surrounded her, some more corrosive than others. Parroting the fascist kids' slogans at Stormfront, or Parker's patient instructions in Native American activism and government betrayal, the dubious and vapid content on her phone, or psychology lectures from the mouth of some associate professor at Montana State. Eventually she would choose which of these to make her own, to build her self on, but his chance to impress any life lessons upon her had probably passed—at least for now.

"You've done a good job here, Hal. I'm proud of you."

"Thanks." Now she had her phone out, scrolling away. A dismissal.

"I'm sorry I suspected you," he said, laying a hand on her arm. "Of hurting him again. That was unfair to you, and I'm sorry." She kept her eyes on her screen, and it took everything he had not to demand she put it down and look at him as he spoke.

45

August
New York City

Resa had planted the seed in the first place, though she would later swear to God she'd only meant it as a joke. Least researched the procedure because she hadn't believed Resa, was so convinced it couldn't be a "thing" that she wanted to settle the argument there and then. But a quick Google search proved Resa was right: "Hymen replacement therapy" was, in fact, a bona fide cosmetic procedure, called hymenoplasty, common in Egypt and places in the Middle East where virginity was a matter of family honor and sometimes of life or death, but available even in the United States. It was an outpatient procedure, not covered by most insurance plans. When Least had jokingly mentioned it to Luka, he told her about an article he'd read profiling a woman named Esmeralda Venegas, who'd branded herself "the queen of virginity." Venegas ran a clinic in Queens specializing in the procedure.

Amid the frenzied preparations in the weeks leading up to the Utah trip aboard Air Force One, which included multiple interviews with Secret Service agents as well as investigations into her employment and credit history and, most important, her voting records, Luka mentioned the President had once again shared one of her posts, along with this comment: "Actual virgin, or more fake news?" When he showed her the remark, Least felt genuine panic and a plummeting feeling in the pit of her stomach. That nagging concern she'd had over the past few months about being called out as an imposter had never entirely gone away, despite Luka's assurances that in 2021 appearances mattered more than so-called "reality." Her cousin's pushing the #notavirgin hashtag had continued to rankle. So when the invitation came, this once-in-a-lifetime opportunity, and she heard about the President's comment, Least decided it was time to take action. But the queen of virginity was booked solid through the end of August, on account of all the Muslim women racing to schedule the procedure before the month of Safar, traditionally regarded as unlucky. So Luka gave Least the number of another doctor in Manhattan who might be able to squeeze her in. Soon after, she'd booked an appointment for the afternoon before the Utah trip at the Upper East Side office of Dr. Chandramohan Mukherjee. She said nothing about it to Resa, of course.

The doctor's offices were not marked on the outside of the building, no doubt due to the discreet nature of his work. She rang the bell of the address Luka had given her, and a voice on the intercom asked for her name and then buzzed her in, first into the marble-floored lobby and then into a small office located on the second floor of the building toward the rear. As Least stepped through the door, a pretty receptionist seated at a desk behind a partition smiled at her and slid aside a thick transparent panel, greeting her by name. "Least Kardashian?" She handed Least a clipboard with several sheets of paperwork to complete and sign, including questions about her medical history, the date of her last period, allergies, and other standard inquiries including the current state of her mental health. Least hesitated at the line asking for her emergency contact information, and then wrote down Luka's cell number.

For the sake of discretion, Least had been informed that only cash would be accepted as payment for the procedure. Along with her completed paperwork she handed the receptionist an envelope containing twenty $100 bills, and the woman smiled at her and told her to have a seat, that Dr. Mukherjee would be with her shortly. Several magazines had been fanned out next to a potted white orchid on an end table, but Least ignored them to stare at the thin braids swirling into tight black rosettes all over the receptionist's elegant skull.

Eight minutes later, during which Least's misgivings about what lay ahead alternately waxed and waned, the door next to the receptionist's compartment swung open and an extraordinarily attractive older man in a white lab coat smiled out at her, and beckoned her inside.

———

As it turned out, the whole experience wasn't any more unpleasant than a pap smear, though it was weird to have such a distractingly hot guy delving into her cooch in such a clinical manner. She wondered what he must have thought when he got an eyeful of her custom bikini wax, but he made no mention of the precise T-shaped landing strip an aesthetician named Olga had given her two days prior. He'd probably seen plenty of pubic landscaping, given his line of work. Once she'd changed into the drab hospital gown, Least had stretched out on the paper-covered surface and fitted her heels into the stirrups at the end of the examining table. When Dr. Mukherjee instructed her to, she scooted down, knees spread apart, and he aimed a warm, bright light at her snatch. Then he began to hum softly, his technique for setting his patients at ease, perhaps. She stared up at the white acoustic tiles on the ceiling as he inserted the speculum, and then she felt the remote discomfort of unseen tools and gloved fingers being inserted into her vaginal canal.

Before she'd undressed, Dr. Mukherjee had showed her the prosthesis, which looked like an oval piece of clear plastic wrap with a ruby-red center. He explained how it worked, releasing a convincing spot of blood-colored liquid when broken during intercourse. Afterward, when he'd switched off the lamp and snapped off his latex gloves with that medical finality that always seemed theatrical to Least, he directed her to sit up again, and issued a few post-procedure instructions: no baths, showers okay, don't insert any sex toys or other objects into the vagina.

Then the doctor shook her hand in a charmingly formal manner, considering where he'd just been, and turned his dazzling teeth on her. "Just one last thing: If I were you, my dear, I'd avoid the Peloton."

46

August
Washington, DC

No sooner had they risen from their knees in the chapel after evening prayers than Mother resumed her energetic carping about the guests who would be traveling with the President on Air Force One. The invitation list had been leaked that morning, and ever since, Karen had been gnawing at this fresh outrage like a Corgi with a butcher's bone.

"It's an absolute disgrace," she told him for the umpteenth time, "to have that Internet floozy along, just because the First Lady had a little snafu with her procedure. Honestly, Mike, the man has no shame!" Neither of them had seen FLOTUS, but the White House grapevine was abuzz about her raccoon eyes and bandaged nose, obviously the result of some badly botched plastic surgery, unless you chose to believe the darker rumors circulating about spousal abuse, which he did not. He knew the President was a man who typically made others do his dirty work. In either case, the First Lady was keeping to her quarters while her face healed, and POTUS had wasted no time in inviting this jezebel, sacrilegiously nicknamed the "Virgin Kardashian," to fill that void. Melania frequently inspired schizophrenic reactions from Mother, who swung between disapproval of the woman for her vaguely scandalous past (because everyone knew "model" was a euphemism for "escort"), barely concealed envy at FLOTUS's superior status and looks, and a grudging sense of solidarity, since Melania was a member of the First Wives Club, after all, even though she had that KGB accent and, as an immigrant, really couldn't be trusted. And Karen had felt genuinely sorry for her when Barron ran off and disowned his father, but who could really blame the boy, with a father like that? "First, he invites that hussy Kim into the Oval Office and gives her an ambassadorship, and now he's bringing another one along on Air Force One. It's an infestation of Kardashians! Really, Mike, you need to have a word with him. It just doesn't look right!"

The Second Lady suffered no illusions about her husband's capacity to influence the President's behavior, but this didn't stop her from clambering up on her high horse at the very principle of the thing. It was hard enough to have to stand by, all smiles, while a truly worthy man, a godly man, a man who served his Maker with every breath, with every thought and deed, was denied his rightful place in the world. Even more galling was that a serial adulterer occupied that place, a faithless fornicator, a phony, and a felon, who by all rights should have resigned his position long ago, but who instead strutted around like Satan himself, wearing his daily scandals like a halo. Clearly, God seemed determined to test them both to the very limits of their forbearance.

Pence looked at her wearily and shrugged. Nothing he said to the man would cut any mustard. POTUS was deaf to advice from all quarters, and ever since he'd been "elected" to a second term there'd been just no living with him. He did whatever he wanted, and to H-E-double hockey sticks with everyone else. If the President wanted to bring along some minor celebrity with big breasts and a pouty mouth, someone to flutter her lashes at him and flatter his *Hindenburg* ego, Pence thought, better to distract the man than let his attention stray to matters where he might do some serious harm, such as national defense or foreign policy. Frankly, Pence had more important things to worry about, such as why

Stephen would be on that flight, and whether that creepy doctor had been invited to the soft opening of Ursa Major.

He'd seen a copy of the flight manifest, and Mobius's name wasn't on it—just that of Stephen and this Kardashian creature, along with assorted aides and staff, including that badger Jim Jordan and the new Republican senator from Utah, Tiff Balderdash, or whatever his name was, and the chinless Senate majority leader. As the vice president, he could never travel on the same plane as the President, for obvious reasons. He didn't particularly care about the project—had in fact argued against it (if his mild suggestion that such a significant Russian investment might be put off for a year or two, for the sake of appearances, could be called "arguing"), but he wanted to be anywhere Stephen was, and that would be at a golf club and luxury spa improbably situated in the middle of a Utah desert, on the site of a former national park.

While Stephen attended the gala at the club—perhaps tucked cozily next to Mobius at a sumptuous banquet, sampling caviar from delicately carved spoons of horn—he and Mother would be boarding a red-eye bound for Belarus to attend the official ceremonies naming Minsk a sister city to Muncie, Indiana. They were scheduled to visit the Holy Spirit Cathedral and be honored as "carriers of the holy flame," though he had his doubts about how warm the reception would be, now that the President had just tweeted something about cutting off millions in aid to that struggling nation. Pence couldn't help thinking back on that embarrassing trip to Ireland when he and Karen had been pelted with a stinging rainbow shower of Smarties when they'd tried to leave their Doonbeg hotel room.

As he perched on the edge of the marital bed, doing up the buttons on his immaculate pajamas, his heart was pierced by a vision (oh, why must his imagination always torture him?) of Stephen and Mobius stripped and lying side by side on paired tables in a dim and scented room, tinkling music playing softly in the background, enjoying a vigorous massage from a pair of muscular Swedish twins. The ache in his chest was so sudden and intense he had to pause and force himself to breathe while the bedroom careened around him. Eventually the pain subsided, and he chided himself for failing to master the tumult of his own mind; jealousy, such a base emotion, was beneath him. Everything he felt for Stephen was holy, an expression of his Maker's ineffable love for them both.

Thoughts of Stephen and Mobius reminded him of that session in the Oval Office when POTUS had blathered on about some super-secret weapon, and of his conversation with Pinkney on the plane while they waited for the all-clear to fly to South Dakota. (Bit of a cool reception at that meeting with the grieving parents of Murdo. One of the mothers had started shouting and had to be removed from the auditorium by his bodyguards.) His aide thought the secret plans might have been about weaponizing television in some targeted way. But wasn't that what they had been doing, the Republicans and their enemies, all along? Firing volleys at each other via campaign ads and through the mouthpieces of those yammering pundits on the right and left. *You lie. No, you.*

Mike Pence was not a big fan of television. Occasionally, he would watch a Pacers game with Mike, Jr., and treat himself to one cold beer, but a trip through the other channels—that profane wasteland of sin, depravity, sex, violence, and godlessness—always left him with a bitter taste in his mouth and the conviction that something had gone very wrong with the American culture. He hated to watch himself on TV, too. When he saw his television self standing at a podium or seated stiffly beside the President at a news conference, the experience always made him feel ill and disembodied. He saw a cardboard cutout of himself, as flattened and immaterial as that illegal alien dressed as a soldier who'd been crushed by the tank on Independence Day.

The land of television was POTUS's natural habitat, of course. Pence didn't believe in evolution, naturally, but he recognized a compelling argument for it in this case. He saw how the President was a product of that diseased environment excreted by the ubiquitous screen on the wall, how entirely it had shaped his fractured, stunted brain as surely as the hand of the Creator had shaped Adam in His own image. It appeared the President had a secret plan to kill off his enemies, by driving them mad with despair, or so Pence had gathered from what his boss had bragged about in his office while Stephen stared at that Mobius character in naked admiration. But, as he'd learned in the previous five years, observing the awful symbiosis on full display, Individual One was nothing without his enemies. He fed upon them, like a tomato bug on a Beefsteak, and when PHAL and the liberals and Antifa were fully vanquished he would look around for another source of sustenance. Ultimately, he would feed upon them all.

Pence looked up from his gloomy ruminations to see his wife's plain country-mouse face, slathered with cold cream and framed by dark curtains of hair, as she padded out of the bathroom in her lavender nylon nightie. Her middle-aged flesh was white and pliable as floured lumps of dough set to rise in a proofing drawer. He didn't want her, had never wanted her, but she was dear to him nonetheless, and he treasured her as the priest had instructed him to do when they were joined in holy wedlock, all those years ago. As they climbed into bed, he prayed fervently that Mother wouldn't reach for his pajama string.

47

Orange Pill Bottle Moon
Sargassa

They had searched late into the night, shouting his name along the channel until their throats burned raw, but they found nothing but an oily paint slick on the surface of the water and some charred remnants of a plastic mouth floating where the puppet had gone under. Benjamina had spoken to the puppet crew and determined that, before the show, the girl originally chosen to embody Chaos had given Luis her place in the costume in exchange for his broken phone. The poor kid, now inconsolable, had no idea he'd meant to do himself any harm. Raiza's daughter, Yael, was distraught and furious and desperate to blame someone, and that person was Petra.

"This was your idea! All yours!" she screamed, her chest heaving, her face distorted with anguish. "You couldn't just leave him alone to wander around, jabbering into his phone—you had to give him a project, to get him out of the way. And now look what's happened!"

Petra had seen the red patch on the shin of the puppeteer. She had been the first to sound the alarm, from where she'd been standing at the back of the crowd. Staring intently into the flickering dark, she had failed to detect any movement along the channel's edge after the puppet disappeared into the water. Adnan's hand had been on her arm and he was saying something to her in a gentle voice, but she kept her eyes fixed on the channel and began running that way, calling Luis's name, and shouting over her shoulder for help.

In the aftermath, it had been a subject of much debate whether Luis had intended to plunge into the water along with the burning head, or if he'd simply become stuck in the costume and dove into the water to extinguish the flames. But Petra knew. After all his talk of sacrifice, of instructions straight from the mouth of his dead mother that something must be offered up to heaven to avert the disaster bearing down on them, Luis had seen his chance and taken it. His body might have been grabbed by a shark and dragged under, though the moonlight showed no blood in the water, or maybe he had drifted under the surface of the Patch and become trapped. They might never know, since bodies vanished quickly once they were submerged, with so many mouths down there to feed.

Petra did blame herself. As a governor of the southern trust she knew it was important she publically take responsibility, and she had been the one to assign him to the project. But she also knew that for someone intent on suicide, the Patch presented countless opportunities. The way he'd chosen to do it, at the height of the celebration, was a message, she believed. Petra remembered how Luis had knelt before Virginia Daria when she stood near the bonfire with a torch in her hand, like a knight bowing before his queen. She found the girl the next morning, shelling peas down near the kitchen tents with her little gang of friends. Petra drew her aside. "Virginia," she asked, "last night during the puppet show, did Luis say anything to you when you lit the head on fire?"

The little girl nodded solemnly. "Yes, Governor. I didn't know it was Luis. He said something to me."

"And what did he say?"

"It was hard to hear him through the mask."

"What did it sound like?"

"It sounded like, 'A god will return with the moon in his mouth.'"

The official investigation into Luis's death would have to wait. As the month grew old, the community came together in a last push to have preparations in place, to finish the shield that might protect them from the coming storm. The boy's death cast a pall over the work, with the most pessimistic of the colonists believing it cursed their efforts. Others claimed Luis had sacrificed himself as part of a protective spell to strengthen their defenses, and they must exert themselves to make sure his death was not in vain. The disappearance of his body was proof, they insisted, that magic was at work. Petra thought of Luis's final words to Virginia, and pictured a divine being clambering up like Adnan's mutt, Wasim, from a swim in the channel with a cracked Frisbee clenched in his teeth. Was it a prophecy, or a warning? Was Luis a new messiah, or a grief-crazed boy speaking in riddles?

Days passed and the moon bulged dangerously in the sky, as Petra paddled her own raft around the trust, checking on the work and encouraging the Sargassans in their labors. Tethered containment pens had been built for the chickens and rabbits, which would float if they were blown off the Patch and could later be retrieved by survivors. Emergency stores of fresh water, medical supplies, and imperishable food were cached in each community, including canned goods from the last trade vessel to make it through the degenerating weather. Designated community leaders worked to finalize emergency plans, so precious time would not be lost in the aftermath locating injured colonists and securing supplies and rebuilding structures shredded by the tempest. Adnan had returned from his travels up and down the eastern edge of Sargassa, supervising work on the shield, and Petra caught occasional glimpses of him, rallying each community in its efforts and uniting them all with his inextinguishable hope.

Only once did their paths cross, when each was paddling a raft in the opposite direction and they paused to speak in the middle of the channel. A rising wind tangled his dark hair as he held the front of her raft to prevent them from drifting apart. She mentioned Luis, whose body still hadn't been recovered, and Adnan reminded her that wherever people were inclined to point fingers of blame, the boy had made his own choice. Then followed an awkward pause, during which the knocking together of their rafts' rough edges and the sound of the sloshing water sounded oddly magnified in the quiet. She forced herself to ask about the work on the shield, how it was advancing and whether he really believed they would complete it in time. Adnan's answer took her by surprise.

"No," he said, laughing grimly, "no shield we can build will ever hold back the wind, not of a hurricane that passes directly over us. You said so yourself, and you were right. What do we have to work with here?" He gestured at the banks of the channel. "Shreds and scraps and fragments of plastic? It's all garbage. But for people who have come from war, whose minds have been shaped by war, this idea of a shield has value, a powerful symbolic value."

"But then . . ." She stopped, puzzled. "Then all these efforts, all your work, everyone's work, has been for nothing?"

"Petra." Her name was heavy in his mouth. "The people think they have been building a shield because that is what we have told them. This effort has given them hope and purpose, and channeled their fears into work. None of that counts as nothing, as you say. For people who have nothing, these things become everything. Don't you know that by now?" He gave her a sweetly chiding look that felt more like a slap. "But they have succeeded in building something else — not a shield, but something that may actually have a chance of saving us: a sail."

It was an ingenious design — a continuous sail running along the eastern coast of the Patch. The massive sail would catch the leading edge of the wind and drag Sargassa out of the storm's path, using the hurricane's own force as a fulcrum. For a storm-battered coastal city, such a plan would be ridiculous. But a floating island built entirely of buoyant materials, riding light on the surface of the waves, a place with no roots tethering it to the earth, such a place might be able to sail out of harm's way. In any case, it was worth a try.

Looking into his dark eyes, his gaunt and intelligent face, animated by the prospect and the madness of working such a miracle, she saw him naked in a way she never had in all the times they lay together, stripped of their clothing, their social roles cast aside. She knew she'd wounded him by how little she seemed to care. She might have loved this man if she'd only allowed herself to.

A cloud passed over, tugging a brief rain shower in its wake before the sun returned. She watched the shining drops collect in his black beard and slide down his neck to pool in the hollow of his shoulder. She had a sudden yearning to put her mouth there, to drink from that cup, but she resisted it.

48

August
Miles City

When Paul heard from Ryan Sugarman that KYUS was going dark, and everyone on staff would be laid off, he expected to feel a horse-kick to the gut, but strangely enough, the first thing he experienced in the wake of that bombshell was a prickling sense of freedom.

Like many, Paul owed his career in television to *SNL*. He and a friend, Brody, had been granted permission to operate a cable channel out of their Great Falls high school multipurpose room, where they put together a weekly hour of programming shamelessly derivative of *Wayne's World* but featuring local news. Back then, his quarter share of Indian blood was still worth something in the eyes of the federal government: enough financial aid to help him earn a two-year associate's degree in TV broadcasting at Montana State. His widowed mom never could've swung it on her own.

Thanks, in large part, to his looks, Paul had been hired on at Channel 3 in 1995 as a production assistant. He and Paige had met in Diversity class at Billings (a freshman year requirement, since discontinued) and married in 1997—and for the first two years they lived with her folks, longtime Miles City residents who Paul got along with just fine until the divorce. Paul's father-in-law knew a senior producer at KYUS, and soon his handsome son-in-law was on-camera reporting on local events like Little Bighorn Days and the Standing Arrow Powwow ("This is Paul Pendegrass, special to Channel 3 news"). He knew he would be pigeon-holed, stuck covering "the Native beat," if he didn't make it clear early on that he had no intention of being a one-subject reporter. Paul's elevation to anchor happened before Grant took over the station in 2015, under the benevolent reign of Grant's predecessor, a big-hearted guy with a prosthetic leg named Randy Pearl who quit the business to try his hand at winemaking.

Since 2017, pressure on the media had become intense. With the profession now squarely in the President's crosshairs, that chickenshit Grant had decreed that job one at the station would be to avoid offending the Great White Father in Washington and not attract the unwanted attention of the newly purged FCC. After Sinclair gobbled up the station in 2019, this mission became even more imperative. Work that Paul had once genuinely enjoyed became an exercise in ass-kissing. The team at KYUS produced innocuous stories that wouldn't rub the station's new owners and sponsors the wrong way, and they ran every must-air handed down from on high, including that *Foxy Friends* teaser. The first time he'd seen it, Paul thought Leash (was that her name?) Kardashian was vaguely sexy, like an Armenian Monica Lewinsky, but after the umpteenth viewing the promo retained all the allure of an air horn.

News of the station's closure meant that, for their final weeks on the air, he wouldn't have to beg Grant to let him do a story; he could say it straight and not have to pull any punches for fear of being fired. He and Helen planned to go live with what they knew on the Wednesday before the long Labor Day weekend. Paul had borrowed a camera and they'd filmed interviews with Mac and some of the other medical examiners describing the yellow cotton candy they'd found crowding out the healthy brain tissue of the suicide victims. He'd interviewed Helen and Tyler, the ranch hand, talking about Ferris—about why he never would have taken his own life under normal circumstances, and explaining how the chickens had died after lunching on his brains. They had other key pieces of the evidence they'd assembled: screen shots of autopsy reports, data from the current Montana voter roles, the images (pixilated, out of respect for the dead) that Helen had snapped of Ferris crushed beneath the Venus, national and state suicide stats, and a blurry photo Helen dug up online of Orlando Mobius at a Midwestern microwave industry function, published in a newsletter called *Waves of Grain*.

Paul and Helen had spent the previous two nights at his place editing the footage—at this stage, he really didn't care anymore if Miles City gums started flapping about the frowsy, pot-scented woman seen leaving his townhouse in the wee hours. While they still didn't understand how everything fit together, they had a working theory, a story of a conspiracy behind the so-called "derangement syndrome"—a mysterious Dr. Mobius devising a top-secret microwave technology to target members of PHAL and drive them to suicide—unless, by chance, they had ingested enough marijuana to blunt its effects. Totally nuts, sure, but it wasn't any weirder than those satanic pedophile conspiracies like QAnon or whatever the alt-right rumor mill kept churning out. Punch-drunk with fatigue, they'd even given their joint venture into investigative journalism a name: EasterGrass Productions.

Before she'd left his place around two that morning, Helen had asked Paul what he planned to do if Grant scrapped the piece or cut away from the report. Her eyes were bloodshot from hours of staring at the monitor, and in the stark side lighting of his foyer he could see the velvet on her jaw that reminded him of his mother's skin, the texture of an aging women's face. Not for the first time, he wondered what Helen might look like with a little contouring and a hot-oil treatment. "We'll post it online right after it's aired, and we'll send it to news outlets that aren't affiliated with Sinclair. They can't keep a lid on this," he assured her with a show of confidence he didn't really feel, not after a long night of crappy pizza and hunching in front of a screen. He reached out and awkwardly patted her cheek. "Go get some sleep, mama—tomorrow's your big debut."

———

By the time Paul had his butt in the makeup chair the following afternoon, Hurricane Pandora was already wreaking havoc with the day's schedule. At the top of the hour, Grant cut right to Sugarman, who was engorged with self-importance at being handed the leadoff slot. The weather segment typically wrapped up the broadcast, but the ferocity of the storm (a Category 4 and counting) currently forming out in the Atlantic, and the fact that it was barreling southwest in the general direction of the Winter White House, meant it was big news even out west.

Ryan made the most of it, yammering about "the cone of uncertainty" and the highly unusual storm track and gesticulating in front of the weather screen where various models for the hurricane's path stretched like multicolored linguini. Though most of the projections showed the hurricane making landfall to the north, the President had already dispatched the Florida national guard to assist in sandbagging the length of Ocean Boulevard and all around Mar-a-Lago. Paul gagged a bit, listening to the weatherman promise that meteorologists were "trying to keep Pandora far out at sea and to bring down wind speeds over the course of the next several hours." During his career in TV broadcasting, Paul had watched this trend catch on, and he still found it grating: how the forecasters all spoke as if they were somehow in charge of the weather events they were describing. How typical of people to act like they had mastery over the uncontrollable, although with human-driven climate change, the warming oceans and the new megastorms, maybe it was time to finally own the unpredictable monsters they'd unleashed.

Paul's piece—which he'd told Grant was a local-interest story on Ferris's posthumous fame as an outsider artist—was slotted in after a report on a mass fatality crash on I-90 when a self-driving semi had strayed across the double yellow and into a church bus. Paul hadn't told Helen about what he was planning to do once he went live with the piece—he'd promised not to keep any more secrets from her, but he'd lied, and eventually Helen would see the logic of that decision. The gun had belonged to his mother, and Paul had never fired it—had kept it secure in its locked black plastic case, buried deep in his closet. Paul had never been a gun guy, despite his Montana upbringing, but after more than twenty years in TV broadcasting he knew something about theater, about how to hold people's attention. That afternoon, he'd stowed the firearm under the news desk inside a Kleenex box kept there for use during commercial breaks. He knew as soon as the true subject of the report became plain, Grant would signal them to cut to a commercial or the *Foxy Friends* promo. So when the camera came in tight on his face at the beginning of the story, Paul planned to reach for the gun, raise it to his head, and cock it. Very calmly, he would inform the station staff that if they cut away during any portion of his report he would pull the trigger. He'd practiced his lines in the mirror, looking directly into the camera and saying, "I'm a middle-aged, divorced, Native American man. In a couple days I'll be unemployed in a profession that's being slowly choked to death. So I have absolutely nothing to lose. You tuned in tonight for entertainment. So I'm going to tell you a story."

And once he got the signal, it all unfolded pretty much as he imagined it would, except that his own voice sounded curiously muffled in his ears. He thought of Helen, and Hallie, and Paige, and Mac, all watching him on the screen, staring at the stubby muzzle pressed tight against his right temple with a shaking hand. But when he cued the director in the production room to cut to the report that he and Helen had prepared, he heard a strange noise, a sudden engulfing silence, as if all the generators in Miles City had powered down at once. Then everything faded to black.

49

September
Belarus

He had always been a guy with butterflies in his belly. As a kid, he'd had to cut short phone calls with friends, as they jabbered about an exciting plan, or a new movie release, in order to bolt for the john, in competition with his five siblings for the family's one bathroom. When talk during a family drive threatened to reveal something big, his brothers would tease, "Don't tell Bubbles until we get in the house!" And even his own children made their father the brunt of this enduring Pence family joke. When he won the governorship in 2012, he'd felt it first in his guts, that familiar churning, before his brain could process the news. When he saw the tweet announcing he'd been tapped to share the 2016 presidential ticket, he barely made it into the stall before his bowels exploded.

Over his life, he'd made an effort to cultivate a placid, controlled exterior to mask the fact that a tornado was slumbering in his entrails. So it was his seismographic gut that first sensed something big had broken, before he saw the news swell and move, tsunami-like, across the faces of his security detail and staff, before Karen rushed toward him with eyes shining and her cheeks all aflame.

———

The mayor of Muncie, invited along to commemorate the new sister-city relationship, was an intense brunette named Nan Zapruder, whose deep knowledge of Indiana's automotive history had managed to exhaust him even before the plane's wheels left the ground. Happily, after several hours during which he'd been told more about the BorgWarner "Vintage Car of the Future" than he'd ever cared to know, the voluble mayor was buttonholed by an aide, a fellow Pacers' fan, on her way back from the washroom. Thereafter Pinkney managed to keep her occupied, going over the program for the ceremony, during the remainder of their flight to Minsk.

Karen, still nursing her grievance about "that Kardashian woman" being invited aboard Air Force One, popped her headphones on and was deep into the audiobook of Francine Rivers's *Redeeming Love* by the time they crossed the Atlantic, skirting the fringes of the weather system churned up by Hurricane Pandora, which was gaining strength farther south. He studied the cameo of his own long-suffering face reflected in the plane's oval window, prayed during the worst of the turbulence, and eventually dozed, his seatbelt pulled snug across his lap. And at last, after a clumsy, skidding landing when he clutched the armrests and held his breath as sheets of horizontal rain swept the Plexiglas, they were there. Despite the early hour of their arrival and the inclement weather, a soggy cluster of women crowned with artificial flowers and clad in the Belarusian national costume (all red and white, with trim little velvet vests and embroidered aprons that reminded him of the hall runner in his great-grandmother's house) had been assembled on the tarmac to greet them, curtsying in welcome.

The irony of the fact that he and Karen had been given the Presidential Suite at the Minsk Marriott had not escaped them. Despite the name, the accommodations proved only marginally nicer than those at the South Bend Radisson, as his wife groused once the bomb-sniffing dog had made its rounds and the door swung shut behind the dark shoulders of the Secret Service agents. She stomped around the suite, pointing out, "Look, Mike, the presidential hair dryer! The presidential microwave! The presidential coat hanger!" That kind of snarkiness did not become her—she didn't have the cheekbones to carry it off, for one thing—but he kept his thoughts to himself, grateful as he was to be out of the plane at last and stretching his bones across a relatively comfortable queen-sized mattress.

Later that afternoon, once they'd rested a bit, they were ushered down countless cordoned-off hotel hallways by his security team, Pinkney by his side. His bleary eyes caught an unsettling glimpse of a meeting room and row upon row of skirted chairs with crimson sashes. On the wall beyond the chairs, an enormous television screen flashed images of a firework crookedly exploding and a map of the U.S. with Utah, instead of Indiana, circled in red. He hoped they'd correct the error before the speeches began.

As mass shooting survivors learn to automatically scan for the exits in any public space, he always took note of the position of the nearest washroom, or the attentive Pinkney made him aware of it with a subtle nod of his head. So when his gut began its urgent signaling, he set his sights on the massive bronze handle of the door marked with the generic male icon (no unisex, thank God) at the far end of the long hall, and he made for it like a relief-seeking missile.

Yet the blesséd door drifted backward beyond his grasp, and the carpet under his shoes began to soften and pulse. He felt a strange pressure in his chest, radiating up from his belly and through his left shoulder. For all his effort, his body seemed to move with the languor of a pearl sinking through Prell shampoo, like in that old TV commercial his mom always brought up when she washed his hair. The hall narrowed, as multitudes of men crowded close along the gauntlet, mouthing words he didn't understand, reaching out with their hands. Somewhere behind him he could make out Mother's voice, but his wife, too, now called out to him in a language foreign to his ears. At last, after what felt like eons, he grasped the deliverance of the cold bronze handle and entered the sanctuary.

He stepped into a place of cold, clean surfaces under dazzling white lights. Struggling to slow his breathing, he took in a row of sinks with gleaming handles, a long metal urinal affixed to one wall, and two stall doors to his right. But when he sought the reassuring sight of his own eyes in the mirror, to ground him and help calm the clamor in his body, it hit him with a jolt: There was nothing there, no familiar, anxious face looking back at him, crowned with its smooth cap of milk-white hair, no reassuring twin in the silvery glass—just a void, a blankness, where his own reflection should have been.

The vice president felt his Maker's hand form a fist around his misfiring heart and squeeze. Then, suddenly beneath his neck, the unyielding surface of a tiled floor. He lay there, gaping at the revelation of the twisting black pipes hidden under the white skirts of the sinks, snaking up and out of sight. He thought again of his mother's topsy-turvy doll, and his own strange dream of the conjoined city, where dark and light, evil and good, death and life met and fused. He struggled to breathe, to shape his breath into a final cry of supplication.

But, much to his surprise, as death emptied his veins, he did not see a host of angels fanning their creamy wings or the glorious image of his Creator beaming at him and beckoning him home. He did not see Stephen's cruel and beautiful mouth bending close to his own, murmuring words of eternal love and torment. Instead, he watched his narrowing field of vision shrink to a pinprick on the black face of a man peering down at him in alarm and saying over and over, "Sir? Sir?"

50

September, earlier
Air Force One

Least Kardashian was in heaven, but she was still a little pissed off. Thirty-five thousand feet above the planet's surface, supple black leather cradling her ass like a giant's hand, she had been relegated to the rearmost seats in the guest section, basically the Siberia of the plane. The staff and the other VIP passengers treated her like an ex-trophy wife gearing up to make a scene at a media mogul's second wedding. She was strategically walled off from Him by an ever-shifting buffer zone of men: assorted GOP senators and cabinet officials and oil barons and that creepy goblin Stephen Miller, who seemed to be everywhere at once.

Earlier that day, after she'd cleared security and been waiting to board Air Force One with the other dignitaries and guests flying to Utah for the Ursa Major event, Least had appraised the glossy skin of the aircraft, with the words UNTIED STATES OF AMERICA racing along its length. Dazzled by the light glancing off the metal detailing, she had to remind herself to breathe as she stood waiting on the tarmac for POTUS to arrive. She remembered Luka's parting words to her, and she mentally fondled them like the beads of a rosary: "Don't forget: It is always the woman who has the power."

When the presidential limo pulled up at last, a scrum of men in dark suits with ear wires erupted from the interior. At the center of the group, like the nucleus of a massive cell, floated a lofty nest of spun sugar. When they reached the bottom of the jet way, the protective shell of agents cracked open to reveal a tall, broad-shouldered figure with an extra-long maroon tie who paused to greet the assembled crowd. His golden crown of hair glistened in the declining sun, and his blue eyes stood out in startling contrast to his Pantone #4546 face, the color of the year.

The waiting men rushed forward, jockeying for the power places at the front of the pack, competing with one another to strike the perfect note of jocular flattery. Finally, an attractive, uniformed brunette gestured to Least, who minced forward on stilettoed feet she could no longer feel. All her extremities seemed to be miles away from her body. In a trance, she moved toward the famous face, at once distant and close-up in her telescoping vision. For a bizarrely attenuated moment she didn't know exactly where, or even who, she was. So she mirrored him, stretching out her hand like a drowning victim seizing a towrope. And he pulled her to safety. Drawing her close, he smiled broadly, and she heard her name tumble like a miracle from his mouth. "Lease Kardashian," he said, "I just love you on television!" Then he signaled to his aide for a wet wipe.

After they'd followed POTUS's back up the red-carpeted steps and into the plane, Least beheld a multitude of television screens, twenty in all on Air Force One, as the President would brag to her later. They were tuned to various news channels, with crawls zipping across the bottom (*Amazon Debuts Same-Hour Delivery, POTUS Appoints Himself Head of Fed, Grammy Winner's Self-Slay Shocks Fans*), and she'd had the surreal experience of seeing her own ass on every one, sheathed like an Oscar statuette in skin-tight gold Lurex, swallowed by the aircraft door she'd just passed through. Now the screens all showed a weather map of the eastern seaboard, and the massive bull's-eye of Hurricane Pandora barreling toward it.

The President had led them all on a tour of the plane's surprisingly roomy interior, showing off its features, including his private office with its burnished wooden desk and wall-to-wall flat screens and the Great Seal with the new presidential motto: *Ego Redintegro Innovare Unius Est*, I Alone Can Fix It. He'd spread his arms wide, as if sweeping the jet's contents and its lucky passengers into a great big bear hug. "It's incredible, right?" The guests erupted into fountains of praise just as Stephen Miller spoke quiet words into the President's ear and then steered him toward the front of the plane. *Of course, he has important work to do.* Still, Least felt her heart, her hopes, deflate like a tube dancer at a car lot. She settled into her window seat, crossed her spray-tanned legs, and buckled the safety belt low over her hips. The aisle seat to her right remained empty.

Soon the pilot made his announcement and the aircraft rumbled to life and gathered speed, racing past SUVs and emergency vehicles lining the runway. The plane's wings lofted through the late-summer haze choking the capital and then arced in a slow turn west into the sun. None of it seemed real to Least—the good fortune and effort that had brought her to this moment, to this place, still barely believable. The fact of His proximity, somewhere toward the front of the plane, made her hands shake and her heart hammer. Knowing the President wasn't a drinker, she almost turned down the offer of a cocktail, but then thought what the hell and asked for a White Russian. During her briefing in advance of the trip, she'd been surprised (and, frankly, a little miffed) to hear she'd have to pony up for the cost of the flight and an on-board meal, even if she was too nervous to eat it. She sipped from the lead-crystal glass, the ice shockingly cold against her teeth, and left a blurred crimson lip print on a napkin embossed with POTUS's golden logo.

Peering at the darkening land, Least could just make out the missing mountaintops of West Virginia. Soon she was joined by the Under-Undersecretary of the Interior, a toothy Oklahoman named Jerry Krupke, who pointed out the faint shape of the Ohio River twisting across the landscape far below, being dammed to create the Midwest's largest effluent collection pond. Krupke had a hard time grasping what an "influencer" was. She sighed and tried her best to explain while his eyes roamed like a buffalo all over her body.

The cabin lights dimmed a little and a meal materialized in front of them, but she ignored it and sipped at the dregs of her drink while Krupke chowed down on his overcooked steak. By the time the flight path took them over Indiana, Least's boredom was laced with desperation. How stupid of her to assume hours of personal grooming and a fabulous dress could do the work for her, and attract the President like a prize bass to a flashing lure. She had no Plan B for what to do if he didn't seek her out, and once they'd arrived in Utah she would be competing with Ursa Major and all the other guests for his attention, a hopeless contest, she knew.

Resa had teased Least that her elaborate preparations for the flight and the gala event to follow rivaled those of a wealthy Iranian bride getting ready for her wedding. Least had her teeth whitened and her eyebrows threaded, her lips plumped with collagen and her anus bleached (courtesy of BeautyBooty), and every inch of her body waxed, save for that T-shaped landing strip. Her hymen implant didn't sting (much) anymore when she peed, so she figured the surgery was mostly healed by now, but she'd gone commando just to be on the safe side.

Her one regret was the choice of dress. The short body-con number had begun crawling up her thighs once she'd taken her seat. Luka had insisted she wear gold rather than her signature virginal white for this very special occasion, but the clingy metallic fabric seemed to have a mind of its own. Five more minutes of this upward creep and the Under-Undersecretary would be getting the surprise of a lifetime.

Just as Least unbuckled her seat belt, then yanked her hem back toward her knees and prepared to stand, a ripple of excitement swept down the aisle. The President came swaggering back to the guest section, where he ejected Krupke with a jerk of his thumb and claimed the seat next to Least's. Even before he lowered his bulk into the buttery leather, his mouth was moving: *Wasn't the food incredible? Did she know his chef had been awarded three Michelin stars? Definitely better than that supposedly healthy crap Michelle Obama served, right?*

He told her about his brand-new club, listing all the fantastic features of the golf and spa resort, which boasted the largest swimming pool in Utah. He scoffed at how all the naysayers had said, You can't do that, keep the grass on the greens so lush and manicured like that in the middle of the desert, it's impossible! But she'd see, when they got there, the most beautiful course in the U.S., in the world, people were saying. He had plenty of ideas for her show, too, and who she should interview, starting with his own daughter, who would boost her ratings bigly. As his fractured monologue washed over her, with its familiar mesmerizing rhythms, she didn't hear the words so much as experience the effect of his supreme confidence in full flow, his assumption that things would be true just because he said they were.

Least became aware that she needed to pee, but she clenched her muscles and kept an inviting smile plastered on her face. Her dress, meanwhile, had resumed its tactical retreat up her thighs. The President was looking at her, he was taking her in, which made her keenly aware of her own body, spotlighted in the overhead beam that bounced off the metallic fabric and shadowed her deep cleavage. She felt herself the sum of all her parts, whether original or more recently acquired: her swelling breasts and hips, her toned legs pressed damply together, and her fingers with their lacquered gel extensions interlaced in her lap.

Time passed and the President was still talking—he'd never stopped, actually—but she didn't dare stand up and adjust her hem, for fear she might appear rude or that he would take the opportunity to step away, and she'd never have him to herself again. By chance or prearrangement, most of the other passengers had drifted to the very rear of the plane, where the accredited members of the press had been sequestered, or into one of the two conference rooms she'd peeked into during the President's tour. Here was the bliss she had fantasized about from that very first rally when she'd felt the power of his maximal charisma, and her joy should have been undiminished by corporeal concerns. Yet somewhere over the dark wastes of Nebraska, the growing pressure in her bladder became impossible to ignore. She prepared to excuse herself, hating her own treasonous body, when the President placed a hand on her knee, and she knew she wasn't going anywhere.

Seeking distraction, Least stared at his mouth, and the rubbery shapes it made became increasingly surreal as her need to urinate grew. The pain in her belly grew sharper and more intense, and the images streaming on all the television screens started to blur together into a swirling circle of light that contracted around them, like Saturn's rings wrapping that planet in a cosmic embrace. In her ecstatic agony, Least pictured the two of them transforming into twin molten stars, locked in orbit, spinning at the white-hot core of the universe.

—

Ultimately, it was that troll Stephen Miller who saved the President from an unintentional golden shower. Good thing, too, because her hemline was mere centimeters away from flashing her custom landing strip at the leader of the free world. The President had parked himself next to Least for over an hour, with Miller hovering nearby, clearly anxious to keep the Commander in Chief circulating through the bloodstream of the plane. At last the advisor's gargoyle presence became impossible to ignore, and the President winked at Least and heaved himself to his feet. "This guy," he told her, "thinks he runs the show."

He lumbered away, heading for the press gaggle at the aircraft's tail section, and seconds later Least bolted for the restroom. The relief was exquisite. Afterward, she blotted her crotch carefully, then fluffed her hair and freshened her lipstick while the floor of the plane shuddered softly beneath her heels. The residual pain of her hymen implant made her feel like she'd just been enthusiastically fucked. Indeed, an hour's proximity to the President had given her a flattering post-coital kind of glow, she noted, as she inspected her face in the mirror.

Least felt gobsmacked by her own good fortune. Just five months earlier, she had been stretched out on a lounge chair in South Beach, bored out of her skull. Then a stranger with Cool-Whip hair and a Rolex came along, and everything changed, delivering her to this amazing place. Sailing above the clouds with the world's most fascinating man, she had succeeded in capturing and holding his attention for what felt like an eternity—without saying a word. There would be more times like these, once they arrived at the gala, now that he and she had broken the ice. She had definitely felt a connection sparking between them. The President was bound to seek her out amid the giddy swirl of the party, maybe spirit her off to a secluded corner for a private tête-à-tête well away from his security detail. She only wished Luka could have been there to share in her triumph, since he was the only friend she had who truly understood what it all meant to her. She would have to text him immediately once they were on the ground.

As Least exited the restroom, the President popped his head around the door of the airborne Oval Office and summoned her inside. "You want a photo, don't you? A souvenir from the trip? Stephen, take a photo for the lovely lady." She stepped into the room and POTUS waved her over behind the wooden desk. And here it was, her big Monica Lewinsky moment, the scene she'd long imagined in her most heated fantasies, spoiled by the inconvenient presence of this third wheel. The man with the hooded eyes and the suspiciously shiny skin aimed his cell phone at Least and the President, who posed a little stiffly side by side.

As Miller framed the shot, Least felt a hand slip down her spine and slide possessively between her buttocks. She kept the photo smile fixed on her face as the hand scurried up under the hem of her dress. It clawed its way into her crevices like a sea star, roughly inserting a probing finger. Taken by surprise, she turned to him, and the President beamed back at her, his shameless grin all sly and knowing, when the plastic explosive implanted in her vagina suddenly detonated.

As the blast engulfed her and the man with his finger deep inside her, along with every other soul on Air Force One, Least Kardashian saw, finally saw with perfect clarity for the first and only time in her life. In the mushroom cloud of her immolating mind, when time slowed and stretched like so much taffy, she saw the skin of that smirking face flayed, the orange mask peeled back by a thousand fingers of flame and, beneath it all, the void, the howling hole of nothingness, at the core of every hurricane.

51

September
Somewhere in the West

They had traveled far enough outside the cities that it was finally safe to claw away the piles of burlap heaped on top of them, to inhale the fresh air, and to look up into the miles of black sky above the open back of the truck. Felo's body ached from bouncing along the rough highways day after day, traveling into the sun that beat down on them through the heavy brown sacks. When he felt like he couldn't breathe, that he would surely begin to scream, Mama would wrap her arms around him and sing softly in his ear, until he grew calm and his breathing quieted.

After Felo had slipped out of the room where the *bruja* had locked him away and darted like a lizard down the long hall, he had been passed from one pair of brown hands to another, hidden in cramped closets and garbage bags piled with food scraps and rolling carts crammed with damp towels, loaded into the back of a laundry truck, and finally taken in the quiet of the night to a small wooden house with a sagging porch flying a ragged American flag. Despite the reassuring words whispered through the slot in the door of his prison, he had felt certain Mama had been murdered back in the camp, taken away and shot in the head with Papa and the other adults. When the *maquinista* had led him down to the dank cellar of the house, to a skinny door hidden by a pile of boxes in the corner, and a woman he knew stepped out from behind that door, sobbing and reaching out hungrily for Felo, he thought he was seeing a ghost and had nearly fainted from terror.

During the long journey west, Felo begged his mother again and again to tell him the story of how she had escaped from the detention camp, of how she had found her way to him. She had heard in the camp that the President's *esposa*, the slit-eyed one, had taken Felo away with her. She told him the story of how she had been zip-tied and brought to the capital to march like a soldier in the parade, how she had slipped away from the buses and hid in the Metro tunnels and the abandoned buildings with the homeless people and the *drogadictos* and the Dreamers. Down in the tunnels people whispered about a network of safe houses and escape routes called El Ferrocarril, of good people called *maquinistas* who might be trusted to help you obtain some money and fake papers and reach the safety of *el norte*. They had heard the rumors, too, of a little Guatemalan boy stolen away from the camps, hidden behind the walls of the White House, and kept like a pet by the President's immigrant wife.

Felo didn't want to tell Mama his own stories about the eternity he spent in the room with no windows. He hoped that time in his life would fade away like an awful nightmare, now that he was finally awake again and in his mother's arms. But one night he had dreamed about the worm with the red tennis shoe. In his dream he saw it twisting on the road and tried to grab it, and it had slithered up his arm and into one of the holes in his nose. He was afraid it might have wriggled into his brain and was living there, and he didn't want Mama to know.

His mama told Felo that Papa had been sent south again, but when he arrived back in the highlands, he'd made his way to the city and set out once more, heading north with Felo's *tia*. *Your papa will keep trying,* Mama told him. *They may catch him and send him back, but he will never stop trying to join us.*

When it was safe, the driver would pull the truck off the road and give them bottles of water and bananas and apples and *cacahuetes* and long wrinkled sticks of peppery meat, and they would hurry to relieve themselves in the ditches at the side of the highway. They were heading west, he told them, to collect other fugitives hiding in the mountains there, and then another *maquinista* would take them all north into Canada. It was much too dangerous to remain here. Mama's name was known to ICE, and her photograph had been posted all across the country.

As they rattled along the road, Felo lay back in his mother's arms and watched as the moon dipped behind the trees and *las estrellas* wheeled in the sky, and he wondered whether it would be cold in Canada. The air grew sharper and the engine gears groaned as the truck climbed and climbed. Then a flower of light suddenly bloomed against the blackness far above him, a glittering blossom of white and orange that broke apart and all its petals trickled slowly down behind the mountains. "*¡Mira!*" Felo pointed, shaking Mama awake.

She had missed it and Felo described it to her, how the star had shimmered as it fell, and Mama said that a falling star was a good omen, a blessing on their journey. Not long after, the truck slowed and pulled over onto the shoulder of the highway. Felo looked fearfully for Mama's eyes in the dark as they sat there for a long while in silence, holding their breath and listening to the *tick-tick-tick* of the truck's engine. Then a door swung open and slammed, and the man's boots crunched on the gravel. He spoke to them through the wooden slats of the truck. The radio was gone, he told them, and his cell phone showed no bars. This was very strange, he said. They were close to Denver, a big city, but most of the power seemed to be out and the lights of the city were dark. It might be best to wait here, safely off the road, until the power returned.

52

Ivanka Bottle Moon
Sargassa

The towering swells that lifted and lowered the surface of the Patch, steadily growing stronger until it felt as if the entire planet was tilting on its axis, told her something terrible was coming. The surface of Sargassa moved constantly; most of the time one scarcely noticed it, though during one of the rare storms that action could become more turbulent, and cooking pots had to be secured until it passed. This new motion was of a whole different magnitude, signaling the approach of something outsized, of such massive power, that even the most hardened skeptics among them felt their pulses quicken and their tongues turn dry with fear.

Regardless of the emergency preparations she had helped to direct, and all the work she had participated in, Petra had never truly believed Hiranur's prophecy might come true. Every decision she made changed her own future, just as it changed her past, altering the meaning of those events. Squinting through some prognosticating telescope at a fixed future looming on a distant horizon? Impossible. She had joined in the storm prep efforts because she knew the importance of a unified

Sargassa. If they would ever be more than a hodgepodge of desperate individuals of warring faiths from embattled homelands, thrown together by the paroxysms of geopolitical policy, they needed a common project to bring them together and transform them into one nation. Her job as a governor had always been to advance such a project.

But as Petra squatted in the entrance of her shelter with a cup of tea in her hand, exhausted after the long day, watching the sun sink through bumpy ridges of magenta and gray, what some called a mackerel sky, she saw the surface of the dark liquid in her cup tilt alarmingly. Sometime later it happened again, and then a while later she felt it yet again. By that time the sky was almost fully black. Like the intensifying contractions of an enormous womb, the swells rolled beneath the surface of the Patch. When Petra heard the signal drums, she tried to stay calm and follow the emergency plan. In her trust, the plan called for all colonists near the Council House to shelter there or in the overflow sheds, and she arrived there after checking into every home she passed along the way, to make sure no one had been left behind.

By now the winds had picked up, sending pieces of loose plastic aloft like startled birds. Alicia Daria met Petra at the entrance to the Council House, her face white with concern. Her husband had left for the coast earlier in the day, to help manage the shield, and her son, Raul, was inside, but Virginia had slipped away while everyone was busy getting settled and was nowhere to be found. Petra commandeered a battery lamp and set out again in search of her, calling the girl's name and squinting against the rising wind, the whipping rain. Soon she could no longer hear the drums.

Petra reached the main channel and worked her way along its phosphorescent edge and then toward the south, in the general direction of the Darias' home, violently peppered by flying debris—her cheek smarting from where the sole of a flip-flop had flown out of the darkness and slapped her face. Even with the lamp she could barely see two steps in front of her. She worried that any familiar landmarks would soon be obliterated, and even if she succeeded in locating the girl, they would never find a place to ride out the storm. She turned in one direction and then another, trying to spot anything in the darkness to help guide her steps. Then the strength of the wind and the battering rain knocked Petra down, and forced her down again when she tried to stand. And when she managed to struggle to her feet again, she knew she had lost her bearings.

Dangerously close to giving way to a wild panic, Petra felt something snag her foot, and in the lamp's weak light she saw her ankle trapped beneath a tether. She recognized the distinctive triple-braided line and realized she'd reached the corner of her own shelter, though she would have sworn she was nowhere near that neighborhood of the Patch. The lamp hooked over one arm, she grabbed the braided line and, hand over hand, pulled herself inside while the winds threatened to tear the walls off and scour the skin from her face.

Prostrate beneath the low roof, which had been lashed down the day before as a precautionary measure, Petra pressed her shaking hands to her ears and tried to block out the wailing of the wind as the hurricane plowed into Sargassa. She had imagined such a storm might sound like an attack, like bombs and drones and machine gun fire and the screams of the dying in the rubble. Those were all sounds she remembered from her last days in Aleppo, sounds that came back to her in dreams, and that she wished never to hear again awake or asleep. But the monster bearing down on them was a different beast, which emitted an unearthly wailing noise, like a ghost train's horrible whistle, or fingernails shrieking on the chalkboard of the sky—like absolutely nothing she'd ever heard before. Petra closed her eyes and began to pray.

———

She must have been lying there for a lifetime—it felt that long and longer—when through her muffled ears Petra sensed a slight ebbing of sound, and by and by the winds diminished and finally fell away, and the rain stopped. She had been flogged by debris and deafened by the screaming wind and had clawed parts of her own scalp raw in terror.

Petra crawled on shaking legs out from under the ruins of her shelter, into a night so bright she could have read a book without a lamp or candle. Staring up, she saw a still, clear sky centered above her and the full moon staring down on Sargassa like a cosmic pupil. She knew they must be in the hurricane's eye.

It was the reprieve she needed to resume her search for Virginia, and she spun around, trying to orient herself. A few yards off, toward what she guessed were the remains of the storage shed at the corner of her yard, judging by what was scattered widely around it, something shiny caught her eye, and she stumbled that way. She tried to call for Virginia as she walked, but her throat was so hoarse only a croak came out. Petra could make out something that looked like a tiny light, winking in the distance. She went toward this beacon, which resembled, as she came closer, a metallic disc floating on a wavering surface. It was a sight so strange, in that blasted place, Petra's brain scrambled to make sense of it. Was this a mirage, a vision, a fata morgana? Only when she was nearly on top of the thing did its meaning become clear.

The corpse lay on its back with its long arms flung above its head, eyes open and glassy and its gaping mouth stretched wide. The mouth brimmed with water, and on the water's surface floated the full moon's reflection, a communion wafer made of light. Luis's words to Virginia echoed in Petra's head: *A god will return with the moon in his mouth.* And here a man lay, dark hair plastered to his skull, with the moon in his mouth like a coin, an obol for Charon. He wore the same ragged shorts and T-shirt he had on when they'd stopped their rafts in the channel and spoke to one another, when she'd watched the rain pool in his collarbone and wanted to drink from that cup. Had Adnan come searching for her, or for Virginia? Had he lost his grip on the enormous sail, and had a wave dragged him under to drown and then flung his sodden body back onto the Patch? Or had a divine hand deposited him there as a reproach to an unbeliever like Petra, who only felt moved to pray when death shrieked its name in her ears? In any case, she knew the trouble that came from worshipping a man as a god. She could not let that happen again.

Petra had fled Aleppo with a mind full of darkness, with nothing but the clothing on her back. In her exodus she had paused and stooped down, and her hand had closed around a heavy gray stone, circular and mottled as the moon's surface. Throughout the long journey back from hell, over land, over water, she had carried that stone, clenched in her fist, warm in her pocket.

On the Patch, she learned that others had brought stones away with them, too, mementoes of the homelands they left behind, which they would sometimes swap for other goods. Over time, Petra had collected a heap of these, stone by stone, rough and smooth pieces of limestone and granite and gypsum and basalt and marble, materials rare and therefore precious on Sargassa. Drop one in the wrong spot and it would plummet out of sight forever. She kept her collection at the bottom of the fresh-water reservoir in her shelter, where the varied colors and textures showed more vividly. In her home country, men had used stones to murder adulteresses, to reduce gay men's heads to pulp. But Petra loved the weight of a stone in her hand, and all the things a stone could be. It was a tool, or a weapon; you can build with stone, or defend yourself with it. It outlasted every stupid human choice, every noble human act, to utter the same message: *Still here.*

The dog Wasim was nowhere to be seen, but he might appear at any moment and start to howl. The survivors would surely begin to creep out in the winds' hiatus, searching for lost ones, assessing the damage. Petra knew she needed to be quick. A side channel wasn't far from where the body lay, and she somehow found the strength to drag Adnan up to its edge and tip him onto his side, letting the silvery water drain from his mouth, before she hurried back to her shelter. She scrambled under the roof and into the far corner. Most of the fresh water in the reservoir had been lost, heaving up and over the rim of the basin as the surface of the Patch bucked in the monstrous waves, but she thrust her hand deep and felt the heap of stones clacking together at the bottom. She stretched out the hem of her shift, woven from plastic rice bags, waterproof and strong, and loaded it with every one.

When she reached Adnan's body, she crammed the stones deep into the pockets of his ragged shorts, all but the last, her own stone from the ruins of Aleppo. One final look to make sure she was still alone, and Petra pressed her mouth to his cold lips, stifling a sob. Then she shoved Adnan's shoulder until he flopped slowly into the channel, like a man rolling over in his sleep, and he sank out of sight.

———

Aching with her efforts, Petra lay flat on her back, a weary sailor lashed to a ship's deck. She was staring up at the moon, adrift in its borderless ocean of sky, when another vivid face suddenly thrust itself before her eyes. "Governor, are you alive?" Virginia Daria crouched beside Petra with a furrowed brow. Her relief at seeing her, at knowing the child had survived the storm and that she hadn't witnessed what Petra had done with Adnan's body, made her laugh out loud as she struggled to her feet. "Virginia!" she rasped. "I'm so happy to see you. Your mama is very worried about you! This is just the eye, you know—the rest of the hurricane will be coming soon. We need to get back to shelter."

She took the child's hand in hers, but it was Virginia who led the way as they headed in the direction of the Council House. She chattered to Petra about how she'd snuck out to look for Wasim and lost the path back, and ended up sheltering with Burak's goats in the shed. "Those goats made almost as much noise as the wind!" she told Petra. They could see very clearly in the moonlight, and though the winds had scattered debris everywhere, they managed to locate the main path leading north. Everything would have to be rebuilt, Petra thought wearily, when it was all over. But Virginia prattled on with excitement, as if riding out a hurricane was the greatest possible adventure. "I'm not afraid anymore," she told Petra with a hopeful expression on her face. "It was just like Luis said—you know, about the god with the moon in his mouth. I saw him, back there. He looked a little like Adnan, but I know he was really a god. So I'm sure we'll be OK. We don't have to be afraid."

At Virginia's words, Petra's body turned cold, her brain emptied of every thought save one. The little girl dashed ahead, giddy to share the good news. And Petra went after her, gripping the stone in her hand.

Epilogue

In the spring of 2047, an older man with close-cropped ice-white hair and a wary face stood with his hands buried in his pockets, his coat collar buttoned up against the March wind blasting off Lake Erie. Watery blue eyes peered through tinted glass lenses to rest on the placid face of the statue recently installed in the redbrick courtyard of the New Armenian Church. *Not a good likeness at all,* he thought. He guessed that the glass sculptor had taken a mass-produced plaster statue of Saint Lucy as his model and simply swapped out what was on the plate she held in her hands. The statue sported the same corona, the same sightless eyes cast downward in an attitude of devotion. But, he supposed, you can't install a sculpture of a voluptuous woman, with plump lips and sensuous curves, smack in front of a Catholic church.

Nominated years earlier for sainthood by the Ann Arbor diocese, after a tireless campaign by Archbishop Bogosian, she had recently been given the Pope's blessing, entirely bypassing the traditional investigation conducted by the Congregation for the Causes of Saints. The canonization was based not on verified miracles (though there were those, many would argue) but on a posthumous Nobel Peace Prize and the Holy Father's own assessment of the breadth of the benefit conferred upon humankind by the candidate's sacrifice. That, and the fact that

317

homemade shrines to the martyred saint had cropped up all through the Bitcoin Belt during the previous decades. Petitions had circulated, too, even among the faithless.

So now it was official: Saint Least, the Virgin Kardashian, molded in frosted glass, proffering her immaculate vagina on a plate. He had hoped to see a Judy Chicago-esque inflorescence sculpted in Carrera marble, a nod to Least's sad little degree in art history, but the object on the plate looked, truth be told, more like a dried apricot. If you believed the testimonies, a prayer to Saint Least had the power to regenerate a torn hymen and restore a woman's virginity. She deserved so much better, he knew, but sainthood was a pretty decent consolation prize.

He'd come to pay his respects, and would be back on a plane to Belarus late that evening, with three days to recuperate from the extreme turbulence before heading on to A_____, where Soo-jin would be waiting. They both knew it was a risk, him making this trip; with every plane change he braced to feel a firm hand clamp around his elbow, to meet the stony mugs of federal agents stationed by the jet way. But he needed to see for himself how Least Kardashian was being honored in the nation she had died to save. The customs agent had given the forged passport on his security app only a cursory glance before she smiled tightly and waved him through. Leaving the U.S. later that day would be a breeze—they'd only have eyes on the incoming flights, if they were looking at all. And at the end of his travels, she would be there to meet him, her face suffused with ardor and relief. The thought of running his tongue along the puckered skin of her right ear—a birth defect he'd always found powerfully erotic—made him flush with desire.

It was his first trip back to the States in all these years, and he'd accumulated enough ration points for the round-trip flight. Over the stormy Atlantic he'd listened to a new EasterGrass seedcast about the Mobius trial, released ahead of the man's sentencing earlier that month. That shady quack with a fake degree had succeeded in bilking the U.S. government out of millions of taxpayer dollars in an effort to fatally kneecap the Democratic voting base, yet none of Mobius's nefarious microwave transmissions had actually accomplished more than irritate the delicate bones of the inner ear. It had taken the feckless FBI more than two decades to track the man down.

He had to laugh at the way the venerable Dr. Helen Easterhunt, with her familiar smoky voice, pronounced "Cottoncandiform encephalopathy," as if it were an especially challenging spelling bee word rather than a degenerative condition caused by toxic ash and heavy metals leaching into the groundwater from countless Montana coalfields. After Rocky Mountain Labs confirmed the widespread contamination, the reconstituted EPA declared the eastern half of the state a Superfund region. According to Pendegrass, the spike in U.S. suicides recorded during 2020 and 2021 that sparked their investigation had, in the end, been a perfectly rational response by the members of an anguished populace, specifically those who didn't have the wherewithal to self-medicate. They had watched in horror and grief as all the hard-worn progress of the western world was undone before their eyes by that madman, abetted by his pack of power-hungry sycophants, and the spectacle had proved too much for many to endure. Deaths of despair, indeed.

He was happy to see that conditions at home had finally begun to improve a bit. The border walls had been torn down and the ports re-opened, and the lingering distrust of the international community had at last begun to abate. Many residents of the Atlantic Patch were able to return to their original homelands, though a significant percentage had elected to stay after UNESCO designated Sargassa a World Heritage Site. He and Soo-jin hoped to visit someday, but visas were notoriously difficult to procure.

Even in the U.S., where a significant portion of the population remained militantly resistant to common sense measures, a nationwide environmental cleanup was well under way. But critical time had been lost, with grievous consequences. The lakes and oceans all had new shorelines, and most of the great American coastal cities, including his hometown, were underwater. New York, New Orleans, Los Angeles, San Francisco, Sarasota, Galveston, and Miami—all uninhabitable.

Mar-a-Lago, confiscated back in 2022 by the federal government, was now a scuba park.

In the month after the Air Force One explosion and the government's emergency shutdown of the energy grid, once the nation's airspace was finally declared safe again, he'd boarded a plane with a false passport and a fresh scar on his chest and disappeared down the rabbit hole for more than twenty years. The tattoo removal took a while to heal, and the ragged patch over his nipple still turned a garish Pepto-Bismol pink in the sunlight, but he hadn't wanted to take any chances — nothing that might link him to the others. After hatching their plot, they'd all visited the same LA tattoo parlor on a drunken whim and asked for different versions of the same design, as a sign of their solidarity and commitment. It wouldn't do to have *Sic Semper Tyrannis* inscribed on his chest, or in his case just the initials. Even in the moment it had struck him as juvenile and ill considered to ink himself with Booth's words. Shouting "Thus always to tyrants!" in a dead language, that pompous zealot had robbed the world of a great and eloquent man, a commander in chief who was a peacemaker at heart. His own crew of co-conspirators had instead dedicated themselves to cutting a metastasizing tumor out of the body politic. Purely by chance, he and Soo-jin's paths had crossed a year later on a group tour of the Guggenheim Bilbao, and they'd stayed together after that. Success felt meaningless without someone you loved to share it with.

As he stood there, his exposed ears aching in the brisk wind, the electronic bells in the church tower began to toll. High noon, and he was late. Gently, he laid a spray of white orchids sheathed in biodegradable cellophane beneath the cold toes of the saint, smeared with the overlapping lipstick kisses of the grateful. Then, like a thing that ceases to exist in the instant its function is complete — a bar of soap, or a plastic explosive — he vanished without a trace.

Acknowledgments

I started writing this book in the summer of 2018 as a means of inoc-ulating myself against the possibility that the nightmare of 2016 might reoccur. This was well before COVID-19 swept in to change the polit-ical calculus in this country and reveal our national dysfunction in the starkest possible light. Some of the events I first conceived of as broad satire would ultimately come to pass during the unfolding horror show that was 2020. Some horrors only a few would foresee. The final surprise of this worst of all possible years was that millions of Americans voted for more of the same.

A loving and functional family is rarely the optimal breeding ground for a writer, but this support network has helped me weather the darkest times and channel my anger into fiction. Love and gratitude to my brothers, Christian and Paolo Vescia; sisters-in-law Lucia Sanchéz and Amelia Hansen; and my quartet of beautiful nieces, Francesca, Carmen, Madeleine, and Natalie.

And *in memorium*, Colleen and Fernando Vescia, beloved parents, much missed.

Generous readers Ted Castanes, Chelle Chase, Rosemary Coleman, Rebecca Hartman, Jennifer Hazzard, Julie Salle, and Liz Zitelli gave me essential feedback in early drafts and boosted my confidence as an aspiring novelist. Encouragement came from Paul Savoia and Sue Rhodehouse, friends lost and then found. Though I never told him I was working on a novel until I'd finished it, my kind husband, Don Rauf, allowed me the space and privacy to empty my brain onto the page. Many thanks to my favorite son, Leo, for his wonderful cover design, and to Mark Lerner for his help with the interior. And a special nod to the überniece, Franny, who never stopped asking, "Have you ever wanted to write fiction?" and who kept my secret once I began.

CPSIA information can be obtained
at www.ICGtesting.com
Printed in the USA
BVHW031942190221
600639BV00008B/178